EDGE
OF
CIVILISATION

TONY
McHALE

CRANTHORPE
—MILLNER—
PUBLISHERS

First published by Cranthorpe Millner Publishers (2022)

ISBN 978-1-80378-002-3 (Paperback)

www.cranthorpemillner.com

Cranthorpe Millner Publishers

Acknowledgements

I have to acknowledge two major contributions to this novel. Firstly, Dawn Norris, an old friend and over the years the source of terrific material. She is also my go-to person for verification and in-depth information. Secondly, I have to acknowledge the West Yorkshire Police, although those police officers involved, I imagine, will all by now be retired. But without them I would never have written this novel.

Back in the late 1980s I wanted to do some hands-on research with the police and via my sister-in-law Jenny Bolton, who had a friend whose husband was a police inspector, it was swiftly arranged. Times were different, no health and safety hurdles, not even a disclaimer form to sign, I just turned up one Monday morning at a small police substation, met the DS I was trailing and off I went. The three weeks were eventful for many reasons and many of the incidents that occurred through that time I've included in some form or other in various pieces of work. But the episode, I won't even call it an incident, that prompted me to write this book, just happened by accident.

My time with the DS was coming to an end and I happened to wander into a room in the station I'd never been in before, and there on a board were the head shots of a number of men, five or six in total. Beneath them were photographs of about a dozen young girls, I guessed aged between about thirteen and sixteen. There were lines drawn connecting each of the men to the various girls. I asked what this 'display' was about and was simply told that these five men, all taxi drivers and part of an ethnic community, were 'running' these girls, all of which were in care homes. They were using them for their own sexual pleasure as well as pimping them out to other men. Payment to the girls often took the form of fish 'n' chips or a packet of cigarettes. When I asked the police officers what they were doing to curtail the men's activities, they replied that they were doing nothing – because they weren't allowed to do anything. It was a monitoring operation. It had been deemed by the powers-that-be that any action could be deemed as being racist.

Over the subsequent years, I tried on a number of occasions to sell this story as a TV drama or part of an existing series. No one was interested. Strange they were queuing up to tell the story once it broke, echoes of what happened with the Jimmy Saville story. Over thirty years later, we are now all well aware of the heinous and despicable crime of grooming vulnerable girls, but it may never have come into the public domain if it hadn't had been for Nazir Afzal.

In 2011 he was appointed the North West Chief Crown Prosecutor, covering Greater Manchester, Cumbria and Lancashire, and one of his first decisions was to initiate prosecutions in the case of the Rochdale sex trafficking gang, overturning an earlier decision by the CPS. He suggested that: "white professionals' over-sensitivity to political correctness and fear of appearing racist may well have contributed to justice being stalled".

This novel does not cover that crime – this novel, like a lot of my writing, is about a 'what if' scenario. The events that unfurl are all fictitious, but I was made aware of the possibility of their existence some forty years ago and it has continued to feature in the press, albeit in a minor way, ever since. The element of this story that I do know to be true, is the existence of the 'dark web' and as long as that continues in the same form, the perverted and the deviant will continue to exploit the vulnerable and the fragile, those people society need to protect.

TONY McHALE

To my wife, Jan McHale

INTERVIEW ROOM. BRADFORD CITY CENTRE
POLICE STATION, NELSON STREET.
09:04 a.m. 10ᵗʰ JANUARY 2020

"Please, sit down. We'll try and be as quick as we can. We're all busy people."

There was an officious air about Superintendent Michael Price, but no malice. He didn't look up from the paperwork in front of him as Wordsworth shuffled onto the chair. Although he'd never so much as exchanged a word with Wordsworth prior to this meeting, Price already knew quite a bit about the man before him, late thirties, known to speak his mind and one of the few black officers in the West Yorkshire Force. Price couldn't help but wonder what made him want to be a police officer, his life must have been full of racist insults and jibes and not just from the public. The Force still had its share of racists in its

1

ranks. Price eventually looked up at Wordsworth and immediately reached the conclusion that if someone had ever decided to racially abuse this man, then he was more than capable of handling it.

Wordsworth looked straight into Price's eyes. His gaze was firm and unwavering. He'd also done his homework. He knew as a police officer in the Internal Investigations Unit, Price tended to be less hostile than others. He had a reputation of being fair to lenient, which was a bit like finding a grass snake in a pit of black mambas.

"Busy, you say?" chimed up Sharvari Rana having let both men take in the other. "Then why not just call off the witch hunt? I'm sure Inspector Wordsworth would be more than happy to get back to work."

Sharvari was Wordsworth's Police Federation Rep, and from the off she wanted the interviewing officers to know exactly what she thought of the whole affair. She was early thirties and resolutely feminine, but she never let her sex, her Hindu religion, or her ethnicity get in the way of her work. She had a job to do and that was all that mattered. Wordsworth was slightly fascinated by her, not in a sexual way, but because this was only his second meeting with her and already she'd committed the entire case to memory.

"I'm sure he would," said Price smiling, "but you must appreciate we have to go through the correct procedure."

"Which consists mainly of the persecution of a police officer," persisted Sharvari with no intention of letting it get all warm and cosy.

"We just need him to answer a few questions so we can clear up some minor details with regards to the investigation." As Price spoke, he pressed the record button, and Wordsworth, having conducted countless interviews himself, knew that both the audio and video recording to the small camera positioned on a tripod, would commence simultaneously.

"The time is zero nine zero four on 10th of January 2020 at Nelson Street Police Station, Bradford. Present are myself, Superintendent Michael Price, Sergeant Miriam Ashburn, Detective Inspector William Wordsworth and the Police Federation Representative Inspector Sharvari Rana."

"I want to make it clear for the *tape* –" chipped in Sharvari.

"Digital recordings these days …" It was Ashburn who was going to be the hair-splitting, the nit-picking, the not-let-anything-slide investigator. This approach matched her rather stiff, uptight demeanour. In her late twenties, her determination to have a stellar career in the police force was still very much her aim, even though her path to greatness hadn't gone quite the route she had originally intended. Her rise up the promotional ladder hadn't been as swift as she had hoped and although she didn't realise it, her ambition had floundered mainly because of her … stiff, uptight demeanour. She had deliberately fashioned herself as a cold, efficient and independent individual. Cold because she thought it came across as inner strength,

3

efficient because the Force functioned on efficiency and independent because nobody, as yet, had proposed to her or even suggested they cohabit. In fact, most of her dalliances with the opposite sex had rarely survived three dates and that was since the age of sixteen.

"I just want to make it clear for the *digital recording* and the pedantic Sergeant that Inspector Wordsworth has come here of his own free will and is more than happy to answer any questions you want to put to him. In other words … he has nothing to hide." Sharvari was rarely intimidated by anyone.

"That's good to know." Price smiled again as he turned over the first page of a pad and picked up his Mont Blanc pen that was lying on the table. Ashburn, in way of a contrast, swiped the iPad in front of her indicating, as far as she was concerned, she was younger and more tech savvy.

"Where would you like to start?" asked Sharvari throwing the ball into the court of the interrogators.

"I think we should start with Operation Clayton," said Price.

"You are familiar with Operation Clayton?" Ashburn asked Wordsworth.

"I am," replied Wordsworth immediately.

"He was heavily involved in the operation. He is more than familiar with it, thank you," Sharvari pointed out.

"Operation Clayton was only set up because of the investigation I was involved in at the time," stated

4

Wordsworth.

"Which investigation was that?" Price's question was casual, no demands, no threats. He was one of those police officers that played the politics. He knew when to speak, when to keep quiet, who was worth sucking up to and who wasn't.

Price's small, tidy frame, his golf-weathered complexion and his immaculate uniform made Wordsworth wonder how long it took him to get out of the house in the morning. But he was known for being particular, and he was good at his job. He had been doing these kinds of interviews for five years or so, and Wordsworth knew his tactic would be to spend time trying to create a false sense of security.

"I was investigating the disappearance of Jodie Kinsella," replied Wordsworth.

"Jodie Kinsella?" asked Ashburn almost casually.

"You know …."

"For the recording."

"Jodie Kinsella was a fifteen-year-old girl who went missing," Wordsworth told the machine.

"When was this?" Price sounded like he was asking about when the next bus was due.

"September 9th, 2019."

"A Monday – right?" said Ashburn.

"Yeah. A Monday. Read my report … It's all there."

"I'd like to hear it from you."

Sharvari stirred in her seat before saying, "What has this

5

enquiry got to do with Jodie Kinsella?"

"That's what we're trying to establish. It may have nothing to do with her, but that's for us to decide," barked Ashburn.

"If you don't want to tell them about the case, then you don't have to," said Sharvari quietly to Wordsworth.

"No. I'll tell them. They need to know it all. Any chance of a cup of tea and some biscuits before we start?"

If Wordsworth was at all ruffled, he wasn't showing it.

CHAPTER ONE

DI Wordsworth's car pulled up outside the small terrace house on Mount Pleasant. Local estate agents classified the houses as 'cottages', but Wordsworth had always called them 'two up two downs'.

Wordsworth was first out of the car and even though it was September there was a warmish morning breeze causing the trees and shrubs to sway. He was wearing a light suit which he wished was Armani, but wasn't. Nevertheless, it wasn't cheap, not on his salary. He was of the belief that as a police officer, you should at least look respectable. He was the face that presented to the public; they needed to feel they were in secure hands and shabby attire didn't breed confidence.

The driver, Detective Sergeant Steve Redhead, who through some quirk of fate had short black hair, followed Wordsworth to the front door of the cottage. Wordsworth had an almost military posture; a ramrod back with pushed back shoulders. Redhead was a couple of inches shorter than his boss, had been his sergeant for about six months and still didn't know what to make of him, but what he did know was that by the time he reached the age of thirty-eight he was going to be further up the ladder than his DI. He knew Wordsworth had made inspector in his twenties, but he also knew that's where his career had stalled. He'd been tipped for the top, but DI was as far as he'd got.

Wordsworth turned his phone to silent and nodded to Redhead to do the same. Ringing phones can disturb a moment of truth. He knocked on the door, which swung open with the force of the knock.

"Hello? Police!" Wordsworth called into the house.

He waited on the doorstep. He could hear movement and then a figure appeared out of the darkness. It was large woman in a t-shirt and leggings, which had a slight split in one of the seams. She was holding a can of Special Brew in one hand and a cigarette in the other.

"Mrs Kinsella?" asked Wordsworth.

"No …"

"Then you are?"

"Trisha … Tidswell. Her neighbour."

"Is Mrs Kinsella in?"

"Yeah."

"We need to have a word with her."

"Come through."

Wordsworth and Redhead followed the woman through what was a small dining kitchen. There were dirty pots and pans piled high in the sink and a half-finished bowl of cornflakes on the table. Wordsworth glanced at a couple of photographs, one showing a mother and baby and the other a school photograph of a girl about twelve. He was pretty sure that both the baby and the schoolgirl were Jodie.

They entered the living room at the back of the house, which seemed crammed with furniture and dominated by a huge television screen. A brown, rather shabby three-piece suite that appeared too large for the room was angled towards the TV and slumped on the sofa, a near empty wine glass in her hand, was another woman.

"Mrs Kinsella?" The woman nodded slowly, confirming that the glass in her hand certainly wasn't the first of the day. "I'm Detective Inspector Wordsworth and this is Detective Sergeant Redhead."

Redhead gave a little smile, then looked round. There was a person missing.

"Where's the police officer?" asked Redhead.

Stacey didn't react. Had she even noticed there'd been a police officer?

"They've gone to the shop," said Trisha the neighbour, taking a sip from her can.

"Shop?" Asked Redhead, instantly dubious. The FLO they had left there to look after Stacey wouldn't have just gone to the shop.

"Stacey needed some more wine," said the other woman blankly, offering no further explanation.

"And you live … next door?" asked Wordsworth.

9

"Yeah … that way." Trisha indicated to the left and then changed her mind and indicated to the right. For a second Wordsworth thought he was watching the Scarecrow in the Wizard of Oz. Then as if to say she didn't care whether she made a mistake or not, she took another swig of beer.

"Is there a Mr Kinsella?" asked Wordsworth.

"Not here, thank Christ," replied Stacey.

"You're divorced … separated …?"

"He's gone," said Stacey, leaving the detectives to fill in the rest themselves.

"Do you have another partner?" continued Wordsworth.

"No … do I hellers like. After him I'd be mad to take on another man. He bled me dry. He tried to sell me shoes once … only pair I had. I caught him though."

"Good for you," said Wordsworth. "Mrs Kinsella, we're here because we need to talk to you about Jodie."

For the first time Stacey looked up at Wordsworth.

"We need you tell us all you can about when you saw her last, who she's being associating with and where she might have gone."

"She already told t'other police," Trisha said.

"All we have is a report of a missing girl, now we need more detail, which hopefully will help us find her," Wordsworth explained patiently.

Wordsworth had been put on this case after Jodie had been missing for forty-eight hours. Before setting out to speak with the mother, Wordsworth had digested what information there was about the missing girl. She'd left

10

home for school on Monday morning and her mother didn't report her missing until the Tuesday afternoon when she didn't arrive home from school. The reason for the delay, she claimed, was that she thought her daughter had stayed at a friend's overnight. Seeing the set up at Jodie's home, Wordsworth knew it could simply have been that the mother had been out of her skull.

Stacey looked at them, draining the last of the wine from the glass. As she did her arm was angled in such a way that Wordsworth could see the track marks that scarred most of the limb.

"Okay if we sit down?" asked Wordsworth.

Stacey nodded.

Wordsworth sat closest to her on one of the armchairs. Redhead looked at the other armchair and decided against it. He pulled up a hardback chair from the corner of the room and sat on it, first scanning a cursory glance over it to make sure it was reasonably germ free.

"Your daughter's full name is … Jodie Tempest Kinsella?"

Stacey nodded.

"Her date of birth?"

"Er … 3rd March … and she's … fifteen."

"So … 2004. And this address is her principal place of residence?"

Stacey just nodded again.

"When was the last time you saw her?"

"I can't remember," said Stacey twisting awkwardly.

11

The movement caused her short denim skirt to ride up her thighs, exposing a couple of large bruises, while her low cut top, with the words 'KINKY' printed on it in silver letters shifted in such a way that Wordsworth could see she wasn't wearing a bra, because it forced her small, emaciated breasts to press against the material.

"And what was she wearing when you last saw her? Do you have a picture or anything?"

"Not sure."

"You're not sure what your daughter was wearing the last time you saw her?" said Redhead, not masking his surprise.

"Hey leave off her gobby!" Trisha leapt to her friend's defence. "She's going through a hell of a time and *she's* done nowt wrong … you need to remember that."

"Monday morning … she left for school?" asked Wordsworth, steering the conversation back.

"Yeah … Monday … morning," said Stacey clearly saying anything to get the police off her back.

"I can vouch for that," Trisha announced. "I saw her."

"Did you speak to her?"

"No, I saw her through the window," Trisha added.

Wordsworth stared at her. He often did this when he was trying to figure out if a person was lying or not. With career criminals, it wasn't too easy. Most of them were consummate liars. But with your average person he had a pretty good hit rate.

"What you bloody looking at?" she almost roared.

"Just thinking," smiled Wordsworth. He decided she was telling the truth. "Did she seem upset in any way?"

"No."

"Agitated?"

"No."

"Did you notice anything that was amiss with her?"

"I saw her through the fucking kitchen window for Christ's sake. I wasn't doing a friggin' psychoanalysis session with her."

"But can you remember what she was wearing?"

"Yeah – fucking clothes."

Trisha stared at him aggressively, but Wordsworth refused to let her rile him.

"It will help our investigation. We can give a description of the girl and what she was wearing to the public so they can call in if they see her."

Trisha shrugged like she didn't believe him but muttered her response anyway: "Short, patterned skirt, off the shoulder jumper... her hair was down. It's long, dark."

"Thank you." Wordsworth turned back to Stacey. "Mrs Kinsella? Is it alright if I call you Stacey?" He normally took a few minutes when questioning someone to decide how best to address them. Stacey just nodded, twisting again.

"Do you know if Jodie had been upset recently?" continued Wordsworth.

"No."

"Had there been anything worrying her?"

"No."

"Had she mentioned running away at all?" Wordsworth was studying Stacey closely.

"Running away?" As she asked the question there was no discernible reaction from her.

"Yeah. Maybe you'd fallen out … or is there a boyfriend you're not happy with …?"

"She hasn't run away," said Stacey with a twinge of annoyance.

"What makes you so certain?"

"It's her daughter, isn't it," snapped Trisha.

"Let her answer …" said Redhead. He was getting frustrated with Wordsworth's questioning technique.

"Yeah … she's my daughter … I know my daughter," confirmed Stacey.

"Really?" Suddenly there was an edge to Wordsworth's voice.

"What do you mean by that?" Trisha snapped.

"Come on … I'm not blind. It's just after half nine in the morning and she's already half cut," said Wordsworth indicating Stacey. "Has she been junking up as well?"

"You can't talk to us like that!"

"I just have. I'm trying to find her daughter; I'm not trying to bust you. Look at the state of her … and don't try telling me that she's only like this because her daughter's missing, 'cos I won't believe you."

Stacey staggered to her feet only just managing to keep her balance. "Who do you fucking think you are?"

"You know who I am … and you know you need to get your shit together if you want me to find Jodie. So did she talk about running away?"

"I've told you … no!"

"What about boyfriends?" Wordsworth wasn't letting up.

"Boyfriends? She's not interested."

"Girlfriends then?"

"Give over.

Stacey almost spat out the words as she took a tentative step towards Wordsworth, who held his ground.

"Let it go, Stace …" Trisha wasn't shouting anymore. She looked concerned.

"He knows fuck all!" Stacey snapped. "She's far too good for any of the little shits round here. No … not my girl. I want her back. I want her back now. You … you fucking … I want her back …"

Letting out a howl, Stacey broke down in tears and collapsed in a heap on the floor in front of Wordsworth. He looked at her for a moment. He could feel Redhead's eyes on him.

Trisha, instead of moving to help her friend, just let out a tirade of abuse.

"You happy now? Got what you came for? Like to see us girls cry do you … you fucking bullies!"

Wordsworth slowly bent down and, taking Stacey gently by the shoulders, eased her to her feet and guided her back to the sofa, where he tenderly sat her down.

"I think it's time for you to go," Trisha announced.

"We haven't finished questioning her yet," said Redhead.

"Are you blind … look at her … Look at the state of her!"

"We'll take a short break," said Wordsworth. "I need to look in Jodie's bedroom anyway." He turned to Stacey, who nodded her assent. "I'm sorry if I've upset you. I just want to find Jodie."

***

Wordsworth and Redhead arrived on the small landing, which lay between two doors. Wordsworth pushed open one door and looked in the room. It was a mess. Clothes on the floor, bed unmade, wine bottles strewn around and even a hypodermic, three quarters full of blood, on the bedside cabinet.

"What do you reckon sir?" asked Redhead as they looked round.

"I reckon we're talking to a couple of smack heads who shouldn't be allowed to look after a hamster never mind a kid."

"It's just the way it is."

"Maybe – but it's crap. If you're shooting up heroin for 'personal use' then we turn a blind eye. What the fuck kind of system is that?"

Wordsworth moved to a door set to the right of the

16

bedroom. He pushed it open.

"Lock 'em up and throw away the key, is that what you're aiming for?" asked Redhead.

Wordsworth looked into the bathroom. Like the bedroom it was a mess. There were dried bloodstains running down the side of the basin and the toilet hadn't been flushed.

"No … what I'd really like is for them to decriminalise the lot."

"You serious?"

"Yeah – sell it over the counter in your local shop with a big sign saying: 'Buy if you want to, but you could be in a coffin this time tomorrow – your fucking choice.' If you're old enough to vote, if you're old enough to fight, then you're old enough to know if you're willing to take the risk or not. That's what I'd like to see."

Redhead was starting to realise why Detective Inspector Wordsworth hadn't gone on to make Chief Constable.

Wordsworth had seen enough so he headed out past Redhead, back onto the landing and into the other bedroom.

Jodie had created herself a little sanctuary in this otherwise screwed up house. The room was predominantly white with odd sections of the walls painted mauve, which matched the bedcover covering the neatly made bed. Wordsworth got the distinct impression that it was Jodie who had acted not only as designer, but decorator too. This was all her handiwork. Under the window was a white desk

17

with a computer on it. Wordsworth was tempted to flick it on and see if there was anything on it that would give them an indication to where she had gone. But he knew better. Leave it to the experts. Leave it to SOCO. Likewise, he didn't touch the expensive looking, empty watch box next to the computer. However, without touching the box, he could see that it was an Armani timepiece which certainly wasn't going to be cheap. A present from some rich friend or something she had desperately wanted and saved up for herself. His betting was on the former. Either way they needed to find it.

He took a cursory look around the rest of the room, knowing there wasn't much he could do without SOCO. There was a phone charger still plugged in, which made Wordsworth think she must have intended retuning home. There were no posters of boy bands, no indication of her likes or dislikes, just a number of books, and pinned to a notice board a few selfie photos, mainly of her and her mum on what were obviously Stacey's good days. The only other item that really stood out was a piece of verse framed and hung over her bed.

These things I have spoken onto you,
That in me ye might have peace.
In the world ye shall have tribulation:
But be of good cheer
I have overcome the world
JOHN 16.33.

Wordsworth was beginning to think they were looking

for a lost soul.

Back downstairs Trisha was cooking up heroin. Stacey was transfixed as if watching a rite of passage. She stared as Trisha mixed the heroin, water and citric together in the bent spoon she kept especially for this ceremony. The liquid turned a golden-brown colour and Stacey started to hum *Golden Brown* by The Stranglers … just another part of the ritual.

"You want a dig, Stacey? Make you feel better."

Stacey just nodded.

Trisha put a piece of cotton wool into the mixture and sucked up the majority of the solution through the white fibres into a syringe, leaving only a tiny bit in the spoon. With the needle in her hand she took hold of Stacey's foot and removed the slipper. She skilfully injected the heroin in between her toes. Almost immediately the drug took effect and Stacey's eyes glazed over as she slumped back onto the sofa. Trisha looked at her for a few moments, then tidied away the paraphernalia, placing it back in a box Stacey kept under the television. Then she took the two little plastic bags that had contained the heroin and stuffed them in her pocket. Job done. She picked up her can of beer and took a swig.

***

Wordsworth and Redhead, in need of fresh air, had just stepped out of the house when PC Emma Williams, the Family Liaison Officer assigned to Stacey, pulled up outside and got out of her unmarked police car carrying a Morrison's carrier bag. From the way the bag strained, Wordsworth knew it contained bottles. Without waiting to be asked for an explanation, Williams gave one.

"She asked if I'd go … I couldn't say no."

"We heard," said Redhead. "You paid?"

"Well she hasn't got any money, has she."

"They won't let you claim it."

"I can stand a couple of bottles of wine. She was in a right state."

"I think that's pretty normal," remarked Redhead. "Kid's run off – I bet you anything. Who wouldn't with that as a mother?"

"No," Wordsworth spoke quietly and decisively. "She's not a runaway."

"What makes you so certain?" asked Redhead.

"Her mother's incapable. She needs her daughter … and Jodie knows it. Two days' worth of pots in the sink. The two days Jodie's been gone. I bet Jodie normally keeps on top of it. Then there's her computer and phone charger – she wouldn't have left them. And the photos, of her and her mum. They're not fake. They show exactly what she wants their relationship to be. Have you checked her bedroom?"

"Yeah," replied Williams.

"Neat, tidy … Schoolwork. There's schoolwork isn't there?" asked Wordsworth.

"Yeah," Williams said again.

"None of this says runaway. Something's happened to her," Wordsworth stated.

Before they went back into the house, Wordsworth quizzed Williams about whether she'd gleaned anything from either the mother or the neighbour. Her reply was just what Wordsworth had expected … the only thing she'd gleaned was that booze and drugs played an important part in their lives. Wordsworth, who had four children and spent the majority of his time trying to ensure their well-being and happiness, for which he got little thanks, was always surprised that total screw ups like Stacey Kinsella were able to generate such devotion from their children. Just another topsy-turvy fact of parenting.

They stepped back into the living room and Wordsworth immediately knew something was wrong. He took in the scene. Trisha was in an armchair, eyes closed, can of beer in her hand. Stacey was lying back on the sofa. Her eyes were also closed, but out of the corner of her mouth there was a trickle of vomit.

Quickly Wordsworth moved to her, he'd seen this scenario too often.

"Stacey …"

He felt for a pulse in her neck …

"Stacey …" he repeated. She didn't stir. "Call an ambulance," he instructed Redhead, but he knew it was too late. He knew Stacey was already dead.

INTERVIEW ROOM. BRADFORD CITY CENTRE POLICE STATION, NELSON STREET.
09:36 a.m. 10th JANUARY 2020

"The ambulance arrived in approximately eight minutes. I made a call that SOCO were needed and then I left," explained Wordsworth.

"By yourself?" asked Sergeant Ashburn, her stern demeanour not wavering for a moment.

"No. DS Redhead was with me."

"Where did you go?" persisted the sergeant.

"Back to the office to write up the report."

"What were you thinking had happened?"

"I thought there'd been an accident. I thought that Stacey Kinsella was in such an emotional state she'd OD'd."

"Do you know a lot about OD'ing?" Ashburn's words dripped with sarcasm.

"I've seen a few in my time."

"When you say a few …?"

"I would think it would be near a hundred."

Ashburn hadn't expected that number and for a moment she involuntarily leant back in her chair.

Wordsworth continued, "When I was in uniform, I worked the City Centre …" Wordsworth paused for a moment, then continued with more than a touch of irony in his voice. "Have you ever frequented Bradford City Centre on a Friday and Saturday night?"

"No, not often," Ashburn had to admit.

"OD'ing is pretty common. Most times not fatal … but occasionally you come across a dead one."

"Had the doctor arrived when you left?" asked Price, bringing them back to the point of the conversation with a far more amiable tone.

"No – just the paramedics."

"You didn't think it necessary to wait for the doctor."

"No."

"Why not?" asked Ashburn with an aggressive air.

"I just said. She was dead."

"You didn't need it confirming then?"

"She was dead – no doubt. You've got to remember my priority at that time was still the missing girl – her daughter. We had no leads; we had no idea if she was in danger. I needed to get working."

"And by now you had been nominated to head up the investigation," Price reeled off what was an obvious fact.

"Yes."

"With DS Redhead acting as your number two?" continued Price.

"Yes."

"Did you and DS Redhead get along?" asked Ashburn.

If there had been any doubt who was good cop who was bad cop, the last couple of minutes had clarified each of the interviewers' roles.

"Get along?"

"Did you … *gel*?" Ashburn almost spit out the last word.

"We managed to … *get along*," said Wordsworth matching the interviewer's emphasis.

"There was an altercation, wasn't there? Back at the office." Ashburn had her hooks into him.

"Yes."

"What happened?"

"I thought he was being a prick and I put him in his place."

"What was the altercation about?"

"I'd rather not say."

"Why not?" Ashburn persisted.

"I just wouldn't …"

"He doesn't have to answer," Sharvari stated.

"No he doesn't, but he isn't doing himself any favours by not doing." Ashburn directed the statement at the rep, whilst not taking her eyes off Wordsworth. "Not answering could easily be construed that he has something to hide. Why don't you want to answer, DI Wordsworth? Is it because you don't want to incriminate yourself?"

Wordsworth remained silent.

"We'll be taking a statement from DS Redhead, so we can learn from him what the argument was about," she continued with a condemnation that Wordsworth found slightly pathetic. He knew she'd get nothing from his partner.

"It might be easier if you told them," Sharvari suggested.

"Okay … if you think so," replied Wordsworth nonchalantly.

"Well …?" challenged Ashburn.

"I said I thought the whole thing was a waste of police time and money, and that the mother had been a smackhead who had lived off benefits and had probably never done a day's work in her life or made one positive contribution to society." Wordsworth paused for a moment, then continued: "I then went on to say that the kid, Jodie, was probably better off as far away from her mother and her lifestyle as possible. From the little we had learnt about her at the time, it seemed she had some semblance of decency, but she was a teenager, and we all know how easy it is for a teenage kid to be swallowed up by the world they live in. At this stage I thought she would be back in a matter of hours." Wordsworth paused briefly, then added, "It was something along those lines."

"And DS Redhead took umbrage to this?" Price couldn't hide the surprise in his voice. He knew that Wordsworth's take on the likes of Stacey Kinsella were pretty much widespread throughout the Force.

"Yeah. He said I shouldn't paint everyone with the same brush … or something like that. Then he kicked off. It all got a bit heated … so I walked out. As far as I was concerned that was it. Me right – him wrong."

Price had a feeling that there was something else at the root of this argument.

"Is this a common occurrence … you and him arguing?"

"We exchange words now and then."

"The Inspector had just witnessed a senseless death. He was very upset, isn't that so?" Sharvari was again trying to protect him.

"I was upset that it kept happening and nobody was doing anything about it. Doling out great big dollops of sympathy achieves nothing. Jodie Kinsella's role-models were junkies. What hope did she have? That's what I was thinking. We all become involved when it's too late. Wasn't it about time someone did something before it's too late?"

"And that was it?"

"More or less."

CHAPTER TWO

Wordsworth had had arguments with Redhead before, disagreements about procedure, even disagreements about a person's guilt or innocence, but they'd never been this bad.

He went to ring his wife, Wendy, with the intention of letting her know he'd be home earlier than expected, but before he could dial, he had another call. He didn't recognise the number, but he accepted it nevertheless.

"DI Wordsworth," he announced into his hands free.

"PC Williams here, sir – the FLO," came the voice through the speaker. "I think I've found something."

"You're not going to tell me she wasn't dead after all, are you?"

"No – she was dead." She wasn't sure if Wordsworth was joking or not. "It's just about the missing daughter,"

"Go on."

"Sir, I don't think she had any intention of going to

school that morning."

"Why not?"

"SOCO have just found her school bag stuffed in the bottom of her wardrobe. If she was going to school, wouldn't she have taken it?"

"Which school does she go to?'

"Buttershaw Comp ... Sorry Buttershaw Business and Enterprise College," there was just a touch of derision in Williams voice.

"You don't like the place?"

"No ... I went there, I did okay. But the Business and Enterprise title ... bit pretentious. A school's a school's a school."

"Okay ... thanks. Oh ... PC Williams ... while you're there, get me a recent photo of Jodie. There are some on her notice board in her bedroom. Check with SOCO first."

"Will do, sir."

Wordsworth hung up the call, wondering whether he should make a trip to the school, but it was the other side of the city from where he lived in Heaton and all the 'business and enterprising' would most certainly have finished by the time he got there, so he decided he'd go in the morning. With the added information concerning Jodie's school bag, he was even more convinced that the girl hadn't run away, at least not permanently. But if she had, she would almost certainly turn up the minute she heard her mother had died. They had found her social media and although so far it hadn't given them any new information, they had reached out to her via the various platforms to let her know something had happened to her mother and she had to get in touch. Maybe she would.

He doubted it.

***

Wordsworth pulled up outside his Victorian terrace house, locked his Vauxhall and headed indoors. He could hear sounds of his family coming from the kitchen and headed in that direction, finding two of the kids – Molly, thirteen, and Oliver, eighteen months younger – at the kitchen table doing their homework. Molly was quite big for her age, while Oliver was quite small, so there seemed a bigger age discrepancy between the two. However, this didn't stop the two of them being very close, with Oliver idolising his elder sister. His wife was preparing her regular stand-by pasta dish.

Wendy smiled when she saw him. She was the same age as her husband but looked younger, and her unguarded expression made people want to open up to her. Her upbringing was very middle-class, and it took her parents a little while to realise that she had never even noticed the colour of the man she'd married. Her parents could never be described as prejudice, but nevertheless the fact their 'precious' daughter ended up marrying a black policeman, did take them a bit by surprise. Wendy was, in virtually everyman's eyes, more than just a pretty face, she was the complete package. She was intelligent, caring and had a wicked sense of humour and out of all her attributes, this was the one that attracted Wordsworth to her the most.

"This is a pleasant surprise. I take it you found the girl," said Wendy.

"No …"

"So what you doing home?"

"I'd had enough."

Wendy stopped what she was doing and looked at her husband. Over the years his cynicism concerning the Force had grown and grown, but she'd never heard him say that he'd had enough.

"Are you not well?" she asked.

"I'm fine."

"So what's wrong? This isn't like you."

"Yeah – well …"

"Do you know where she is – this girl?"

"No – but hopefully she'll turn up."

"In ten minutes you two need to pack that lot away so we can eat," said Wendy.

"I'll do it now."

And before either parent could object, Molly's books were being whisked away and Oliver was quickly following his big sister's lead. Homework was over. Books in hand, Oliver headed out of the kitchen.

Wordsworth opened the fridge door and took out a bottle of Bud. He then rifled through a drawer for a bottle opener and clicked off the cap off his beer. He took a long swig and immediately felt better.

"Bad day," said Wendy.

"It's like every day's a bad day."

"You should quit."

Wordsworth just smiled a wry smile. He could just about manage to pay the mortgage on their house, changing jobs could prove financially catastrophic.

"I could see if I can get some extra shifts," suggested Wendy. Her job as dentist's receptionist didn't pay great, but it was better than nothing.

"And have the kids come home to an empty house? No."

"Then we could downsize."

"And have the kids sharing bedrooms. Can you imagine how that'd go down …?"

"Like a leg of lamb at a vegan convention," Molly interjected.

"That's what I was about to say," laughed Wordsworth.

"I know," was his daughter's quick reply, "I thought I'd save you the effort."

At that moment, Nathan, the youngest in the Wordsworth household hit the kitchen at speed, using a copy of *Shout* magazine to destroy imaginary missiles. Quite naturally, Molly snatched her *Shout* out of his hands, and Nathan, without faltering, just kept on running.

"So I'll do what I have to and no more," continued Wordsworth, oblivious to Nathan's sudden igneous arrival. "No more eighteen-hour days … because there's no point."

"Not like you to be defeatist," said Wendy as she stirred the penne.

"I'm not being defeatist, I'm being realistic."

The door was flung open and Izzy, the Wordsworths' eldest child, entered. She was just fifteen, but looked older, deliberately, and was her mother in the making.

"What you doing home? Have you got the sack?" she asked without any real seriousness, but in an almost identical fashion to Wendy.

"No."

"You're not normally home at this time."

"And that worries you, does it?"

"No," said Izzy too quickly. Then she glanced at Wendy, a glance that Wordsworth knew that Izzy and her mum had a little secret going on between the two of them.

"All right … what am I not party to?" asked Wordsworth.

Izzy was trying to not give anything else away.

"Well?" demanded her father.

It was Wendy who eventually cracked. "Pinks' are having an under eighteens night, I said she could go."

"On a weeknight …"

"We didn't expect you to be home," said Izzy without thinking.

"Well I am."

"All my friends are going."

"Yeah – right."

"They are. Please, it's one night," Izzy pleaded. "I

33

promise I won't do anything stupid."

"Oh? Like what?" Wordsworth said, his concern peaking.

Izzy looked away. "Well, you know …"

"No, I don't."

"Billy …" Wendy only ever called him 'Billy' when she was growing exasperated with him.

"Drugs. Is that what you're talking about? Drugs?"

"I promise you, Dad, I don't do drugs and I *never* will. I've heard you go on about them too much … and there's the photos …"

"What photos?" asked Wendy, apprehensively.

"He showed me some photos. Case photos."

"When?"

"A couple of weeks ago."

"It's important she knows the reality …" Wordsworth tried to sound as if he was in charge, but he was regretting his actions now in the face of his wife's ire. "She has to see what can happen. What these people look like…"

Izzy looked at her father. When he showed her the photographs he had specifically asked her not to mention them to her mother, but now, somehow, here they were discussing them.

"Junkies?"

"Dead junkies," corrected Izzy.

"You're telling me you showed our fifteen-year-old daughter photographs of dead junkies?"

"Yeah."

"Why?"

"I would have thought that was obvious."

"He did right, Mum," said Izzy, suddenly on her dad's side. "I think it's a good thing. Jesus … I'll never touch anything after seeing those." She turned to her dad. "I mean, I bet that bloke you work with wishes he'd shown his sister."

There was a slight pause in the discussion.

"What?"

"That bloke you work with – is it Steve? Steve Redhead?"

"He's got a sister …?"

"Yeah … Zara. She goes to our school."

"I didn't know … he never said …"

"Well he has and I'm guessing he never showed her the photos or she wouldn't be in the BRI as we speak."

Wordsworth was stunned. He couldn't believe he hadn't known.

"She's in hospital?"

"OD'd. It's all round school."

"How well do you know her?"

"I don't … not really … She's in the year below me. I just picked up on the name and asked her one day if her dad was a copper … She told me it was her brother … there's like eleven years between them."

"And she took an overdose?"

"That, or someone said it could have been a bad 'E'."

Now Redhead's earlier reaction made sense.

35

"He never said anything to you?" asked Wendy.

"No."

"You'd have thought he would."

With a quick good-bye, which everyone took for normal, Wordsworth headed out of the kitchen.

***

Bradford Royal Infirmary is a large fusion of buildings, featuring most styles of architecture from the mid-1930s to the present day. It's on a major bus route from the city centre and the majority of visitors arrive by public transport as it's easier. Wordsworth however arrived in his car and eventually managed to find a place to park. He headed straight to the ICU where he found Redhead with his parents outside Zara's room. Redhead had to look twice at Wordsworth as he approached. He was the last person he expected to see and surprised himself when he realised he was pleased to see him.

Redhead introduced Wordsworth to his parents, both of whom barely managed a glimmer of acknowledgement.

"How is she?" asked Wordsworth.

Redhead just shrugged; he didn't know what to say.

"You should have said something."

"I didn't realise it was this serious. I thought … she'd just been stupid. Fuck … we've all been stupid."

"Do they know what she took?"

"Some fucking thing off the internet."

36

"Legal high?"

"Yeah - that's what they think. By the time the ambulance got to her she'd been out for twenty minutes. Massive cardiac arrest."

"They revived her?"

Redhead nodded before he steeled himself to say: "Her brain had been starved of oxygen for fuck knows how long."

"Is there anything I can do?"

"No ... but I appreciate you coming."

"Sorry about earlier ... I was just ..." Wordsworth trailed off.

"Saying how it was ... how it is ... that's what you were doing."

Wordsworth looked in the room where Zara lay, pipes and tubes breathing air into her, but not life. A clever middle-class girl, from a happy caring family, if she couldn't steer clear of the drug world, what chance did Jodie Kinsella have?

CHAPTER THREE

Buttershaw Business and Enterprise College was a short walk from where Jodie and her mother lived. Wordsworth and Redhead arrived just as the day's lessons started, the headmaster, or headteacher, as he insisted on being called, felt their arrival then would be less disruptive.

En route, Wordsworth had asked Redhead about Zara and he'd simply replied that there was no change. They'd driven for another mile in silence before Wordsworth asked if Redhead had thought about taking some compassionate leave. He replied that he needed to keep occupied and sitting by her bedside wasn't going to achieve anything.

At the school, after speaking briefly with the head, who didn't seem to really know who Jodie was, they were shown into Jodie's class. They were in the middle of a French lesson and by the teacher's withering stare in their direction, she wasn't happy about the interruption.

Wordsworth looked at the sea of mainly blank faces,

topped with masses of hair in the girls' case and shaved heads in the boys. Was there any serious hope for these kids, or were they just walking into oblivion?

"As most of you know," Wordsworth started, "Jodie Kinsella has gone missing."

Both Wordsworth and Redhead scoured the class for a reaction – nothing.

"We need to know where she is and that she's all right. If anybody can tell us anything about where she might be or why she's gone off, we would be very grateful."

Still nothing from the class.

"I'm going to give you my personal mobile number. And if you do know anything, or you remember anything, then you need to call me. If I don't answer, leave a message and I'll get back to you as soon as I can. Ok?"

Wordsworth articulated the number, then took another look at what seemed to him the personification of inertia. But in this cauldron of apathy, he did pick out one girl. She had short, black, spiky hair, which certainly set her apart from the majority of the girls in the class. She was staring at Wordsworth like she wanted to tell him something. But whether she would or not Wordsworth hadn't a clue. He hoped she would.

***

Back in the car, Wordsworth and Redhead made their way back through the council estate that surrounded the school.

There were the ubiquitous boarded up houses amongst the mixture of run-down dwellings and those smarter homes that the tenants had obviously purchased. In various doorways or on street corners, overweight residents were matched in number by their anorexic counterparts, both types watched with suspicion, while either pulling on a cigarette or taking a mouthful of the omnipresent Special Brew. They could smell a copper at a hundred paces.

"There was a girl in that class," Wordsworth said without preamble.

"Short dark hair," Redhead interposed, nodding.

"You saw her."

"Yeah."

"What did you think?"

Redhead took couple of moments before replying. "I thought she knew something."

"So did I."

Then, right on cue, Wordsworth's phone rang. Wordsworth looked at it: unknown number. He answered. Wordsworth listened to the caller and eventually said, "We're coming straight back. See you in a few minutes," then he hung up the call.

"Was that her?" asked Redhead.

"That's what I'm guessing."

Redhead signalled and started to do a U-turn.

***

The girl's name was Chloe Moreno. It wasn't just her look that made her an outsider; there was also something about her attitude that set her apart. A quiet confidence, not bravado, that came from a knowledge of her own abilities and not that she could chew gum louder and longer than anyone else.

Wordsworth and Redhead had been given the school's theatre studio to talk to Chloe. The headteacher, having got the go ahead from Chloe's mother, insisted a member of staff was present. Wordsworth and Redhead could hardly object, even though they wanted to.

Chloe came into the studio with the languages' teacher, Miss Laura Radsma. Wordsworth hadn't really taken any notice of her earlier, but now her presence had a more powerful significance. Miss Radsma could get in the way of them learning what Chloe was hiding. She looked in her late twenties but could have been older. Her dress was inexpensively smart and there was something very neat about her whole appearance. The overall impression Wordsworth got from this committed teacher was that she wanted to set an example.

"I'm recording this on my phone," said Miss Radsma with a slight Dutch twang in her voice.

"Of course," Wordsworth acquiesced politely.

"Any time you want to stop, or you don't want to answer these gentlemen's questions, you just say. Alright, Chloe?"

Miss Radsma's tone was gentle, reassuring. Chloe just

41

nodded.

"Okay if we start now?" asked Wordsworth.

"Okay." Miss Radsma nodded, pressing record on her phone.

Wordsworth was about to pitch in with a question when Redhead beat him to it.

"You wanted to talk to us about Jodie?"

Chloe nodded.

"What did you want to tell us?"

Chloe couldn't help but glance nervously at Miss Radsma. It was obvious that the teacher's presence was making her feel uncomfortable and when she'd rung Wordsworth, she'd assumed she'd be speaking to him by herself.

"How well do you know her?" asked Redhead, sensing Chloe's sudden reluctance.

"She's my best friend," Chloe replied.

Redhead seemed to be gently easing info out of the girl, so Wordsworth just sat back and let him get the preliminaries out of the way.

"Sat next to her in class?" asked Redhead as if he already knew the answer.

"Not every class ... but most ..."

"Did you see her outside of school?"

"Yeah."

"How often would you say?"

"Er ..."

"Twice ... three times a week?"

42

"Weekends ... I see her most weekends. But we're never off Facetime ... and we text each other all the time."

"When you meet up, where do you go?"

"Nowhere special ... we'd just hang out."

"Just the two of you?

"No ..." Chloe paused, a meaningful pause. Wordsworth realised that without really trying Redhead had arrived at the information that Chloe had wanted to tell them about all along ... *This* is why she had rung him. "There's a gang of us. Me and Jodie and some lads," she said, deliberately not looking in the teacher's direction.

"Lads ... which lads?"

"Just some lads."

"Lads from school?"

"No ... not this one."

"Which one then?"

Chloe looked at him for a moment, considering her answer.

"Which school do they go to?" Redhead asked again.

"Fulneck."

"Over the other side of the city ... that Fulneck?"

Chloe nodded.

"It's a boarding school isn't it?"

"Yeah – but they're day boys."

"And what age are they ... these lads?"

"Same as us – fifteen ... sixteen."

Wordsworth's head tilted slightly as an involuntarily action to what he'd just heard. He hadn't expected them to socialise with pupils from a school at the other end of the academic spectrum. His prejudices were inbred; he had to admit that, if only to himself. And prejudice was something he had been the butt of on various occasions. It was way back in first school he'd realised in a city peppered with immigrant families; few were Afro-Caribbean.

"Can you give me the names of these boys?" continued Redhead.

"Not sure of all of their surnames … and a couple I only know their nicknames …"

"Could you write them down for me please," Redhead said holding out his notebook and a pen.

Chloe started to scribble down the names without pausing. It took her no time at all. She handed the notebook and pen back to Redhead, who started to study the names.

"What's the real reason you rang me Chloe? It wasn't just to give us a few names was it?"

Chloe shrugged.

Wordsworth decided to put her on the spot, see how she reacted.

"What are you keeping from us Chloe?"

"Nothing."

"That's a lie. I bet Miss Radsma here knows it's a lie, so let's not mess about any longer."

"I'm not lying. I rang you – remember?" Chloe protested, but there seemed a lack of belief in her protest.

"You're not in any trouble Chloe, but we need to know everything so we can find your friend."

44

Chloe looked at them, weighing up her options. Wordsworth sensed the quandary within her and decided they needed to press her even further.

"We don't know what's happened to Jodie, but we have to consider that it's something bad, otherwise she would have been in touch."

"Jodie's a bright girl, I can't imagine she's done anything stupid." Miss Radsma decided she needed to join in the conversation.

"Even bright girls can find themselves in situations they can't handle," was Wordsworth riposte.

Both Chloe and Miss Radsma said nothing, but both knew Wordsworth was right.

"Look," continued Wordsworth, "we've left messages on her phone, Facebook and Twitter, telling her that she needs to contact us about her mother … we said it was serious. You'd think if she was ok she'd have got these messages, right? And the least she could have done is make a call."

"Her mother …? What about her mother?" asked Chloe.

"You hadn't heard?" Wordsworth pretended to be surprised.

"No … has something happened?"

"She died."

"What?" Chloe was genuinely shocked.

"Died …? When?" asked Miss Radsma.

"Yesterday." Wordsworth paused for a moment to let it sink in, then went a step even further, maybe a step too far.

"She overdosed on heroin."

Redhead looked at him, unable to hide his shock.

"She was probably distraught about her missing daughter and wasn't thinking."

"Heroin? She took heroin?" said Chloe in a quiet, incredulous voice.

"Didn't you know?"

"No."

"I thought with you and Jodie being such good mates…"

"I didn't know," said Chloe quietly.

Miss Radsma knew Wordsworth had crossed a line.

"That's enough. I think we need to get Chloe back to her class."

"Just one last question …" Wordsworth gave her no option. "I was under the impression Jodie and her mother were close and if that was the case, why wouldn't she take time out to call?"

Wordsworth waited for an answer. None was forthcoming.

"I know of one possible reason;" he continued, "she can't. Something's happened to her and she can't get in touch. That seems a plausible reason to me, don't you think?

"Come on Chloe … let's get you back to class." Without turning off her phone, which was still recording, Miss Radsma moved to guide her pupil out of the studio. But something was still troubling the student.

46

"She'd been offered some money," she blurted out halting her teacher in her endeavour to get her out.

"For what?" asked Redhead, now understanding Wordsworth's tactics.

"To meet this man."

"What man?" Redhead pressed.

"I don't know."

"She told you this?" Wordsworth joined in.

"Yes."

"What did she say – exactly?"

"That her mum was ill …"

"But you didn't know she was an addict?"

"No – I swear. I thought she had cancer – that's what Jodie told me. She said if she met this man, the money would help …"

"And you're sure you don't know who this man is?"

"She didn't say. She couldn't tell me anything about it."

"Nothing at all? You're sure? Because any little snippet could help." Wordsworth was pushing hard.

"No … Honest, I don't know anything," Chloe replied with a tremor in her voice. She was thinking exactly the same as Wordsworth – something very bad had happened to her friend.

"Did she meet this man online?"

"No."

"So how did she meet him?"

"I don't know. I just know she needed the money."

"How much was he offering?"

"A thousand pounds," said Chloe hesitantly.

"A thousand pounds, just to meet him …?" asked Wordsworth incredulously.

"That's what she said."

"Didn't Jodie think it odd?" Wordsworth questioned.

"I guess not."

"She must have had some sort of reassurance," Miss Radsma joined in. "Jodie isn't stupid."

"So you said," Wordsworth couldn't help thinking that it was a pretty dumb idea for any fifteen year old to go and meet a man for a thousand pounds and expect it to be kosher.

"She was desperate … really desperate. She needed the money to help her mum … there were bills to pay and they had nothing. She even asked if I could loan her anything."

"Did you?"

"Ten pounds. That's all I had."

Wordsworth suddenly had a surge of pity for Jodie. If she was really that desperate for money, where could she go?

"Is there anything else you need to know?" asked Miss Radsma.

"Not at the moment. We might need to speak to Chloe again later. You've got my number Chloe. If you think of anything else, I would really appreciate you getting in contact."

"I will," replied Chloe, but her eyes confirmed his suspicion that she wouldn't.

48

Miss Radsma ushered her pupil out of the studio and Wordsworth looked at his subordinate.

"Not good," he said, his eyes turning towards the departing Chloe. "Not good."

***

As Wordsworth and Redhead were climbing back into their car, they were stopped by Miss Radsma.

"I need to tell you something. Jodie did speak to me about her mother. I knew she was having problems and I'd been to see her, because I didn't want anything interfering with Jodie's schoolwork."

"You went to see her at her house?" enquired Redhead.

"They had no electricity … they just had some candles. I thought you should know I paid for some electric for them. It was obvious they were desperate for money."

"At the time did you realise her mother was an addict?" asked Wordsworth.

"No … I knew she wasn't on this planet. But like Chloe, I just thought she was ill and had taken something … something that had made her drowsy. It just didn't make sense …"

"What didn't?"

"Jodie is in line for straight A's. She is Oxbridge material. That's virtually unheard of at a school like ours. Her and her mother just … didn't match."

Wordsworth, slightly relieved he wasn't the only one

susceptible to the idea of stereotypes, realised then that Miss Radsma not only admired Jodie, but she was in fear of losing one of her few star pupils.

"Let's hope we can find her and she can get back on track."

"Please…"

Redhead, believing Miss Radsma had said all she'd come to say, turned and headed for the car, but the way she trailed off told Wordsworth there was more. He didn't want to pressure her, so he looked away and waited patiently.

"There is one other thing …"

Wordsworth turned his gaze back to the teacher. Redhead, not being too far from them, just kept his distance, but was able to hear everything that was said.

"Jodie asked me not to mention it to anyone," she continued.

"Obviously if it's relevant to our enquiry then I'll need to share it with my colleagues," clarified Wordsworth.

"I don't know if it's relevant or not."

"What is it?"

"A couple of weeks ago, actually a week last Wednesday, I know it was the Wednesday, because that's the day I give Jodie extra tutorials …"

"In …?"

"Spanish. She's not doing it as one of her core subjects, she just wanted to do it because she thought it would be useful. She started teaching herself and had asked me for advice … I offered to give her a couple of hours each week, if she wanted. She bit my hand off."

"And a week last Wednesday you'd had one of these tutorials."

"That's right … and generally we left together."

"What time?"

"Five-ish."

"And that Wednesday was no exception."

"That's right. We'd just come out of the school gates. I'd said good-bye to her and gone over to the bus stop and as I was waiting there, I watched Jodie go off down the road and suddenly a man appeared. He grabbed her by the arm. I was going to go over and see what was going on, when I realised she was talking to him. There was some sort of heated discussion happening, but it was obvious she knew him."

"You didn't go over then?"

"No I just stood watching. She eventually pulled away from him and he went in one direction and she carried on to her house."

"And that was it?"

"I wasn't going to say anything, but I couldn't get it out of my mind. And then Chloe's story just now …"

"Did you ask her about the incident?"

"Yes. I needed to check all was okay."

"And did she tell you what it was about?"

"No – she said it was nothing to worry about, just some annoying bloke. She actually said – 'Fue sólo un tipo que se presenta de vez en cuando' which is Spanish for: 'It was just some bloke that turns up now and then.' But she was lying."

"How can you be so certain?"

"I know Jodie … she's a bad liar. It's not in her nature."

"Have you any idea who this bloke was?"

"No … sorry."

"Can you give us a description of him?"

"He wasn't very tall … 1.6 … maybe 1.7 metres at a guess. Could have been anywhere between thirty and forty. I couldn't see if he had hair or not, because he had on a baseball cap – black with an inscription I couldn't read. He was wearing jeans and a t-shirt, a white one, which was nearer grey it was so filthy. He also had tattoos … on both arms, but I was too far away to see what they were."

"Thanks. That could be very useful. If you think of anything else, however small, please give me a ring."

"I will do."

Wordsworth turned to go and join Redhead by the car, but was stopped once again.

"There was one other thing," said Miss Radsma.

Wordsworth turned back to her.

"She gave him something. She handed him something, but I couldn't see what. It was at that point she was able to walk away from him, so whatever it was, it was enough to get him to back off."

Taking on board what he'd just been told, Wordsworth climbed back in the car. He spoke quietly as Redhead pulled away, "We have a suspect."

INTERVIEW ROOM. BRADFORD CITY CENTRE POLICE STATION. NELSON STREET. 09:45 a.m. 10th JANUARY 2020

"You'd met the woman for all of an hour and you decided she had a crush on one of her pupils."

"I never said or even insinuated that. What I saw was a bloody good teacher who was upset about the possibility of losing her best pupil."

Ashburn had deliberately ignored the whole point of Wordsworth's account of the man who confronted Jodie outside her school. She seemed more interested in trying to goad him. Little did she know Wordsworth didn't give a toss and saw right through her pretensions.

"Can we get back to the business outside the school?" Price suggested almost apologetically.

"Just to make something clear for the DS – assessing people's characters is what I do for a living. It's called being a detective. I figure out what makes people tick, what

53

makes them vulnerable, what makes them get up in the morning. I work things out from previous experience, just like you're trying to work me out now. Already you're wondering whether by the end of today you're going to have enough to take this interview onto the next stage. At the moment you're trying to figure out what sort of man I really am. Our paths crossed fleetingly a few years ago, but that wasn't enough for you to have gained a complete picture of me. Now you've done some digging, got some facts on me. You know about my wife of course … my gaggle of kids. You know I have a huge mortgage I can't really afford … and you believe I was promoted to DI at the age of twenty-eight because I was black and not because I was good at my job. And you feel justified in thinking that because I was never promoted further. But the truth is I haven't been promoted because I have my own form of turrets. I can't keep my mouth shut, I have to say things as they are, diplomacy isn't one of my attributes – that's why I'm still a DI. It's the Northern upbringing in me.'"

Ashburn was about to interrupt, but Wordsworth didn't give her chance.

"Physically I'm not big, 5'11" last time anyone cared to measure. I feel like I could lose a few pounds, but technically I'm not overweight, so generally not very intimidating. You can see that. But when you look at me, like you're looking at me now, you know I could kick your sorry arse from here to Barnsley if the mood took me. I never suggested Miss Laura Radsma had a crush on Jodie, I never once speculated on her sexuality, I don't believe it has any bearing on this case. But clearly you do."

Ashburn was seething. If she could have got up and hit him, she would have. Sharvari was more than aware of the tension in the air and decided she should do something about it.

"I don't see what any of this has to do with your enquiry."

"The investigation into the disappearance of Jodie Kinsella seems to be key to our enquiry," added Price. "So can we continue please."

"Sooner this is over the better. I wouldn't mind getting back to work. I spend my time going after real villains. Going after fellow police officers is a bit like shooting fish in a barrel." Wordsworth looked at Ashburn and smiled, leaving her in no doubt what he thought about her.

Price cleared his throat. "So, after going to the school, learning what you did from Chloe Moreno and Laura Radsma … what did you do next?"

"I contacted the Chief Super and filled him in on what was what and that I now believed that the girl was in danger."

"An about turn," Ashburn almost sneered.

"I hadn't met her, but I'd grown to believe that she didn't seem to be the type of girl that would act without serious thought. And we needed to find the man she met outside the school to either eliminate him or find evidence he was involved. If her mother hadn't have died, then we might have been able to learn more. But ..." Wordsworth's statement was left hanging in the air.

"So the team was assembled?"

"That's right. Myself and DS Redhead ... two DCs and three uniforms." Wordsworth took a breath and looked at the table a moment, then back up. His expression steeled. "I believed the girl was in danger ... extreme danger."

CHAPTER FOUR

"Okay Hannah ... I want you to contact Missing Persons Bureau, Missing People, Missing Kids, Salvation Army and that other one ..."

"Look4Them," Redhead proffered.

"Yeah, that's it. And Child Exploitation." Wordsworth was doling out the workload and DC Hannah Harvey had got the slog job of ringing round all the missing people agencies seeing if anybody had any news on Jodie. But she didn't complain. The team had picked up that Wordsworth was worried about this girl, and he wasn't the type to go off half cock at the first sign of a problem.

"It's PC Wheeldon, right?" Wordsworth was indicating one of the uniformed bobbies in the incident room.

"Yes sir."

"You and PC Harlow can do a door to door in the area, see what you can find out. PC Morehouse I need you to check the shops, cafes, what have you, see if anyone remembers seeing Jodie that morning."

"Will do."

"And Declan you're on the nonces. See who's in the area, see who might have got out recently … you know the ropes."

"Okay."

"One other piece of information, you've all got photos of what she looks like, well she may also be wearing an Armani watch. Right, let's get to it."

The team immediately, with minimal chatter, headed off to attack their assigned tasks. Wordsworth turned to Redhead.

"I need you to stay here, co-ordinate and log everything, whilst trying to find out who the man outside the school was. I don't want us to miss anything."

"Sure."

"Any news on your sister?"

Redhead shook his head before replying. "She's still in a coma."

"How old is she?"

"Fourteen."

"Something needs to be done."

"But what? We're fighting a losing battle."

Wordsworth just nodded his head. Redhead wasn't in any mood to hear about anything proactive, he was hurting so deeply he couldn't see past his sister in hospital on life support. Wanting revenge would come later – whatever the outcome. Wordsworth started to head for the door.

"I'm on my mobile if you need me."

"Where you going sir?" asked Declan

"Speak to the neighbour."

"Again? She didn't give us anything last time," Redhead reminded him.

"As far as we know, she was the last person to see Jodie. Not to mention she was also there when Jodie's mother died. I think she's worth another crack."

***

There was blue and white police tape barring the way into the Kinsella house. SOCO were still going over the place and Wordsworth was speaking with PC Emma Williams who had been helping out SOCO with what she knew.

"The mother didn't give you anything … no thoughts about Jodie?"

"Nothing," said Williams. "I was surprised she even noticed she was missing."

"What about Jodie's dad? Was he ever mentioned?"

"Not to me he wasn't."

"And there's no sign of any partner?" asked Wordsworth.

"No. Nearest she's got is her next-door neighbour – the *lovely* Trisha. SOCO found two sets of drug works, both minus any drugs … seems Stacey shot up all she had. Trisha's also a junkie, just more controlled than Stacey. I first picked her up when I was in the pandas … she was

59

soliciting in the Ancient Foresters. The landlord called us. He was well pissed off. Then I'd see her round and about … always trying to get drug money from somewhere."

"Another socially responsible citizen that doesn't work but finds enough money to shoot up." Wordsworth looked at Trisha's house next door before asking, "Is she in do you know?"

"I saw her go out earlier."

"Can you ring if you're still here when she comes back?"

"Sure." Williams gave a little smile.

Wordsworth headed back to his car glancing at his two uniformed PCs, each on a doorstep talking to Stacey's other neighbours. As he slid behind the wheel of his car his phone went. It was Redhead.

"Boss, it's me. A girl answering Jodie's description was seen on Monday morning getting into a car at the junction of Smith Avenue and Wibsey High Street. There's a pub there, The White Swan. A Mrs Pearson, who cleans there every morning, saw her. She's there at the moment. Do you want me to send someone to check it out?"

"No … I'm five minutes away … I'll go."

***

The White Swan had that smell of stale beer and desperation. A lot of its regulars started drinking way before lunchtime and continued until they either ran out of money, fell over, or couldn't cadge anymore.

Wordsworth was glad to get out of the place, he'd learnt nothing from the very amiable Mrs Pearson. She'd seen a girl, which from her description could have been Jodie, short, patterned skirt, off the shoulder jumper, long dark hair, but that's as far as it went. She didn't know the make of the car, the one that Jodie had 'possibly' climbed into, she wasn't even sure of the colour. It could have been blue, but it might have been black … or even red. She didn't even see if it was a man or a woman driving and she thought it went off down Smith Avenue, but she couldn't be sure. As Wordsworth drove away, he was already instructing Redhead to get Wheeldon, Harlow and Morehouse into the area as soon as possible. Mrs Pearson can't have been the only person around at nine o'clock that morning.

Wordsworth went back up Fair Road and drove past the Ancient Foresters pub. He slowed and came to a halt across the road. PC Williams had mentioned earlier how it had been one of the places Trisha Tidswell frequented. Yeah – it was worth a try. He parked the car on Upper George Street and headed for the pub.

It was nearing lunchtime, so the pub was getting busy. Trisha was sitting at the bar knocking back a vodka. She didn't see Wordsworth as he came into the pub.

The barman asked him what he wanted to drink and Wordsworth just held out his warrant card, then sidled over to Trisha.

"How you doing Trisha?" he asked.

Trisha turned to look at him, trying to remember where she knew him from.

"I went to your home, but you weren't there, so I came here … on the off chance," continued Wordsworth.

Trisha's eyes widened as she slowly realised who was talking to her.

"Has she turned up?" she asked.

"Afraid not …" Wordsworth paused, looking directly at her.

"She will do. She's a teenager. When I was her age, I ran away from home every other day. Half the time my mum never noticed I'd gone."

"What made you run away? Looking for the bright lights and the big city?"

She scoffed. "It was normally 'cos of lads. They'd say we should run away together. We'd shack up on somebody's floor or couch for a couple of nights, then I'd come home. After a while, I'd had enough."

"Had enough of what? The sex … the booze … the drugs?"

"Everything … of everything. I never let anyone push me around."

"These lads tried, did they … tried to push you around?"

"Sometimes. But I gave 'em it straight back. Let 'em know where they stood."

There was no conviction in Trisha's words and Wordsworth guessed she was lying. She didn't walk away; she was driven out.

62

"Right …" said Wordsworth nonchalantly. "You said you saw her leave? Monday morning?"

"Jodie?"

"Yeah. What was she carrying?"

"Carrying?"

"In her hands. What was she carrying? You're familiar with the verb I take it … 'to carry'. The act of holding something whilst moving along. It could have been a slice of toast, a Labrador pup, or maybe a bag."

"A bag?"

"If she was going off to shack up with some fella, then I thought she might be carrying a bag with her personal belongings. Toothbrush, make-up, that sort of thing."

"I didn't notice …"

"But you probably would have done, if she'd been carrying something."

"I don't know … maybe," she said knocking back the rest of her drink.

"You and her friendly, were you?" continued Wordsworth.

"Yeah."

"How long you lived next door?"

"A couple of years," Trisha replied holding out her empty glass. "This answering questions thing is thirsty work, you know."

"What did you and her talk about?" Wordsworth fired another question.

"You know …"

"No. You tell me."

"This and that."

"I'm just trying to get a picture of Jodie. Did she do drugs?"

"No … not Jodie." She smiled at the thought. "She didn't even do booze."

"But her mum used, that's no secret. And you use."

"No … I don't. I drink, I don't do drugs. I um … I don't agree with drugs."

Wordsworth couldn't resist a smile. "You see now I know you're lying …"

"Just buy us a fucking drink, will you?" Trisha's patience had run out.

Wordsworth just moved his hand slightly, indicating that he'd buy her a refill.

"Here … here …" said Trisha immediately, whilst gesturing toward the barman with her empty glass.

The barman came across.

"Make it a large," she said without looking at Wordsworth.

The barman took the glass and pushed it twice up the Smirnoff optic, while Wordsworth put a tenner down on the bar.

"I know you do heroin … you were there the other day, when Stacey shot up enough to kill herself. When we went to look at Jodie's bedroom, she was fine. Next thing we know … she's dead. She shot up there and then, didn't she?"

Trisha took a hit of the vodka and without looking at Wordsworth said, "Yeah, okay … so what?"

"She fucking died – that's what. Did she cook up more than normal?"

"No … just her normal hit."

"Did you know she had two sets of works?"

Trisha didn't answer.

Wordsworth continued: "My guess is she kept a spare for when she was desperate. Did you have the spare that morning?

"No."

"She took both lots herself."

"I … I don't know." Trisha's eyes glassed over in shock. "That means … that means when I gave her a hit that morning, she'd already had … oh, my god." With shaking hands, she threw back a large gulp of vodka, leaving a trail of spittle down her chin. She repeated, "oh my god," and hung her head.

Wordsworth changed tack. He needed her to keep talking. "Were Stacey and Jodie living there when you moved in?"

"Yeah." Trisha's voice was quiet.

"How long had they been there?"

"I think about three or four years."

"And over that time did Stacey have any regular partners?"

She shook her head irritably. "No, I told you she wasn't interested."

"A couple of weeks ago, when Jodie left school, she was stopped by a man. She clearly knew him but they were having an argument. I need to trace him. Any idea of who it might be?"

"Some man? Not much of a clue. There's lots of men around, you know."

"In his thirties, about 5'6" ... 5'7", wore a black baseball cap, jeans, t-shirt and had tattoos on both his arms."

"I know who it sounds like ..."

"Who?"

"Jodie's dad – Boyd Kinsella."

"I thought her dad wasn't around," stated Wordsworth.

"He isn't ... he's showed up a couple of times whilst I've been here. Always on the make. Always after something."

"You met him, did you?"

"Too fucking right. He tried to sell me some smack and if it hadn't been for Stacey, I'd have bought it. Fucking baking powder wasn't it. I'm surprised nobody's done him in. He's a rat. Stacey hated him. He's older than she is. Promised her the world, got her pregnant, then disappeared. Stacey was fourteen ... thought she was in love. Soon worked out that he was a pile of shite."

"Do you know if Jodie's had any contact with him?"

"No. Not a clue."

"Do you know where I might find him?"

"Again – not a clue. But if you do find him, keep an eye

on your wallet. He'd steal anything, the toe-rag."

Trisha downed the rest of her drink and once again held out the empty glass. This time Wordsworth ignored it, turned and left the bar.

INTERVIEW ROOM. BRADFORD CITY CENTRE POLICE STATION, NELSON STREET. 09:52 a.m. 10th JANUARY 2020

"At that point did you consider this Boyd Kinsella to be a suspect in his daughter's disappearance?" Price asked.

"I don't know what I … *considered,*" replied Wordsworth.

"But you wanted to speak to him," asked Ashburn rhetorically.

"Of course. It seemed, although he wasn't a regular figure in Jodie's life, he'd certainly been around at some point. There was no real reason to suspect the man outside the school was Boyd Kinsella, but it was a possibility. Jodie wouldn't be the first daughter to have a covert relationship with their father after an acrimonious separation."

"And the neighbour, Trisha Tidswell, what did you do about her?" asked Ashburn.

"Nothing."

"It sounds at the very least she should have been facing a manslaughter charge."

Wordsworth just shrugged. "If I could have proved she was involved, I couldn't agree more."

"Did you ask her?"

"If she was involved?" asked Wordsworth with a touch of humorous disbelief.

"Yes."

"No."

"Why not?"

"Because there was no point."

"You don't know that."

"I do. She would never come clean about anything. It's not in her DNA. There's more chance of me walking a tight rope over Niagara Falls while tap dancing to *Singin' In The Rain*."

"This facetious attitude is only going to slow things down," said Price taking the heat out of the situation.

"Not sure we could go any slower," quipped Sharvari. "Have you many more questions for DI Wordsworth?" she continued.

"Quite a few," Ashburn replied coldly.

"You said you didn't intend being long."

"And I don't …"

"It's been an hour. My client needs to get back to work."

"Unless we get this whole business cleared up satisfactorily, he won't be going back to work."

Sharvari wasn't going to let Ashburn's comment go

unchallenged. "I detect a definite shift in the tone of this interview. The sergeant seems to have her own agenda and if this is about suspending DI Wordsworth from duty, then we should have been informed from the very start."

"If your client was more forthcoming, then *the tone* would have remained the same."

"My client is answering your questions to the best of his knowledge."

"By his own admission, your client didn't conduct an interview with a murder suspect. He chose to ignore it."

"It was a hunch … no proof. If I arrested everyone I had a hunch about, then they'd need to build a new prison every week."

"For someone who thought the girl was in danger, aren't you being a bit cavalier."

"Okay DS Ashburn," said Wordsworth, "what would you have done? How would you have handled it?"

"That's irrelevant."

"And yet you seem to think my client went about it the wrong way," said Sharvari. "During your career, DS Ashburn, how many arrests have you actually made?"

"That's none of your business."

"I presume it's none of my business because your grand total of arrests total just four. DI Wordsworth's arrests number in the hundreds. If nothing else, you need to show some respect."

This time Price sighed a sigh of relief, unable to hide his momentary allegiance with Sharvari. Wordsworth let a little smile cross his lips. Ashburn was slowing up the procedure with her blatant bias and, as far as he was concerned, that was just fine. He knew where this was headed, he knew what they would eventually get to. But the more Ashburn displayed this clear prejudice, then the less meaningful the interview would be.

However, Wordsworth couldn't help but admire her tenacity. She was hurt, her professional integrity had taken a definite hit when Wordsworth had blocked her career path in CID, but she'd fought back and here she was working with the Internal Investigation Squad and the officer that they were trying to nail, was none other than the officer that had stood in her way. He knew Ashburn would go to great lengths to see him disciplined, but her fanatical approach could also prove to be her undoing.

CHAPTER FIVE

Wordsworth arrived back in the office to find Redhead looking at an e-mail Hannah had just sent him regarding the missing persons' agencies. Wordsworth leaned over Redhead's shoulder to read it: no leads. Hannah's trawl around them had brought up no new information.

Wordsworth wanted to ask Redhead about his sister, but he somehow knew this wasn't the time or the place, instead he went through his own e-mails. Only one was of any significance and that was the pathologist's report on Stacey Kinsella. Just as anticipated – a heroin overdose.

"Okay," he said, addressing his team in the room without any preamble, "what does anybody know about the girl's old man ... Mr Boyd Kinsella? There's a name that has a definite ring about it."

He'd called ahead after his meeting with Trisha and got Redhead on the case.

"Twenty-seven convictions," Redhead said, reading off

his computer screen. "Fifteen for drug possession, five for burglary, six for shoplifting and one for drunk driving … on a stolen moped. Most of the drug offences ended with a caution or community service. But he has served nearly five years in total."

"In other words a low life scumbag."

"He's thirty-eight, 5'5", shaved head and both arms are tattooed with numerous inscriptions, but the main ones are a nude covering his entire right forearm, the devil riding a motorbike on his upper right arm and the whole of his left arm is a snakeskin designed sleeve … which, it says here," Redhead squinted at Boyd Kinsella's profile on his computer, "is cobra-like."

"Do we have an address?"

Redhead nodded.

"Okay. Let's get someone round there, check it out. In the meantime, let's keep knocking on doors. And have we made any progress with those lads that her mate Chloe said they hung with?"

"Not yet," replied Redhead.

"We've got their names, haven't we?"

"I've got two nicknames, Pizza Boy and Diesel," explained Redhead.

"Isn't that your nickname, Declan … Pizza Boy?"

"If I didn't eat pizzas doing this job, I'd starve to death."

"And we have one possible real name," continued Redhead, "Herschel Berkowitz."

"Herschel … that's a chocolate bar isn't it?" Declan said

with no certainty.

"Hershey … Hershey Bar," corrected Hannah.

"What sort of fucking name's that?"

"Jewish," said Wordsworth.

"And Berkowitz … are they Poles, do we know?" Declan wasn't sure why he was bothered about their name, perhaps he just wanted to get some sort of handle on the family.

"Or they could be German."

"Or they could be English," Hannah pointed out.

"What's more worrying is … does anyone remember the name David Berkowitz?" asked Wordsworth generally.

"Son of Sam serial killer in the 70s. Let's hope there's nothing in a name. We'll take a trip to Fulneck after I've had a word with Creepy Caroline."

Caroline's office was at the other side of the building and Wordsworth used the walk through the corridors to give more thought to Jodie, who was proving to be something of a conundrum. He tried to reconcile this carer of junkie adults with the aspirational schoolgirl. If Chloe's story of her agreeing to meet some man for a thousand pounds was true, then it just proved how desperate she was for cash and how deep her love was for her mother. Nevertheless, he thought there had to be more to it than just a thousand pounds.

Caroline was at her desk writing up a report. She looked more like a Sunday school teacher than a woman who revelled in blood, guts and DNA. Her not-so-secret nickname, Creepy Caroline, didn't originate from the nature of her job, but from her love of reptiles, of which she had a number. She had on what looked like a skirt Laura Ashley could have designed in the seventies, along with a blouse that had too many frills. Her hair can't have seen any conditioner for at least a year, and it was probably the same length of time since she'd visited a hairdresser, as there was no shape or style to the frizzy mass on her head.

"Anything?" asked Wordsworth as he entered the room.

"Nothing you'll get excited about," Caroline replied. "Nothing you wouldn't expect at that house."

"The pathology report says it was a heroin overdose. It seems she injected between her toes, something she'd been doing for a while."

"I know … I have it all here." Caroline produced a number of photos from a file on her desk. They were autopsy snaps that showed Stacey Kinsella in various stages of being cut open by the pathologist. Wordsworth started to thumb through them.

"He reckons there wasn't much life left in her anyway," Caroline commented. "She had collapsed veins, which had caused infections of the blood vessels and heart valves. She also had TB and hepatitis C2, which means her liver was pretty much fucked."

Profanities seemed odd coming out of Caroline's prim little mouth.

"Which explains why she died so quickly."

"Yeah … she was nearly there as it was."

"There was nothing in the daughter's bedroom?"

"Nothing that will help with your investigation."

Wordsworth was hoping for something that explained everything, but no such luck.

"We did take a laptop away, they might have found something on that," Caroline added hopefully.

"Okay … thanks."

The Computer Forensics Investigators offices were just further down the corridor. Peter 'Gatesy' Harding was the CFI who had been assigned the computer. He had on a short sleeved white shirt and a tie that he tucked into the front of the shirt in between the second and third button. He was in his early forties, but could have passed for nineteen. When Wordsworth walked into the office, no one was surprised to see him. SIOs were rarely seen, unless it was DI Wordsworth.

"That the girl's computer?" said Wordsworth pointing at the laptop in front of Gatesy, who nodded. "Anything?"

"I think so, yeah. We've got access now to her social media. She sent a private message to an Ethan Cartwright the night before she went missing."

"What did it say?"

"I'll let you read it."

The message came up on the screen and Wordsworth scrutinised it. It read: *'I know you're angry with me, but just remember I love you. Please believe me.'*

Scrolling up from this message, he could see forty or fifty more. He read a few, each young and bordering on intense. "Serious relationship then," he mused.

"The start of one at least."

"Slow burn."

"From the messages I don't think they were having sex. But they were obviously close. And you can see the relationship building."

"Dating … but not having sex. Novel this day and age."

"Not really dating … not as we know it anyway. It sounds like they always met up with a group of others … never by themselves. But you can see from their conversation they were just waiting for the opportunity to take it to the next stage."

"Do we know who these others were?"

"Chloe … she features big."

"That's her school mate."

"Someone called Pizza Boy and Herschel."

"So that would make this Ethan Cartwright character Diesel."

Gatesy just looked at him, not understanding what Wordsworth was talking about.

"I'll need a copy of all of it," said Wordsworth, indicating the laptop.

"Sure. The interesting thing about that last message is that it's the first time she used the word love."

"And that's interesting why?" asked Wordsworth.

"Well …whatever she got herself into, whatever she was about to do, he was angry with her. By saying 'love', my guess is she was trying to win him round."

"She knew she was taking a risk," Wordsworth thought out loud, "that's what this is about. Anything else?"

"Nothing as yet."

"What about her other activity on social media?"

"She has accounts, but it seems she didn't really use them much, besides messaging. When I was going through it all, I thought I wouldn't mind having this girl as my daughter. She seems so together."

"Let's hope she's stayed together."

CHAPTER SIX

After Wordsworth left the Ancient Foresters pub, Trisha Tidswell went in search of Boyd Kinsella. She'd lied to Wordsworth when she said she hadn't seen him for a year, she saw him at least once a week. Stacey never knew it, even though she'd met him through her.

After he tried to rip her off by trying to sell her baking powder, Trisha had tracked him down to his favourite haunt, The Commercial Inn on James Street. There she proceeded to kick the shit out of him, then watch from a distance as he was loaded into an ambulance.

As far as Trisha was concerned, he still owed her money and he needed to pay it. After her conning her way into A & E she cornered him in a cubicle and demanded payment. For Boyd he was facing tenacity on an unprecedented level and he quickly capitulated. Only he didn't have any cash, so he settled the debt with heroin, this time the real deal.

Kinsella was small time, which suited Trisha fine. She'd have never got anything like the same price from one of the big boys. A relationship was quickly established: Trisha got her heroin cheap and Kinsella had his profits cut by a third, but his balls remained intact.

Again Trisha had no trouble finding Kinsella – he was at The Commercial Inn – where else?

He was in his usual seat, a half-finished large gin on the tacky table in front of him. He stared at her as she came into the small bar.

"I've got some info that you really want to hear," she said without introduction.

"What sort of info?"

"What you prepared to pay?"

"It depends what the info is."

"Info that could save your skin."

Kinsella was beginning to lose patience. "Just tell me what you want."

"Ten wraps for forty quid."

"You've got to be fucking joking."

Trisha stared at him.

"You're going to break me."

Again, she made no attempt to reply. She just kept quiet, let him sweat.

"There's no way you know something that could be worth so much. Fuck off."

There was a long pause as Kinsella tried to weigh up what could possibly be worth that much to him. What he did know is that Trisha wouldn't risk giving him bum information, the heroin deal she had with him was far too precious to her. Finally, with a resigned shrug of the shoulders, he acquiesced.

"Okay … what's the info."

"The cops are going to be paying you a visit."

"What? When?"

"Soon … Real soon."

"Why would they suddenly come after me? I'm small fry. You're bullshitting me."

"Really? Jodie's gone missing and the cops think you may have something to do with it."

"Missing?"

"Yeah."

"What the fuck has that got to do with me?"

"That's between you and the cops, I just thought you probably wouldn't want a lot of junk hanging around when they come knocking on your door. I'll be round later in the week collect my wraps …."

Trisha smiled. Kinsella was a snivelling little rat. The thought of him in a panic amused her.

**

Kinsella rushed back to his place – a house in Manningham that had been split into ten bedsits. He raced up to his room, where he gathered up the small bit of junk he had, along with all his drug paraphernalia, and a few other things he thought might be of interest to the police. He put it all in a Morrisons carrier bag and headed out of his bedsit. The room across the landing was occupied by Jarmila, a Slovakian prostitute.

Kinsella knocked on her door, praying she didn't have a punter in there. A few moments later the door opened and the statuesque Jarmila was standing there in shorts and a loose shirt. Sex was rarely on Kinsella's mind, drugs took precedent over everything, so there was no stirring within, he just needed to find somewhere to hide his drugs stash. Jarmila didn't speak much English but through some uncoordinated gesticulating between the carrier bag and the inside of her bedsit, Jarmila seemed to understand what he wanted. He could hear the doorbell ringing, someone was trying to gain entry, so he thrust the carrier bag at Jarmila and headed back to his room.

The doorbell rang a couple of times more, then stopped. Kinsella waited, but he didn't hear it again. Could they have gone away? He was just starting to relax, believing they may have given up, when there was the sharp rap of knuckles on his door.

Kinsella remained still and quiet. Then a female voice: "Mr Kinsella … we're police officers. Please open up."

Not knowing what to expect, Kinsella opened the door. Harvey and Cosgrove both stood there displaying their warrant cards.

"DC Harvey and DC Cosgrove … can we come in, Mr Kinsella?" asked Harvey.

Kinsella knew there was no point in objecting, so he just went back into the room, followed by the police officers. It was quite small, the largest piece of furniture being a bed with no sheets, just a blanket. There was a small cooker next to a sink that if you'd washed up anything in it, it would have come out dirtier. Then there was a Formica topped table. On the table was one tell-tale sign of Kinsella's predilection: a bent spoon.

"Mr Boyd Kinsella?" asked Harvey.

"Yeah," replied Kinsella with as much aggression as he could muster.

"We're here about you daughter," continued Harvey.

"She's gone missing, hasn't she?"

"Yes."

"When?"

"Monday."

"And you've just got round to telling me now? If a friend hadn't told me, this would be the first I'd have heard. Thanks a fucking bunch."

"It's not our responsibility to keep you informed of your own daughter's whereabouts," Cosgrove chimed in. "If you can't be bothered …"

"When was the last time you saw her, Mr Kinsella?" asked Harvey.

"I don't know … some time ago."

"A week, a month, a year …? What's some time ago?" asked Cosgrove with more than a hint of impatience.

"I don't know. Months."

"So it wasn't you that stopped her outside school two weeks ago."

Kinsella tried to remain unshaken, to remain cool. He just shook his head and muttered: "No."

"That's funny, because someone saw you," smiled Cosgrove. "Someone described you. Said you stopped her on her way home from school. Now you're telling us it wasn't you. Do you have a twin?"

"Funny man."

"No of course you don't," continued Cosgrove. "So I'm guessing you're lying to us."

"Well I'm not," Kinsella protested limply. "They must be mistaken."

"Do you want to tell us what happened?" asked Harvey almost amiably. "Did you and Jodie argue about something?"

Kinsella looked at the detectives and, in that moment, decided he wasn't going to say another word. He'd been lawyered up enough times, he knew if he didn't say anything, he couldn't say anything wrong.

"Well?" prompted Harvey.

Nothing.

"Do you understand what we're asking you?"

Still nothing.

"If you don't answer our questions it'll only make things worse for you."

"One last chance, Mr Kinsella … what happened when you saw your daughter outside of her school approximately two weeks ago?"

Kinsella just stared at the ground.

Harvey and Cosgrove exchanged a look.

"Boyd Kinsella," Harvey started, "we're arresting you on a charge of attempting to pervert the course of justice. You do not have to say anything, but it may harm your defence if you do not mention when questioned something which you later rely on in court. Anything you do say may be given in evidence."

Harvey rattled off the caution. She knew that they didn't have a case against Kinsella, but if they got him in an interview, he might just let something slip. Kinsella seemed totally unmoved by the situation and remained quiet as they led him out of the bedsit. All he was thinking was he needn't have panicked about his gear; they never even mentioned it. What was worrying him now was what the Slovakian hooker might do with it.

***

Cosgrove had a firm grip on Kinsella's upper arm as they made their way down the stairs. There was no way Kinsella was going to make a run for it. Harvey was following them asking Kinsella questions on the move.

"Any weapons on you, Mr Kinsella? Knives, guns or anything?"

"No," came the derisive reply.

"What about needles, razor blades … anything like that?"

"No."

Then Harvey had a thought: the only sign that Kinsella was a junkie was the bent spoon. He'd cleaned up before they arrived. So where was all the gear? It might be useful to know; they could use it as leverage.

"Won't be a minute." Harvey headed back up the stairs. Kinsella had shown no interest in locking the door of his bedsit, so Harvey just turned the handle and entered the room. Straight away she started to look around the place, checking the cupboards, under the mattress, beneath the sink – there weren't many places he could hide anything. Harvey came to the conclusion there was nothing there. Not a needle, a wrap nor a tourniquet. Kinsella had clearly been tipped off.

Harvey came out onto the landing and looked around. There seemed nowhere it could be hidden. There was no loft hatch, in fact the only other thing was the bedsit across the way. She decided to check it out.

Harvey knocked on the door. Almost immediately it was opened by Jarmila, holding Kinsella's carrier bag.

"Oh sorry … … I thought you were man," she said, pointing across the landing at Kinsella's door.

Harvey looked at the carrier bag and smiled. Two and a half minutes later she was headed off down the stairs, stealing a quick glance in the bag as she went, just to make sure it was what she thought it was. And there it all was: syringes, cotton wool, a couple of bent spoons. This was what they were looking for.

The contents of the bag were not checked fully until Kinsella was installed in an interview room along with a duty solicitor and Harvey and Cosgrove had related to Wordsworth and Redhead what had happened at the house in Manningham.

Creepy Caroline, wearing gloves, had carefully removed each item from the carrier bag and put them into evidence bags, which she then sealed. Laid out, neatly bagged, was all the drug paraphernalia that Harvey saw when she first glanced in the carrier bag, but there was something else there too. Something far more interesting. Wordsworth took out his phone and took a photograph.

In the interview room Wordsworth and Redhead took up their positions across the table from Kinsella and his court-appointed lawyer: a bald-headed, smartly dressed, thirty-year-old who said little but made lots of notes.

"Mr Kinsella it's your choice to speak or not, I'm certainly not going to force you ... no wet towels or electrodes on the nipples ..."

Wordsworth smiled, but Kinsella didn't.

"We have a witness who says you gave them a Morrisons carrier bag to look after."

"She's lying," was Kinsella's instant reply, forgetting his decision not to say anything.

"You know it was a girl then?" said Wordsworth, enjoying Kinsella's ineptness.

"I don't know … No … I … What carrier bag?"

"She lives right opposite you and she certainly knows you."

"Her word against mine."

"I'm not going to waste my time arguing with you about whether you gave her the bag or not. She says you did and I have no doubt your fingerprints will be all over it and its contents. I just have one question to ask you … whose is this?"

Wordsworth put his phone on the table in front of Kinsella. It was open on a photo, a photo of a woman's Armani watch with a pink strap.

INTERVIEW ROOM. BRADFORD CITY CENTRE POLICE STATION, NELSON STREET. 09:58 a.m. 10th JANUARY 2020

"What was his reaction to seeing the photo? Not that you had any proof that it was actually Jodie's watch," stated Ashburn, who felt like they may be inching somewhere, but far too slowly.

"He stared at it for two ... maybe three minutes," replied Wordsworth, "nobody in the room said a word, then eventually his lawyer whispered something in his ear and guess what Mr Kinsella said?"

"No comment?" asked Price, knowing full well.

"Spot on."

"Did he know anything about her disappearance?"

"Course he did ... but he was lawyered up, so he wasn't going to admit to anything."

"Not even that the watch was Jodie's?"

"No. But I knew it was."

"What made you so certain?"

"Gut instinct."

"I thought gut instinct had been superseded by DNA," Ashburn said with a supercilious smile.

"Not by real detectives," Wordsworth hit back.

"Do you think you should have waited for the forensic results before confronting him?" Price asked calmly.

"No."

"That would be too obvious," Ashburn jibed.

"No," Wordsworth replied again.

"You don't have a lot of time for the forensic team, do you?" There was an accusatory tone in Ashburn's question.

"That's not true."

"But you thought your gut instinct was more reliable than the forensics."

"It's not even that. We had no reason to hold Kinsella. If we didn't get lucky then he'd have walked at the end of forty-eight hours. And I'm pretty certain he would have disappeared. I needed to see his reaction and besides, he virtually admitted the carrier bag was his. But he wasn't owning up to the watch. He never owned up to the watch. And there were no prints or DNA – nothing we could use anyway. In that moment we had nothing concrete to link him to Jodie's disappearance. Therefore I was relying on that age-old tool that police have relied on since they found Abel stiff as a board – no fingerprints in those days … no DNA … no CCTV … just a couple of brothers having a barney. Along comes some Hebrew cop, weighs up the

90

pros and cons … uses his gut instinct and guesses that a certain Mr Cain has offed his own brother. Case forever enshrined in the bible."

"So how did you proceed?" Price asked.

"My hunch was that when they met at the school, Jodie gave him the watch. That's what she handed over. But I couldn't prove it, so I had to let him go. I just made him think that we'd dropped him from our list of suspects. I thought there was a better chance of him making a mistake if he thought we'd given up on him. In the meantime, I decided we should concentrate on Jodie's relationship with Ethan Cartwright aka Diesel. I knew they were close, so he might just know who Jodie had arranged to meet the morning she disappeared."

"And this was down to your gut instinct?" prodded Ashburn.

"No … Instinct's not like a tap, you can't just turn it off and on. And I'd never even met this kid. He could have been Billy Liar or Ghandi for all I knew."

"And when you met him?"

"I knew he was covering for her. I was fairly sure Jodie had spoken to him about her Monday morning meeting."

"And how did you work that out?" sneered Ashburn.

"Gut instinct."

CHAPTER SEVEN

"Zara's still in a coma."

The suddenness of Redhead's update on his sister's condition caught Wordsworth off guard. He wasn't sure how to reply. They were in the car on their way to Fulneck, the independent school, which the three boys Chloe had told them about, attended.

Redhead continued, "It's now twelve days. My mum and dad still think she's going to recover ..."

"You don't," stated Wordsworth.

"I want to think that ... I want to believe she'll wake up and be as she was. But ..."

"What do the doctors say?"

"It's more about what they don't say and that look they give you when you ask. That sort of non-committal look, which is meant to give you hope and does the exact opposite."

"Were you close, you and Zara?"

"Yeah."

"That's nice."

"She's adopted. After my parents had me, they found they couldn't have any more children. So they adopted Zara. She was just three. Had some problems. But she loved the idea of having a big brother and I loved the idea of having a little sister … I could play the big man … protect her." Redhead paused momentarily and swallowed. "Didn't do a great job there, did I?"

"There's nothing you could have done."

"Not let her use the fucking internet would have been a start," Redhead blurted out before letting out an inarticulate sound. Wordsworth knew he was angry with himself for not doing more to shield his younger sister from taking that step over the edge.

On their arrival at the school, a young girl met them at the big double doors. She politely took them into the main building and along a wide corridor, its walls adorned with photographs and certificates of the school's achievements, until they arrived at an office door. The name on the door was clear for all to see: *DR W. GRIFFITHS – VICE PRINCIPAL*. There was a little entrance bell, which the girl pushed. After a few moments, the top indicator light went green and the girl entered the office, holding open the door for Wordsworth and Redhead. Griffiths, a small man with a head of dark wavy hair and wearing a suit, rose from behind his desk to greet the detectives.

"Thank you, Esther," said Griffiths and the girl left,

closing the door behind her.

"I did get your message, but I'm afraid you may have had a bit of a wasted journey," said Griffiths as he shook hands with first Wordsworth then Redhead.

"Wasted?" asked Wordsworth.

"Please sit." Griffiths indicated the two chairs in front of his desk. Wordsworth and Redhead took the seats.

"We've been in contact with the boys' parents and I'm afraid neither of them will allow their sons to be questioned without them being present. I would have rung and told you, but we've only just managed to get hold of them."

"Okay ... then we just need to ask you a few questions." Wordsworth didn't give Griffiths a chance to object. "Herschel Berkowitz, how old is he?"

Griffiths hesitated for a moment as if he were trying to figure out whether this was a trick question or not. "Sixteen."

"And Ethan Cartwright? Who we understand has the nick name Diesel?"

"Also sixteen, but I didn't know about the nickname."

"Have you any idea why he might be called Diesel?"

"Sorry – not my domain," said Griffiths affably.

"Then can you tell us who Pizza Boy is?"

"Sorry ... as I said nicknames are not my expertise."

"Could you give us the two boys' addresses then?"

"Of course. It's important for the school to get these things sorted out as soon as possible."

Griffiths had obviously been anticipating the request

94

and had Cartwright's and Berkowitz's addresses and phone numbers already typed out for the police officers. Redhead took them and placed them carefully into his inside pocket.

"Now if you'll excuse me." Griffiths stood up, indicating that the meeting was over. "I'm sorry you had a wasted journey."

"One of those things," said Wordsworth, happy to move on. This man was just an extra, he wasn't a lead player. He had no information for them.

Their guide was quickly summoned and as they made their way back along the corridor, they became aware of a group of boys and girls coming towards them. They were around the sixteen-year-old mark and Wordsworth decided he'd take a punt.

"Excuse me," he said stopping the pack. "I'm looking for Pizza Boy."

Nobody looked confused or surprised. It seemed Pizza Boy was known to them all. One of them, a petite Asian girl, said, "He's not in this class. He doesn't take Humanities."

"What's his name?" Wordsworth asked.

"Sebastian Mancini," said the girl without a moment's thought and Wordsworth and Redhead suddenly knew why he was called Pizza Boy.

After acquiring Pizza Boy's number and address they climbed back into the car and Redhead started the engine.

"What now?"

"We need to make arrangements to question these three

lads. While that's been sorted, let's go and speak to Chloe Moreno again … see what she knows about Boyd Kinsella."

"You think Boyd Kinsella's involved, don't you?" said Redhead as he steered the car onto the main road.

"He's a druggie, he'll do anything so he can buy gear to stick in his veins, which could include selling his own daughter."

They drove on a little further before Wordsworth said quietly, "Do you sometimes wonder whether we're fighting a lost cause?"

Redhead answered without taking his eyes off the road. "Everyday day … every fucking day."

CHAPTER EIGHT

Chloe had been sent home early that day. Her mind was on her missing friend and not on her schoolwork. She kept bursting into tears, something she seemed unable to control. Laura Radsma had tried talking to her, but to no avail and it was decided the best course of action was for her to go home.

Chloe, like her friend Jodie, was the product of a single parent family, but her mother was a 'grafter' not a junkie. Chloe's dad, a civil servant, left them when she was just three, running off with a man he'd met and fallen in love with. Until that moment Sandy, Chloe's mum, had no idea that her husband was gay and it wasn't something she made public. Sandy just dug her heels in, refused to talk about it and set about providing for Chloe, and Chloe's two older brothers and younger sister.

Their home was a semi on Reevylands Drive, just a short distance from school and Jodie's house. She always kept it neat and clean, even if she couldn't afford the finer things in the way of furniture and furnishings.

When the knock came on the door, Chloe decided not to answer it. She was curled up on the sofa with a blanket round her watching *Legally Blonde* for the countless time, her favourite film.

The knocking persisted and Chloe stubbornly continued to ignore it, until Redhead's face appeared at the window.

She opened the door and led the two police officers into the sitting room.

"You haven't found her, have you?" she asked in a quiet voice as they all sat down.

"We will," assured Wordsworth. "We've located the three boys you told us about."

"And?"

"We haven't spoken to them yet."

"They won't know anything."

"You never know." Wordsworth moved to the window and glanced outside before continuing, "Jodie's father … Do you know him at all?"

"I wouldn't say I know him. I've seen him."

"When was the last time?"

"A few weeks ago."

"Where?"

"Outside school."

"Did you speak to him?"

"No. Why would I talk to that loser?"

"But you've spoken to him in the past?"

98

"Sort of. Said hello … that's about it."

"You didn't speak to him a couple of weeks ago then?"

"No, I didn't."

"Do you know if he spoke to Jodie?"

"Yeah, he spoke to her," said Chloe tentatively.

Wordsworth looked at her. He knew there was something else she was nervous of telling him.

"Do you know what was said?" asked Redhead.

Chloe just shook her head.

"Jodie didn't talk to you about it at all?" continued Redhead, disbelieving.

Again she shook her head.

"I think she did," said Wordsworth. "You're her mate, there's no way she wouldn't talk to you about her father.

Chloe still didn't say anything.

"Look," said Wordsworth sensing a breakthrough was imminent, "we have reason to believe that Boyd Kinsella is involved in Jodie's disappearance. And if we can get a lead, if we can get just one little light at the end of the tunnel, then there's a chance we'll get her back safe and sound."

Still Chloe was silent.

Wordsworth took out his phone and opened up the photo of the watch that had been found in Kinsella's possession. He showed it to Chloe, the pink strap almost screaming out.

"Recognise it?"

Chloe nodded.

"Do you know whose it is?"

"Jodie's"

"Do you know where we found it?"

Chloe just looked at him.

"Her father had it," said Wordsworth, "And I need to know how he got it."

Wordsworth looked at her, willing her to tell him.

"I guess, she half gave it to him and he half took it."

"Go on," urged Wordsworth.

"Look if I tell you what I know … I'm not going have to go to court to testify or nothing, am I?"

"I can't promise anything. What if he's kidnapped Jodie, what then? What if your evidence will get him convicted? What if what you know means we can find Jodie and get her back safe? Would you still be worried about testifying?"

Wordsworth knew he'd struck home. He could tell from Chloe's expression that she knew it could be dangerous for her mate if she withheld information. How would she ever live with herself if something happened to Jodie and she could have prevented it?

"Well?" prompted Wordsworth.

Chloe looked at Wordsworth, then at Redhead. She took an audible intake of breath and looked at the floor.

"Jodie doesn't want anyone to know about her dad … what he's like. Like she didn't want anybody, including me to know about her mum. Jodie wants to go places. Her life has been hard … and she wanted to break out of it. Having

100

a junkie mum … she knew would hold her back. You go for your interview for uni and they ask what your parents do and you answer, 'Well my mum's a full-time junkie, and my dad uses, but he's not a slouch, he does push drugs on the side, which is where I get my enterprising approach from.' Whichever way you couch it, it ain't going to open no doors."

"I take it she didn't get on with her dad," said Redhead.

"Too right," Chloe confirmed. "Hardly surprising - every time he showed up, it was because he was after something."

"Like what?"

"Usually money. He had this habit of buying gear to push, then sticking it in his own veins."

"And that's what he wanted this time, was it?" asked Wordsworth.

"No … he wanted something worse."

Wordsworth and Redhead resisted looking at each other. They didn't want Chloe to lose focus.

"He wanted her to push gear at school for him. He had people after him for cash. He had this idea Jodie could make him a fortune pushing at school."

"She told you this, did she?"

"Yeah."

"Did she agree to do it?"

"Did she fuck … Sorry, didn't mean to swear … but there was no way she was going to push anything anywhere. He had this 'plan'. Get kids hooked at eleven …

or twelve, and you have an income for life. He knew how popular Jodie was so he thought it was a no-brainer."

"But she wouldn't entertain it," confirmed Wordsworth, not for a second doubting Chloe's account.

"No. But he cried the poor tale, said these people would kill him if he didn't give them something, so she gave him the watch ... told him he could sell it ... but there was no way she was going to turn into some drug pusher for him."

"It was an expensive watch to give away," declared Wordsworth.

"Yeah."

"Where did Jodie get it?"

"She had it given."

"By?"

"I don't know."

"Don't start this again, Chloe. Of course you know. If your mate comes to school one day sporting an Armani timepiece you are going to ask where she got it. Where did she get it from?"

Chloe paused again before answering.

"Diesel."

"Ethan Cartwright." Redhead said. She looked briefly surprised they knew his name. "You knew that was his name, didn't you?"

Chloe paused for a moment, then nodded her head.

"Why wouldn't you tell us his real name when we asked before?"

"Don't know," muttered Chloe. "I just didn't want to

get anyone into trouble.

"You gave us Herschel's name."

She shrugged.

But Wordsworth thought there might be another reason she didn't give up Diesel's name. Just the look in her eyes when she mentioned him said to Wordsworth that she had a thing about him and she didn't want to put him in the firing line. She didn't want to be the person to give Ethan's name to the police. She wanted to protect him. He understood why she said what she did, hormones and all that, but he also knew that this might mean there are other things she's not being entirely truthful about.

CHAPTER NINE

Boyd Kinsella hadn't left his bedsit since being released from police custody. What he'd told his daughter about him owing money was a lie, but because of his history, a plausible lie. Cocking up was as habitual to Kinsella as drug taking. He told Jodie the story about him being in danger, hoping to generate some pity from her and in doing so extract some money. The idea of her pushing smack at school had only come to him moments before speaking to her. He didn't just think it was a good idea, he thought it brilliant. Why hadn't he come up with it before? Get a kid to push to kids. Genius. For him it was like having a business plan. Of course his plan hit a stumbling block when Jodie said she wouldn't be part of it, but he'd not given up hope. He knew his daughter hankered after a father. He'd never been there for her, but she had consistently helped him when she could. Give it time and he was sure she'd go along with it.

In the meantime he had to find some cash to score. After all the little bit of gear he did have was now in the possession of the West Yorkshire Police after the 'stupid whoring bitch' handed it over to them. The way he saw it, she owed him.

He knocked on Jarmila's door, which was quickly opened by Jarmila dressed in just a silk robe covering her nakedness.

"You remember me, don't you? I live just over there," said Kinsella pointing to the door of his bedsit.

"Kinsella … Mr Kinsella," she said, smiling. She still had no idea she'd done anything wrong.

"You gave my bag to the cops."

"Sorry?" She smiled at him, not understanding him.

"My bag," he said loudly and slowly, "you gave it to the cops."

Jarmila just stared, a slight look of puzzlement appearing on her face.

"Bag … my fucking bag, with my gear and a watch … a fucking watch." Kinsella started to tap his wrist furiously.

Jarmila took a guess at what he was ranting about.

"Lady … lady …"

"What?"

"You send … you send her."

"You thought I'd sent her?"

"Your friend … I gave …"

"Why would I send someone to pick up my gear that I'd only given you five minutes before? Why would I do that? How fucking stupid are you, you fuckwit Polack? You owe me and I want paying."

Without warning he pushed past her into her neat and tidy bedsit, the complete opposite to his shit tip.

"Money, you owe me money!" he shouted, pointing at her then pointing at himself. He rubbed his fingers together indicating cash then said, "Fifty quid. You must have fifty quid."

"My money – mine," she understood money perfectly well and was used to standing her ground when it came to haggling.

"Now suddenly you understand English. Listen I want some money. Forget your pimp. I've fucking seen him, I'm not blind. Just give me some cash."

"I have boyfriend," she said defiantly.

"Yeah like fuck you have a boyfriend. Just give me the money."

"No. I am protected."

"You're protected?" Kinsella half laughed the words. "Well unfortunately your protection isn't here at the moment, so ..." he grabbed her by the throat, pushing her against the wall. "Give me fifty pounds now, and we'll let it go at that ... eh?"

"My money!"

"It's money you owe me, you fucking bitch!"

"You not get money," Jarmila choked, grabbing at his hand around her throat. "I not give you money."

Without warning Kinsella just smashed his fist into the face. Her head cracked loudly against the wall and her nose burst open, spraying blood down her face and into her

106

mouth. She crumpled to the floor.

***

Wordsworth and Redhead turned off Manningham Lane and pulled up directly outside Kinsella's bedsit.

They were about to ring Kinsella's bell, when the door of the house opened and two men appeared, both obviously drunk. When confronted by Wordsworth and Redhead, they did some exaggerated apologising and started to stumble off down the street.

"Which is his place?" asked Redhead.

"9A," replied Wordsworth.

They started to climb the stairs. They were only halfway up when they heard the sound of someone screaming out in some Eastern European language. They charged up the rest of the stairs and there, through the open door of Jarmila's bedsit they saw Kinsella kicking Jarmila's body as she lay curled up on the floor. Wordsworth raced into the room and grabbed him by the scruff of the neck, then with his right foot, he whipped away Kinsella's legs, who ended up face down on the floor.

Redhead immediately started to assess the damage to Jarmila. Apart from the bloody nose, Kinsella hadn't inflicted a lot of damage, some bruising here and there, but it was nothing she couldn't handle.

Redhead helped her to her feet. "You okay?" he asked.

"Bastard ..." screamed Jarmila. Then taking everybody

by surprise, she started to lay into Kinsella.

"Hey … hey … no … stop …" said Redhead, restraining her.

Wordsworth grabbed Kinsella and hauled him to his feet.

"Check her out, see if she needs an ambulance," Wordsworth said. "I'm going to have a word with Mr Kinsella."

Leaving Redhead with the girl, Wordsworth literally dragged Kinsella into his bedsit and slammed the door behind him. He sat Kinsella down on the edge of the bed.

"If in the next five minutes you tell me a single lie, I'll beat you so badly you'll wish you were dead. Do I make myself clear?" Wordsworth threatened.

Kinsella just nodded.

"Good," continued Wordsworth. "If the girl across the way wants to press charges against you, then I'm not going to stop her. That's between you and her. But if you go near her again … and by that, I mean if you so much as speak to her again, I will put you away for possession, intimidation and assault. Understand?"

Kinsella just nodded again. Wordsworth was pretty certain the girl wouldn't even think about pressing charges. An obvious prostitute, probably an illegal, she'd just want to keep her head down, not get involved with the police.

"What I want to know," Wordsworth carried on, "and remember what I said about lying … Did you have anything to do with the disappearance of your daughter?"

Kinsella shook his head.

"Do you know anything about the disappearance of your daughter?"

Kinsella shook his head again.

"So why did you go to see her the other day?"

Kinsella shrugged. "I just wanted to see my daughter."

Wordsworth grabbed Kinsella and dragged him to his feet. "You are a total dickhead, aren't you? I know why you went to see your daughter. Now you have one last chance to tell me the truth and if you don't, I *will* beat the living crap out of you here and fucking now and in court I'll blame it on the seven and a half stone prostitute."

To underpin his statement, Wordsworth smashed Kinsella up against the wall, causing his head to bang loudly against it.

"I needed cash," Kinsella blurted out. "I needed cash … to score."

"Did she give you any?"

"She gave me the watch … I didn't steal it, she gave me it," Kinsella rambled.

"Did you or did you not ask her to push drugs at her school?"

"I … I … might have suggested it," Kinsella stammered.

"Pushing drugs to school kids … that's not clever."

"No … no … I know. I wasn't thinking."

"Well think about this, Boyd … if I ever hear that you've been near another school again in your life, I promise I will personally hunt you down and rip your fucking head clean off."

Kinsella just looked at him. There was sheer terror in his eyes.

"Let me ask you again … do you know anything about Jodie?"

"No – I swear it."

Wordsworth looked at him, then let him go.

Kinsella was literally shaking – he was a mess.

Wordsworth put his hand in his jacket pocket and took out his wallet. From it he plucked a twenty-pound note and lay it on the shitty table.

"That's for a fix. Don't waste it on food or anything like that."

INTERVIEW ROOM. BRADFORD CITY CENTRE POLICE STATION, NELSON STREET.
10:07 a.m. 10th JANUARY 2020

"So you broke rules and questioned him by yourself."

"I didn't break any rules. I just spoke to him. He told me that he had nothing to do with his daughter's disappearance and I believed him. His story matched Chloe's – Jodie gave him the watch so he could sell it." Then in an even more contemptible tone, he said: "No rules were broken in the obtaining of this information and no animals were harmed."

"Well we wouldn't know, would we, as no one else was there?" said Ashburn. "And I just find it hard to believe that this man was suddenly an open book, when previously you could hardly get a word out of him."

Sharvari came immediately to Wordsworth defence. "Sorry … what are you suggesting?"

"Are you seriously telling me that DI Wordsworth didn't use some coercion to get the answers he wanted?

And if that was the case, then maybe the answers were totally unreliable."

"I asked and he told me," said Wordsworth.

"According to PACE?" persisted Ashburn.

"If you're asking me if I treated this man as if he was a fully functioning human being, with a modicum of intelligence, then the answer would be no. I asked him in a language that he readily understood."

"You threatened him."

"No … I just didn't pander to him. Boyd Kinsella is a lost cause … way past redemption."

Ashburn liked what she was hearing. To her it seemed they were tantalisingly close to Wordsworth unwittingly making an admission to witness intimidation. So she pressed on. "He's still a person who deserves our respect"

"Yours maybe. Not mine."

"It's attitudes like yours that give the Force a bad name."

"Not so. It's attitudes like yours, pretending we're dealing with rational individuals that makes everybody mistrust us. The public know the score. They know the truth. We're the ones that try and gloss over everything, try and create something that isn't true."

"I'm a police officer with a great deal of experience," Ashburn countered, her volume level rising. "I think I know the truth. And I would also ask you to show *me* a degree of respect."

"Come on, do you think I don't know what this is really

112

all about?"

"I advise you not to go down that road," Sharvari cautioned.

"Okay …" Wordsworth smiled at Ashburn, "I'll listen to my rep's advice, but it doesn't stop me knowing what your game is."

"My game …?"

"Yes. You're out to get me."

"You think this is some sort of personal vendetta?"

"Yes."

"You're wrong," said Ashburn, rather unconvincingly.

"I'd agree with you, but then we'd both be wrong."

This time it was Sharvari that couldn't stop herself from smiling.

Ashburn couldn't decide where to go next. She knew she'd lost the point – she wasn't able to ruffle any of her prey's feathers – so she decided on a different tack. "This enquiry seems to be having an adverse effect on you," she offered.

"In what way?" Wordsworth answered, not even trying to disguise his bemusement.

"Mentally, you appear … troubled."

Wordsworth couldn't help but laugh. "No … this is just how I am."

"We're not here to discuss the Inspector's mental state." Sharvari said.

"I don't mind discussing mine, as long as she doesn't mind discussing hers," challenged Wordsworth.

Sharvari gave him a warning look.

Price cleared his throat. "Respect Inspector Wordsworth."

"Respect as in an Aretha Franklin song which you can only sing if you have soul – something I think your sergeant is definitely lacking."

"Can we return to the agenda?" Ashburn knew her ploy hadn't worked and wanted to try and regain the initiative.

"Isn't this the agenda? If this is not about wanting to nail me to the metaphorical cross, then what is it about? You're trying to pin something on me because I don't fit into your unreal world. Well, let me tell you, I do my job as well as I'm allowed," continued Wordsworth. "Do you think half the people I come into contact with care about the police? To them we're just a nuisance."

"We need to move on ..." Price attempted, but Wordsworth continued, ignoring him.

"I do my job in spite of the incompetence of some senior officers, in spite of the fact that junior officers know more about political correctness than actual detection and in spite of the fact the law is an ass. It's a jungle out there ... Of course, it's a jungle that's surrounded by nice middle-class suburbs, but it's still there. A small area isolated in the middle of relative sanity, that takes up ninety per cent of our time. So what do we do ...? We talk about giving them respect. Respect! You're on a different planet. They have no comprehension of what respect actually means. Most of them are way past the point of respect. They just want to

114

blitz out on any drug they can lay their hands on. They don't contribute to society on any level. And the government's perennial answer to the problem is to throw more money at it … money that just goes into the drug barons' coffers. They need to get on the streets and actually see what's going on. The underbelly is growing unchecked … because we're doing nothing."

"It sounds to me you are rife with prejudice," said Ashburn thinking at last she had rattled him.

"It's not prejudice," continued Wordsworth who was on a roll. "I don't care who these thieves, junkies and low-lifes are … they can be black, blue, white or green as far as I'm concerned. If they've broken the law, I want to nail them. But the system's archaic. It's not fit for purpose. Laws that were introduced in the Victorian era to try and protect the genuinely poor, those in genuine need, now apply to people who have enough money to buy drugs, go on holidays and get drunk seven nights a week. It's wrong. A mother who can't afford food for her kids doesn't give up her cigarettes, getting pissed or going to bingo. She carries on in the same way, because the only person she truly cares about is herself. We all know it's wrong, but nobody does anything to change it."

"Except you. Is that what you want us to believe?"

"Grow up sergeant. Are you ever going to see the truth? We didn't hit it off because you have always been more concerned with how things look on paper, rather than trying to create a better safer place for people to live. Do you want the majority or the minority to run the show? Because as things stand at the moment, we're running scared of the minority … giving them a nice route into damaging this society forever."

"Can we please get back to what this interview is really about?" demanded Sharvari.

Wordsworth had enjoyed his rant and to prove he was still in the driving seat he looked Ashburn right in the eyes and with no malevolence just an undercurrent of passion and belief, he said, "Like it or not we're creeping closer and closer to the edge of civilisation."

CHAPTER TEN

Out of the three schoolboys, their first interview was with Sebastian Mancini: Pizza Boy. He lived with his parents and four siblings, two brothers and two sisters, in a large, newly built, stone house with views of Thackley West Wood. The exterior of the property was tastefully finished and showed that whoever built it had some style. The interior, however ... was different. Both the décor and furnishings were on the garish side, with enough ornaments and trinkets to supply a souvenir shop on the front at Blackpool.

Sebastian's mother, Danielle, a rotund brunette in her mid-forties, wearing a purple velour tracksuit, showed in Wordsworth and Redhead. Redhead had done his homework on Google. He'd discovered that Danielle, the mother, used to be a waitress in Giovanni Mancini's first restaurant. Giovanni was second generation British Italian, who came from a large hard working but poor family. He clearly wanted more for his own offspring. His father had always been the hired help; Giovanni was determined to be the man that did the hiring. Over the past twenty years he'd opened five restaurants, both sides of the Pennines. An empire big enough to control and not too big to run out of control. He'd watched Jamie Oliver with jealousy as his empire expanded and expanded, but then he watched as it ran into trouble and his envy turned to thankfulness that he hadn't gone down the same path.

Giovanni, a small dapper man who had just turned fifty, was sitting on one of the two large sofas, positioned in front of the large TV, in the large living room. Next to him was Sebastian, a very confident, good-looking youth, who towered over his father, but at the same time showed him total respect.

Introductions over and done with, Wordsworth and Redhead sat on the sofa opposite the three family members.

"I understand you see Jodie Kinsella socially," Wordsworth said. Sebastian was about to just agree with him when his father stepped in.

"He knows her." There wasn't any trace of an Italian accent; he was Yorkshire to the core.

"Were you in a relationship with her?" Wordsworth looked directly at Sebastian.

"No he wasn't," Danielle said, not allowing her son to answer.

118

"If you could let your son tell us himself, I'd be very grateful."

All eyes went to Sebastian.

"No I wasn't,' he said in a soft voice which didn't seem to fit with his large physique.

"But you'd meet up with her?" Redhead asked.

"Her and some other mates."

"Which mates?" asked Redhead.

"Normally me, Diesel …"

"Ethan Cartwright?" checked Redhead.

"Yeah … and Hershey Berkowitz and … of course, her mate, Chloe."

"Moreno?" asked Redhead, once again making sure their facts were correct.

Pizza Boy nodded.

"Where do you meet?"

"All over … Café Nero … That place up Westgate … the market … Just depends."

"On what?"

"What we feel like."

"There are just the five of you that hang around together?"

"Yeah."

"How come?"

"How come we hang out together?"

"Yeah. You're from this side of town. Jodie and Chloe live, what, eight or nine miles away. You go to different schools. How did you become friends?"

"Through Hershey originally."

"Go on …" Wordsworth prompted.

"Jodie was waitering at some do or other … and so was Hershey."

"Waitering?" asked Redhead looking for clarification.

"Waiting tables. It's a catering company that uses school kids … cheap labour. My dad always pays his staff over minimum wage, isn't that right, Dad?"

His father hesitated before nodding his head, which told Wordsworth that despite what his son believed, there were some staff at the Mancini restaurants that were only getting the minimum.

"And Jodie and Herschel met waiting tables … for minimum wage?" confirmed Wordsworth.

"Yeah. Jodie did it 'cos she needed the money, Hershey did it because his mum made him. She just wanted him off his Xbox."

"And Jodie and Herschel just clicked?"

"I wouldn't say that. Hershey is a bit of an acquired taste. They just got talking and arranged to meet up. She said she wanted to bring a mate. She didn't want to see him by herself. I think she thought it would send out the wrong signal."

"That it was a date, you mean?" asked Wordsworth.

"Yeah."

"She didn't fancy Hershey?"

"No."

"Why not?"

"You not met him, have you? He's just a bit of a plonker."

"Sebastian …" his mother reprimanded gently.

"How do you mean?"

"He's always telling you what he knows, even though no one ever asks. Nobody even understands half the stuff he comes out with."

"If he was such a plonker," Wordsworth asked, "why did Jodie agree to meet him?"

"I think she thought he was smart … which I suppose he is. We all are. Jodie preferred hanging with us because we're all going to Oxbridge."

"You don't actually know that dear, do you?" his mum said.

"Okay … we're going to uni – good ones – and Jodie liked that. She didn't want to end up at some uni no one's ever heard of, in a town nobody wants to visit, studying tourism and origami."

"Sebastian!" It was Giovanni's turn to caution his son.

"Sorry," his son apologised immediately, "but I got where she was coming from. What good's a degree in glass-blowing? She wanted to go to the best. Do a subject that was academic. And she thought rubbing shoulders with the likes of us wouldn't do her any harm. Something might rub off."

"And so she brought along her friend Chloe and Hershey brought along you and Ethan Cartwright."

"Yeah."

121

"It was like a blind date …"

"No. It was just some mates meeting up with some girls. See how it went. If I hadn't have got on so well with Chloe, I'd have just had a drink and that would have been it."

"But you did get on."

"Yeah … I got on with her."

"And Ethan got on with Jodie," said Redhead.

"Yeah. He couldn't take his eyes off her. Mind you, she is something else. You'd have to be blind not to fancy her."

"So poor old Hershey was left out on a limb," Wordsworth remarked.

"Hershey's always on a limb. He sort of just hangs on and we let him. Me and Ethan did try and get rid of him a couple of times, but we couldn't shake him. He was always there. Once we lied to him about meeting Jodie and Chloe, said we were staying in to do homework, but he texted one of the girls and found out we were meeting up, so he just turned up. He didn't even think we were trying to get rid of him. He just thought we'd changed our minds."

"Was Hershey jealous? You two had girlfriends and he'd been left behind."

"Jealous? No, I don't think so."

"He must have felt something."

"Hershey's used to it. Wait till you meet him. You'll see what he's like. If he wasn't so bright, you'd think he was a retard."

"That's enough of that sort of talk!" his mum remonstrated.

"All right … mentally challenged or whatever you want to call it. You know Hershey, Mum … He isn't the full ticket."

"He's a very nice boy … just a little odd," Danielle commented, shuffling uncomfortably.

"When did you last see Jodie?" Wordsworth asked.

"Friday night."

"Did you all meet up?"

"Yeah."

"Who instigated it?"

"Nobody … it was just something we did most Fridays."

"What did you do?"

"Just hung around. There's a couple of bars up by the university that get real busy on a weekend, we normally go to one of them."

"How do you get in? Don't they want ID?" asked Redhead.

"Yeah. Why do you think we let Hershey hang with us? He sorts all that."

"That's against the law!" Danielle sounded horrified.

"You don't mind me drinking. I've been drinking wine since I was a kid."

"That's different. That's when we're having a meal."

"How come it's different? Alcohol's alcohol," protested Sebastian.

Wordsworth thought he had a point.

"It's not just the alcohol … what about the ID."

123

"Everybody would do it if they had a Hershey."

"Well I don't want you to do it again," continued Danielle. "Do we, Gio?"

"No."

"And any false IDs I want you to destroy."

"And there was I thinking I was part of a liberal family."

"I don't want to see you in jail."

"In jail? Get real, Mum. I'm not going to end up in jail. You should see some of 'em … falling over, fighting, throwing up … police do nothing."

"Still …"

"Did you go to one of these bars Friday?" asked Redhead.

"Yeah."

"Which one?"

"The Varsity. It's on two floors, so if you stay upstairs, you're normally okay."

"Did anything happen?" Wordsworth asked.

"Like what?" asked Sebastian defensively.

"Anything out of the ordinary between the five of you … anything between Jodie and Ethan?"

Wordsworth sensed Sebastian was thinking whether or not to tell him about something. Wordsworth knew not to press. If he did then he was fairly certain Sebastian would clam up, or his parents would move in to protect him. So he just looked out of the large window with the view of the woods, as if there were no pressure at all.

"Great view by the way," he remarked nonchalantly.

Giovanni half smiled and nodded in agreement. Danielle just kept her eyes on her son.

"Jodie and Ethan were talking about something," Sebastian eventually said. "It got pretty heated."

"Do you know what they were talking about?"

"No."

"But they were arguing?"

"I suppose you could call it that. It ended up with Jodie walking out."

"She just walked out and left you all."

"No Hershey went after her. He told Ethan he was a moron and left the bar."

"Do you know what happened then?"

"We just finished our drinks and left."

"I mean with Jodie and Hershey?" Wordsworth clarified.

"You'll have to ask Hershey. By the time we came out, they'd gone."

"You didn't ask him what happened?"

"He said nothing happened. I really didn't care."

Wordsworth and Redhead were about to leave when Wordsworth had one last thought: "Ethan Cartwright … why is his nickname Diesel?"

"From the designer label. One day, years ago, we were going out and he arrives dressed head to toe in Diesel gear. It sort of stuck after that. He spends a fortune on clothes … well his mum and dad do."

Redhead and Wordsworth set off to leave again and

125

were stopped by Sebastian.

"Aren't you going to ask me why I'm called Pizza Boy?" he asked with a sardonic smile.

CHAPTER ELEVEN

The Berkowitzs lived in Calverley, a rural village about 4 miles away from Fulneck school. Well, 4.1 miles, to be exact. Herschel Berkowitz tracked the journey every morning and evening, just to check it never changed – and it never did. Hershey was next on the list, and Wordsworth was hoping that he would at least confirm Pizza Boy's account of last Friday night.

The house was a modest detached Yorkshire stone building in a residential area. Unlike the Mancinis' place, nothing lavish, nothing extravagant and it looked directly across the road at a similar house.

The front door was opened by Ruth Berkowitz, Herschel's mother. Ever since Herschel was born, Ruth assumed the role of full-time mum. Even now, with her son turned sixteen, she felt she needed to be there when he came home just in case he needed something … anything. And Herschel normally needed a lot from this ridiculously devoted parent.

Ruth explained to the police officers that her husband wasn't home, but it wouldn't be too long before he was back.

"He's got a client who's being investigated by the Inland Revenue. They need to go through his books for the morning," she explained, giving the police officers far too much information.

"I take it he's an accountant," stated Redhead.

"Yes." There was a pause. Then, "He's upstairs."

Ruth had been preparing mentally for the police's arrival all day, ever since she got the phone call from the school. She was quite calm, but she knew if she hadn't been forewarned, then this would have been very difficult for her. In her wildest nightmares, and she had some pretty wild ones, she had never even considered the possibility of her precious son being interrogated by the police.

Herschel was in his bedroom playing *Call of Duty* on his Xbox. He heard the door open at the same time he heard his mother's voice asking if it was okay for them to come in. Herschel grunted a reply, his concentration still on the game.

Wordsworth and Redhead stood awkwardly in the doorway for a few moments while Herschel continued to rapidly press buttons on his wireless control. Ruth hovered just behind, smiling proudly. Wordsworth's patience quickly ran out.

"Herschel? We need to talk to you about Jodie Kinsella."

128

"One second … let me just …" Herschel said without looking at them.

Wordsworth took a deep intake of breath and exhaled it rather noisily. Ruth looked at him, wondering what his problem was. This was her son; he was playing with his game and interrupting was simply not on.

Then he cried out, "No! No!" and his arms dropped, his expression defeated.

"Finished?" asked Wordsworth sarcastically.

Herschel seemed inured to Wordsworth's little dig. He just looked at the detectives through his frameless glasses, which seemed so far down his nose they were about to fall off. His mouth was slightly open, his hair curly and cut badly, his posture hunched, and he was podgy verging on fat.

"Jodie Kinsella … I understand you were with her on Friday night." Wordsworth made no attempt to hide his slight annoyance with Herschel's lack of engagement.

"Is this some girlfriend you've been keeping secret?" Ruth asked, hardly able to hide her excitement.

"No," replied Herschel curtly.

"But you were with her Friday?" persisted Wordsworth.

"Yes."

"Along with Chloe Moreno, Sebastian Mancini and Ethan Cartwright."

"Yes."

"Sebastian said you visited a bar up by the university," Wordsworth continued.

"The Varsity," Herschel offered.

"A bar…?" asked a shocked Ruth.

"Don't be so prudish, Mother."

"Your father will have something to say about this."

"Only if you tell him." Herschel looked directly at his mother. And both Wordsworth and Redhead knew that Herschel's father wouldn't hear a word about his son's misdemeanour.

"We understand Jodie and Ethan had an argument."

Herschel shrugged.

"Do you know what about?"

"Not really."

"You followed her out of the bar, didn't you?"

Herschel glanced at his mother before replying, "Yeah. I told Ethan he was behaving like a knob and went after her."

"But you didn't know what they were arguing about?" Redhead kept pushing.

"I knew it involved her meeting up with someone, but that's all."

"And she never said who?"

"No."

"And Ethan didn't tell you?"

"No."

"You went outside and what happened then? What did you say to her?" Redhead persisted.

Herschel looked at him for a moment, then at his mother.

"Herschel ... tell the policeman." His mother demanded.

Herschel paused for what seemed forever before he spoke. "I told her I thought she was beautiful and she should forget about Ethan."

Nobody in the room was expecting this.

"You didn't ask what they were arguing about?" queried Wordsworth.

"I didn't care what they were arguing about," said Herschel. "I just wanted to make her happy and I thought I could. First time I saw her I thought she was the most amazing girl I'd ever seen. Then when I talked to her ... I realised she wasn't just beautiful, she was also intelligent. She was really smart. She could talk with me about things most girls don't understand. She was like nobody I'd ever met before."

"What was her reaction?" asked Wordsworth quietly, not wanting to disturb Herschel's stream of honesty.

"She didn't laugh at me ..." Herschel said almost with pride. "She said she thought I was really 'sweet' ... she said 'sweet'. And that I was 'kind'."

"Then what happened?" Wordsworth spoke again quietly.

"She touched my face ... just gently ... I didn't know what to do. I asked her what *she* wanted to do ... Did she want to go back into the bar ... or go somewhere else? She said she wanted to go home and could I walk her to her bus stop? So I did."

131

"Where was that?"

"The bus stop?"

"Yeah."

"Outside the ice rink."

"Was anything else said?"

"No …"

"Nothing?"

"Nothing. We walked in silence. I was just happy to be walking with her. She seemed a bit preoccupied …"

"What about?"

"I assumed her row with Ethan … and I didn't want to go there. I didn't want to talk about Ethan. For those few minutes Ethan didn't exist … which was fine by me."

"And the bus stop … anything happen there?" Wordsworth was feeling sorry for this boy. Here was a kid totally besotted by a girl who he knew he'd never get.

"We waited for about five minutes … which seemed like five seconds … and her bus arrived. She turned to me and said 'Thanks.' And I … I …"

"You what?"

"I tried to kiss her."

Ruth's mouth opened as if she was about to say something, but nothing came out.

"Tried?" questioned Wordsworth.

"Yeah."

"You didn't succeed."

"No … she just turned her face away from me, she wasn't awful or anything … and I … I realised that … it

132

was never going to happen between me and her. She got on the bus and that was the last time I saw her."

Wordsworth could see Herschel's eyes filling up. The youth turned away from them, determined not to cry in front of these people, which not only meant the cops, but also his mother.

"What did you do then?"

"I went and got my bus. Came home."

"What about Ethan? Did he know about ..."

"No."

"You didn't tell him about the conversation you'd had with Jodie?"

"No ... he never asked. I think he might have found out from Jodie. He was just ... distant with me when I saw him at school on Monday."

"And you're certain she didn't say anything else to you?"

"I remember everything she said. I'll always remember."

Wordsworth and Redhead asked a few more questions, mainly going over the same ground, then Redhead reminded his boss that they still had to speak with Ethan that night, so they took their leave. As they were climbing into their car, another car pulled up. It was Herschel's father Shimon Berkowitz. A short man, bald head, glasses, with not an ounce of excess fat. He apologised profusely for his late arrival offering the same explanation that his wife had given earlier. He then asked about his son.

Wordsworth told him that his son wasn't completely out of the woods yet, they would more than certainly have to question him again.

As they pulled away from the Berkowitzs', Wordsworth asked Redhead his opinion on Herschel's story.

"I think he was telling the truth."

"So do I. But we can't rule him out … has it crossed your mind he could have been the person she was meeting."

Redhead hadn't even considered that possibility.

CHAPTER TWELVE

Ethan Cartwright could have been a male model. He was magazine cover good looking. His expensive hair cut was longer than his contemporaries and his dress - casual high designer, fashion jeans and a loose tee shirt. At first glance it was clear to Wordsworth and Redhead that he was more than comfortable in his own skin. The family home was a large property only half a mile or so from where the Berkowitzs lived. But it was easily three times the size, with electric gates and sizable grounds. The other houses in the road were all of a similar size and quality. This was an expensive property and Wordsworth envied it. He liked his own house, but this location he knew was far better for bringing up kids.

Ethan answered the intercom and opened the gates for them. As they approached the front door, it opened and there was Ethan Cartwright. He politely ushered them through to a large kitchen where Ethan's mother, Virginia

Cartwright, was already making coffee with the very latest Nespresso coffee maker.

"Coffee?" she asked as Wordsworth and Redhead sat down at the large kitchen table.

"Thanks," replied Wordsworth.

"Americano, espresso, latte …?"

"Americano thanks." Wordsworth would have been quite happy with instant.

"And for you?" asked Virginia looking directly at Redhead with a smile that was both welcoming and well-practiced.

"Americano's good for me too."

"Two Americanos." At first glance, Virginia could have been in her late twenties: slim, long dark hair and like her son dressed in fashion jeans and tee shirt. Wordsworth knew her age was actually late thirties, thirty-eight to be precise, he'd checked her out and found out she was born the same year as himself.

"I take it this is about Jodie," said Ethan.

"That's right," said Wordsworth.

"Has she turned up yet?"

"Not yet. We know you saw her on Friday night." Wordsworth studied Ethan.

"Yeah – that's right."

"And you had an argument."

Ethan registered a sliver of surprise when Wordsworth hit him with the argument detail, but he was soon back in his stride.

"It was something or nothing."

"She walked out on you," Redhead joined in.

"These things happen," Ethan said with a slight smile and a sense of maturity beyond his years.

"What was the argument about?" Redhead persisted.

"I don't know … she looked at some guy and I got jealous … you know, something like that."

"That's funny," Wordsworth interrupted, "that's not what we heard."

Ethan's confidence ebbed slightly, but only momentarily. "What did you hear?"

"Coffee." Virginia placed the two coffees in front of the detectives, followed by a small jug of heated, frothy milk. The word sugar obviously wasn't in her vocabulary. "Do you want a drink, Ethan?"

"I'd love a coffee."

Wordsworth picked up his black coffee and took a sip. He had to admit it – it was good coffee. Despite himself he could tell the difference between this and the cheap instant stuff. "So what did you two really argue about?"

Virginia looked at Wordsworth, sensing the mood had changed and the detectives' questions had suddenly developed an edge.

"Does it matter what we argued about? It was forever ago."

"We believe that the argument you had may be directly related to Jodie going missing." It wasn't necessarily true but it also wasn't quite a lie.

"Are we in need of a lawyer here?" asked Virginia. She had an almost jokey quality to the question.

"I wouldn't have thought so, but if you want one, we can continue this conversation down at the police station."

"It's okay Mum."

"Let me put our cards on the table," Wordsworth said directly. "You, Jodie Kinsella, Chloe Moreno, Sebastian Mancini and Herschel Berkowitz all ended up at The Varsity on Friday night. You and Jodie argued; we know it was about her meeting someone … a man … a meeting for which she was being paid a thousand pounds. Jodie stormed out of The Varsity, you and Herschel exchanged words and then Herschel went after her. Am I correct so far?"

Virginia had stopped making coffee and watched as her son nodded his head.

"Who was she was meeting?"

"I don't know. She wouldn't tell me."

"She just said she was meeting a man? That was it?"

"Yes."

"Out of the blue."

"Sort of. Obviously she didn't want me to hear from someone else."

"And you went mad."

Ethan paused for a moment. He looked down. "Yes."

"So she left, and that was the last time you saw her."

"No. I saw her on the Sunday. We met up."

"Where?"

138

"In town."

"Where did you go?"

"We just walked around … ended up going to Nero's. She said she was sorry, but then she tells me she still has to go see this bloke."

"Is that when she told you his name?" Redhead asked.

"She didn't tell me his name. She never told me his name."

"She must have told you something about him."

"No."

"You just accepted your girlfriend going off to see some bloke for a thousand pounds."

"No … I didn't just accept it … What do you think we were arguing about?"

"Did she mention this bloke's age? What he did? Or why he wanted to see her? Anything at all."

"No."

"All she said is that she was going to see a man and he was going to give her a grand?" Wordsworth persisted, highlighting how ludicrous it sounded.

"Yes."

Wordsworth looked at Ethan for a moment. Ethan didn't flinch. Virginia placed his coffee on the table in front of him and he muttered a thank you. Wordsworth took a sip of his coffee, without taking his eyes off Ethan.

"Why are you lying to me?" Wordsworth asked quietly.

"Excuse me …" For the first time Virginia let her cool façade drop. "He's told you what he knows."

139

"I don't think he has."

"Look if you're going to become aggressive …"

"Ethan, have you told us everything?" Wordsworth pushed.

Ethan stared at the table, avoiding anyone's gaze. Then he mumbled, "No."

Virginia was visibly upset by the admission.

"Ethan …"

"What did you omit?" Wordsworth asked.

"It was her mum …"

"What was her mum?"

"That wanted her to see this bloke. That's what she told me. That's why she had to do it. She said she couldn't let her mum down."

"When did she tell you this?" asked Wordsworth.

"That night – Sunday. She said her mum was ill and desperate for money."

Chloe had said the same thing. But they didn't need to tell Ethan that.

Wordsworth wondered why Ethan hadn't asked his wealthy parents for the money. Maybe as laid back as their relationship seemed, loaning a girlfriend's mother some cash wasn't part of the bond. Maybe this relationship wasn't what it seemed. Whatever this parent/offspring connection was, it wasn't like Jodie and her mother's. In Wordsworth's mind there was no doubting the depth of feeling between Jodie and Stacey, but Ethan and Virginia … there was just something off kilter.

"You know she's just died … her mum?" Wordsworth said mater-of-factly, whilst scrutinising Ethan's reaction.

"I read it in the papers."

"But by the sound of it, you didn't believe Jodie when she said the reason she needed the money was because her mum was ill."

"I didn't know what to believe."

"What did you think when you heard Jodie had gone missing?" asked Redhead.

Ethan took a few moments before answering. "I thought … I thought … why didn't I stop her. I should have stopped her."

Wordsworth considered this to be the most genuine statement the boy had made throughout the entire interview.

***

Ethan, like the polite teenager he'd been brought up to be, showed them to the door. As they walked to their car, they became aware of a pair of headlights coming up the drive. They belonged to a Mercedes that pulled up outside the house. They watched as the driver turned off the engine and got out of the car, followed by a younger man getting out of the passenger side. Wordsworth worked out straight away that the older man, who was in his late forties, bearing a confidence that's reserved for the rich and highlighted by his expensive designer glasses, was Ethan's father,

Prentice Cartwright. The younger man was in his early thirties. He was dressed in a checked shirt and jeans, wore a pair of heavy dark rimmed glasses and had a fashionable beard, but was also losing his hair quite extensively. Wordsworth had no idea who this person was.

"I'll be in in a minute, Robin. Virginia will get you a drink."

The young man headed off into the house as Prentice turned back to Wordsworth.

Sorry I'm late … we had a business meeting that went on. Ethan told you everything you needed to know I trust," said Prentice amiably.

"Yes … thank you," Wordsworth replied as he studied Ethan's father.

Again, he was someone Wordsworth had Googled. Wikipedia summed him up as a property and business entrepreneur. Wordsworth had discovered he'd inherited a healthy sum from his father who had owned a number of amusement arcades in Blackpool. It wasn't clear from the web entry whether he still owned those arcades or not. Whatever he'd used his dead father's money to expand the Cartwright Empire. And having now seen the man in the flesh and met his wife, who he married just twelve years ago, he was fairly sure she hadn't married him for his good looks. Of course, what he gained was a ready-made family in the form of Ethan, whose biological father wasn't revealed on the web page.

Wordsworth and Redhead were about to get in their car

142

when Cartwright stopped them. "This girl … Jodie Kershaw."

"Kinsella," Redhead corrected him.

"Sorry, Kinsella. What do you think has happened to her?"

"We don't know."

"And you wouldn't say if you did," smiled Cartwright.

"Probably not."

Wordsworth decided this was an opportunity and took it. "What do you know about her?"

"Nothing really – only that she was a friend of my son."

"Did he tell you anything about a man she'd arranged to meet … that had offered her a thousand pounds."

"No. A thousand pounds, just to meet up – sounds a bit far-fetched to me," said Cartwright. "Would she really go to meet some man she didn't know just for money? Ethan tells me she was smart. If she did go, she wasn't that smart. There'd be less of a worry if there was no money involved. The thousand pounds stinks of it being dodgy."

"Or maybe if you're that desperate, you'll believe anything," said Redhead.

"Yeah – maybe. But if it was so important to her, then why didn't Ethan ask me for it? He knows I'd have given him it."

Between Ethan and his father, they'd managed to create even more ambiguity about the case. Wordsworth felt the investigation had slipped further into an abyss of uncertainty.

INTERVIEW ROOM. BRADFORD CITY CENTRE POLICE STATION, NELSON STREET.
10:14 a.m. 10th JANUARY 2020

"And at this point, there'd still been no further sightings of the girl?" Ashburn asked.

"No."

"Leaving you to think what?"

"Surely what DI Wordsworth was *thinking* is irrelevant. He could have been *thinking* about his children … going on holiday … his thoughts don't really matter, which you made quite clear by dismissing the idea of gut instinct."

"We're just trying to discover what the actual chain of events was and whether there is evidence for us to progress further."

Ashburn was like a pit bull, she had hold and she wasn't going to let go, but at twenty-eight, she didn't have the maturity to switch the questioning back to the ascendancy.

Her veiled threat that this interview was just the prelude was intended to throw Wordsworth and Sharvari off course. She hadn't bargained on Sharvari's instinct, which was to drive back hard.

"Progress further to what?" Sharvari pressed.

"I think we all know." Ashburn tried to sound in control, but her lack of a complete answer showed she had now been pushed onto the back foot.

"We may or may not know what your intentions are, but as his representative, if you continue to overstep the mark, we will leave this meeting. DI Wordsworth has been honest and open about the investigation, but I get the feeling that you two are not being entirely truthful."

Price decided he needed to regain the upper hand. "That's not the case. We're being totally truthful."

"Then why do I feel like there's another agenda kicking around here?" demanded Sharvari.

"I think you must be misreading our intentions." Price leant back in his chair; the one thing he didn't want is for Wordsworth and his lawyer to walk out, because he had no intention of going through all this again,

"Really?" said Sharvari sardonically. She then turned and spoke quietly to Wordsworth. "Should I move to get DS Ashburn removed?"

Wordsworth considered the idea for a few moments, his eyes darting a look at Ashburn, letting her know they were talking about her. Then he simply said, "No … let her carry on," loud enough for her to hear.

Wordsworth knew if she didn't get anything worthwhile from this meeting, then any case they were hoping to build against him would start to fade into the recesses of the dead file room.

"After interviewing the three boys," Price said, rushing past the interlude, "did you feel you'd learnt anything of any significance?"

"Nothing that would tell us directly what had happened to Jodie, but somethings could prove useful later."

"I'm sorry … I don't understand," Ashburn said curtly.

"I felt that if we managed to slot in a few more pieces of the jigsaw, then it could be a different story. I believe it's what's normally referred to as police work," Wordsworth's sarcasm was obvious.

"You widened your enquiries," Ashburn confirmed.

"As I've said the team wasn't huge, Jodie Kinsella wasn't a high priority, as far as West Yorkshire was concerned – we all knew that. It was no Maddie McCann. Jodie was virtually old enough to leave home legally, her mum was a junkie so there was a good motive for her to get out and there was no evidence of foul play. There were people who thought we should just let it drop – stop wasting the manpower. So, whilst the majority of the team continued with the normal lines of enquiry, DS Redhead and I were looking at the possibility of her being involved in an accident, or an abduction. Just trying to understand what might have happened. I knew that there was a clock ticking, if we didn't come up with something soon, then they would pull the plug. After all her mum was dead, her dad didn't give a toss about her – if she disappeared off the face of the earth, so what?"

"Are you saying this was the attitude of officers in Bradford?" asked Ashburn scornfully.

"Not all, but some." Wordsworth replied calmly. "And just one was enough to spur me on to prove them wrong."

CHAPTER THIRTEEN

Wordsworth had been summoned to Chief Superintendent Stephen Lumb's office. It was now just over a week since Jodie went missing and Lumb, always with an eye on the cash flow, wanted to know whether the investigation was, as he put it, 'paying its way'.

Wordsworth reported the team's activity so far but had to admit they had little to show for all of their effort.

Lumb was an obsequious character who thought man management was all about being wily and making people believe that he was working for their best interests. In truth there wasn't an officer in the West Yorkshire Metropolitan Police Force that didn't see right through him. Everything he did was totally self-serving, which is how he'd risen so swiftly up the ranks. He was in his early fifties and a couple of inches over six foot, but he had a slight stoop, which coupled with the weakest handshake known to man, made him much less formidable than he thought he was.

"It sounds like you're convinced it was foul play," Lumb stated.

"No ... not convinced. At the moment it's just a feeling."

"Well you know what they say about feelings. There are two types ... the feelings you should ignore and the feelings you should ignore."

This was Lumb's way of having a joke, letting Wordsworth know they were all one big, happy, law enforcing family. But it just made Wordsworth think, *What a prick.*

"We can't conduct serious police work on feelings. We need evidence," continued Lumb with a supercilious smile.

"Of course – but early days yet," was Wordsworth's defence, which even he knew was weak.

"Get on to the public relations people. Let's get the word out more. You know the type of thing. Let's explore the runaway route ... Check train stations ... bus stations ... etcetera."

"We don't think she's a runaway ... plus we have positive sightings of her after leaving home – one lady saw her getting into a car on Smith Avenue. There was no mention of buses or trains."

Wordsworth guessed Lumb knew all this already, he'd have read the reports, he just wanted to prove a point.

"What's not to say she was running away with the driver of that car? Eloping possibly," Lumb seemed very pleased with his hypothesis.

"I just think it's highly unlikely."

"Indulge me. Have a look into the runaway theory."

"Yes sir."

Wordsworth waited for Lumb to continue … there was something else, he knew it, especially when Lumb smiled at him, a benignly sycophantic smile.

"Will that be all, sir?" Wordsworth asked.

"Yes … well no," said Lumb rapidly changing his mind. "We need to cut the team down. I don't want to do it. I'm against it, let that be known. But budget restrictions make it impossible for you to continue with the size of team you have at the moment. When will she be sixteen?"

"Not for six months."

"So if this drags on for six months, she will legally be able to leave home and we'll have wasted all this time and resources for nothing."

"That's assuming she's run away."

"Which, as I say, is a possibility you shouldn't ignore."

Wordsworth hadn't ignored it; he'd worked through it and had decided it was highly unlikely.

"Press enquiries … has there been any interest?" asked Lumb tentatively.

"No, not really."

"Just another runaway to them. They know what's what." Then without pausing he simply said, "You can have three in your team. You, DS Redhead and one other."

"That's hardly a team sir," objected Wordsworth.

"If something comes up and there's proof of foul play,

then we'll up the numbers, but until then, sorry … it's going to be just the three of you. I'll let you pick who you'd like."

Wordsworth, stunned, stood looking at him for a few seconds. What the hell was he meant to do with just the three of them?

CHAPTER FOURTEEN

Wordsworth made the announcement to his team that morning; there was no point delaying bad news. When he explained that the directive had come from the Chief Super, it was greeted by various comments, all of which were derisory. They believed they were only just getting started.

Wordsworth let them know that the new team would be just himself, DS Redhead and DC Hannah Harvey and the rest would be returning to the CID pool. And that was that. Wordsworth left it until the afternoon, hoping the dust would have settled, to let the two remaining officers know that Lumb had demanded they go back to the runaway theory. They were both as sceptical as he was, nevertheless they knew they had no choice. Wordsworth met with the PR people and they drafted a statement between them, covering all the usual bases. He couldn't help but feel they were going backwards.

Behind a desk bedizened with computer screens sat Robin Adams, Prentice Cartwright's associate, the man whose path had crossed with Wordsworth and Redhead's the night they visited the Cartwrights' house. On the surface, Adams was an average sort of a guy, the sort of guy who had mentally never left university. He still went to gigs and played computer games. But fact was, this was a man you should never cross – never. Not because he'd attack you physically, that wasn't his style. Robin Adams would come at you from a different perspective entirely. Robin Adams was able to hack into most computers and extract, destroy or implant information without anyone knowing he'd ever been anywhere near their hard drive. Of course, this ability had its drawbacks. Computer tampering was just a step below murder in the top five most punishable of crimes, which prompted Adams to steer away from hacking, he was happier earning his money other ways and Prentice made sure he was rewarded for his expertise. And as DI Wordsworth arrived home from work, Adams had just finished uploading their next 'little earner.'

Adams hit the return key, then picked up a manga comic book off a pile of about twenty on his desk. He studied the front cover for a moment, then settled back in his chair to go through it.

At the Wordsworths' home supper had been a relaxing time, even if Wordsworth's mind had partly been on something else other than his family. Izzy was helping her mum clear away, while her father, still at the table, continued to worry how he was ever going to find Jodie with his newly depleted team.

"Have you heard anything else about Zara Redhead?" asked Izzy.

Wordsworth shook his thoughts from Jodie. "No," he said. "Steve hasn't said anything."

"You haven't asked, have you?"

"No."

"Don't you think that's a bit rude, Daddy?"

"He doesn't talk about it."

"Because you don't ask."

Wordsworth had to agree she was probably right.

"Do you think she'll ever come out of the coma?"

"I don't know … I hope so."

Izzy started to leave the kitchen when Wordsworth stopped her. "Do you know if Zara was happy?"

"I don't know … as I said she's the year below, so I didn't really know her."

There was a pause. Then, "Would you say you were happy?" he asked tentatively.

"Most of the time."

"The times you don't feel happy … how do you cope with it?"

"Like most other fifteen-year-olds – I play my music …

loud."

"Ever thought about running way?"

"No … never."

"Never?"

"Never."

"There must have been times when I've got you really wound up … just wanted to scream and leave."

"Yeah, a few."

"So why didn't you just go … runaway?

Izzy thought for a moment, her eyes flicking between her parents.

"Because I knew it would hurt you too much."

Which was a much better reply than Wordsworth could have hoped for.

"What do you know about girls who do runaway?"

"How do you mean?"

"Have any of your friends ever run away?"

"No."

"Have they talked about it?" he pressed.

"Yeah … all the time."

"You … have you talked about it?"

"Yeah course, but like I said I'd never do it."

"But you all talk about it. What would make you discuss something like running away?"

"It's not really a discussion," Izzy corrected her father. "It's more like … my parents have grounded me and I didn't do anything wrong. If I ran away that'd show them."

"But that's about it?"

155

"Yeah. Nobody ever does it."

"Okay. Thanks."

Izzy stayed where she was, she was thinking.

"There was one girl though …"

"Who?"

"I didn't really know her. You know my friend Kelly? Kelly Finch? She's been round here a few times. Her parents had fostered her."

"The girl that ran away?"

"Yeah. Kelly said she left and never came back."

"What happened to her?"

"Not sure. I know she was a couple of months off sixteen … so I suppose everyone's stopped looking for her by now."

"Do you know her name?"

"It could have been Mandy … or Melanie … not sure, but something like that."

"Do you think Kelly will mind me talking to her about it?"

"Why should she?"

"I just wanted to clear it with you."

"Is this about this Jodie girl? You think she might have run away."

"What do you think?"

"It's possible. Did she hate her mum … she only had a mum, didn't she?"

"Yes. And as far as I can tell she didn't hate her. She wanted to look after her."

156

"At fifteen it's all about your mum and dad. They might drive you mad, but if deep down you respect them, then you try not to hurt them. So …"

Izzy left the thought unfinished. Wordsworth felt good. He felt his daughter was telling him something and he liked what she was telling him.

Kelly Finch he knew as one of Izzy's interim friends. They were in the same class at school and for a time were quite chummy, but then they seemed to go their separate ways, the way kids do. When he was first introduced to Kelly he knew she wasn't the type that Izzy would team up with long term. All teenagers want to be older than they are and Kelly was definitely achieving that aim. She would have been fourteen when Wordsworth met her, but she could have passed for eighteen. Her whole being was very sexualised - her look, her mannerisms and the way she spoke. He was glad when they went their separate ways. What was now interesting Wordsworth was the fact the fostered girl, whose name he wasn't sure of, hadn't turned up somewhere. She seemed to have disappeared for good. And Jodie had done just the same … she'd disappeared, vanished … he was hoping not for good.

CHAPTER FIFTEEN

Kelly Finch lived on High House Road in a pebble dashed semi. From here it was a short walk to hers and Izzy's school – Hanson Academy.

Wordsworth pulled up just down the road from Kelly's house. He'd decided not to bring Redhead. It was probably all a wild goose chase and if there were anything to be learnt then hopefully Kelly would be more forthcoming with his friendly approach.

Wordsworth waited patiently in his car. Being able to wait and not let the situation frustrate you was an important asset for a copper. If frustration did creep in, then concentration often started to dwindle and mistakes were made. Izzy had told him that Kelly normally went straight home, got changed, then went and met her current boyfriend, who Izzy described as a nineteen-year-old 'creep'. It was now ten minutes to three and he was expecting her at any time. Two minutes later Kelly appeared, walking down the street. She had tousled long blonde hair, and wore a very short skirt, a white shirt and school tie which was loose at the neck. She carried her blazer over her arm; the days still being quite mild even though it was mid-September.

As she arrived at her house, Wordsworth got out of his car and called her. At the mention of her name, Kelly turned around and looked at Wordsworth. Her house keys dangled from her fingers as she tried to remember where she knew him from.

"Izzy's dad," he said, prompting her memory.

As soon as she heard this, she relaxed. She now recognised him and remembered he was a cop. She wondered what he was doing there. He wouldn't be the first father of a friend that had tried it on with her, but as Wordsworth traversed the short walk, she'd worked out that this was no social visit.

"Hi … You looking for Izzy?"

"No, I want a word with you, if you have a minute?"

"Have I done something wrong?" She wasn't worried; there was a flirtatious tone in her question.

"No. It's about the girl your parents fostered – the one who ran away."

"Madison?

"Yeah," Wordsworth replied, making out he'd known her name all along.

"I haven't seen her for weeks, not since she left."

Kelly from a very early age had learned to distance

herself from anything that smelt like trouble.

"She just upped and left?"

"Yeah."

"Do you know why?"

"No."

"Did she have a boyfriend?"

"So she said," replied Kelly, slightly petulantly, "but I never met him."

"What can you tell me about her?"

"Nothing really. She wasn't here that long."

"You two weren't close then?"

"No way," said Kelly indignantly. "She thought she was Little Miss Somebody and she was just a nobody."

"Did you try contacting her?"

"My mum rang her load of times but she never answered. I think she was trying to make them look bad. She was a bitch like that."

"And you've no idea where she went?"

"No."

"She's not shown up on your social media at all?"

"No."

This was like pulling teeth for Wordsworth.

"A bit odd … her just packing up her things and going."

"She didn't really pack," Kelly offered half-heartedly.

"What do you mean?"

"She left her things here."

"All of them?"

"Yeah … except what she was wearing of course, and

one of my bags. It was a Louis Vuitton … a real one. My mum got me it for my birthday. I loved that bag. It was one of them shoulder bags, just big enough to get your make up in."

"Bit dressy was it?"

Kelly nodded.

"What clothes did she have on then?" continued Wordsworth.

"She was meeting her boyfriend, so it wasn't a lot. Black shorts … a loose, white top that showed the top of her tits …"

"No jacket."

"I didn't see her leave, so I don't know. But she could have taken her jean jacket."

"It's not with her things?

"No …" She hesitated. "I don't think so."

"Where are her the things now … the ones she left?"

"In the garage."

"Can you show me them?"

"Sure."

***

The garage, a prefabricated structure, was at the back of the house. The driveway to get to it was hardly big enough to accommodate a car and Wordsworth was pretty certain that rarely did a car navigate this unkempt thoroughfare. His suspicions were confirmed when Kelly pushed open the

161

up-and-over door and revealed a space bursting with everything from lawn mowers to piles of magazines, from old furniture to rusty peddle bikes. A proverbial dumping ground. Kelly knew exactly where Madison's belongings were and went straight to them. Three boxes, side by side, next to a work bench that was covered with tools, most of them rusting, and bits of wood. They were all marked 'Madison' with a blue felt tip pen and were assorted. One was an old washing powder cardboard box, the second was a just a plain brown cardboard box and the third was a red plastic box, the type used in offices to store documents.

"How come your parents kept all this stuff? Could they not have sent it back to the agency where they'd fostered Madison?"

"The agency didn't really care. They left it to my parents to deal with."

"Did they file a missing person's report?"

"They might have, I don't know. Probably."

"Alright if I take a look?" asked Wordsworth.

"Go ahead," said Kelly nonchalantly.

What Wordsworth really wanted to do was take these three boxes and examine them more closely. Rooting through them, here in the garage, with Kelly Finch looking over his shoulder, wasn't going to achieve a lot.

"I don't really have time to look at these here. I'm going to take them with me," he said as if it were just natural to take personal possessions.

"Okay … they're not heavy," replied Kelly,

unsuspiciously. Wordsworth had been prepared to offer a bogus receipt for the boxes, but Kelly had probably got what she wanted from them and just wanted rid.

Wordsworth carried the soap box to his car and came back for the other two. Kelly helped out by carrying the red document box, which contained what looked like mainly papers and photographs.

As they walked to the car, Wordsworth chatted to Kelly trying to glean more information about Madison.

"What was she like?"

"A bit of a show-off," Kelly replied dismissively.

"How?"

"Always saying she'd pulled some boy or other. And they were always mega rich or good looking, or they'd been on TV."

"TV?"

"Some guy she met she said he'd once been on X Factor … like fuck. Sorry … just slipped out."

"That's okay. Did she say anything else about him?"

"She said that he'd reached the finals …"

"Of X Factor?"

"Yeah. I looked him up. Couldn't find him anywhere. Then I tried Facebook. Found him. He'd *auditioned* for X Factor … didn't get through. She was just a liar."

"Do you remember his name?"

"No. It was ages ago. When she first came to stay. As soon as I pointed it out to her that the only place he'd seen Simon Cowell was on the telly, she soon ditched him … on to the next fella."

"Was she pretty?" asked Wordsworth trying to get handle on this missing girl.

Kelly dropped the box she was carrying on the floor and at first Wordsworth thought he'd offended her in some way, until he realised she was looking in the box trying to find something.

"Here … you tell me." Kelly handed Wordsworth a photo.

It showed a young girl. Short blonde hair, cut in a boyish style, which helped extenuate her high cheekbones. She was petite and her eyes displayed a sadness that she was unable to hide. He was half hoping that she was going to look like Jodie Kinsella, with her long dark hair, but there was no resemblance. He knew he was grasping at straws, but at the moment that was about all he could do.

INTERVIEW ROOM. BRADFORD CITY CENTRE
POLICE STATION, NELSON STREET.
10:27 a.m. 10th JANUARY 2020

"In your report you say you eventually discovered what happened to this girl," Ashburn stated scornfully. "This Madison ..." she glanced at her notes, "Bradshaw.

"Yes."

"But you have no proof."

"That's correct."

"It's pure speculation."

"Not in my mind."

"Without actual proof ... surely it can only be speculation."

Price was being forced into taking a back seat as his Detective Sergeant fired the questions at Wordsworth. Sharvari put down a pen she'd been making notes with and once again stepped in.

"DI Wordsworth instigated a thorough investigation which led him to believe that Madison Bradshaw was indeed the victim of a serious crime."

"Look, I don't want to dwell too long on this," said Ashburn not wanting to take her foot off the gas, "but it would be nice to understand DI Wordsworth's thought pattern. How he got to this point."

Wordsworth looked at Ashburn for what seemed an age. During this silence Ashburn never took her eyes off him. Sharvari looked down at her notes, while Superintendent Price slowly turned his gaze on Wordsworth, who after another minute or so, quietly started to speak.

"I was once involved in a case – the murder of a teenage girl. She was proving real hard to identify, the reason being we should have been trying to identify a boy. Until the post-mortem we had no idea that she was transgender. Her friends called her Tammy, but her birth name was Arif Tripura. She lived with her parents, who were a traditional Bangladeshi family. She would change in various secret places after leaving her flat, something that had been going on since she was thirteen. When we got involved, she was just fifteen, but looked older. After her body was discovered and her identity established, our first suspicions went directly to the father and who was truly rattled by the whole notion of transgender. 'Not my boy, he kept saying. 'You fucking liars – you are all fucking liars. Not my boy.' And for a very brief moment he was our number one suspect, but he was quickly eliminated because his alibi was rock solid. His alibi included Tammy's mother, so she also was in the clear. The pathologist then stepped in and

166

stated that Tammy had been anally raped just prior to her death. The motive for the murder suddenly had a sexual aspect.

"Tammy's life was quite simple. Most of the time she hung out with a group of other teenagers on the Holmewood Estate. It seemed most of them knew that Tammy was really Arif and just accepted it. That's how it had always been. Then enter two brothers – Kyle and Brandon Gledhill. They were seventeen and eighteen, bit older than most of the other kids and they had no idea that Tammy was transgender. According to Tammy's friends she flirted with them, because she flirted with everyone. It didn't mean anything. Brandon thought sex was on the cards and in one of the tower block lifts he got something he hadn't bargained for - a hand full of male genitalia. Tammy managed to escape, but two days later she was found dead on a stretch of waste ground not fifty yards from where she lived. She was held down while she was anally raped.

"Brandon and Kyle were brought in for questioning. Their alibis were shaky, but they denied everything despite the fact Tammy's blood was on one of Brandon's shirts Brandon claimed the blood was from the altercation in the lift and the CPS decided to drop the case. Insufficient evidence. The boys walked. Now you ask me what my thought pattern was that led me to believe that Madison Bradshaw was the victim of a serious crime, simple - it was bloody obvious ... just like it was bloody obvious who killed Tammy. Good old Brandon and Kyle just eight months later were charged with kidnap, rape and torture of a twenty-two-year-old transgender woman. When they eventually released her, she walked straight down to the ring road and threw herself under the first bus that passed. Sometimes you just know ... I knew those lads were guilty as sure as I knew Madison Bradshaw wasn't coming back."

"We still need facts," persisted Ashburn.

"Yeah – but it doesn't stop me from being right."

"Just because you believe something doesn't make it lawful. We can't put people away just because you had a *feeling*."

There was a long pause as Wordsworth just stared at her, then quietly, not even trying to hide his disdain for the sergeant, he said: "So what the fuck are we doing here?"

CHAPTER SIXTEEN

Wordsworth placed the last of the three boxes he got from Kelly's garage next to the other two on his living room floor. He chalked it up as another misdemeanour to add to his ever-growing list. He just assumed one day that all these acts of circumventing the red tape would catch up with him, when they did, he wasn't sure what would happen or what he'd do.

Wordsworth opened the first box, the soap box, the one that contained her schoolwork. There were various exercise books all with *'Madison Bradshaw'* scrawled across the front, which is how he learned her surname. He meticulously and methodically went through the books looking for anything that might give him a clue to why she ran away. There was nothing. He was about to go through the second box when his wife came in.

"I thought I heard you … What's all that?" she asked, referring to the boxes.

"Some runaway's possessions."

"What they doing here?"

"Technically I obtained them illegally, so I thought I'd better not take them down the station."

"Do you need to hide them?" Wendy was used to her husband's slightly idiosyncratic police methods and was always prepared to protect him in any way she could.

"I do if anyone comes asking about them ... but I don't think they will."

"Have you got five minutes?"

"Sure."

"There's something I want to show you."

Wordsworth followed his wife out of the living room and up the stairs to their bedroom. The room was done in a light blue paint with colour matching curtains and bedspread, something Wendy designed, and Wordsworth certainly hadn't objected to. Although he never said it, he'd often thought that after the squalor and degenerates he dealt with on a daily basis, then the light blue was a calming colour.

On the bed was a black suit bag. On it, in white lettering, was the word *BOSS*.

"Open it," she said.

Wordsworth smiled at her and moved to open the suit bag, not really knowing what to expect. He unzipped the bag and there it was: a black, single-breasted suit, not too shabby at all. But there again Wendy did have great taste.

"Do you like it?" she asked.

"I love it. Where did you get it?"

"Manchester."

"You've been to Manchester?" he said as if it were the end of the world.

"It's only an hour. You're sounding like your dad."

"Why did you go to Manchester?"

"Because it was the nearest place that stocked the suit I wanted."

Wordsworth paused for a moment while he took in what she was saying. Had he heard right? Wordsworth looked down at the suit. He opened the jacket and without looking at the label he slipped it on. It was a beautiful cut, a beautiful fit. This wasn't the normal type of suit he wore. This was indeed special.

"It's BOSS," he said, quietly shocked.

"It is," she replied.

"I don't understand."

"I've been saving up."

"But ..."

"It's something you've always wanted ... and I wanted to be the person to give it to you."

"I don't know what to say."

"Thank you?" she proffered.

"Thank you, thank you ... thank you." Wordsworth took hold of her and kissed her. "I don't believe it ... it's amazing." He was fighting for words as they fell back onto the bed.

"I'm never going to go out in it ..."

"You better ... it cost too much to just leave hanging in

171

the wardrobe."

"How much?"

"What does it matter? I've paid for it … the kids haven't gone hungry and the bank hasn't repossessed the house."

"It must have taken for ever – saving for it."

"A while …"

Wordsworth slowly started to unbutton her pink cardigan to reveal her black bra, a stark contrast to her pale skin. Wendy didn't stop him immediately and then she said, "If that's what you have in mind, you take that jacket off right now and hang it up."

Wordsworth smiled at her and took off the jacket and hung it in the suit bag in the wardrobe, then flipped the lock on the door. When he turned back she was lying there, in just her bra and knickers. She'd always told him she was an any time, any place sort of girl … but with only one man – him.

They made love passionately, they always did. Her orgasm happened before his, which was often the case and just as he reached his climax, they heard someone come in downstairs.

"What time's tea?" shouted Oliver.

"Not for another hour or so … get something from the fridge. I better go pick up Nat …"

"I'll go," offered Wordsworth.

Wendy just smiled at him. After all these years, she loved to make him happy. They rarely argued, discussed things yes, but seriously cross words were few and far between.

With the suit and sex firmly on his mind, he wasn't quite sure which was more dominant; he went to pick up their seven-year-old.

***

After they'd all had something to eat, Wordsworth decided he better continue looking through Madison's belongings. What immediately struck him was that there seemed to be nothing from her previous life. There was no indication why she was in care, but he knew a few judicious phone calls the following morning would give him all that type of information.

Izzy, who was trying to do her homework, looked across at where her father was methodically going through the missing girl's boxes.

"She didn't have a lot, did she," stated Izzy.

Wordsworth knew that a lot of times kids that are shunted from pillar to post often don't have a lot and it seemed Madison was no exception. They just managed to hang on to a few possessions that they considered important to them.

Wordsworth pulled from one of the boxes a scruffy, old pink teddy.

"And this is about the only really personal item I can find …"

"Whow … that's been round the block."

"Certainly has. I bet she's had it since she was a kid. And my guess is if she'd planned to leave, she'd have taken it with her. She wouldn't have left this behind."

"And that's the type of thing you're looking for?"

"I'm looking for anything that tells me something." He held up a phone charger. "There's no mobile, but there is a charger. My guess is she was planning on coming back, or she'd have taken her charger."

"She could have just forgotten it," said Izzy.

"Could have. But let me ask you this … you're going on a night out, do you take your computer?

"No course not."

"So where is Madison's computer. Everyone has a laptop – right?"

"Right. So maybe she did take it with her."

"The only thing she was carrying when she left was a small designer handbag … just big enough for her make-up."

"So where's her computer?"

"That's what I want to know."

CHAPTER SEVENTEEN

Wordsworth spoke to Child Services the following day and managed to glean a fair amount of helpful information.

Madison first went into care when she was seven because her mother, a single parent, was a junkie who was turning tricks to feed her habit. She had a series of foster parents, twelve in total, all of which reported a steady decline in her behaviour. At the age of twelve she was deemed unmanageable in a domestic environment. Madison would literally go on the rampage, smashing up rooms and attacking anyone who tried to stop her. If she wasn't causing havoc in her foster home, she was out shoplifting and breaking into cars. It was decided that it was necessary for her to be placed into a residential care home for problem kids. The home, Tall Trees, was in Greengates, a suburb of Bradford and had always had favourable reports. The Residential Manager found Madison a real problem. The home was for twelve to sixteen-year-olds and for at least a year Madison was their most troublesome resident. But by the time she'd turned fourteen she'd started to calm down. At fifteen they considered her stable enough to return to foster care. It took some time to find the right placement, but eventually Kelly's parents were deemed the best match. In a report to Social Services, made by Kelly's parents shortly after Madison went missing, they stated she hadn't been any real bother – stayed out late a couple of times, but all teenagers do. Then without any real warning she ran away. The Finches thought she must have been planning it all along, the only thing that made them doubt it was the fact that she'd left the majority of her belongings behind.

The care workers continued to explain it was just two months before Madison's sixteenth birthday when she decided to abscond. She would have guessed that by the time she turned sixteen, the authorities would probably ease up looking for her, if not forget her entirely. Which is exactly what had happened. The Finches had no idea where she'd gone. They knew she'd been seeing a boy, but who he was, or where he came from, they hadn't a clue. The truth was Madison had nobody in the world that really cared about her. Why wouldn't she run off with the first boy that showed her just a glimmer of attention?

"Madison was a lot worse than some of the kids we have here, and a bit better than a few," stated the Tall Trees manager, but that was all he really had to say on the matter. So Wordsworth thanked him for his time and left. He knew it was no push over being the manager of a home like Tall Trees, and this man was certainly feeling it. He was jaded and exhausted, but who wouldn't be thought Wordsworth.

**

Kelly was just leaving school when Wordsworth pulled up next to her in his car.

"Have you got a minute, Kelly?" asked Wordsworth through the open passenger window.

"I'm a bit busy." Kelly was nervous. Wordsworth sensed it immediately.

"You going home?" he enquired. "I can give you a lift."

"Er …" she wanted to say no but knew it would sound ridiculous. Where would she be going in her school uniform? She had style … everyone knew that. She climbed into the car.

Wordsworth headed off. He said nothing. He wanted Kelly to speak and she did.

"What … what's this about?"

"Madison …"

"What about her?"

"It's about her computer."

Kelly tried to appear unruffled, but Wordsworth knew at a glance she was panicking. It was blazing from her eyes.

"We know she had one," bluffed Wordsworth, "but it's not in her possessions. We can't find it anywhere. We were wondering if you knew what happened to it."

"Me? Why would I know?" protested Kelly at little too vehemently.

"Because you had her things."

"I've not seen it … not since she left," Kelly continued.

"When was the last time you saw it?" pressed Wordsworth.

"Not sure …"

"But you haven't seen it for a while."

Kelly wasn't liking this.

"She didn't take it with her when she left … You said she only had a designer handbag … so it must be in your house somewhere …"

"No …" This time it was a sharp interjection from Kelly, not a trace of scorn, just straight denial.

"But if she didn't take it …"

"It's not in the house …"

"I can get a search warrant … check thoroughly …"

"It's not in the house," repeated Kelly.

"So where is it?" Wordsworth tone was firm but not threatening.

Kelly was looking down at her lap, trying to work out what was the best thing to do. Suddenly she threw her head back, and then level again, so she was looking straight out of the front of Wordsworth's car.

"I took it," she confessed.

"So you do know where it is?"

"I know what I did with it."

"What?" asked Wordsworth.

"I sold it … It was to make up for her stealing my bag."

***

The Trading Post was on Morley Street, two minutes from Bradford's city centre. The building that housed the ramshackle shop was made of Yorkshire stone, as were the other buildings around it, except for a newish concrete building, directly across from the second-hand emporium, which offered 'safe and secure' student accommodation. There was a van parked outside the front of the shop, which was apparently used for clearing houses. Wordsworth parked next to the van.

Inside the shop, which resold all manner of items, Wordsworth explained what he was looking for. The owner was reluctant to talk about buying any computer from any young girl, but when Wordsworth let it be known that he would have to return with a warrant and a full search team, he suddenly remembered the computer and that it was in fact in his home. It was so good; he'd given it to his eldest boy. He would bring it into the police station himself.

The second-hand shop owner, not wanting to attract police attention, was true to his word. The next day the computer was sitting on Wordsworth's desk directly in front of him.

Gatesy was of course the one Wordsworth presented

with the problem.

"I need anything that's left on the computer that pertains to Madison Bradshaw – she once owned it," said Wordsworth.

Gatesy looked quizzically at the HP Pavilion x360. He seemed reluctant to touch it, as if he might contaminate it in some way. He slowly lifted the lid to reveal the screen, then pressed a button and the screen faded up into life.

"Well?" asked Wordsworth.

"All I can say is - I'll see. If there's anything there I'll find it. Might take some time though, I'm a bit snowed under," replied Gatesy.

"Oh come on … computer crime is hardly big in Bradford," Wordsworth remonstrated. "If you were in charge of abacus fraud, then you might have a good excuse…"

"That's what you all think, don't you? We just sit on our backsides, playing on our PlayStations." Gatesy was actually a little hurt.

"Not at all. I was just trying to push my job up from the bottom of the pile to the top," said Wordsworth diplomatically.

"William … you know I'll do it as soon as I can."

"Thanks."

And with that word of gratitude Wordsworth left. Not sure whether Gatesy would give him the lead he so desperately needed. He knew time was running out and the next stage after scaling down the investigation would be to close it down, whilst pretending to the world it was still active. Wordsworth needed to find something quick, if not, Jodie Kinsella and Madison Bradshaw would both become just another couple of runaways that disappeared into the underbelly of humanity.

CHAPTER EIGHTEEN

Wordsworth took his place at his desk just as Harvey came to the end of a call. She had an ease on the phone that Wordsworth had never noticed before. She was twenty-six, but had a knack of speaking to young and old alike as if they were her best friend. She always wore smart suits to work, which Wordsworth appreciated, whilst having no idea that she was subconsciously emulating her boss. She thought him sexy and she had thought of making a play for him. But hey – they worked together, own doorstep and all that.

"How we doing?" Wordsworth asked both Redhead and Harvey. Between them they'd made over forty phone calls, looking for other missing teenagers ... male and female.

"Nothing relevant so far," was Redhead's reply as his phone rang. He picked it up.

Wordsworth looked at Harvey who shook her head.

"No ... nothing."

"Okay ... I'll ... I'll be straight over." Redhead replaced

the receiver. He sat there for a moment. Wordsworth and Harvey looked at him.

"What is it?" asked Wordsworth.

Redhead just stared at the phone then quietly said: "They're turning off her life support."

He then looked up and there was a strange pleading in his eyes; he was begging for someone to do something. Make it not be true.

Wordsworth drove him to the hospital. The journey was completed in silence. As they parked up outside Wordsworth asked if he wanted him to go in with him? Redhead just nodded. He needed the support.

On the ward, Redhead entered Zara's room and Wordsworth waited respectfully outside. He could hear the rhythmic sounds of the various machines keeping his sister alive. Wordsworth just waited and couldn't help wondering how he'd react if it had been one of his children. He couldn't imagine it.

Then the sounds stopped. Despite the general noise of the hospital continuing, for Wordsworth there was a deafening silence.

Two nurses emerged from the room; one of them in tears, the other looked at Wordsworth and gave him a little smile that had no joy in it. Shortly afterwards a doctor emerged from the room. She spotted Wordsworth. "Are you a relative or a friend?"

"Friend," answered Wordsworth.

"They might be a while … so …"

"Thanks."

The doctor went on her way. Wordsworth didn't know how long it was, it could have been five minutes, it could have been five hours, he didn't once look at his watch as he waited, but eventually Redhead appeared with his parents. Wordsworth just expressed his sorrow, for there was nothing else he could say.

Redhead's parents had the nurses ring them a taxi … Wordsworth urged Steve to go with them, but he needed company and although he didn't say it, he didn't want it to be his parents. Their grief was full of shock and disbelief, his grief was full of anger.

They ended up at the Hare and Hounds on Toller Lane. It was a respectable place, which didn't attract any real villains. The last thing they needed was to bump into some old lag with a grievance. There was just the one person in there that they knew, Joe Carter, another DI working out of Nelson Street. He was a big man, a fish 'n' chips, six pints a night man. They exchanged a few pleasantries and Carter was about to settle down with them, when fortunately, his phone went. After a quick exchange he downed what remained of his pint and headed out of the pub, turning to Wordsworth and Redhead as he went.

"She who must be obeyed … I'll catch you another time."

And Carter was gone, much to Wordsworth's relief.

Quite early on Wordsworth decided he wouldn't be driving home. Redhead needed a drinking companion, not a sober wise owl. They drank and talked about everything but Redhead's sister.

After the fourth drink, Wordsworth rang Wendy and arranged for her to pick them up later.

After the sixth drink Redhead started talking about Zara. It was like the verbal floodgates had been opened. He explained how he felt responsible for her, how she'd always looked up to him, how she was a sensible girl and how he still found it hard to understand how this had happened. And the more Wordsworth listened the more he thought that Zara's drug fuelled death wasn't as straight forward as he'd first thought. His brain, sodden with alcohol, couldn't figure out what was troubling him, but his instinct told him there was definitely something.

CHAPTER NINETEEN

Redhead took some time off work, he just had to. Although he'd been told quite early on that the chances of his sister coming out of the coma were virtually non-existent, it was still a shock for him when she actually died.

His parents were racked with guilt, believing that they were responsible for their daughter's death. Their daughter was taking drugs and they had no idea. How could that be?

It was soon determined by the pathologist that the reason for Zara's condition was an overdose of a mixture of the drug AMT – Alpha Methyltryptamine. Her dosage had probably been somewhere in the region of 100 milligrams – a seriously strong dose. So why had Zara been so reckless and where had she obtained the drug? When Wordsworth woke up the morning after his drinking session with Redhead, he decided to look into what actually happened with Zara. He felt if nothing else he owed it to his colleague. But instead of his usual methods he decided to take an alternative track … his daughter Izzy was going to be his eyes and ears on the ground. He needed her to ask around about Zara Redhead. Was it known she was on drugs? Who was her supplier? Who were her friends?

Izzy loved the idea of playing detective. Although Zara was the year below her, she knew the crowd she hung with. They were the type that liked to think they were 'cool,' but in fact they missed 'cool' by a mile. They would talk about boys, sex, drugs and music, but talk is as far as it went. Izzy easily recognised this teenage posturing, because that's how she was a year ago. Now she considered herself mature. She'd had a couple of boyfriends, with whom there'd been sexual fumblings. She'd been offered drugs on numerous occasions and once tried smoking cannabis, but seeing how she didn't smoke cigarettes, she'd had to do some fairly skilful acting to fool the others she was inhaling.

She soon learned that Zara's best friends were Candice and Melissa. As the news circulated that Zara Redhead had died, they had become the centre of attention They cried a lot, held court a lot and spent a lot of the day in the sick bay being counselled by the school nurse. At lunchtime Izzy came across them with a coterie of mourners, having a cigarette on the playing fields out of sight of the school building.

Izzy approached them, posing as another concerned school colleague with sadness etched on her face. "I'm so sorry to hear about Zara," she said.

Candice and Melissa both nodded, giving a small sad

smile of thanks.

"Do you know when the funeral is?"

Candice shook her head.

"I think most people will want to go," Izzy said earnestly.

"Her parents might want a private funeral, family only," said Candice. "There'll be a memorial service though."

"Yeah of course," Izzy said. "Poor Zara."

"Yeah," Melissa mumbled.

Izzy lowered her voice to a conspiratorial whisper. "Do you know what it was she took ...?"

"No," said Candice.

"Do you know who she got it from then?" asked Izzy as if she was part of some drug taking fraternity.

Both girls shook their heads feeling slightly left footed. Really as the self-imposed role of Zara's best friends, they should know all details.

"It wasn't that spotty kid in year ten was it?"

Candice and Melissa looked at each other, not sure how to reply.

"No, it wasn't him," Candice was suddenly positive. She couldn't allow somebody she didn't even know to be more knowledgeable about her dead friend, than herself. "I'm pretty sure she got the stuff off her boyfriend."

"Her boyfriend ... who's that?" Izzy questioned.

"I never met him."

"Does he go to this school?"

"No."

"So who is he?"

"Not sure," Melissa added. "She met him at a party."

"Which party?"

"There was this big house party ... Catherine Brown put it on Facebook ... and half the world turned up."

"Did you go?"

"Yeah ... we went."

"And that's where she met this boy?"

"Yeah."

"Did you see him?

There was a pause. Izzy sensed that whatever had happened at the party, Candice and Melissa were embarrassed about it.

"We left," Candice said eventually.

"It wasn't our sort of party," Melissa continued haughtily. "The neighbours called the police and my dad would have killed me if I'd have been arrested or anything."

"So would mine ..." agreed Candice. "We told her we were going ... didn't we Melissa?"

"Yeah, we both told her. But she wanted to stay."

"You just left her?"

"It wasn't like that. It wasn't like it sounds."

"So she was with this boy? And she started seeing him?"

"Yeah. A couple of times a week. I know he thought she was older than she was."

"How do you know that?" asked Izzy.

"She told me. She said she was nearly sixteen ..." said Candice.

"The night the police found her ... had she been out with him?"

"Yeah - I think so."

"I heard they found her by the Cenotaph ... unconscious."

"That's what we heard as well, didn't we?"

Melissa nodded.

"If there's bad gear going around ... then I need to know. If you ever find out who the boy is ..."

"We'll let you know ..." said Candice.

"Straightaway," added Melissa.

Pleased with what she'd learned, Izzy walked back towards the school.

***

Izzy told her father about her conversation with Candice and Melissa. Wordsworth was impressed and he told her as much. But he still needed more and he needed her to continue with her covert exploration. Someone had to know who this boy was.

Wendy who had listened to father and daughter exchanging information, cornered her husband in the kitchen as he started to cook supper ... chicken chasseur. "This isn't going to become a regular thing is it?" she asked.

"Me cooking?" he replied knowing full well she wasn't referring to his culinary efforts.

"Getting our daughter to play detective … 'cos she seems to have really got into it."

"It was only because Zara went to the same school as her."

"I just worry about her. Please don't get her mixed up with this stuff."

"What stuff?"

"I know more about what you get up to then most coppers wives …"

"You ask … so I tell."

"Which is great … makes me feel like we're not leading separate lives," she said slipping her arms round his neck. "I just worry, if Izzy were to become too involved …"

"She's won't … this was a one off," said Wordsworth as he added tomato puree to the pan. "I'll tell her to call it quits."

"It's nothing new for you – you know how to handle it. You take it in your stride …"

"What?" he asked, stirring the sauce.

"Every day you mix with junkies, rapists and murderers … and you can handle it. You're used to it. And I've sort of got used to it … at arm's length. I just don't want Izzy to get used to it. She's too young to know that on every other street corner there's a whacko sicko."

Wordsworth turned to his wife. He looked at her for a moment and simply said, "Agreed."

Wordsworth kissed her on her lips. She normally felt safe when he did that … and this time was no different.

CHAPTER TWENTY

DC Hannah Harvey had been doing just as Wordsworth had asked - looking into missing girls. She had once again spoken to the residential manager at Tall Trees and had asked all the relevant questions, including whether she could possibly have been groomed by any individual or individuals ... The Manager honestly replied that he didn't think so, but he couldn't know for certain. These days after Rochdale, Rotherham and Sheffield everyone was 'ultra-cautious' and 'mega vigilant.' But these girls were vulnerable; all that was important to them was to feel somebody wanted them. Hannah had asked him about other girls that he may have been concerned about. Reluctantly he told her about one other missing girl, Britney Atkinson, who the manager described as being shy and quiet. Apparently, she'd run away a couple of months before her sixteenth birthday, just like Madison had and according to some of the other occupants of the home, there

193

was a 'friend' involved.

Back at the office Wordsworth wanted to know more about this friend. "Male or female friend?" he asked Hannah.

"They don't know for sure, but the girls closest to her were convinced it was a boy. She'd mentioned picking up 'a lad' at a bus stop a couple of weeks before she ran off. Nobody knew who he was, because none of the other girls had ever seen him. The manager said he'd shown the authorities the note Britney had left, stating she was running away with a friend, but I haven't been able to find any record of it. He may just have been protecting his job. Then he let something slip."

"What?" asked Wordsworth.

"He didn't use these exact words, but he implied that because the girl was nearly sixteen, spending resources or trying to find her was a waste of taxpayers' money, so nothing was really done. In other words, same old, same old."

"That's basically what he said on the phone to me about Madison." Wordsworth ran his hand over his face, something he did when he was trying to work his way through something. "So how many missing girls in the last few months are we looking at now?"

"Five," Harvey said, looking at her notes. "I spoke to a few different homes and we're up to five now, including Jodie."

"Which homes were they?" Wordsworth continued.

"One called Oak House in Low Moor, the other in Shipley, called Dove Place."

"And I take it you have the other names?"

"Skye Chapman and Abigail Davies."

"So now suddenly we have five missing fifteen-year-olds, four who have been in care and one with a junkie mum. Certainly all vulnerable. How the fuck has no one noticed this after what happened? Didn't we learn anything from Rochdale and Rotherham. We need to get out a description of each of them ... then let's see what we can turn up."

"Do you want me to go to these places?" asked the DC holding up a piece of paper with the addresses of the latest missing girls. "See if I can get a photo of them?"

"Yeah. And let's do it pronto."

Harvey started to gather up the details of the missing girls and as she did, she asked about Redhead.

"He's doing okay," Wordsworth said. "But he feels responsible in some way. He did right coming back to work – keep him busy."

"Do we know where she got the drugs?"

"No. But I intend to find out."

Then, unassumingly, Gatesy arrived in their office. He had in his hand a photograph. Wordsworth hoped against hope this meant he had managed to find something on Madison's computer. He was in luck.

"It's the only thing I've found that might be relevant. It was on Facebook."

Wordsworth and Harvey studied the photograph. It was a selfie of Madison Bradshaw and a boy. She was in her school uniform and the boy had a scarf wrapped around his face and a baseball cap pulled low down over his eyes, making him totally unrecognisable. Madison was laughing.

"Any good?" asked Gatesy.

"Could be," mumbled Wordsworth thoughtfully.

"I'll leave it with you."

"Thanks. And if you get anything else …" prompted Wordsworth.

"I'll let you have it faster than … than a new Mac." As Gatesy left he was laughing at what he thought was a funny line, sadly nobody else saw the humour.

Wordsworth and Harvey studied the photograph. The boy was dressed in jeans and a black jacket zipped up to the neck.

"What do you think?" asked Harvey.

"Was he having a joke with the scarf and cap, or was he trying to disguise himself?" Wordsworth mused.

"Well … she thinks it's a joke."

"And I'm betting it wasn't …" said Wordsworth as he continued to study the photo.

INTERVIEW ROOM. BRADFORD CITY CENTRE
POLICE STATION, NELSON STREET.
10:42 a.m. 10th JANUARY 2020

"You clearly thought the youth in the photograph was important," Ashburn stated.

"Obviously."

"And why did you think he was covering his face?"

"He didn't want to be recognised.. Maybe because he was two-timing her, or he was supplying her with drugs … or he should have been at home studying."

"At the time did you have any thoughts about the identity of this youth?" Price asked.

"No."

"None at all?"

"None at all."

"And regarding the missing girls – by now you were certain they were all linked."

"I considered it a distinct possibility … but the fact the

Super also agreed that it could be the case, gave me impetus to dig some more."

"You had another meeting with the Chief Super?"

"Yes … a reassessment meeting."

"And after the meeting – what was the recommended course of action … assuming there was one?"

"There was nothing really new, so I decided my course of action was to try and find out where these girls had gone. If they were just living on the street or in squats, then at least we'd know they were still alive and we could try and do something."

"And the Chief Superintendent didn't offer up any alternatives?"

"He did make one suggestion."

"What was that?"

"That we quietly let it disappear."

"Disappear?"

"I need to have a word with the Inspector," demanded Sharvari, worried Wordsworth was about to say something that would be held against him whatever the outcome of this investigation.

"No … it's fine. I'm fine. Chief Superintendent Lumb said I should let it slide … so I could get on with some real detective work." As Wordsworth spoke, he looked directly at Ashburn – she needed to know the truth about policing, she needed to have her eyes opened to what was really going on.

"That's a serious accusation," Ashburn said.

"Accusation? I'm not accusing him of anything. He agreed there could be a possible link between these missing girls, but at the same time it was in the interest of the Force to let it slide. You asked me what I was instructed to do, and I've just told you."

"Are you accusing him of negligence?" snapped Ashburn.

"As I said … I'm not accusing him of anything. I'm telling you how it was. He told me to forget them, I said I wasn't going to, he said I shouldn't push my luck and I said he could discipline me if he wanted, but I wasn't going to stop trying to find out what happened to these girls. Then I walked out of his office. The next time I saw him he didn't say anything about the case. It was as if the conversation had never happened."

"You deliberately disregarded your superior's instructions."

"Yeah. And I'm glad I did. If I hadn't then we'd never have found out what happened. Those girls were used and abused … I guessed that from early on."

"Now suddenly you're psychic."

"There were too many coincidences. Coincidences are for bad soap operas and Ripley's Believe It or Not."

CHAPTER TWENTY-ONE

Following Wordsworth's instructions, Hannah Harvey spent three days learning what she could about the lives of the four new missing girls.

She visited Tall Trees, Oak House and Dove Place where she spoke with the staff and a number of the residents.

It was clear that Madison Bradshaw had not been well liked at Tall Trees. The staff thought she was trouble and the majority of the residents that knew her were slow to defend her. She spent most of the time by herself and socialised very little. As for Britney, it seemed she was popular with most people. A very pretty girl who wasn't that bright. If someone showed her any affection, she would give them *everything* she had. She had dated various boys, but nobody seemed to know the identity of the boyfriend she was seeing before she disappeared.

Skye Chapman and Abigail Davies were apparently

well liked and relatively well behaved. Skye was quite the little artist while Abigail was a bright apple in what was frequently a dull crop.

As Harvey was looking into the girls' lives in care, Wordsworth was trying to track down their families.

Madison Bradshaw's mother lived in a small terrace house in Sheffield. The place was dark inside and the smell of spices was dominant. There were kids' clothes scattered around, as if someone had literally just undressed and left their clothing either on the floor or over the back of some piece of furniture. There were also too many ornaments of various shapes and sizes, which Wordsworth guessed had come from the Indian sub-continent. Madison's mother was now married with two children and when Wordsworth came knocking, Sylvia Jadoon, as she was now called, had on a sari and a headscarf and was clearly nervous. Apparently, her present husband Aamir, knew nothing of her previous life. She had converted to Islam and despite appearing to be clinically depressed, told Wordsworth that being a Muslim had changed her life forever.   She proclaimed loudly that she loved her family, whilst also stating the biggest thing Islam had given her was that she now didn't fear death. Wordsworth couldn't help but think that having to live with all the ornaments and the total mess, death would a blessed relief.

He assured her he had no intention of undermining her world, he just wanted to know when was the last time she'd seen or heard from Madison? Sylvia took a little time thinking before saying it was about ten years ago; Madison was five or six.

"Which was about the time she was put into care," said Wordsworth.

"Yes."

"Why was she put into care?" he asked.

"I couldn't cope. Her dad had left me …"

"What's his name?"

"Kobe Bradshaw … but he's dead now."

"How did he die?

Sylvia looked round just to check no one was listening, even though the house was empty, before continuing:

"He was a pimp …"

"Okay …"

"Tried to move into somebody else's turf and paid the penalty."

"Was he your pimp?" Wordsworth asked matter-of-factly.

Sylvia just looked at him; Wordsworth wasn't sure which way this was going to go. Was she about to fly at him shouting and screaming, or was she going to tell him the truth? It turned out to be the latter.

"Yeah … but Aamir knows nothing about it. He doesn't know anything about Kobe or Madison … or the other two," she confided nervously.

"Other two?"

"I had three children …"

"They all went into care?"

"Yeah ... all three."

There was a pause as they looked at each other.

"Don't judge me," she said rather pitifully. "Don't you dare judge me. You don't know what it was like."

***

The stories revolving round Britney, Skye and Abigail were all of a similar ilk - broken families, abusive parents, extensive drug use and economic deprivation. He felt both anger and pity about these various families. But he knew he had to focus on the job in hand; he had to find these girls. Sorting out society's ever recurring problems was not his job; he would leave that to the politicians.

It was Hannah Harvey that opened up another course of action, a very obvious course of action.

"Boss," she said totally out of the blue, as they sat in a coffee bar just below John Street Market. "Five girls all go off ... yeah?"

"Yeah," replied Wordsworth, taking a sip of his coffee.

"And there's not been a single sighting of one of them."

"Jodie was spotted getting into a car ..." Wordsworth said.

"But that was it. Then she vanished." Hannah paused momentarily before continuing. "Maybe they're not here any longer. Maybe they're not in Bradford."

Wordsworth's cup stopped before it reached his lips. It hovered there for a few moments, while Harvey then raised her eyebrows demanding a reaction from him. Wordsworth placed the cup back onto the table.

"Maybe they're not," Wordsworth spoke quietly with a dawning realisation. "But if they've all left Bradford, where are they? Where would they go?"

"That's down to you find out," Harvey smiled at her boss and he couldn't help but smile back.

***

Wordsworth had to leave the coffee bar in a hurry. He'd forgotten there was a school concert he promised he'd attend. Both Izzy and Molly were in it – Molly on her violin and Izzy on the drums. Molly practiced a lot at home, and Wordsworth, not knowing the first thing about the violin, other than they weren't cheap, thought she was doing rather well, considering she'd only been playing for a year.

While Izzy and her drums worried him.

About six months ago Izzy had announced that she wanted a drum kit. Wordsworth had been there before with Izzy. There'd been so many times that she'd *discovered her heart's desire*, and every one of them was going to be *the thing* that she would really work at. Most fell by the wayside in a matter of weeks, quite often it was just days.

When they heard that this time it was the drums, they both agreed that to buy her a drum kit was not a good idea. They were expensive and chances were it would be a total waste of money.

With no kit at home, Izzy had to practice at school. Her Mum and Dad had never heard her, so the impending concert was viewed with a degree of trepidation.

Wordsworth arrived just in time and met up with Wendy in the school's impressive foyer.

They settled down and waited patiently as trumpeters blew more bad notes than good ones and pianists played everything from chopsticks to hardly recognisable Chopin. A choir took to the stage to perform a strange and rather apposite version of the Beatles number – *She's Leaving Home*. Wordsworth noticed Kelly Finch in the choir, and for a moment wondered if Madison had also been a member.

Harvey could very well be right. They've been looking too close to home. As the song continued, the stats started to swirl round in Wordsworth's head, making the task seem impossible. Of course, different organisations varied in their estimates, but they all had a figure of over two hundred thousand people reported missing each year. He knew that many of those returned home quite quickly, but there were a significant number that just disappeared. He also knew that the majority of the missing under eighteens, approximately one hundred and forty thousand, seventy-one per cent of those were girls and the majority came from single parent families or were kids in care. All his missing girls fell into this category. The vulnerable category.

They were on the last verse of the Beatles song when he

once again thought about the fact that the only positive sighting of any of the missing girls was that of Jodie. As Hannah had said earlier, the others had literally just disappeared. Why hadn't there been a sighting of at least another one of them? There are over thirteen million CCTV cameras in the UK; he would have thought one of them would have recorded one of the girls somewhere. Maybe it was time they started looking for bodies. Maybe that was why there had been no sightings: they were dead. And as much as the thought thoroughly depressed him, and as much as he knew certain members of society found it acceptable that runaways were allowed to just disappear, he also knew corpses of teenage girls was something nobody ignored, nobody could ignore.

He was pulled back into the school concert when Wendy nudged him. The song had come to an end and Molly was taking the stage with the other members of her quartet. They attacked the piece with gusto and Molly held her own. As far as Wordsworth and Wendy could tell she didn't play any bum notes and as she left the stage, she cast a smile at her parents, who, almost bursting with delight and affection, beamed back.

Various others came and went until it was the turn of the band, which was also the climax of the evening. And there was Izzy taking up her position behind the drums.

A guitar riff that Wordsworth recognised – *Seven Nation Army* by The White Stripes. Then Izzy was hitting the drums. Thud – thud – thud – thud. A steady beat. It sounded okay. It sounded good. Wordsworth and Wendy watched with growing pride and amazement. The number progressed without incident and with a flourish the song ended and the audience applauded enthusiastically, nobody more enthusiastic than Izzy's overjoyed parents.

Afterwards, as they walked to the car, Wordsworth and Wendy lavished praise on both their daughters. Izzy was unusually quiet, until she said, "That song's dead easy to play."

"Easy or hard, you still played it," said Wendy, trying to figure out why Izzy wasn't happy with her achievement.

"Truth is, it's the only song I could play. They all wanted to play something else, something more modern … but I couldn't do it."

"Why not?" asked Wendy.

"I could only practice at school … so it didn't give me much time. Next concert I'll be a lot better."

Wordsworth exchanged a look with his wife. A look they'd exchanged many times in their marriage. It was a look that said … *Should we?* This was followed by the slightest of nods from Wendy and without saying anything, the decision to buy Izzy a drum kit had been made.

CHAPTER TWENTY-TWO

Against Wordsworth's advice, Redhead was adamant that he wanted to continue to work on finding the missing girls, and Wordsworth knew it was pointless trying to change his mind. He secretly thought that Redhead's rage at what happened to Zara would come in useful.

So Wordsworth set Redhead and Harvey to checking the CATCHEM database, and before long, they came up with all the statistics of dead teenage girls over the last six months. Wordsworth scoured the list. All that concerned him were the girls that were as yet unidentified. Only one fit the bill. This was a girl who had been found on the Embankment in London. Wordsworth asked for Harvey to make travel arrangements for him and Redhead. If Redhead really wanted to keep busy, then Wordsworth would oblige.

The train journey down to London was done in virtual silence. Wordsworth tried to strike up a conversation, but

Redhead was not up for talking. Next to him on the seat was his briefcase, which contained photographs of all the missing girls. Around about Peterborough, Redhead opened the case and took out the photographs. Without saying a word, he looked at them individually. Wordsworth assumed this was about him refreshing himself with the case, but in fact Redhead was testing himself. There was a chance that he'd be looking at one of these girls in a mortuary; he had to know he could cope.

They caught a cab that took them to the Westminster Public Mortuary, where they were admitted to a small reception area. They only had a short wait before they were joined by DI Peter Wilson. Wilson was mid-thirties, quite stocky, with a shaven head. He would fit in a football crowd nicely.

Before they went in to view the body, Wilson, his South London accent very obvious, gave his two Yorkshire co-workers a brief synopsis of what his team knew. The girl, who they believed to be between fourteen and seventeen, was found eight weeks ago under some large pieces of cardboard in a well-known homeless spot near the Festival Hall on the Embankment. At first it was thought she'd died of a drug overdose, which was the most common cause of death amongst the homeless, and she did have numerous track marks on her arms and thighs, but the pathologist quickly determined that the cause of death was strangulation with some form of ligature, possibly a stocking, which was logical as when she was found, she

209

was wearing only one. She had also been raped both vaginally and anally, and due to the horrific tearing and bruising and the fact she had a mix of old scar tissue and fresh wounds, it was suspected she had been raped numerous times over a span of days or weeks. When they found the body, the pathologist determined that she'd been dead for nearly a week, but when they questioned the others who were living rough in the same area, nobody could remember seeing her. A suspicious death team was assembled, over thirty officers in total, but they discovered nothing. Nobody had seen the girl; nobody knew the girl and nobody appeared to care about the girl. Various possibilities to her identity were investigated, but all were a dead end.

"When they found her was she clothed?"

"Skirt and a tank toppy thing, with black underwear, suspenders, one stocking …"

"Not the normal homeless attire then," said Redhead, confirming Wordsworth's thoughts.

"No. And the sexy underwear is an odd one on someone so young. Not right. You think you might know who she is?"

"We've five missing girls, all around that age … we're just following every lead we can."

Wordsworth and Redhead flanked Wilson as they walked down a corridor and through another door. They found themselves in a large room with body drawers lining either side. Already there, dressed in a white coat with a shabby beard and wispy, prematurely grey hair, was a mortuary technician. He'd obviously been prepped, because without asking he went straight to a drawer and pulled it out.

Lying there, covered in a white sheet, was the body Wordsworth and Redhead had come to look at. Wilson nodded to the technician and he pulled back the sheet.

Redhead's eyes were transfixed on the body and Wordsworth was transfixed on Redhead. Wordsworth noticed that his breathing had changed; it had become shallower and more rapid as he tried to keep his emotions in check. Wordsworth wanted to tell him to get out, he should be anywhere but here, this was too close to what had just happened to him, this was too difficult for him. But Wordsworth knew that Redhead needed to stick it out. He needed to do this for himself.

Wordsworth looked at Redhead for what seemed like minutes, but was in fact only seconds, before tilting his eyes down towards the dead girl. She was young ... too young. Wordsworth wanted her to be peaceful, but for some reason even in death she seemed troubled. He stared at the girl in silence, a silence that was eventually broken by Wilson.

"Well?" asked the London detective.

"What do you think?" Wordsworth in turn asked Redhead.

Redhead tried to speak, but no words came out of his mouth. Instead he undid the brief case and took out a photograph. He handed it across to Wordsworth who looked at it. He was right. The girl was Britney Atkinson.

CHAPTER TWENTY-THREE

There was talk about how they would carry out the formal identification and what the procedure would be with regards to acquiring DNA that would officially confirm what they already knew. It was also agreed that the Met would continue with the murder investigation – there was a large team of detectives who had been on it since the discovery of the body – while Wordsworth and his team would try and discover the dead girl's movements before she travelled to London. Then with firm handshakes all round and a promise to keep each other informed of any developments, Wordsworth and Redhead climbed into a taxi and headed back to Kings Cross.

"What do you think happened?" Redhead asked as the two of them sat down with a beer each on the train. "I mean with society. What happened with this society we live in? I know it wasn't always like this."

Wordsworth knew he was referring to his sister Zara as

much as Britney Atkinson. It was also a question Wordsworth had asked himself more than once. After all he had four children, how do you protect them? It was a seemingly impossible task.

"I just want to know what happened." Redhead hit his beer hard.

"You know she had a boyfriend?" said Wordsworth.

"Britney?"

"Zara."

Redhead stared blankly at him.

"He could be the one who supplied her with the drugs," continued Wordsworth.

"She never mentioned any boyfriend to me," stated Redhead. "How do you know she had a boyfriend?"

"A couple of girls at school told Izzy. They didn't know his name, but they thought he might be older than her."

"This is fucking rubbish," Redhead said through clenched teeth. "I would have known if she'd had a boyfriend …"

"She was a teenage girl. She might not have wanted you to know."

"That's fucking bullshit," was Redhead's angry retort. "There's no fucking way she had a boyfriend."

Wordsworth looked at him for a moment, internally debating whether to continue with this conversation. He decided it was pointless backing down. It was now or never.

"She was fourteen, Steve. Fourteen-year-olds have

214

boyfriends … they have relationships … they have sex."

"What're you saying?"

"That we have to open up the way we're thinking. These girls are not little innocents. They may be naïve, but they have been further than Sunday school."

"You're saying Zara was like this Britney Atkinson …?"

"I'm saying she had a boyfriend like her … that she kept secrets like her … She'd also talked about trying out drugs … I'm saying she was fourteen, not a child."

Redhead just looked at Wordsworth, then after what seemed like an eternity to Wordsworth, Redhead lowered his eyes and turned his head away.

The silence was all encompassing; even the noise of the train seemed to fade into a soundless void. Wordsworth started to get up.

"I'm going to get a couple more beers."

Wordsworth, without waiting for any input from Redhead set off to the buffet carriage. Redhead didn't stir.

As he stood at the bar, he couldn't help but think that he'd been thoughtless. He ordered a beer. He thought it best to give his colleague a bit more time. As he stood sipping his can of Carlsberg his mind remained with Zara. Strange how she too had this secret boyfriend. In fact all the missing girls except Jodie Kinsella, had secret boyfriends. Had Wordsworth been missing something that had been staring him in the face all along? Teenage girls liked to boast about their boyfriends, especially the undesirable ones; they didn't usually like to keep them secret. Then the possibility hit him ... the crazy notion rushed into his brain - could it be that each of these girls had been seeing the same secret boyfriend. Jodie told Ethan she was seeing a man for cash, what if that wasn't the case, what if she was seeing a boyfriend ... a secret boyfriend.

Wordsworth bought another couple of beers and headed back to his colleague. As he opened the beer he told Redhead about the idea of a 'secret boyfriend.' This was the common denominator they had been searching for. Redhead couldn't help but take notice, his interest becoming more concentrated as Wordsworth expounded his theory.

They were still discussing it as the train approached the station in Bradford. It was slowing down, preparing to stop when Wordsworth announced, "We need you to go through Zara's things again. We've missed something. We need to find out who her secret boyfriend was. That way she stays in the theory ... or she drops out of it."

Redhead felt sick at the idea, but knew he would have to do it.

INTERVIEW ROOM. BRADFORD CITY CENTRE POLICE STATION, NELSON STREET.
10:59 a.m. 10th JANUARY 2020

"A bit of a stab in the dark, introducing Zara Redhead's death ..."

"Possible murder," interrupted Wordsworth.

"... into the scenario," continued Price, writing something on his pad.

"How did your sergeant feel about it?" asked Ashburn.

"When something like this happens, then what anyone wants is to find someone to blame. They don't want it to be the fault of their little angel ... there has to be another reason. Steve was no different to anyone else, except he knew he had to tread carefully so as not to prejudice anything we did find," explained Wordsworth.

"Did you get a warrant?" asked Ashburn trying to find a flaw.

"Didn't need one, Steve's parents gave us permission to

search their house and their cars."

"And that's what you did?"

"That's what we did."

"Where was DS Redhead when the search was taking place?" asked Ashburn knowing that Wordsworth wouldn't have been so stupid as to directly involve him.

"Back at base," replied Wordsworth, just managing to hide his smile.

"And according to your statement you found something?" announced Price.

"We did, we found something that we considered to be our first major breakthrough. For us it was a turning point … a real turning point."

CHAPTER TWENTY-FOUR

Robert and Rose Redhead, Zara and Steve's parents sat in the kitchen. Robert had suggested they went out while the police conducted their search, but Rose wanted to stay. Now she was wishing she was anywhere but there. Steve hadn't told them much about the investigation, but he had told them that Zara's death may not be as straight forward as they first thought.

"I think we should go for a walk," Rose announced. Robert didn't argue.

Neither of them noticed the weather, pouring rain and a fierce wind. They just walked off down their street, not speaking, just suffering.

***

In Zara's bedroom, Wordsworth and Harvey were methodically going through the dead girl's belongings –

her wardrobe, schoolbooks, travel brochures, make-up, everything. They weren't sure what they were looking for and they'd certainly never dreamt of what they did find.

Zara had a diary. A goldmine of potential information. It was a strangely old-fashioned thing to do, but there it was a page per day diary, with entries written neatly, always in black. Her entries were not consistent. Sometimes it was every day for three or four continuous weeks, then sometimes there was nothing for a couple of days, or even a week.

As Wordsworth continued with the search, Harvey started to take a cursory look at the diary. It soon became clear that there was a boy on the scene. A boy she referred to as 'J'.

'J promised he'd get me some sweets, but I had to promise not to mention his name to anyone ... so I'm not even going to write it down. I'm not really bothered about trying them, although everybody does use them these days, but J wants me to. He said how can I comment on something I hadn't even tried.'

Harvey showed Wordsworth the passage and Wordsworth couldn't help but smile. 'J' had to be the mystery boyfriend they'd been looking for. 'Sweets' was clearly a thinly disguised euphemism for drugs and if 'J' was responsible for providing drugs to a minor, he could be in serious trouble.

As Harvey studied the diary, Wordsworth started to concentrate on Zara's laptop. Her father had given them the password, he'd always known it, and Wordsworth got access to Zara's emails, as well as her Facebook account, Instagram and Twitter. It was the emails that proved to be the most interesting. Wordsworth knew few teenagers exclusively used email to communicate with their friends, it was all social media these days. But here were over a hundred to a recipient who changed his email address all the time. Wordsworth's guess was that whoever Zara had been emailing had been using public computers, they definitely didn't want to be traced.

Through the emails and the diary, they quickly discerned that 'J' was older than Zara and that she was besotted with him. They'd always arrange to meet in quiet, obscure places and she never questioned this decision. The emails were all intelligently written, suggesting the boy was well-educated, and more than once he mentioned that his family had money. Then in a later email, J had said he'd meet her straight after school and he'd be leaving FN at about 4:30 … could she get to see him then?

FN had to be Fulneck. Now there was a clear link.

"Am I hallucinating or wasn't Pizza Boy the nickname of one of those lads you interviewed," Harvey chimed up.

"Yes," answered Wordsworth. "Why?"

"He's mentioned in her diary."

"What does it say?"

"I'll read it … *'Met J and he was with his mate. I'd never met him before. J called him Pizza Boy and Pizza Boy had a crap nickname for J. Diesel. I'm going to get*

221

him to change it.'" Harvey paused, looking at her boss for a reaction. They both knew this was major.

"J is fucking Diesel! And Diesel is fucking Ethan Cartwright. Fuck! I think we've found our mystery boy."

INTERVIEW ROOM. BRADFORD CITY CENTRE POLICE STATION, NELSON STREET.
11:10 a.m. 10th JANUARY 2020

"At that stage, the truth of the matter is, you had nothing but a hunch," Ashburn was in there as soon as Wordsworth took a pause for breath. "A hunch that would never stand up in court."

"Would you like me to just skip to the end, because that's all you really bothered about, isn't it?" Wordsworth challenged Ashburn.

Ashburn was about to reply, but her moment's hesitation allowed Price to intercede, "How did Sergeant Redhead react when he realised that you may have the person responsible for his sister's death in your sights?"

No one in the room knew Price had lost his brother when he was quite young, hit by a drunk driver; he'd never really got over it. The driver spent a few years in jail before being released. Price always wondered what he'd do if he came across him again.

"Professionally," Wordsworth replied. "Once we made the connection, I informed him that he'd have to move off the case; we couldn't risk being accused of tarnishing the evidence."

"He understood?"

"Totally. He didn't want some smart-arsed lawyer using him as a reason to get the case thrown out. He packed up his personals and moved into an office a floor below. After that, as far as I'm aware, while the investigation was still ongoing, he never even set foot on our floor."

What Wordsworth failed to say was that during the course of the investigation, he and Redhead met regularly on the pretext of having a drink together. In reality Wordsworth was giving him a step-by-step account of what was happening with the case.

"Did you manage to get a replacement for him?" asked Price, really knowing the answer.

"No. I got a promise there would be one forthcoming, but they never materialized. It was just the two of us. Our office was like the Mary Celeste on dry ground."

"But you soldiered on in search of justice," said Ashburn sarcastically.

"We were just doing our job, like you're doing yours. Only our attitude was neither vindictive nor bias."

Wordsworth smiled at Ashburn who failed to come up with a retort; instead she just sucked in her anger and let it fester.

CHAPTER TWENTY-FIVE

It was decided that with the help of a number of uniformed officers they'd pick up Sebastian Mancini and Ethan Cartwright simultaneously. They wouldn't be arrested; they'd be told they were helping with police enquiries. The decision was made to leave out Herschel Berkowitz for the time being. The idea being that the other two might wonder if their geeky mate had said something to the police, something that was enough to allow him his freedom.

They tried the Cartwrights first, but were met with an empty house. So in the end, only Sebastian and his parents came in.

Harvey started the questioning, but even with his nerves, Sebastian seemed relatively sure of himself.

"Tell us about Zara Redhead. We know you know her."

Sebastian didn't seem at all rattled by Wordsworth's declaration.

"I'm not sure, I may do," was Sebastian's reply.

"Either you do or you don't," chimed in his mother.

Wordsworth opened a file that he had brought into the room with him and took out a photograph of Zara. He placed it in front of Sebastian.

"That's Zara Redhead," said Wordsworth.

Sebastian didn't hesitate. "Yeah I know her. Her name's Zara is it?"

"Was," stated Harvey quietly.

"Was?" Sebastian was either a brilliant actor, or he had no idea about what had happened to her.

"She's dead," continued Harvey. "Bad drugs."

"Dead ...?" There was genuine shock in Sebastian's voice.

"Yeah. Did you know she did drugs?" asked Harvey.

"No ... I only met her the once."

"Was she by herself?" Wordsworth joined in.

"Yeah."

"There wasn't a boy with her?" persisted Wordsworth.

"A boy?"

"Yeah ... was she with a boy?"

"Yeah ... Ethan. Ethan was with her. That's how I met her. He knocked around with her for a couple of weeks, but I only saw her the once."

"Ethan Cartwright?" Wordsworth confirmed.

Sebastian nodded.

"What do you remember about that meeting?"

"I wasn't supposed to be there. I just hadn't got his

226

message."

"Where did you meet them?"

"Nero's … centre of Bradford. We meet in there a lot. I thought we were going on somewhere, but when I got there Ethan was with … that girl." He nonchalantly pointed at the photograph.

"Then what happened?"

"She went to the loo and Ethan said he needed me to get lost."

"He wanted to be by himself with her?" Wordsworth asked.

"Yeah … and I'd better not say anything to Jodie. This girl was his bit on the side …"

"Jodie knew nothing about this girl - Zara?"

"No."

"And you were ok with keeping it secret?"

"It was no big deal for me. It wasn't the first time Ethan two timed his girlfriend."

"He did it regularly?"

"Now and then. Hey, you're not going to say anything are you? 'Cos if you are then …" Sebastian couldn't finish the sentence because if they had have told Ethan, he wasn't sure what he'd do.

"No … this is between you and us …" Harvey said reassuringly.

"We might …" Wordsworth stared at Sebastian coldly.

Sebastian looked at him shocked, as did Harvey.

Sebastian's parents were also taken aback by

227

Wordsworth's veiled threat. Danielle was about to say something, but her husband just squeezed her hand. Giovanni had realised the boy they were after was Ethan, not Sebastian. His son's best bet was to tell them all he knew.

"I've a dead girl on my hands," continued Wordsworth, "a girl who was given some drugs that killed her."

"I've never known Ethan do drugs ... and I don't do 'em."

Wordsworth just ignored his protest and carried on "I've another girl who's missing, maybe dead, also linked to Ethan Cartwright. I need to know what you know, before another girl turns up dead."

"I said ... I only met her the once."

"Did Ethan ever talk about her to you?" Wordsworth asked still keeping the tone of the interview hostile.

"No."

"And what about Jodie ... did you say anything to her about Zara?"

"No ... no. I wouldn't."

"Why not?"

"Cos ... he's my mate. Ethan's my mate."

"What you not telling me. I know you're keeping something from me," his voice still quiet.

Danielle had had enough and despite Giovanni trying to restrain her, she stood up and spoke out.

"I'm sorry, this is not on ... my son's told you all he knows. It's time for us to leave."

Sebastian looked at his mother nervously; he didn't want her intervention to make things worse for him.

Wordsworth leant back in his chair and eyed up Danielle. "Fine," he said. "DC Harvey, show them out please."

With a sense of relief, Sebastian's parents headed for the door, which Harvey opened for them. Sebastian for a moment didn't move, then he slowly stood up. He looked at Wordsworth – he'd made a decision

"J. She kept calling him J. That's all I know, I swear it."

Wordsworth looked back at him, giving nothing away.

"I don't know why she thought his name was J, but she did." Sebastian was now offering information without even being questioned. "I should have asked, but I didn't. Ethan has a way with him …"

Wordsworth still said nothing, so Sebastian just continued.

"You know straight off if he's not happy with you. And usually it's just best to just keep your mouth closed, or he'll get mad with you. There was nothing else … I promise."

Wordsworth looked at him for a moment; then just nodded his head, almost imperceptibly. Sebastian took this as a signal that Wordsworth believed him and he could go.

They needed to talk to Ethan Cartwright.

CHAPTER TWENTY-SIX

Over half the girls that had been at Dove Place when Abigail had been there had now gone onto pastures new, which in most cases meant foster homes or the big bad world. Harvey managed to find a couple of girls that had known her. Erin Nowak and Willow Hallman.

She quickly got them onto the subject of her boyfriends.

"She talked about them a lot," replied Erin in her street patois accent. "She said most boys she met weren't good enough for her ... didn't know shit from Shinola."

"She didn't say that," said Willow. "She didn't say that, 'cos she never swore."

"Never?" asked Harvey.

"Only when she was doing the crossword. She used to swear then," replied Willow.

"She did a crossword?" asked Harvey.

"I know ... She was smart," said Erin, "I got to give her that. But I did get pissed off with her now and then, giving it large all the time. Coming on like Miss fucking Mensa.

She might have been bright, but she wasn't that fucking bright."

"So there were no boyfriends? None at all?"

"There was one guy," chipped in Willow. "She talked about one guy."

"Did he have a name?"

"I don't know about a name but she called him J."

***

At Oak House, Wordsworth was having no joy. He'd interviewed all the residents and staff that were there the same time as Skye Chapman. Of course they knew her, but none of them could tell him anything that helped to point the finger of suspicion at Ethan. By all accounts Skye was slightly withdrawn and immersed in her love of art. She talked little, drew a lot. When it came to socialising with the others, she was reluctant to become too involved. It seemed all she wanted to do was get back to her mum, who had her own problems.

Wordsworth realised that Skye wasn't in care because of something she'd done, but because of something her mother had done. Even though he asked, no one was prepared to say what that was, that is until one of the carers spoke quietly to him in a deserted corridor. "She made her smoke crack, then forced her to have sex with her uncle and couple of his mates. Skye swore it had nothing to do with her mum, it was all her fault, but the police found text messages on her mother's phone, setting it all up. But despite knowing the truth Skye always said as soon as she could, she'd go live with her."

It seemed he'd hit a brick wall and decided to call it a day. As he headed towards the exit, passing the communal lounge he became aware of some paintings and drawings on the wall: a mini art gallery. He stood looking at the artwork, which comprised of an eclectic mix of methods of drawing and painting and varying degrees of technique and talent. But there was one pen and ink drawing that caught his eye. It was framed in a black wooden frame and showed a youth walking down a street, his jacket open, hands in jeans pockets, similar to the famous James Dean poster. Only the youth wasn't James Dean, but it was someone Wordsworth recognised … it was Ethan Cartwright.

There were a couple of girls in the room, he reckoned around fourteen or fifteen, playing FIFA on an X-box. Wordsworth waited until there was a natural lull in the action before he spoke. "Do you know who did this drawing?"

The two girls both turned and looked at him. One shrugged.

"No idea?" persisted Wordsworth.

"Name'll be on the back," said the other girl.

"Thanks."

Wordsworth moved to the drawing and carefully removed it from the wall. He knew what he was hoping to see, and there it was neatly penned – *Skye Chapman.*

Wordsworth stood staring at it for some time. Both girls were just looking at Wordsworth, wondering what the big deal was.

"Hey mister, are you some art man?" asked one of the girls.

"No, I'm a copper."

The two girls looked at each other and turned their attention back to their game.

Wordsworth leant the drawing against a tatty armchair, and took half a dozen photos on his phone both of the signature and the drawing. And having got more than he could have hoped for – he left. The two girls never noticed him go.

CHAPTER TWENTY-SEVEN

Back in their small incident room, Wordsworth and Harvey exchanged information. They now had proof Ethan Cartwright was not only linked to the disappearances of Jodie Kinsella, Abigail Davies and Skye Chapman, but they could also link him to Zara Redhead.

Convinced they were on the right track, the big question now was how to proceed from here.

Wordsworth decided it was time to fill in his boss with where they were and hopefully persuade him to allocate them more manpower. The Chief Super warmly welcomed Wordsworth into his office and then, as he often did, started the conversation with the question: "So … what can I do for you?"

Wordsworth explained where they were in the investigation and how he considered the intelligence they had gathered pointed directly at Ethan Cartwright. But he wasn't certain he had enough to issue an arrest warrant;

they were short on both motive and forensic evidence.

"If you're right," said Lumb, edging his bet, "then motive is surely power. He's exercising his power over these girls."

Wordsworth didn't contradict his boss, but his expression showed he wasn't convinced with that theory.

"You don't think so?" asked Lumb, picking up on Wordsworth's doubt.

"No, I don't. I believe there's something more kicking around here."

"Like what? Vulnerable girls, he woos them with his suave charm, it seems pretty straightforward to me."

"We have one girl strangled, another die of a drugs overdose, but where are the others?"

Lumb silently and reluctantly could see his point.

"I need some more men, then we can keep an eye on Cartwright, get him to lead us to where there *is* evidence."

"But like you say Bill, we still don't have anything that would justify us taking officers off other more pressing matters …"

"More pressing than four missing teenage girls, one of them definitely murdered, and all linked to the same boy? More pressing than that?"

Lumb looked at him, he knew when it was put like that, he couldn't argue. "Ok, I can give you one more," acquiesced Lumb. "You can have DC Cosgrove."

"I was hoping for twenty …" was Wordsworth's disappointed retort.

Lumb just laughed. "Bring me something concrete and then we'll see about finding you some more bodies." Wordsworth couldn't believe his boss hadn't noticed his un-PC pun.

***

The Hare and Hounds where Wordsworth and Redhead had their night of drunkenness now became the location for Wordsworth to brief his small, but enthusiastic team. Everything about the investigation wasn't following normal procedures and to make that more evident their first briefing was in a pub. He told Harvey and Cosgrove that they were going to have to be slightly underhand. They had to find proof that Ethan was involved with the missing girls, once they knew where that proof was, then they would get the warrants. They couldn't risk getting the warrants and then finding nothing.

Before they got a chance to discuss anything, they were interrupted by Joe Carter, who was now seeing out his last few weeks before retiring. He was on his fifth pint and very talkative. He wanted to tell his fellow officers about what he considered to be his last case. It'd involved some Ukrainian - Sergey Klochkova, who he'd nabbed for armed robbery and was now awaiting trial.

"He was a right hard case," boasted Carter. "Really fucking fancied himself. Didn't fancy himself too much when he was laid on the ground twitching 'cos I'd tasered the bastard." Carter laughed at the thought and the others laughed politely. "He started blabbing about a stash of weapons. Thought if he told me where they were then I'd do a deal. Might have worked in Polack land, but not here. I didn't give a fuck about them. If I'd gone down that route, and I'd found them, I'd still be on the job now, trying to figure out which gun was used in which fucking hold up ... No thank you – someone else can sort that lot out."

Wordsworth thought he was never going to go, and he was having definite second thoughts about having briefing sessions in a pub, then relief appeared in the shape of one of Carter's team. Carter saw a fresh pair of ears to assault and without a word immediately went over to the new arrival and bought him a pint.

Satisfied Carter was now happily engrossed with his compatriot, Wordsworth got back to the business.

"We need to worry Ethan Cartwright. Make him think we have more than we have," Wordsworth said.

"How do you see that working?" asked Cosgrove.

"We put a tail on him." Wordsworth gave a little smile at the thought of his plan. The other two didn't seem very impressed.

"With just the three of us?" asked Harvey with an incredulous air.

"It doesn't have to be a genuine tail; he just has to think it's genuine. He has to think he can't make a move without us seeing him. Force him into making a mistake."

Wordsworth said they would start the trailing the

following day. Harvey would take the first shift outside his home, while Cosgrove would appear outside his school at lunch time. Wordsworth would pick him up after school and Harvey would be waiting outside his house when he arrived home. Hopefully it would create an impression that there was a 24/7 surveillance on him, when in fact there were large chunks of the day when there were no eyes on him at all.

While Wordsworth was talking, Harvey and Cosgrove had come to the conclusion a weak plan was better than no plan. Harvey asked, "Do you think this kid is some perverted serial fuck up who has watched too much porn, or are we looking at something else?"

"Sex is involved, certainly. But I don't think that's all this is about," replied Wordsworth. "Normally a teenage boy who's desperate for sex is not very choosey, and any girl will do. He just wants to fuck, doesn't he? But these are all vulnerable girls … that isn't a coincidence, I believe they've been specifically targeted."

"So what's he playing at?" asked Cosgrove.

"We're obviously missing something, a piece of the jigsaw, but what?" said Harvey.

"Chances are it's staring us in the face," said Wordsworth, downing his drink and getting up to leave. "I'll see you in the morning. Harvey you be outside his house at 7.30. Make it look as if you're trying to be incognito."

And with that instruction Wordsworth left. There was

238

one thought that had been nagging at the back of his head, but so far there had not been one shred of intelligence that backed up his thought, which was … what if Ethan wasn't working alone. What if someone else was involved?

INTERVIEW ROOM. BRADFORD CITY CENTRE POLICE STATION, NELSON STREET.
11:40 a.m. 10th JANUARY 2020

"You were basically trying to harass this young man."

Wordsworth looked at Ashburn, unable to hide the slight grin that appeared on his face. "I had no choice. Here was a kid who I believed was involved with the disappearance of multiple girls and may even be a serial killer. We were only had three officers. How many worked on the Yorkshire Ripper Case and they still didn't get it right? In the end that team just got lucky. I wasn't prepared to wait until we just got lucky. Have you got a teenage daughter, Sergeant Ashburn?"

"Of course not," was her indignant reply.

"I've got two and if anything happened to either of them, I would appreciate the police doing all they could to find the culprit."

"Let's not get bogged down in hypothetical arguments,"

240

Price said. "Sergeant Ashburn has a point about harassment. What you did contravened police policy."

"Okay – what was I supposed to do, forget about it?" Wordsworth knew what had happened had happened, and no way was anyone going to dole out punishment for a low-grade piece of harassment that had consequences nobody could ever have foreseen.

"This tailing," said Price, ignoring Wordsworth's intervention, "how long did it go on for?"

"Six days."

"And in those six days did your men see anything … anything at all that pointed the finger at Ethan Cartwright?"

"Not directly," Wordsworth replied.

"So it was a waste of the valuable manpower you've been complaining you didn't have, whilst at the same time you were opening up the department to accusations of harassment."

Wordsworth once again looked directly at Ashburn; his eyes oozing.

"Considering what occurred I think the sergeant's line of questioning is crass and insensitive." Sharvari looked at Price, waiting for an explanation.

"I think it would be beneficial for us all if the Inspector explained what actually happened while his team were tailing their suspect," Price said.

"What happened was we discovered that Ethan Cartwright was an over-indulged prick who thought he was above the law. But that was only part of the aim of the

241

surveillance. We also wanted to rattle him. We wanted him to start having trouble sleeping. We wanted him to start thinking that we were round every corner. And in that, we succeeded."

Wordsworth looked at Ashburn who was trying to be defiant, but she knew she was getting nowhere.

CHAPTER TWENTY-EIGHT

As Ethan was coming home from school, he spotted Cosgrove outside his house. *This isn't fucking right,* he thought. That was the third person he'd seen watching him that day.

Ethan walked into his house and headed straight for the kitchen, still thinking about the man in the car. Both his mother and father were discussing the approaching weekend.

"I'll be away one night ... that's all."

"Whatever," his mother said nonchalantly.

"It's work."

"I know." Virginia never questioned her husband about his movements. He paid for hers and her son's lifestyle and she was happy with that arrangement.

Ethan came into the kitchen and without saying a word opened the fridge door.

"Hello ... how are you mummy dearest?" Virginia

teased while prompting her son to at least acknowledge her.

"Hi," said Ethan taking out a bottle of Bud.

"You can at least be civil to your mother."

"Sorry … Hi mum …" he said, moodily.

Prentice sensed that something was troubling his stepson. "Is something wrong?" he asked.

"Did you see a car parked outside?"

"No, I didn't. Did you, Virginia?"

"What sort of car?" she asked.

"A shitty Ford or something," Ethan informed them.

"I didn't see anything," Prentice said with just a touch of concern. "Why are you asking?"

"Nothing … it's probably nothing."

"No come on, what's worrying you?" persisted Ethan's stepfather.

"It looked like a policeman."

"Outside?" Virginia wanted it confirming.

"Yeah …"

"What made you think it was a policeman?" Prentice asked.

"He just looked like one."

"And you thought he might be coming here?"

"I don't know what I thought …" replied Ethan.

"Probably just a coincidence," Prentice said dismissively. "He'd have been having a sly takeaway, or a cigarette."

Despite, or probably because of his stepfather's paltry reassurance, Ethan couldn't get the man in the car out of his mind. He lay on his bed trying to imagine what scenario could have led to them having suspicions about him, suspicions that were great enough to warrant someone keeping an eye on him.

Over the next few days Ethan became very wary of any parked cars. He would check them out, without appearing to, or so he thought. Cosgrove and Harvey tried to be as inconspicuous as possible, whilst being very conspicuous. Ethan started to see a number of other vehicles that he was convinced were part of the team tailing him and slowly the paranoia grew.

The following Friday, Ethan arrived at school in an agitated state. He'd become aware of a grey Ford parked outside a terrace house just a short distance from the sixth form entrance. For the first time he was able to see the driver - it was Wordsworth. He immediately recognised him as one of the two detectives who had come to his house to question him. That confirmed it: he was being followed.

Once inside the school, away from other pupils, Ethan cornered Sebastian – Pizza Boy.

"What the fuck did you say to the police?" Ethan spat out.

"What you fucking talking about?" Sebastian replied, bewildered.

"Don't fuck with me, Seb. They've been on my arse for the last four fucking days! There's one parked up the road as we speak."

"I still don't know what you're talking about."

"I'm being watched … big time. Twenty-four hours a day they're following me around."

"Who is?"

"The fucking coppers, who do you think!"

"Don't get shitty with me. Why would they be following you? They're not following me."

"Yeah. Exactly." Ethan glared at Sebastian.

Sebastian started to think about the interview he'd had with Wordsworth. How he'd told them about Zara. Had he somehow opened up an investigatory avenue for the police? Had he placed Ethan in jeopardy? If so, Sebastian decided Ethan would never know. He was not going to risk incurring Ethan's wrath.

"I never said anything, I swear," Sebastian sounded both innocent and offended.

"Well somebody's said something."

"Maybe *you* let something slip," suggested Sebastian.

"No way."

"We were the only two they questioned, and seeing how it's *you* they're following I'm guessing it's *you* that's fucked up."

Ethan looked at him. For a moment it looked like he might hit his mate. His fist was clenched and his anger was palpable. Sebastian was well aware of what might happen, so he braced himself. But the punch never came, and the anger gradually faded from Ethan's eyes as another explanation started to formulate.

"What about Hershey?" Ethan muttered.

"They never took him in," Seb pointed out.

"No but they did question him … earlier."

"Yeah but … if he'd said anything then why would they wait until now to put the tabs on you?"

Ethan knew he had a point, but then he also knew there was another explanation.

"What if they questioned him a second time and he never told us?"

Pizza Boy saw where he was going and liked it because it took the pressure off of him.

"That's what I'm thinking," said Ethan.

"So what do we do?"

"We put him on the spot. We ask him straight."

***

During a physics class that afternoon, Ethan casually informed Herschel that they were meeting up that evening in Bradford. There was a little pub, The Parry, a proper pub, none of this student bar stuff, a real pub, where they wouldn't need IDs. They thought they'd give it a whirl. Herschel was all for it.

A taxi dropped the three of them off at around quarter to nine and sure enough no one asked for any ID when they ordered three pints of bitter at the bar. Herschel wasn't a big drinker and went onto a half for the next round. After finishing their second drinks, Ethan announced, "Let's move on."

"Where to?" asked Herschel.

"Another pub. Follow me."

The three boys came out of pub and started off down the road. Within minutes they were passing Parry Lane Motors, which had been closed for at least a couple of hours. Just past the garage there was a little recess. There were a few bushes and some iron gates that led into what was some sort of rough field. Ethan walked into the recess, the others followed, they always did.

"Where we going?" asked Seb.

"I need to check something out."

"What?"

"Just go with me will you."

Seb gave a little shake of the head and followed Ethan who already had Herschel with him.

Ethan stood at the end of the recess by the iron gates.

"We need to give it a few minutes," he announced.

By now the normally compliant Herschel was beginning to wonder what they were doing. "What …. what we waiting for?" he asked.

"I think you know," replied Ethan ominously. "Seb – check the road."

"For what?"

"See if we've been followed."

Seb walked back to the opening of the recess and looked up and down the dark road both ways.

"Anything?" called Ethan.

"No – nothing," said Seb as he turned and headed back

towards Ethan and Herschel. He'd only gone a few feet when there was the sound of a car. He stopped, turned and looked back at the road. Ethan froze as he listened intently. Herschel wondered what the problem was. It was a road ... cars tend to travel up and down roads. Within seconds a car had flashed past the entrance to the recess. There was a silence.

"Check again," instructed Ethan.

"No point."

"Check again." Ethan's eyes flashed telling Seb this was an instruction not a request.

As Seb walked back to the lane and once again looked both ways, Herschel couldn't stop himself starting to feel concerned. He had no idea why he was worried, but he was.

"Still nothing," reported Seb.

"No parked cars ... or vans?" Ethan persisted.

"No – nothing. Zilch ... zip ... zero ... nowt. Not even a fucking scooter." Seb bowed, a mocking bow, at the end of his declaration, but neither Ethan nor Herschel smiled.

Herschel looked nervously at Ethan who was just coldly staring at him.

"You got something you need to tell us, Hershey boy?" Ethan's tone was menacing.

"About what?" Herschel replied.

"How long have we known each other?" asked Ethan, not taking his eyes off his prey.

"About ten years ..."

"Since we were kids."

"Yeah … since we were kids."

"Do you know what that means? It means I know when you're lying. I know when you're trying to bullshit me."

Herschel frowned; he was genuinely confused. "I … I … don't … I don't … I really …. Look … tell me … Can you tell what you're going on about, 'cos I've no idea? I wouldn't lie to you … It was me that nicknamed you Diesel," he stammered, as if that was some proof of his truthfulness.

Sebastian debated stepping in, but he didn't. He just watched.

"How many times have you spoken to the police?" continued Ethan.

"What – since I was born?"

"Don't be a cunt, Herschel, or I'll give you a kicking here and now. About Jodie … how many times have you spoken to the police about Jodie?"

"Once. And I didn't speak to them, they spoke to me. They came to see me."

"You've only seen them the one time?"

"Yeah. "

"You're lying, Herschel."

"Why would I lie?"

"You tell me."

"I'm not lying. They came to see me once."

"What did you tell them?"

"I don't know …"

"What did you tell them?

"Fuck this …" Herschel turned and headed for the road.

"Where you going?" said Ethan as he grabbed him by the arm.

"Home."

"I haven't finished."

"I don't care."

"Stop him," Ethan ordered and Sebastian instinctively stood directly in Herschel's path.

Herschel tried to move round Sebastian, but he just continued to block his way. Ethan came up on the back of Herschel and grabbed him by the hair, yanking him backwards. Unable to see where he was going, he tripped and fell to the ground. Ethan was left with a clump of hair in his hand.

Herschel lay with his back on the gravel surface staring upwards. Ethan came and stood over him threateningly.

"Now stop fucking me about and tell me what you said to the cops."

Herschel was angry and the words just blurted out: "I told them you'd argued, I told them I looked after her, I told them you were a prick, a real fucking prick."

Ethan kicked him, hard, in the ribs. "You said I was a prick?"

"You are a prick … you always have been. … Nobody likes you …"

Ethan kicked him again, this time even harder.

"You told them I had something to do with her

251

disappearance, didn't you?"

"No! Why would I?"

"Because they're following me, so someone said something and it wasn't me and it wasn't Pizza Boy. So it has to be you."

"Well it wasn't."

"Tell me what you said."

"Nothing."

Swiftly Ethan bent down and grabbed the collar of the Fred Perry shirt Herschel was wearing. "Tell me!" he shouted, then he smashed his fist into Herschel's face. Herschel let out a scream of pain. Sebastian was suddenly taken aback.

"I said nothing!" Herschel croaked back at him.

"Liar!" Ethan punched him in the face again. Blood was now flowing from Herschel's broken nose.

"Ethan ..." warned Seb. This wasn't right. This needed to stop.

"He's lying!" Ethan hit him again and again and again. With each punch he screamed in his face: "Liar ... Liar ... Liar!"

Sebastian moved to pull him away from the now severely hurt Herschel, but Ethan was on a roll. He started kicking him in a frenzied attack, while Sebastian tried to restrain him. Herschel laid there, semi-conscious not even making any attempt to protect himself.

"Ethan stop it ... stop it!" Seb yelled.

Then quite suddenly Ethan stopped the attack. He was

252

panting hard. He doubled up to catch his breath.

"Come on," said Seb. "You need to get away from here. Go."

Ethan lifted his head and looked at Sebastian uncomprehendingly.

"I'm doing you a favour ... Go!"

Ethan stood up straight. The anger seemed to have totally left him. He took one step away from Herschel's prone, bleeding body. Then for no apparent reason, he just rushed at him and stamped on Herschel's arm.

It snapped. The sound rang out in the silence.

That was the moment Pizza Boy turned against Diesel for good.

Ethan moved off and disappeared in the direction of the pub. Sebastian took out his phone and dialled for an ambulance.

INTERVIEW ROOM. BRADFORD CITY CENTRE POLICE STATION, NELSON STREET. 11:54 a.m. 10th JANUARY 2020

"It wasn't until after lunch on the following day that I heard about Herschel Berkowitz. DC Harvey had followed Ethan Cartwright to school that morning and had reported nothing odd. In fact, when she returned, she questioned whether it was worth continuing with the operation, as the youth didn't seem at all phased by the idea of being followed," explained Wordsworth.

"So how did you eventually find out about the assault?" Price asked sombrely.

"A patrol car had responded to a 999 call. An ambulance had also been called. When they got to the scene they found Berkowitz and Mancini. Mancini's story was that he'd found his friend already beaten up, he didn't know who'd done it. Which was obviously bollocks. Anyway, Berkowitz was taken to the hospital and it was his parents who alerted the bobbies to the fact he had recently been interviewed regarding the Jodie Kinsella case – that's when we were notified."

"So your actions in having Ethan Cartwright followed, tipped him over the edge. That must have made you very proud. I need to get a glass of water," said Ashburn without a pause, and got up and was about to leave the room.

"I'll get someone to bring us some water in," said Price stopping her and picking up a phone.

Ashburn sat down again and looked at Wordsworth, the whole purpose of the sudden thirst was to try and throw Wordsworth of balance. Break up his rhythm, it was all too easy for him.

"Could you bring us some water in … four glasses please." Price gently replaced the phone.

"Well?" asked Ashburn.

"Well what?" Wordsworth replied.

"You must have known you were responsible for this atrocity," challenged Ashburn.

"At that stage for all we knew Pizza Boy was telling the truth."

"So you went to the hospital," Price stated calmly pulling them back on track.

"That's right."

"And the boy … how was he?"

"A mess. Fractured cheek bone, broken nose, fractured jaw, five broken ribs, a broken arm and internal bleeding. When we got there, he was still in theatre. I was directed to a relatives' room where his mother was waiting, alongside her husband…"

"Ruth and Shimon …" Ashburn filled in the blank.

"Yeah. She was bordering on hysterical. I thought at first she was accusing us, saying the beating was in some way our fault, but it wasn't that at all, she was complaining about how long it had taken us to show up. Her old man managed to calm her down. They told me that they thought Ethan had attacked their son."

"Why did they think it was Ethan? Had Mancini said something to them?" asked Price.

"Possibly. I got the impression they just didn't trust Ethan. Parents' instinct." He looked at Ashburn for a reaction.

"When did you eventually speak to the injured boy?" asked Ashburn.

"Much later. There was a problem in theatre."

"Collapsed lung … yeah?" Price had read the report several times.

"Yeah."

"So what did you do next?" asked Ashburn coldly.

"Went to speak with the Mancini boy and then Ethan Cartwright. Whatever had happened, we were certain they were involved."

CHAPTER TWENTY-NINE

Sebastian had always known Ethan was unpredictable, but this latest incident had shocked him to the core. It was as if he didn't really know his friend at all. What if he was involved in Jodie's disappearance? It was something he had briefly thought before but not with any real conviction. Now? He just didn't know. What he did know, was what happened wasn't right.

When Wordsworth and Harvey arrived on the Mancini doorstep Sebastian wasn't surprised, but he was unsure what he was going to tell them about the previous night. His father, as usual, had gone off to one of his restaurants, but his mother was at home. She'd never seen her son in this state and she had a feeling it didn't bode well for what might happen next.

She showed the police officers into the living room and went off to fetch her son, who she knew was in his bedroom.

"Whatever you do, tell them the truth," she instructed him. Sebastian just looked at his mother and the look gave her no inclination of what he was about to do.

They sat down opposite Wordsworth and Harvey. A silence lingered in the air. This time there were no offers of coffees or teas.

"Hi Sebastian," began Wordsworth cordially.

"Hi," Sebastian replied quietly.

"Do you know why we're here?"

Sebastian just nodded.

"You're here about last night," said Danielle seeking clarification.

"That's right. Do you want to tell me what happened?"

Sebastian glanced as his mother for guidance. Her eyes were willing him to explain what actually happened, it was for her as much as the police.

Sebastian just sat there, not saying anything. Harvey eventually had to prompt him: "There was a fight, wasn't there …?"

Sebastian waited a few seconds before he gave a slight nod of the head.

"Who was fighting?"

"You know."

"Ethan and Herschel?" she asked carefully.

Sebastian nodded again. Wordsworth had quite naturally let Harvey take the lead in this interview; he knew her non-confrontational, almost passive approach was the way to go.

"What were they fighting about?"

"I'm not sure."

"They just started fighting for no reason?"

Sebastian clammed up again; he was torn between what he wanted to say and what he was scared of saying.

"Look Sebastian," continued Harvey, "we understand Ethan's your mate, but so is Hershey and he's in hospital in a bad way. A very bad way."

Sebastian suddenly looked up. "He's going to be okay, isn't he?"

"I hope so. But he's pretty beaten up … he's in theatre as we speak."

"You want to do what's right," Wordsworth joined in, "and what's right is to make sure Ethan doesn't do this to anybody else."

"Sebastian, we know it was Ethan."

Sebastian went quiet again, he felt sick.

"We know Herschel had a crush on Jodie Kinsella," said Wordsworth.

"How do you know?" Sebastian asked, shocked.

"He told us," replied Wordsworth. "Is that what it was about?"

Sebastian shook his head.

"Come on Sebastian, whatever it is isn't sitting right with you. Just tell us what it was all about."

Dannielle opened her mouth about to try and encourage her son, but before she could say anything, Sebastian spoke.

"Were you having him watched?"

"Having who watched?"

"Ethan. Had you put a tail on him?"

"I don't think we can ...." Harvey started but Wordsworth interrupted her.

"Yeah, we were having him followed."

"He wasn't just being paranoid then?"

"No."

"Why?"

"Why do you think?"

"Because of Jodie?"

"That's right." Wordsworth paused for a moment before continuing. "That's what it was about – yeah?"

Sebastian nodded. Danielle looked puzzled.

"Herschel thought Ethan was making it up – him being followed – was that it?" offered Wordsworth.

"No."

"What then?"

"He thought Hershey had said something to you, something that made you get on his case."

"Why did he think that?" Harvey asked.

Because I lied and said it wasn't me, Sebastian thought, his stomach giving an uncomfortable, guilty twist. "That was the only reason Diesel could come up with as to why you were following him."

"And for that he attacked him?" asked Danielle unable to remain silent any longer.

Shame just oozed from Sebastian as he leant forward,

looking down at the floor.

"And you saw this?" continued Danielle. "You just watched him do this?"

"Mum, please, I couldn't do anything. Diesel was acting all crazy," Sebastian pleaded.

"Did you join in with the attack?" Wordsworth asked, pretty sure he knew the answer.

"No!" replied Sebastian indignantly. "I wouldn't ... I didn't ... I promise."

"Because if you did, now's the time to come clean."

"Ask him ... ask Hershey ... I did nothing."

"But you didn't try to stop it either," said Harvey pointedly.

The statement pulled Sebastian up immediately. Again that sick feeling. Again, the guilt threatened to overwhelm him.

"I did – I tried to stop him." There was little conviction in Seb's declaration.

"You're going to have make a statement," said Wordsworth.

"He'll do that, I'll make sure of that," Danielle stated firmly.

"What we need to know now is anything you can tell us about Ethan's relationship with Jodie."

Sebastian looked directly at Wordsworth. He thought, maybe if he was honest now, and helpful, then that guilty feeling might go away a bit. But ... what did he actually know about Ethan and Jodie?

"I don't know what I can tell you," he said eventually.

Danielle once again couldn't stay out of it: "Don't you go protecting that animal. You speak up and speak up now."

Sebastian wasn't the least bit scared of his mother; this was all about his own conscience, but he was genuinely struggling to think of anything that may be relevant.

"How did he meet her?" asked Harvey.

"I already told him," said Seb, nodding in Wordsworth's direction.

"Could you tell me?"

"Through Hershey … waiting tables, at some do or another. It sort of went from there."

"When you all hung around together, can you remember anything that Ethan said to her, or she said to him, that could be relevant to her disappearance?" asked Wordsworth

"We all just chatted … about all sorts. Nothing in particular. I think Jodie would have loved to have gone to Ethan's home, but it never happened."

"Why not?" Harvey was wondering if this was the age old story of a girl from the wrong side of the tracks.

"I don't know. But it wasn't just her. I don't ever remember him taking any girl home."

"Why do you think she wanted to go there?"

"Wanted to see how the other half lived."

"She had aspirations …" confirmed Harvey.

"Yeah. And I don't see anything wrong with that. She

had nothing like we have. Ethan wouldn't take her to his home, but she certainly didn't want to take him to hers."

"What about Chloe Moreno, was she the same?" Wordsworth asked.

"Maybe – I don't know."

"You don't know?"

"She never asked to come here, but why would she, I didn't go on about how rich my family were …"

"But Ethan did?" probed Harvey knowing the answer.

Sebastian just nodded. Pizza Boy wasn't like Diesel. His nickname was about his ethnicity; Ethan's was about his wealth.

"Tell us about the first time you met. What happened?" Wordsworth felt they were treading water.

"We met in Nero's."

"In Bradford?"

"Yeah. We stayed there for an hour or so."

"Doing what?"

"Just talking. Ethan kept taking photos of Jodie on his phone … getting her to pose for him."

"He liked to show her off? Like a trophy." There was an undisguised revulsion in Harvey's voice.

"I don't know why he did it."

"Showed them off in school, did he?" persisted Harvey.

"I never saw him if he did."

"Didn't show them to you then?"

"No. He just took them … for himself."

"He didn't show them to anyone?" Wordsworth found

this unlikely. What teenage boy doesn't want to brag about his hot new girlfriend?

"All I know is I saw him texting them ... more than once."

"Texting them to who?"

"I don't know. Honestly, I have no idea. Diesel can be really private. I never asked him questions about things he didn't want to talk about."

Wordsworth knew they couldn't get hold of Jodie's phone. After her disappearance it was soon established that the phone was off and they couldn't track it. What they needed to do was get hold of Ethan's phone, or if not the actual phone – his call details. They needed to know whom he was sending the photos to.

CHAPTER THIRTY

It was late afternoon and the road was quiet. It was always quiet. Virtually every house had already placed their recycling bin onto the normally perfect street, ready for the following day's collection. Ethan spotted Wordsworth, waiting patiently for him in his car. His walk slowed for a moment – *What now?* He took a deep breath and headed for his house. Wordsworth was out of his car before Ethan got anywhere near his house's electric gates.

"Ethan, have you got a minute?" said Wordsworth affably as he approached the teenager.

"No," Ethan replied curtly.

"I think you have." Wordsworth still sounded pleasant enough, but there was no denying the underlying, threatening tone. Ethan started to head for his house again, but was stopped when Wordsworth grabbed his arm.

"What do you want?" Ethan cringed inwardly at his false bravado.

"Give me your phone."

"What?"

"I want to look at your phone."

"No way."

"Don't make me take it off you."

"What?" Was this detective serious? He was a copper – coppers can't behave like this.

"You heard. And let me tell you something, I'm no Herschel Berkowitz."

"I don't know what you're talking about," Ethan replied too quickly.

Wordsworth leaned towards him. "Last night you beat the living crap out of your mate."

"No I didn't."

"He's in hospital, unable to talk at the moment. But when he does speak, when he points the finger at you, you little fuckwit, then you're screwed."

"I didn't do anything. His word against mine."

"Actually we have another witness, and you know we do."

"He wouldn't say anything, not Sebastian."

Wordsworth smiled triumphantly and Ethan cursed inwardly at his stupidity.

"So you admit there is something for him to keep quiet about."

"I don't admit anything."

Wordsworth was now just inches from his face. "I know exactly what happened. When you saw we were onto you,

266

you decided someone must be responsible, that someone had talked, and had pointed the blame squarely at you."

"Yeah – right," said Ethan derisively.

"And you decided that that someone was Herschel Berkowitz."

"That's bullshit."

"You then kicked three shades of shit out of him."

"Think what you like," said Ethan, trying to move off.

Wordsworth grabbed Ethan with one hand, holding him by his blazer lapels.

Give me your phone – now. If you don't, I'll make what you did to Herschel look like a love-in."

Ethan put his hand in his pocket, but then stopped. He knew this wasn't right. "Why do you want my phone?"

"Cos I do."

In that moment Ethan believed Wordsworth was capable of carrying out his threat. Later, when questioned by his father he told him he was just playing along - he never had any intention of handing over his phone. Nevertheless, he had the phone half out of his pocket when the electric gates opened and Virginia appeared, pulling their recycling bin after her.

"What's going on?" she demanded to know as soon as she saw them. "Ethan, come here."

Ethan returned his phone to his pocket and obediently moved to his mother.

"What do you want with my son?"

"We were just talking," replied Wordsworth, thinking

shit – bloody recycling.

Virginia turned and looked at her son, "Is that right?"

"Yeah."

"We were talking about Herschel Berkowitz," explained Wordsworth.

"What about him?"

"He was attacked last night." Wordsworth stared at Ethan, waiting for a reaction. Ethan just looked back at him, meeting his stare. He felt confident again, now his mother was playing bodyguard; so confident he couldn't resist a little smile.

"Hershey was?" said Virginia. "Who would want to hurt him?"

"We have a witness who says that your son was responsible for the attack."

"Don't be ridiculous. My son wouldn't do a thing like that." For a moment Virginia's confidence faltered as she tried to figure out what was the truth and what was a lie. As always, she decided her son was being the truthful one. "I need you to leave."

"And I still need to ask your son some questions."

"Go inside Ethan."

"Don't listen to what he tells you …" Ethan almost stuttered.

"Just go inside," ordered his mother.

Ethan headed into the house. Virginia approached Wordsworth.

"What were you asking him, before I came out?"

268

"As I said – I was asking him about the attack on Herschel Berkowitz."

"And that's all?"

"Yes."

"Because to me it looked like you were threatening him. Look up there." She moved nearer to the gateway and pointed to the gutter. Wordsworth looked up. "See it?" asked Virginia smartly.

Of course Wordsworth saw it. He'd spent time surreptitiously checking out the security cameras, making sure any confrontation happened behind the gate pillars, masking him from the camera.

"If you take one step on our property, pictures will immediately appear on your superior's desk. I'll have you dragged off the force, you hear me? If you think it necessary to question my son any further, then you better let me know, so our solicitor can be present. Nice speaking with you."

Virginia moved back through the gates into her driveway. After pressing numbers on a keypad the gates closed, Virginia on one side, Wordsworth on the other.

***

Ethan knew his stepfather would want to talk to him as soon as he got home. His mother would undoubtably waste no time in relating the story to him in full. As expected, not ten minutes after he heard Prentice come home, he was summoned into the sitting room. Prentice, with his mother obediently listening, asked his son various questions about Herschel and Sebastian. Ethan told him the same story he'd told his mother earlier. Prentice seemed satisfied and for the first time since he'd arrived home, he sat down on the large leather sofa, which looked out onto the garden.

"Could you get me a glass of wine?" he asked Virginia.

"Sorry … yes. I should have got you one earlier." Virginia headed off back into the kitchen throwing the half rhetorical question as she went, "Pinot okay?"

"Yeah fine."

Ethan and Prentice sat in silence for a few moments before Prentice checked over his shoulder to make sure they were alone.

In the following second Prentice's whole manner changed.

"What the fuck's going on?" Suddenly the pleasant, easy-going parent was a stern, no nonsense individual that had a darkness lurking behind his eyes.

"I had to sort out Herschel," Ethan replied apprehensively.

"Why?"

"Because every time I turned round there was a cop car. Somebody's told them something and I figured it must have been Hershey."

Prentice took a pause, trying to work out what the hell was going on. Why had the police latched on to his son? He got up and walked to the window, then not because he doubted his son's story, more because he was still searching for some clue he asked, "And that's all that copper wanted to talk about … Herschel?"

Ethan hesitated for a moment. His father picked up on the sliver of indecision quicker than a rattlesnake's reaction to being stepped on.

"What else was there?" demanded Prentice, looking sharply over his shoulder.

Ethan paused before answering: "He wanted my phone."

"Your phone?"

Ethan just nodded.

"Shit."

"I didn't give it to him … I wouldn't give it to him."

"You're going to need to get rid of it."

"But it's got all my mates in it …"

"Give me it."

Ethan just looked at his stepfather, reluctant to give up his line of communication to everyone he knew.

"Give me it!" Prentice wasn't playing nice. "I'll get rid of it for you."

Ethan took his phone from his pocket and handed it over to his stepfather, who slipped into his pocket.

"I'm sorry … I should never have lost it with Hershey."

"Forget it – it's done."

Virginia came back into the room holding two glasses of wine.

"You're just like your mum," Prentice said, smiling.

"Smart and together."

"No … he gets that from you. You're looking at nurture, not nature. Amazingly, I sometimes think he's more like you than me."

Ethan smiled at his mum, but the smile was tinged with worry and doubt.

CHAPTER THIRTY-ONE

The house was a large detached Georgian dwelling in St Johns Wood. Somebody said that a Beatle had once owned it, but nobody had proof. The house had been occupied by squatters for over a year which had so far scuppered the new owners plan to renovate the place and resell it. Now their patience had run out, they couldn't afford another year messing about with court orders and eviction notices.

So they employed Land Force Securities.

Land Force had undertaken similar jobs before and knew very well how to best get results. It involved half a dozen ex-service men, a chainsaw, a building company and a locksmith.

The six ex-service men, three of whom used to play with the SAS, arrived outside the property at 11 o'clock precisely.

When the sound of a chainsaw cutting through the middle of the front door was heard, all the occupants froze,

273

unsure what the noise was. A white Rasta went into the hall to take a look and was greeted with the sight of the main front door being sliced in half. He rushed up to the first floor where a number of others had appeared from various rooms to see what the noise was all about. When asked what was happening, the white Rasta simply said, "They're coming... they're coming."

By the time the front door had been destroyed, at least half of the squatters had made a dash for it through the back garden. The others, frantically packing their bags, intended doing the same.

The last few squatters who didn't manage to get out before being confronted by the Land Force personnel made no objections when they were escorted from the house through the front door, which was now in two halves.

The body was found in a bathroom on the second floor.

The door had been locked, but there was still a pervasive smell throughout the house. It was a teenage girl who had been placed in the bath which was full of putrid water. Her head had been pushed under the surface and held there with a large brick. The naked body was bloated, but because of the water the flies were few.

DI Wilson from the Met rang Wordsworth three days after the discovery. He'd compared the corpse to the photographs the West Yorkshire Force had provided and was fairly certain this was Skye Chapman. A week later her dental records confirmed this was indeed the missing girl.

The autopsy report showed she'd been severely

sexually abused and death was by strangulation. However, the strangulation was not like Brittany Atkinson's. Skye had been strangled with a person's bare hands; red marks were still clearly visible on the girl's windpipe.

***

They now had mounting evidence that Ethan was involved with at least some of the girls' disappearance. Most of the girls had a mystery boyfriend, and in all but Britney's case they had as good as confirmed that this boyfriend had to be Ethan.

Wordsworth turned all his attention to the Cartwrights. He set about finding out what he could about the family. Prencart Holdings was Cartwright's mother company and after that his business became very complex with various companies, branches, partnerships, subsidiaries and arrangements. There was a company, Glee Amusements, that owned amusement arcades in Blackpool, plus a few pubs, shops, restaurants and clubs. There was also PC Developments that renovated properties or knocked them down to build flats and housing developments. There was another company involved in casinos and another that leased plant hire. There was a small insurance company and a larger car parts distribution company. At first glance most of these companies were either just breaking even or ran at a loss. But with his fingers in so many pies, Prentice could stay afloat by just moving money around. It was certainly a complicated state of affairs, but Wordsworth couldn't immediately find anything illegal. He could get the Fraud Squad to dig further, but he knew this could take months, maybe even years, by which time the chances of finding any of the girls would be non-existent.

That night Wordsworth met up with Harvey, Cosgrove and Redhead in their regular haunt the Hare and Hounds. He had given strict instructions that the meeting should appear jolly and social. This had to look as if it was nothing to do with work.

Wordsworth told them they had one shot at nailing Ethan; if they got it wrong, going after him a second time would be virtually impossible. The CPS wouldn't entertain it.

Redhead, who had said little up until this point, then came out with a suggestion: "Let me take him out."

The others didn't know if he was serious or not. "Take him out?" asked Harvey half smiling.

"Kill him. He killed my sister … why don't I just rid the world of this piece of scum and everyone will be happier."

"You're not serious?" Cosgrove said with disbelief.

Redhead looked at the other three, his expression remaining serious and sombre, then he let out a little laugh that was totally devoid of humour and said, "I wish I was serious. I really do. I don't have the guts."

There was a pause as they all looked at each other, waiting for someone to come up with an alternative and more realistic solution. Redhead broke the silence, "What about going back to good old-fashioned harassment. It rattled him last time. Why not try it again … but this time you up the ante?"

"How do we do that?" asked Cosgrove. What *he* didn't want to do was incur the wrath of the Chief Super. This was his career and he had a long way to go yet, as well as a pregnant girlfriend that he'd committed to.

"You find something to bring him in for … and you make it every other day," suggested Redhead.

"He'll just lawyer up," Harvey pointed out.

"Let him. We can still turn on the pressure. If he thinks we're getting close and we're as tenacious as a pack of hungry wolves, then he could just make a mistake. He could just give us something that we could use to go to court."

The group had been hoping for something more inventive. Hoping for something more … definitive. Ethan was protected because of his name, but what else could they do but give it their best shot.

INTERVIEW ROOM. BRADFORD CITY CENTRE POLICE STATION, NELSON STREET.
12:14 p.m. 10th JANUARY 2020

"We have information that you had a meeting with DS Steve Redhead in the Hare and Hounds pub," said Ashburn. "What did you talk about?"

"We met for a drink, if that's what you mean?" replied Wordsworth dismissively.

"So you're not denying you met up with Steve Redhead?"

"No. I'm not denying that for one minute. DCs Harvey, Cosgrove and myself often go for a drink after work, wind down. And on a number of occasions DS Redhead was in there. There was no directive not to communicate with him full stop, just to not discuss the case. Which we didn't."

"Is that right? So what did you discuss?" asked Ashburn.

"Football … Bradford City … What was on at the

cinema … Normal stuff."

"Are you saying you never discussed the case with DS Redhead?" Ashburn couldn't hide her ever increasing frustration.

"That's exactly what I'm saying."

. "I believe you were emotionally involved in this case because of Zara Redhead's death. You wanted to give your colleague a reason for the drug overdose. It couldn't just be self-indulgence on the part of the dead girl. It couldn't just be teenage stupidity; it had to be something else, some other influence that caused her to take this overdose. You were determined to link her to the other cases – weren't you?"

The other three in the room just looked at her, no one sure how to respond.

"Let's have a break," Price said after an elongated silence. "I think we need one."

Nobody objected.

CENTENARY SQUARE. BRADFORD CITY CENTRE.
12:48 p.m. 10th JANUARY 2020

Wordsworth sat opposite Sharvari in the coffee bar. He had a clear view of the artificial lake which had officially been called Bradford City Park. It was the middle of the day, so none of the fountains were illuminated. Wordsworth had a cappuccino, Sharvari a peppermint tea and they each had a toasted sandwich.

"Any time you think they're going too far, we can leave. You're here because you agreed to be," Sharvari said.

"I want to put it to bed, one way or another," said Wordsworth. "I don't want it to go on forever and always be hanging over me. I want to finish it. Today."

"I understand that. But I'm here to protect your rights and I want to make sure I do just that."

Wordsworth felt a momentary lurch of guilt. Sharvari was fighting tooth and nail for him and he was deceiving her. The feeling passed though. He was only doing what he needed to.

"You're doing just fine," said Wordsworth smiling at her. "How do you think I'm doing?"

"I think you're succeeding in pissing off our Miriam very nicely." Sharvari smirked. That was the first time anybody had used Ashburn's first name all day and Sharvari managed to be so derogatory in her annunciation of *'Miriam'* Wordsworth was sorry he couldn't use it all the time. "Have you come across her before?"

"Oh yeah ..." was Wordsworth's loaded reply.

"That sounds ominous. Did you piss her off?"

"I think I must have."

Wordsworth looked at Sharvari and gave a little smile before taking another sip of coffee.

CHAPTER THIRTY-TWO

Prentice was being shown around Brigella Mills on Little Horton Lane, just a mile or so from Bradford's city centre. It used to be an old worsted mill, but since its closure in the early seventies it had housed a large variety of businesses from sales of cheap furniture to sales of cheap suits. Prentice was there with his location scout, architect and the sales agent. His plan was to convert the whole of the property into flats. He was a long way off achieving his aim. He knew without plans he couldn't get permission, but he was confident it wouldn't be a problem. Bribing his way through life was just a matter of course for him. A new car for someone's son, a trip to Pakistan, a crate of Dom Pérignon, and on one occasion he'd paid for a pair of identical twin hookers – he was used to getting the desired results.

His mobile rang and as soon as he saw it was Virginia he excused himself to speak with her. He knew it must be important because she'd learnt not to ring when he was at work unless it was urgent.

And it was urgent: the police had been back and wanted Ethan down at the station.

"Did they say what about?" he asked, hiding his concern.

"Something else has turned up, some more evidence. They didn't say what."

Prentice thought for a few moments before telling Virginia to get in touch with Faiza Amran at Kahn Solicitors. She'd handled the only criminal case he'd been involved in before, a case when he was accused of fraud, but charges were dropped and that was mainly due to her.

He told Virginia to let Faiza make the arrangements with the police. She would attend the interview and they'd be there as support.

"What the hell's going on Prentice?" asked Virginia. "Why are they doing this?"

"It's this Wordsworth chap. He has to put a name in the frame and he's gone for Ethan."

"You don't think he could have anything to do with this girl's disappearance, do you?"

"Ethan?" asked Prentice, feigning surprise as well as innocence. "Of course not, she was just some girl that obviously thought she'd got first prize. He's smart, good looking and has plenty of cash. She's poor with a drug addict mother and zero chance of ever getting out of the gutter. I reckon this is some scam. Someone hopes to make money out of this, somehow."

"Who? The only way would be a ransom … surely it can't be that."

"I don't know … Look I have to get back. Give me a ring and let me know what's going on."

Prentice hung up the call and went to re-join the others.

**

Wordsworth and Harvey came into the room, Harvey carrying a buff-coloured file, which she held on to tightly. Already there was Ethan and Faiza Amran. Ethan was still wearing his school uniform, obeying an instruction from Faiza.

"Sorry to have to drag you in like this. Shouldn't be too long," apologised Wordsworth. "Miss Amran, a pleasure to see you, as always." Wordsworth smiled at the lawyer as he and Harvey took their seats opposite her and Ethan. Wordsworth had sat in many interviews with Faiza. She was an attractive woman in her mid-thirties that you could tell was a lawyer from fifty paces. Her suits were always expensive and always black, the colour of her shoulder length hair. Wordsworth had a lot of respect for her.

"Do you know why you're here, Ethan?" asked Wordsworth, his voice still light and non-aggressive.

"No," replied the youth.

"Which makes two of us," said Faiza, leaning slightly forward. "What is this concerning? My client is at a crucial point in his education and unless there's a good reason for him to be here, then we shall take our leave. Already I think your treatment of him is bordering on harassment."

"Skye Chapman." As Wordsworth said the name he looked directly at Ethan, he just needed a twitch or some tiny tic from him to be convinced they were on the right track. And there it was … Ethan blinked three times in quick succession. He wasn't expecting this shot across his bows. "Do you know her, Ethan?"

Faiza looked at Ethan. She had felt his body language change. She knew Wordsworth had hit a nerve.

"You don't have to answer that if you don't want to."

But Faiza knew they were onto a no-win situation. She knew Wordsworth would have picked up the change in her client; he was far too savvy not to notice, so if Ethan didn't answer, then it would immediately suggest that he did know her. On the other hand, if he answered, she felt it would be impossible for him to hide what she instinctively felt – that Ethan knew this Skye Chapman, whoever she was.

Ethan paused for a moment, then: "No … never heard of her," he said self-assuredly.

If it hadn't been for the earlier tic, he might have got away with it.

"We're under the impression you did know her."

Ethan shrugged. Faiza narrowed her eyes. She was well-versed in police interviews. She could sense something was coming like a dog senses a storm.

"Oak House Youth Care Home ring any bells?" Wordsworth asked.

"No," replied Ethan too quickly.

"Who is this Skye Chapman?" Faiza cut across, wanting to take the pressure off her client. "My client doesn't know her. Is she missing as well?"

"She was missing ..."

"But she's not anymore?

"No. She was found dead last week. In London. She'd been sexually assaulted and strangled."

Faiza felt Ethan's breathing suddenly change, it had become shallow and rapid. Faiza just knew she needed to take control.

"You're not suggesting my client had anything to do with that, are you?"

"We believe he knew her."

"He went to London, sexually assaulted a girl, then came back home in time for tea? Really?"

"We believe the victim was killed in Yorkshire and transported to London," said Wordsworth grasping at straws.

"Therefore it must have something to do with my client. Is that what you're saying?" Faiza said almost with a smile in her voice. "Can I see the forensic report? I would like to see what it says in black and white."

"It's only a preliminary report ... they have some more tests to do."

"The truth is you have no idea where she was killed, do

286

you? Come on Ethan, let's go. This is a waste of time."

As Faiza made to leave, Wordsworth indicated with one finger to the buff file in front of them. Harvey opened it and took out a photograph. It was a photograph of the painting Wordsworth had taken in Oak House showing a youth that looked remarkably like Ethan.

"Recognise this person?"

Even the usually imperturbable Faiza was momentarily thrown.

"Anybody got any suggestions? No? DC Harvey, what do you think? That look like anyone you might have seen? Anywhere?"

Harvey pretended to study the photo carefully as if this was the first time she'd ever seen it, prolonging Ethan's discomfort.

"D'you know what, Inspector, I think this looks remarkably like Ethan."

"Do you, now? How funny – that's exactly what I thought."

"All right, enough of the theatrics," Faiza said assuredly. "This is all just supposition. Have you any proof that it's meant to be my client?"

"Sadly no … because the artist is dead."

Wordsworth signalled again to Harvey, who this time produced the photo of the signature on the back of the painting. They could all clearly read: Skye Chapman.

Suddenly Ethan lost all composure. He leapt to his feet, his hands resting on the table and he started shouting, "I didn't know her all right! I didn't fucking know her!"

"Ethan ... Ethan ..." Faiza was trying to calm her client.

"So she did a painting ... it doesn't mean anything. Charge me ... go on charge me. You won't, will you, because you'll be laughed out of court."

Faiza stood up. "Ethan, let's go."

"Come near me again ... you'll be sorry. Don't fuck with me detective. I'm Prentice Cartwright's son!"

"Ethan ... that's enough!" Faiza knew this was getting out of hand. He'd already said too much. "Come on. We're through here."

Faiza took Ethan by the arm and led him out of the interview room.

Wordsworth turned to Harvey as the door closed, "Well?

"Guilty as sin."

Wordsworth couldn't agree more.

CHAPTER THIRTY-THREE

The following morning, Prentice arrived at his office nice and early. He liked avoiding the rush hour. The four-storey building, of which Prencart Holdings occupied every inch, was just off Thornton Road. Prentice loved these premises, he felt at home. He'd purchased the building ten years ago and converted it to suit his needs. His own office was on the second floor and even though the structure was Victorian, everything inside the building was ultra-modern and it was from this fairly low-key establishment Prentice ran his empire.

On the ground floor was a receptionist, a young girl called Whitney Smith, who had a strong Northern accent that seemed to disappear when she answered the phone. She was conscientious and saw herself staying with the firm if not for life, for a few years at least. She knew Prentice rewarded loyalty.

She was in the process of writing a message down from Faiza Amran as Prentice came through the door.

"One second please," she said into the phone. "Prentice, I've got Faiza Amran on the phone for you."

"Okay, put her through."

Prentice headed off upstairs as he heard Whitney saying, "He's literally just walked in through the door, so I'll be able to put you through once he gets to his office."

As Prentice came into his office the phone started to ring, Whitney's timing was always perfect. Prentice picked up the phone, wasting not a second.

"Faiza. What happened in that room?"

"It wasn't easy."

"What do you mean? What you talking about?"

"They had a painting … done by some girl called Skye Chapman. Do you know her?"

"No. Never heard of her," Prentice answered too quickly.

"She was living in a care home in Low Moor – Oak House. She disappeared just over six months ago. She was fifteen, today would have been her sixteenth birthday."

"Happy fucking birthday …" mumbled Prentice.

"They found her dead in a squat in London."

"Drugs was it?" asked Prentice indifferently.

"No, she was killed … strangled."

Prentice said nothing.

"The police have a drawing that the girl did. It's a

youth and he looks remarkably like Ethan."

"And that's it?" blurted out Prentice. "That's what they've got?"

"For the moment that's all they're telling us they've got. But I'm guessing they have more."

"I hope you told them to go whistle."

"I didn't get chance; Ethan went off the deep end. When they mentioned this Skye Chapman and produced the photo of the drawing, he lost it."

"The fucking little idiot."

"It made him seem like he had something to hide."

"He has nothing to hide."

"Like he knew something about the girl."

"That's ridiculous.'

"I hope so."

***

On the same day, just after one o'clock, Prentice walked into the Grill Room in the Midland Hotel. He often lunched there mainly because it normally wasn't too busy and the food was good.

As he ate his sea bass, he couldn't get Wordsworth and the situation out of his head. But he knew if he kept his cool, then there would be no problem.

He'd just been served with coffee and was about to check his messages on his phone, when he was aware of someone sitting down at his table. He looked up expecting to see a friendly face; instead it was the face of Wordsworth.

"Mr Cartwright." Wordsworth spoke quietly as if he was worried their conversation might be overheard.

"What the fuck do you want?" Prentice's didn't even try to disguise his contempt for Wordsworth.

"I thought we should have a talk."

"I have nothing to talk to you about.

Wordsworth didn't move. Prentice tried to carry on with his coffee, but eventually he gave up.

"If you don't leave immediately, I'll call the management and get you removed."

"You're not going to do that."

"Want to bet?"

"You're not going to do it, because you're going to listen to what I have to say. You're going to listen and then you're going to get very worried, so worried that sleeping nights will be a problem – I guarantee you. We're coming for your son ... sorry stepson."

"Is that a threat?" Prentice was trying to appear in command, but Wordsworth was starting to unnerve him.

"No – that's a promise. And if you were smart you'd get your son to tell *you* the truth, before I make him tell *me* the truth."

"What you going to do – waterboard him?" said Prentice mocking him.

"No. I'm going to scare the shit out of him. After all dealing heroin is a serious offence. He could find himself doing a long stretch for that. Or of course there's that accusation of rape … "

"What you talking about? Ethan hasn't raped anybody."

Wordsworth raised his eyebrows and smiled slightly.

"I promise you Prenny … you don't mind if I call you Prenny do you?" Prentice said nothing. "We're going to nail him … one way or another."

Wordsworth having made his point got up to leave. He was stopped by Prentice screaming at him, "You leave him alone! You go near him I will fuck you … I will ruin you … you will not have a life!"

Prentice's raised voice had attracted the attention of the rest of the restaurant, both customers and staff. The maître d' started to move to his table.

As Wordsworth made his way past the other tables, he could hear the maître d' trying to calm an irate Prentice.

Wordsworth walked out of the door, pleased with his little lunchtime tête à tête.

"No of course I didn't harass him." said Wordsworth indignantly. "I just happened to run into him, and I thought it was an opportune moment to have an informal word with him. Stupidly, I thought he might appreciate it."

Ashburn looked at him with total scepticism. "He claimed you harassed him. He claimed you had a personal vendetta against him and his family …"

"I hardly knew them."

"You knew they had money."

Wordsworth rolled his eyes. "Oh please!" He took a deep breath to compose himself. "Look, you've read the file, you know what I had against him, and you know what roadblocks I was facing in trying to get to him. Prentice Cartwright thought they were protected because of who they were. He thought they were above the law. I had to let him know, no one is above the law. But I was hitting my head against a wall just trying to find a way to get to them. So maybe my methods were a little unorthodox but, Jesus, I had to do *something*."

CHAPTER THIRTY-FOUR

Wordsworth's team were really putting their backs into it. Cosgrove and Harvey were gathering new statements from friends and families, as well as wading through the behemoth of girls admitted to hospitals or who had run-ins with the law. Wordsworth was surreptitiously still digging for information about the Cartwrights; surreptitiously because Prentice Cartwright had complained to the powers-that-be and Lumb had given strict instructions to back off the wealthy and powerful family. This warning hadn't stopped him getting Gatesy to try work out the machinations of Prencart Holdings; it had only strengthened his conviction that the answer to all this lay with that hermetically sealed household.

Redhead came into the office, the edict that he shouldn't go anywhere near the investigation wasn't being taken seriously anymore, a clear indication they were running the operation down.

"Do we have a plan B?" asked Redhead, referring to Lumb's latest order to back off the Cartwrights.

"Yeah – *we* have a plan B, we always have a plan B."

"Which is?"

"The same as plan A, except less blatant."

"You're going to carry on harassing them?" said Redhead as if he hadn't heard correctly.

"That's exactly what we're going to do."

Before Wordsworth could expound how he intended to carry out plan B, he got word from the hospital that Herschel Berkowitz was now well enough to be interviewed, so he and Harvey set off to Bradford Royal Infirmary.

Herschel's parents had been a constant presence at the hospital, while their son was recovering. Shimon intercepted the detectives before they went into question him.

"We've tried talking to him, but …" Shimon just shook his head.

"What's he scared of?" asked Wordsworth.

"He's scared if he says anything, he'll get beaten up again. I'm guessing anti-Semitism"

"But it could be something else?"

"It could be."

"I think it might be useful for us to question him without you being present," suggested Wordsworth.

Shimon didn't look at him directly, but stared at the floor as he gave the suggestion some thought. "I better ask my wife," he suddenly said before heading back into the room. Wordsworth could just see Herschel propped up in bed, still heavily bandaged and horrifically bruised.

Ruth Berkowitz came out with her husband and exchanged greetings with the two detectives. She then started to talk quietly and earnestly.

"I want whoever did this caught," she said. "I don't want them getting away with it. They could have killed him. They're just animals, they need locking away. Herschel's a brave boy, he isn't keeping quiet for nothing, he must be terrified."

"When we first met him," Wordsworth offered, "he didn't seem the sort to be afraid of anything."

"Normally he isn't. We've brought him up to speak his mind. But this … this is something different."

"Will it be all right if we talk to him by ourselves?"

Ruth paused for a moment in thought. Unlike her husband she stared straight into Wordsworth's eyes.

"You can have ten minutes."

Wordsworth didn't wait for them to change their minds and in he went followed by Harvey.

Herschel wasn't expecting them, his parents obviously hadn't said anything about the detectives being there.

"How you feeling Herschel?" Wordsworth asked.

"Why you here?" was Herschel's slightly aggressive reply.

"We need a statement … about what happened."

Herschel paused for a moment; he had the same

298

mannerisms as his father and he looked downwards whilst deciding what to do. "Nothing, nothing happened to me," he said almost mumbling.

"There's no need to be afraid. We've spoken to Sebastian and he told us exactly what happened. We just want to hear it from you."

"He wasn't even there."

Wordsworth and Harvey exchanged a look.

"Yes he was …" exclaimed Harvey.

"No he wasn't. I ran into him just after it happened. He didn't see a thing." Herschel was adamant.

"So why is he telling us different?"

"I don't know. Likes the drama."

"Come on, Herschel. We know what happened."

"Whatever Sebastian told you is a lie. Don't listen to him."

Then a thought struck Wordsworth,

"Has Ethan been in to see you?"

"No." Herschel looked away.

"So why are you so scared?" For the first time Wordsworth's tone was less than sympathetic.

"I'm not."

"You're shielding the person who put you in here."

"I'm not shielding anyone."

Wordsworth leaned into him and spoke quietly. "Why you lying to me?"

Herschel didn't look at Wordsworth, he just kept staring straight down.

"I don't feel well, I need a nurse."

Harvey tapped Wordsworth on the shoulder and indicated they should leave. Wordsworth looked at Herschel for a moment, before giving a little sigh of defeat. He and Harvey left the room.

Shimon and Ruth were waiting in the corridor. There was an air of anxiety about them.

"Well?" said Ruth as soon as she saw Wordsworth and Harvey.

"Have you been here the whole time?"

"One of us has been with him every hour of every day. We wouldn't leave him."

"Then you know who's visited him."

"There's been no other visitors, isn't that right Shimon?"

"That's right," her husband concurred earnestly.

"Well somebody's got to him," said Wordsworth.

"Has he got a phone … a mobile?" asked Harvey.

"Yes … of course. Which child hasn't?"

Wordsworth found it almost amusing that Ruth referred to her overweight - been shaving for two years – son, as a child. "Do you know if he's had any calls?"

"He's had a few."

"Who from?"

"I wouldn't know, friends I suppose."

"We need to get a look at his phone," said Harvey.

"Shimon – get the phone," ordered Ruth.

Shimon started to go into the room, when Wordsworth

300

stopped him.

"Don't let him know why you want it … In fact you need to get it out without him knowing."

Shimon, not sure how he was going to achieve what was required, took a deep breath and entered his son's room.

"I don't want to see the police again," said Herschel without any prompting.

"You're going to have to," said his father running his hand over his bald head. "They need to know what happened."

"I've said - I can't remember."

Shimon looked at the mobile on the top of the bedside cabinet next to his son's laptop.

"You need to relax …" Shimon moved to the bedside cabinet and picked up the laptop. "What do you fancy?"

"Nothing," replied Herschel rather tetchily.

Shimon ignoring his son, hit an icon on the desktop and up came a list of movies. He clicked on *X Men: First Class*. The screen came alive with the movie's opening credits.

"Seen it." But by three minutes in, Herschel was hooked – eyes glued to the screen and without him noticing Shimon picked up the iPhone and putting it in his pocket left the room, closing the door behind him.

Shimon triumphantly produced the phone from his pocket and handed it straight to Wordsworth.

"Any idea what his password is?" he asked.

"1-9-6-2." There was no hesitation from Ruth. "His favourite film is set in 1962."

Wordsworth tapped in the numbers and the phone opened. He then checked recent calls, scrolling down to the date of the attack. There were six calls, all from Herschel's mum. After that there were a dozen other numbers, all showing they were received during his time in hospital. All of the numbers, except one, had names attached, Sebastian being one of the callers, the rest Wordsworth imagined were other concerned schoolmates, but tellingly there was no Ethan. The one unknown number – 07454 264587 – had called six times. The first five times had remained unanswered, but the sixth one had been answered and had lasted just over two minutes.

Wordsworth showed the parents the number and asked them if they recognised it. Neither did. So Harvey made a note of the unnamed number, as well as the names of all the other callers, then handed the phone back to Shimon, who went straight back into Herschel's room.

Five minutes later, Wordsworth and Harvey were headed across the car park towards their car.

"Do you think this could be a lead?" asked Harvey.

"It better be … it's all we've bloody got."

CHAPTER THIRTY-FIVE

There was no doubt in Wordsworth's mind that Herschel's refusal to talk was directly related to the phone call, but the optimism that this may be the breakthrough they were hoping for was shattered in a matter of minutes. The unknown number was a pay-as-you go mobile which at that point was turned off, impossible to trace. The original call to Herschel was made from somewhere in the city centre at twelve minutes past two. So their first port of call was to establish where Ethan Cartwright was at that time. They expected this to be a nightmare, and they were forced to go through Faiza, but it didn't take long to confirm that Ethan was at the dentist at that precise time and disappointingly there was CCTV confirming it.

So who else could it have been? If it wasn't Ethan then who else? All logic told Wordsworth it had to be either Prentice or Virginia Cartwright. But he had no proof, nothing and he wasn't sure how he could get proof.

Later that evening, Wordsworth was settling down to supper with his family when a mobile started to ring. Nobody went to answer it and it was left to ring out.

"Whose phone's that?" he enquired.

"Mine," said Molly.

"Why didn't you answer it?"

"It's dinner … you don't like us using our phones over dinner," she explained smugly.

"I couldn't have left it," said Izzy. "It drives me mad if I can't answer my phone. It happens at school all the time. I can feel it vibrating in my pocket, but we're not allowed to answer it. Really frustrating. The rest of the lesson I'm trying to figure out who it was."

"I've got to admit," confessed Wendy, "if I hear my phone ringing, I just have to answer it."

"I don't have a phone," said Nathan rather forlornly. "Can I have one?"

"You're seven," was Wordsworth's answer. "Seven-year-olds don't have phones."

"Why not?" asked Nathan. "Everybody else has. Oliver's got one."

"I'm twelve," said Oliver. "When you get to my age you can have one, isn't that right Dad?"

"Yeah," said Wordsworth rather distantly. Something was going through his mind.

The next day, he pulled up in the car park in the front of the offices of Prencart Holdings. He got out and glanced across the road. Parked in a side street was Cosgrove. They exchanged a look just before Wordsworth went into the building.

Whitney was still there manning the receptionist desk and after a brief word with Prentice on the phone, directed Wordsworth up to her boss's office.

As Wordsworth climbed the stairs, he pretended he was on his phone. He arrived on Prentice's floor and he stopped outside Prentice's door. A couple of young women came past gossiping with each other. He made as if he was finishing a call, but in reality he was sending a text to Cosgrove that read: *'Going in now.'* Then he knocked on Prentice's door and a voice from inside told him to enter.

In the side street Cosgrove's phone made that distinct pinging sound, notifying him of the text. It came quicker than he'd expected. He checked it was from Wordsworth and then set the stopwatch on his phone for three minutes.

Wordsworth stood in front of Prentice's desk. Prentice looked at him, scrutinising him, trying to figure out what his play was going to be.

"You really want the sack, don't you?" said Prentice, leaning back in his chair nonchalantly.

"I don't think that's going to happen."

"We'll see." smiled Prentice, a cold icy smile. "People like you always get what's coming to them."

When Wordsworth first met this man, he considered him to be a weak, insipid, good-luck-boy who had inherited daddy's business, but quickly he'd become aware of the true nature of the beast. A man who was cunning, devious and most likely dangerous.

"What did you say to Herschel?" asked Wordsworth straight out.

"Herschel? You mean Herschel Berkowitz, the overfed Jew boy?"

Wordsworth didn't give him the satisfaction of replying, as he glanced surreptitiously at his watch.

In the waiting car Cosgrove watched as the seconds ticked by. The alarm sounded; the three minutes were up. He pressed 'Send' on his phone.

In Prencart Holdings Prentice delivered his ultimatum: "I can ring and make a complaint, or you can leave and never come back,"

Wordsworth said nothing and just glanced at his watch again. Nothing. He could hear nothing. There was no phone ringing. Maybe he was wrong. Maybe Prentice wasn't the one that threatened Herschel. Wordsworth just turned and left.

Prentice's office door clicked closed behind him – then he heard it. A mobile ringing. It was definitely a mobile. And it wasn't coming from Prentice's office, but from somewhere close by. Could it possibly be the burner phone?

He knew he had to be quick. He started to move right, but quickly realised it was the other way. He followed the sound to an office adjacent to Prentice's. He tentatively knocked on the door. No reply. Cautiously he tried the handle. It turned and the door eased slowly open.

Wordsworth stepped into the office, preparing to be confronted by whoever. But no one was there. It was empty except for a large three-sided desk which had on it five computer screens, various computer accessories and a pile of Japanese manga comics.

The phone was still ringing.

Wordsworth quickly closed the door and listened … Where was the phone? Then it stopped. *Shit!*

Quickly, Wordsworth took out his phone and dialled Cosgrove's number. Cosgrove answered immediately.

"Ring it again," was all Wordsworth said before hanging up.

He waited in silence. He could hear another phone ringing somewhere in the building. *Could that be the phone he was looking for?*

Then the mobile in the office rang again.

Wordsworth headed for the desk and started to open the drawers - all were empty. Nothing. It had to be there somewhere. Then silence. It stopped ringing. Wordsworth once again quickly dialled Cosgrove. "And again," is all he said. He waited. Why was it taking so long? Then a sound. Not the phone, someone was approaching the office. Wordsworth froze. Being caught he knew would be terminal. He held his breath as whoever it was went straight past … and the phone started to ring again.

Then he saw it - there under the desk, a Calvin Klein backpack. Quickly Wordsworth unzipped it, rummaged around inside and victoriously, from in between a number of manga comics, pulled out the phone. Once out of the dulling confines of the bag, the ring seemed deafening. Wordsworth fumbled with it some more before he was able to answer it.

"Got it," he whispered into the Samsung Galaxy phone, then he quickly hung up.

He glanced towards the door. What was the best thing to do now? His original plan was that the phone would ring and he would confront Prentice Cartwright with the fact he had it in his possession. But that plan was now defunct. He could just take it, but he would have obtained it illegally and as evidence it would be useless. He also realised if he just replaced it, whoever's phone it was, would see the missed calls. He needed to get rid of those calls.

With constant glances towards the door he fired up the phone. The screen was locked.

Shit! What the fuck do I do now?

He took out his phone and quickly called Gatesy. Gatesy took what seemed like forever to answer.

"Gatesy, it's me," whispered Wordsworth. "I've got this pay-as-you-go mobile and it's locked. I need to get into it pronto."

"You'll need to bring it back here?"

"I can't. I need to get into it now!"

"I'm not Jesus. I don't do miracles."

Wordsworth, frustrated was about to hang up the call, when he heard: "Try 1-1-1-1, it could be the default code."

Wordsworth pressed four ones … but nothing.

"Then try four zeros."

Wordsworth pressed the '0' button four times and the phone immediately unlocked. "I'm in ... I'm in."

"I'm going to try walking on water next week," said Gatesy smugly and hung up.

Wordsworth quickly deleted Cosgrove's calls, put the phone back in the backpack and left the office.

He'd found it, but what now? He needed to confirm whose it was. He needed to know whose office it was.

As he headed out, he paused at Whitney's desk.

"The office next to Mr Cartwright's, on the right? The door was open and I couldn't help but see in. Very smart."

"I know," said Whitney with a smile.

"Who's the lucky so-n-so who gets to work in there?"

"Head of IT."

"And who's that?"

Whitney didn't hesitate, it wasn't a secret. "Robin Adams."

"Good work if you can get it," said Wordsworth. He smiled at the girl and left.

CHAPTER THIRTY-SIX

Wordsworth was excited about the lead they'd obtained, albeit illegally. He knew there was no way he could ever tell anybody, other than Cosgrove and Harvey, how he'd found out that a call to Herschel Berkowitz had been made from someone in the Prencart offices. It could have been Prentice himself, or it could have been this Robin Adams character, but of course it could also have been any one of the Prencart staff. But the finger of suspicion was pointing directly at Robin Adams, simply because the phone was discovered in his office.

Harvey and Cosgrove spent the rest of a week trying to find out what they could about Robin Adams. There was plenty to find out, but nothing that appeared crooked. He was brought up in Aylesbury where his father ran a successful IT company, supplying IT infrastructure to numerous corporate clients. His parents divorced when he was fourteen and he chose to live in the paternal home. By that time Robin was well and truly entrenched in Berkhamsted School, a far from cheap independent all boys' school. The twelve years he spent at the school seemed to be marked by his lack of prominence. He was on the school register, but that was about it. Cosgrove managed to track down his old mathematics teacher, who could only remember him for one thing – his addiction to video games, a skill he was told Adams excelled in. He ended up studying IT at Bradford University, his school masters being happy that he'd at least managed to achieve a university place, even if it wasn't a redbrick establishment. Again, his years there were uneventful. That was until he was caught hacking into the university's mainframe and tampering with the exam results. This misdemeanour was looked on as being stupid and in no way evil, but he still paid the price and was sent down. On leaving uni, earlier than expected, he joined various companies, quickly rising from being a programmer to the head of department. Eventually he was picked up by Prencart Holdings. That was four years ago and by all accounts Adams and Prentice had become firm friends. It didn't take long for Wordsworth to realise it had been Adams he had seen at the Cartwright home when he was first there.

Clearly, they needed to speak with him.

The problem was – they couldn't tell anyone they'd found the phone or where they'd found it, so they had no reason to bring Adams in. Wordsworth needed to get him alone. He couldn't risk Adams making a complaint that could be verified, but if no one saw them together, then no one could prove that the encounter ever took place.

Adams owned what was termed 'a luxury apartment' in Clarence Dock in Leeds. Wordsworth decided he needed to speak to this enigmatic character alone. So one night Cosgrove followed him, the next night Harvey, then it was Wordsworth's turn. This went on for a couple of weeks and a pattern of behaviour soon became clear. If Adams didn't go out with Prentice for something to eat, then he would head back to his flat, picking up one of three takeaways on route. He'd either have Chinese, Indian or Kebab. That was his life. The only variation was which of the three he'd choose. He didn't have a pattern, but it would always be one of the three. For Wordsworth this was the best opportunity to confront him. If he waited until he got back to Clarence Dock, then they would almost certainly be caught on CCTV at some point. He needed somewhere they couldn't be recorded.

The night the actual confrontation happened, Adams decided he felt like a kebab. He parked his Lexus directly outside Mill Hill Kebabs on a double yellow line, while Wordsworth drove past and parked legally further up the road. Quite quickly Adams appeared out of the shop, his kebab neatly wrapped and placed in a small white plastic bag. He climbed into his car, as Wordsworth jumped into the passenger seat next to him. Adams was more than shocked to see him. He looked at the police officer anxiously unsure. In reality Adams was trying to assess the situation. Trying to figure out what this was all about.

Wordsworth had expected a more aggressive response, but he was confronted with a man nervously clutching a kebab, who appeared in fear of his supper being stolen.

"Robin Adams?"

"Yeah … yeah. That's me. Who the fuck are you?" Adams recognised him from somewhere, but he couldn't think where.

"DI Wordsworth."

"What … I … er … what the fuck are you doing in my car?" stammered Adams.

"I want to know why you called Herschel Berkowitz and what you said to him."

Adams looked at him. He now knew where he'd seen Wordsworth before and he also knew Wordsworth was pushing his luck, or he wouldn't have Shanghaied him in this manner. He quickly realised he was the one in the strong position and Wordsworth was the one out on a limb.

"Look, if you want to speak with me then invite me down to the station. But right now, I'm starving, and the more we sit here, the colder my kebab gets. So if you don't mind - get out of my car before I call a policeman."

Wordsworth looked at him for a moment, realising his ploy had been hopeless from the start. He opened the car door and started to get out. He was about to close the door when he stopped and leaned back in. "You can tell your boss I'm not giving up. I'm coming after him and I'm coming after the lad … who is three sentences off telling me what happened to Jodie Kinsella."

Wordsworth slammed the car door and walked off back to his own car. Adams drove away, waving politely to Wordsworth as he passed him.

***

Ethan had been summoned to his dad's office. A car had been sent to pick him up straight from school and now he stood before both Prentice and Adams. He hadn't been offered a coffee, a water or even a seat. He just stood there feeling very uncomfortable and vulnerable.

"We have a little problem," Prentice began. "The police are not letting up. It's nothing to worry about, we just need to know you're strong enough to handle anything they might throw at you. We need to know you'll be able to keep your mouth shut."

"You don't have to worry about me; I won't tell them anything. They can pull out my fingernails and I won't say a word," said Ethan confidently.

"If they start following you, take a photo on your phone, take as many as you can. If there's proof of harassment they'll have to back off," said Adams.

"No worries," was Ethan's casual reply.

"And no beating up anybody," added his father.

"He asked for it. He was getting out of his box."

"I don't care if he was crapping all over your face. We'll

deal with it. Understand?"

"Yes," said Ethan quietly.

"Didn't hear you," said his father again softly and menacingly.

"Yes. I'll keep my mouth shut and my eyes open."

"Good. Wait downstairs … in reception. I'll be ten minutes."

Ethan just nodded and left the office.

"What do you think?" asked Prentice turning to Adams.

"I'm worried. He's a kid who's watched too many movies. He thinks he's Sonny Corleone."

"Let's see what the cops next play is. Then we'll decide our next move."

"It's one man … this DI William Wordsworth …" Adams virtually spat out the name. "He's a pain."

"Shame he didn't just stick to poetry …"

Adams looked at Prentice for a moment, then he got it. He let out a little laugh. Prentice wasn't renowned for his joke telling.

***

As stepfather and stepson made their way homewards, they chatted about various dad and son stuff. Football, cricket, Ethan's schoolwork. It was Prentice who brought up the topic of girlfriends.

Ethan shrugged. "Nothing going on at the moment. But there'll be someone soon."

"Good."

They drove on in silence for about half a mile of stop start traffic, then Ethan asked: "What happened to the last girl? What happened to Jodie?"

"Why do you want to know?"

"I'd like to see her again … at some point?"

"Ethan … we're running a business here. And you're an important cog in that business. Think about the future not the past. She's gone, she's living a new life, so move on."

Ethan sat back, looked out of the window, he wanted to keep his mouth shut, he knew he should keep his mouth shut, but he couldn't help himself. "I really liked her."

Prentice's eyes darkened and if Ethan had thought his stepfather had been intimidating earlier, this was a whole new ball game

"If I hear you say anything like that again, I'll cut your balls off and make you fucking eat them."

Ethan didn't say another word and they drove the rest of the way in silence.

CHAPTER THIRTY-SEVEN

Nathan who had reached the ripe old age of seven just six weeks earlier, was having his first sleep over. Izzy, Molly and Oliver were all left doing their homework, while Mum and Dad dropped off their youngest. The friend's house was in Heaton, not far at all, and on the way back home Wordsworth took a detour and they ended up in a backstreet off Canal Road. There were no houses, just industrial units. Wordsworth had often taken Wendy to somewhere resembling this when they were younger. Wendy's parents had been strict Presbyterians and there was no 'carrying on' while she still lived under their roof.

Wordsworth switched off the engine and the headlights that had been lighting the street were extinguished. Wendy couldn't help but smile.

"This takes me back," she whispered.

"Yeah – doesn't it."

They kissed and hurriedly made love in the passenger

seat, spurred on by the thrill of possibly being caught. Minutes later they both lay back in their seats as they made themselves decent.

"You know we have a bed at home and a room all to ourselves."

"I'm big on nostalgia," Wordsworth said, raising his eyebrows and smiling.

"Don't worry … I'm not knocking it."

"And I'm going to be very busy over the next few weeks. Seriously busy."

Wendy looked at her husband, concern etched on her face. "Can you tell me what's happening?" she asked.

"Ethan Cartwright … I reckon I have one last shot at finding out what happened to those girls … and I need to put the pressure on the little smart arse."

"Aren't you already doing that?"

"Sort of. But we have to up our game. He's the weak link … I'm sure of it. This is going to be 24/7."

"Okay … if that's what it takes. Wait, you didn't just screw me so I would be more pliable when you told me, did you?"

"No … I screwed you 'cos I fancied you."

"That's all right then."

Wordsworth started the car's engine and with Wendy's hand resting in his lap, they drove off.

***

From the screen of his laptop, Ethan watched Chloe Moreno push her hands distractedly through her cropped hair. She was thinking what to say next.

"She must have gone somewhere," said Chloe eventually.

"Yeah," was all Ethan could reply.

"I told the police ..." she trailed off, glancing at her screen to see Ethan's reaction.

"Told them what?" he asked, trying to hide the trepidation in his voice.

"That she was meeting some guy for money." Chloe saw Ethan's expression change. He hadn't expected this. "I made it sound like it was her mum's doing. Like she was forcing her to go."

"Why did you say that?"

"Maybe ... I didn't want you to get into trouble."

Ethan had known for some time that Chloe had a thing about him. He always knew that she had gone for what she considered second best with Sebastian, but Ethan had left her no choice. He'd made it clear from the off Jodie was the girl he was interested in.

"Thanks," he muttered.

"I had to tell them something. I'm so worried about her. And you don't seem to know where she is..."

"Why the fuck would I know?"

"She told me how you'd set it up for her."

Ethan just looked at her. His concern was now growing at such a rate, it felt like it was about to rise up in his throat and choke him. He had no idea Jodie had told Chloe so much. He'd been shocked when the police had heard the story of the man and the offer of the grand, but it had seemed they didn't know the full story at least.

"She said you'd told her to meet this guy … it was easy money. It was daytime … it was safe. Look good and talk was all she needed to do. No sex. She was still nervous about doing it, but she kept saying you said it could be the end of all her mum's money worries."

"She told you that?" he said, trying to suppress his feeling of anxiety.

"We tell each other everything."

"But you didn't tell the police any of this? About my involvement, I mean?"

"I said I didn't and I didn't. The police, they could have easily blamed you for her going missing." Then almost seductively, "And I wouldn't have wanted that."

Still Chloe's reassurances that she'd not said anything didn't fully alleviate Ethan's growing panic.

"That night you argued, and she walked off, she told me it was because she didn't want to go, but you insisted she went," continued Chloe. "She knew why."

"Why?"

"You were embarrassed you couldn't help her out. She told me how you'd tried to get cash off your dad, but he wasn't giving you any. So you set up this escort job and…"

"Look … I …"

"You don't have to explain it to me. You were only

320

trying to help her."

Did Chloe really believe this? He said he had to go and hung up the call, closing his laptop. For a moment he couldn't move. He was experiencing something he'd never really experienced before …. and that was fear.

*****

"When was the last time you saw Jodie Kinsella?" asked Ethan tentatively.

Prentice appeared not to hear as he just kept on watching Sky News; he was big on current affairs.

"I'm not saying I want to see her or anything, but one of her mates was asking after her … and I couldn't answer."

"This mate … why would they expect you to know?" Prentice took off his glasses and started to clean them.

"'Cos she knew me and Jodie were like together. She just thought I might know." Ethan had no intention of telling him the truth, he wasn't going to risk that.

"What did you tell her?"

"That I didn't know."

"And she believed you?"

"I think so."

Prentice placed his clean glasses back on. "You think so? Well you better find out for certain, because if this 'mate'…" the word dripped out of his mouth like sour milk, "… thinks you're involved in anyway, we might have

321

to take action."

"What sort of action?"

"That doesn't concern you."

"Dad ... I set her up. I have a right to know what the fuck's going on!"

Prentice's hand flashed out. Ethan was caught off-guard and reeled backwards from the vicious slap Prentice gave him round his face.

"Don't start swearing at me."

Ethan was holding the side of his face, the hurt of his stepfather's action more devastating than the force of the physical blow. And Prentice was already regretting the uncharacteristic flash of anger. "I'm sorry. I shouldn't have done that ... I just ... I'm sorry."

Ethan looked at his father, his hand dropping to his side. Why had he not stopped to think before? He'd just blindly done what had been asked, desperate to impress him, desperate for his approval.

"At this stage the less you know the better," continued Prentice. "You must have guessed what we're doing isn't exactly legal, but it does benefit everybody. It benefits us and it benefits the girls. We get cash that pays for your lifestyle ... your education ... our holidays, cars ... and they get a life they never even dreamed of. Everybody's happy ... It's a win-win situation."

"It's nothing to do with being escorts, is it? It's drugs that's what it is," said Ethan believing this was the only explanation.

322

Prentice didn't answer for a few moments, then he simply said: "Yeah … yeah. It's drugs."

"You're using them as mules, aren't you?"

"That's right. And we choose the girls we do, because they're the ones that benefit the most."

"How did Britney and Skye benefit …"

"Accidents happen."

"What sort of accidents? How did they die?"

"They got greedy. They both decided they wanted more than we were giving them. They swallowed some bags of cocaine, hoping we'd never find out. But the condoms burst. They were stupid. They had everything and they blew it."

"But Jodie's all right?"

"Yeah … more than. And you know what Ethan … she has never once asked about you. As far as she's concerned you were just a stepping-stone to a better life. Don't spend your time fretting about her, because she has never given you a second thought."

Prentice looked at Ethan, he was unsure how he was going to respond. Eventually Ethan, with a depressed air, just nodded his head, turned and left the room.

Virginia came into the room carrying a half full glass of Merlot passing Ethan on the way out. Ethan didn't give her a second glance, head down he just kept on going.

"Is Ethan okay? "

"Yeah … we just had little …" Prentice puts up his fists to indicate they'd had a fight, but at the same time giving the impression that it was almost playful.

But Prentice knew there was nothing playful about it. Ethan had expressed his concern for the girl and was now becoming very inquisitive about what they were actually doing.

***

On the outskirts of Halifax there stood a number of empty industrial units built in the nineties to house various businesses from clothing companies to plastics manufacturers. Round the back of the property was a parking area secluded from the main road. Parked there was Adams' four-by-four, which was in need of a wash. Prentice pulled his car up alongside the dirty vehicle.

Prentice let himself into one of the units and made his way through a maze of corridors and rooms that he knew like the back of his hand. In a darkened room sat Adams, a bank of computer screens in front of him. On the screens were various videos, all showing young girls being violently sexually abused, mainly by middle-aged men. A couple of the girls struggled to get free, but this only seemed to excite their abusers even more and resulted in vicious punches and kicks.

When Prentice walked in Adams was just in the process of pouring himself a large Jack Daniels, a manga comic book open on the desk in front of him. He seemed oblivious to the grotesqueness of the situation.

"I wasn't expecting you tonight," he remarked casually

when he noticed Prentice.

"I wasn't expecting to be here," was Prentice's reply.

"There was a problem with one of the servers, so I had to do some re-routing. Something wrong?"

"Not yet, but could be."

"What?"

"Him. Ethan. He's starting to concern me."

"In what way?"

Adams poured Prentice a shot of whiskey and handed it to him. Prentice took a sip.

"He's just become a little too inquisitive."

"It was bound to happen." Adams seemed totally unperturbed. "I wouldn't worry about it."

"I wouldn't normally … but that DI … it's like he's on some sort of mission. If he pressures him enough, I'm worried he might say something."

"Every girl we've used for the last year has come from him. What's he going to do, shop us to the police?"

Prentice took another sip of the whiskey and looked at the screens, "Busy tonight?"

"Oh yeah – really busy. You won't have to worry about paying your gas and electric this month."

"Her …" Prentice indicated one of the screens. There was Jodie being raped by middle-aged men.

"What about her?"

"I think he's got a thing about her."

Adams squinted at the screen. "She is quite special."

"I don't care - I want her gone."

"Shame. She gets lots of hits."

"Is there anybody lined up to go the whole way?"

"Quite a few … we're spoilt for choice."

"Decide who's the best bet. I'll put a stop to his infatuation once and for all."

"I think you need to bring him here, show him the whole action. Let him see what he's actually part of."

Prentice knew it wasn't entirely a bad idea, but wasn't yet prepared to risk it.

"When the time's right."

"Don't leave it too long … we can't gamble what we've achieved on the whim of a sixteen-year-old."

CHAPTER THIRTY-EIGHT

It was first time Wordsworth had asked Gatesy if he fancied a drink after work. Gatesy was unsure. What was Wordsworth after? Wordsworth decided the best way forward with Gatesy was to come clean and he said he needed to ask him a favour. Gatesy thought for a moment, shrugged and accepted the invite.

As they sipped away at their beers, Wordsworth did attempt some small talk, but realised that small talk wasn't Gatesy's 'thing,' so he just got straight to the point.

"Can you hack into other people's computers?"

Gatesy didn't like the sound of this. There was a long pause, while he took another mouthful of beer without looking once at Wordsworth.

"Well ... can you?" persisted Wordsworth.

"Two questions. Whose computer - and why?

"Prencart Holdings. And the reason I want you to do it is because I would like to take a look at the company's accounts, as well as Prentice Cartwright's own personal accounts."

327

Gatesy still couldn't look Wordsworth the eyes. It was something he found difficult to do. Wordsworth waited patiently, preparing for a disappointing outcome. Then after what seemed like an eternity, Gatesy said: "I can get into his emails … if that's any good."

"That's good for me."

Two days later they were looking at an email sent from Kirkgate and Co Accountants to Prentice Cartwright. Attached were the accounts from the previous year for both Prencart Holdings and Prentice Cartwright's personal accounts, now visible on a split screen.

"Anything scream out at you?" asked Wordsworth.

"No. Salary isn't excessive … and his draw down at the end of the year is only what you'd expect for a company that size. His personal expenses … again not excessive."

"Shit!" said Wordsworth. He'd convinced himself that they would find something wrong with the monies. But no. "Better get rid … asap."

Wordsworth went back into his office, where Cosgrove and Harvey were working away, but again without any success. It seemed Prencart Holdings had consistently paid the taxman his due, never missed a VAT return and generally ran their business in what appeared to be a legal fashion.

But rapid expansion meant the company flew close to the wind financially, borrowing large amounts of cash to buy premises like Brigella Mills and then convert them into offices or private dwellings. But it was all above board.

The breakthrough came via Redhead, who wasn't even supposed to be on the case. He had spent hours going through Zara's belongings. He'd thought of giving up the search on a number of occasions, thought he was wasting his time, but each night he would find himself back in his dead sister's bedroom – searching, looking ... staring.

The night he actually found something that could be of use was no different to any of the others. He started going through things he'd gone through before, things he felt he'd examined a thousand times. Personal possessions, schoolbooks, anything and everything. Then there it was, amongst a number of magazines and brochures, something he'd never really noticed - a holiday brochure for the Seychelles. It was stashed full of beautiful holiday places to rent. What he couldn't figure out was why Zara had a copy. He turned a page and there was a fabulous all white villa, set right on the beach, but just further back from it was an even larger villa. It was quite difficult to make out much detail, only the size, but that wasn't what really caught Redhead's attention.

Zara had circled the villa and next to it had simply written: 'Mine and J's'.

***

Since the 'incident' with Herschel Berkowitz, Ethan had not gone to school. He had gone from the boy most others envied, to a pariah, the person nobody wanted to know.

329

Herschel hadn't told anybody the truth about what happened that night, but Pizza Boy had. Hardly anyone doubted his version of events and in that very British way all seemed to relish in seeing the number one man being knocked off his perch. All this meant that Ethan's life changed overnight. His father had basically grounded him and his mates had ditched him. Ethan was starting to climb the walls.

He chose his time carefully, Prentice was out and had announced he wouldn't be back until late, so there was only his mother to manipulate. As if it was totally natural, he slipped into the conversation that he was going out that evening. Virginia, who for some time had started to question, if only to herself, what it was Prentice actually did and how her son fitted into that world, immediately baulked at the idea. But Ethan told her not to worry and he'd be back home way before his stepfather.

Wordsworth watched as Ethan climbed into a taxi and set off. Keeping his distance, he followed. Having not gone far, Wordsworth's mobile started to ring.

"Yeah?"

"Hi – it's me. Am I interrupting something?" asked Redhead.

"No ... nothing."

"I was looking through Zara's things and found a holiday brochure for the Seychelles."

"Like the way she was thinking."

"Flicking through it something jumped out at me. It's

330

all villas … holiday lets. In one of the photos you can just about make out another villa, in the background. Zara had ringed it and put 'Mine and J's' next to it."

Wordsworth took in what Redhead was telling him.

"What I was thinking, why ring a place that you can hardly see? If it was just her fantasy, why not fantasise about a place you can see? Think about it."

The phone went dead and Wordsworth drove on.

The cab dropped Ethan on Market Street. Wordsworth guessed he was going to his favourite meeting place, Nero's. Sure enough that's where he was headed. Then he watched as Ethan bought two coffees and went and sat in the window. A couple of minutes later, Chloe Moreno showed up and joined him.

Wordsworth sat patiently watching Ethan and Chloe chatting away. They were there about an hour, before Chloe got up and left. Shortly after, Ethan came out of the coffee shop and headed for the taxi rank across the road on Bank Street. But before he could reach any of the waiting cabs, Wordsworth intercepted him, grabbing him by the arm and forcibly guiding him back to where his car was parked.

Ethan tried protesting but Wordsworth ignored him. He opened the passenger door and pushed Ethan in with the command, "Stay!"

Ethan didn't argue.

Wordsworth started the car and then as if he were a cab driver he casually asked: "Where you going? Home?"

"Yeah," replied Ethan tentatively.

Wordsworth pulled away.

Not a word was said until they were driving up Church Bank past the Cathedral. It was Wordsworth that broke the silence.

"Chloe Moreno … smart girl. I think that should be the last time you see her."

"You don't tell me what I can or can't do, who the fuck do you think you are? You're in deep shit for this, do you know that?"

"How do you make that out?" asked Wordsworth calmly.

"You're meant to stay away from me and my dad. You were warned … no more harassment."

"You think this is harassment?"

"Yeah – this is harassment. Definitely," said Ethan defiantly.

Wordsworth turned off the main road onto Byron Street, past the old school that was now apartments to further down the street where both sides were lined with terrace houses, virtually all with loft conversions. Wordsworth brought the car to a halt. There was no one around.

"Let's be clear about one thing," said Wordsworth switching off the engine, "whatever you claim, it's going to be my word against yours."

"Well, we'll see who they believe," said Ethan not backing down.

"I think they'll believe me, because I have a rock-solid

alibi. I have at least half a dozen people who will testify that I am not in this car right now. And if you think we'll have been caught on CCTV, think again - I know exactly where all the cameras are."

For the first time Ethan looked unsure.

"As things stand," continued Wordsworth," we have three missing girls and three dead girls."

"Nothing to do with me – none of it."

"It has everything to do with you."

A sudden panic rushed through Ethan's veins - how much does this police inspector actually know?

"Whose idea was it to choose those specific girls … young girls that no one gives a monkey's about. That wasn't your idea was it? It was your dad's. He told you - go pick up the ones that are most needy, show them the villa in the Seychelles … deed done." Wordsworth pitched in his newly obtained information, just on the off chance. Ethan said nothing, which told him everything.

"The villa was a nice touch. A really nice touch. But you made one huge mistake. Zara and Jodie - they're not in the care system."

"I don't know what you're talking about."

"And … did you know Zara's brother is a police officer?"

Ethan's slight upward tilt of the head told Wordsworth that this was news to him.

"You didn't, did you. Wonder what your dad would say if he found out how badly you'd fucked up eh?"

"I … I …" stammered Ethan and for a moment Wordsworth thought he was about to admit to something, but then Ethan repeated: "I don't know what you're talking about."

"Everything we've found out is just coincidence, is it? The drawing of you in the care home?"

"Could be anybody …"

"And that wasn't you in the photograph sitting on a bench with Madison Bradshaw."

"I don't sit on benches," said Ethan flippantly.

"And it wasn't you in Zara's diary? Or you who showed her a photograph of a villa and said it was yours."

"Diary? … what …"

Wordsworth had wrong-footed him and smiled at the thought. "Now you'll tell you don't own a villa in the Seychelles."

Then something shifted in Ethan's expression. He was angry. "No, we don't own a villa in the Seychelles," he said. "We own two." Ethan smirked before continuing, "Because that's where my dad's clever and you're just some Mr Plod who would have difficulty making enough to buy a shed in your back garden."

Wordsworth said nothing. He knew he was onto something and thought there was a chance Ethan was about to hang himself. Whilst Ethan, complete with youthful arrogance, thought he'd been clever.

"You jealous?" jibed Ethan.

"Too right I'm jealous. I get a couple of weeks in the

Canaries if I'm lucky and there you are in the lap of luxury in The Seychelles. Who wouldn't be jealous? Do you go out there a lot?"

"What's it to you?"

"Just curious."

"Yeah, we go out there a lot."

"Nice," said Wordsworth slightly nodding his head as if he was trying to imagine what that would be like.

Ethan was clearly enjoying this. He was smiling now; he was on a roll. "But sometimes we go to the Cayman Islands, because we have a couple of villas out there as well. Have you been there, Mr Plod?"

"What do you think?"

"I think you thought it'd be easy to get one over on me. I'm only sixteen … sitting target. But I'm not that stupid. I bet you've been recording all of this conversation, haven't you?"

"I'm not here – remember," answered Wordsworth.

"You want me to say something," continued Ethan totally ignoring Wordsworth's denial, "something incriminating. Well tough, I've said all I'm going to say."

"Nothing more to add?" asked Wordsworth.

"Nothing."

Wordsworth pondered for a second then got out of the car. He moved round to the passenger side and opened the door.

"Out."

Ethan didn't move, he just looked at him, wondering

what he was playing at.

"Out of the fucking car ... now!"

Ethan hesitantly climbed out of the car.

"You know what," Wordsworth said, "I feel sorry for you. You don't realise you're being used. Or maybe you do and you're just too scared to do anything about it."

Wordsworth went back round to the driver's side and climbed in behind the wheel. Ethan continued to watch him, as Wordsworth, without warning, started the car and drove off. Ethan was left there. Alone.

CHAPTER THIRTY-NINE

Ethan felt like a disobedient ten-year-old who had got lost on his way home. But at least he had a mobile phone and he used it to call an Uber. It took what seemed like an age for it to show, and by then Ethan knew he was running late.

Prentice arrived home just minutes before his son. He dismissed Virginia into the kitchen. Ethan just stood there, bracing himself for what he knew was to come. He had used the time on the drive home to fashion a version of the night's events. He'd considered not saying anything about his encounter with Wordsworth, but decided he had to. If he didn't and his stepfather found out some other way, then Ethan knew that would be the end of their relationship. Any respect would have gone. The only reason Ethan had gone along with the covert manipulation of vulnerable girls was to earn his stepfather's respect.

His story claimed he met with Chloe because she'd been asking too many questions about his relationship with Jodie, and he was worried she might say something to the police. As it was his concerns were unfounded and he felt confident that Chloe would remain loyal. The truth was he needed his ego stroking and Chloe was the girl to do it. Stuck inside, little contact with anyone, he was having a self-esteem melt down.

He then began to relay the details of Wordsworth's attempt to scare him into some sort of admission, omitting anything he said about their exotic villas. As Ethan talked, Prentice said nothing; he just listened, a darkness descending on him. Ethan finished his account and waited. Eventually Prentice spoke, quietly and with no sense of anger, which was even more disturbing for Ethan.

"I'm going to get a home tutor. If you go out again without my permission, then I *will* be angry. Is that clear?"

"Yes," was all Ethan could say.

"Now go to your room."

Prentice just turned his back on him and started to pour himself a drink. A dejected Ethan left and went to his bedroom.

***

When Wordsworth arrived at the office the following morning Harvey and Cosgrove both realised something positive had happened.

"What do you know about the Cayman Islands … and The Seychelles?" asked Wordsworth with no preamble.

"Had enough have you?" asked Cosgrove.

"Yeah – but that's not why I'm asking."

"They're both offshore tax havens," said Harvey. She'd once spent eighteen months trying to catch a money laundering gang from Belarus, so she knew all about places out of reach of the Chancellor of the Exchequer.

"Well guess what … it turns out our dear friend and all-round nice guy – Prentice Cartwright, has villas in both The Seychelles and the Cayman Islands."

"Definitely dodgy," chipped in Cosgrove. "They don't show up on any of the paperwork."

"I'm guessing there's probably others scattered around the globe. To get that amount of property you're talking serious dosh. This isn't just about cheating the tax man for a few grand, this is real money."

"He has a secret source of income," Harvey declared.

"Drugs … he's pushing drugs," Cosgrove offered.

"I don't think so," said Wordsworth. "I believe we'd have seen some signs of drug pushing if that's what he was up to. Drugs always attracts people with flaws, desperate people who can't keep their mouths shut. One of them would have given the game away by now. No, I think there's something else."

The rest of the day involved the team, such as it was, trying to discover concrete evidence showing the properties that Cartwright owned had been obtained illegally with dirty money. But all they discovered was that the properties were owned by various companies, companies that weren't based in the UK. To figure out who ran these companies, who controlled them and what they actually did was a hurdle too high for the team. They soon realised to have any chance of cracking Cartwright's complex business set up, they'd need a financial forensic team and Wordsworth doubted very much that he would be given the go ahead to spend money on one.

Frustrated, Wordsworth reached for his phone. He dialled Cartwright's mobile number, knowing full well the call would be recorded.

"Hello," said Prentice pleasantly and casually. Wordsworth wondered how long this sunny disposition would last when he found out it was his least favourite copper that was calling.

"Mr Cartwright – hope this isn't an awkward time for you," said Wordsworth without a hint of harassment in his voice.

Prentice recognised Wordsworth's voice immediately and moved to hang up the call.

"Don't hang up," Wordsworth knew that's what he'd naturally do. "I promise there'll be no harassment and the call won't take two minutes."

There was a pause. Then: "What do you want?"

"We've just realised you have multiple properties in both The Seychelles and the Cayman Islands. Are they owned by Prencart Holdings or are they owned privately, by you?"

The line went dead.

After hanging up on the DI, Prentice tried to figure out what had just happened. That wasn't just a lucky guess by Wordsworth, he mentioned two of the four places he owned property. How had he found out? The intricate network of bogus companies meant it virtually impossible for anyone to trace the properties to him. The only way Wordsworth could have found out about them is if someone had told him. And the only person who could have done that was his stepson. His first instinct was to go upstairs and have it out with him, but Virginia coming into the room stopped him. He immediately told her what he thought had happened, and she had to forcibly stop him from confronting her son. She told him nothing would be achieved. Believing this was all about tax evasion, she persuaded her husband to concentrate on deflecting Wordsworth away from their extensive nest egg and leaving Ethan to her.

Later that night, Virginia did speak to Ethan. As soon as she explained what had happened, Ethan knew he was the source. He tried thinking of some excuse, which would shift the blame, but he couldn't think of anything. Stoically Ethan prepared himself to face his punishment.

But Prentice had gone past the point of wanting to punish his stepson. He was now more concerned with damage control. He had to put a stop to the police investigations as soon as possible. The question was how.

INTERVIEW ROOM. BRADFORD CITY CENTRE POLICE STATION, NELSON STREET. 13:52 10TH JANUARY 2020

"So these villas he had in The Seychelles and the Caymans, how did you find out about them?" Ashburn asked the question and Wordsworth, for some reason, was fairly certain she already knew the answer.

"A paper trail," he lied. "Credit card receipts, flight receipts, phone receipts …"

"Are you sure that's how you discovered them?" continued Ashburn.

"Me and my team … yeah." Wordsworth glared at her. *Prove otherwise, bitch.*

"You see, I heard different," said Ashburn.

"From whom?" asked Wordsworth with apparent innocence.

"You know I can't tell you that."

"Why not?" asked Sharvari. "This is meant to be all open and honest, isn't it.?"

Price didn't say anything; he just looked at Ashburn.

"It would mean betraying my source," Ashburn said with just an air of nervousness.

"We have to guess what someone told you and who that person was?" Sharvari wasn't letting her off the hook.

"She has a point," said Price in a conciliatory fashion.

"Well?" prompted Sharvari. Wordsworth said nothing. He just sat back and enjoyed Ashburn's unease.

"I heard that DI Wordsworth had been harassing Ethan Cartwright …"

"Not this again," exclaimed Sharvari. "Who's planting these ideas in your head? You tell us here and now, or we're walking right out of that door."

Ashburn said nothing.

"Fine," said Sharvari gathering her things together. "Let's go, Bill."

Wordsworth, enjoying the drama, started to stand. Price knew he had to do something.

"Sergeant, tell them what they want to know."

"But …"

"Tell them." Price didn't raise his voice, but the severity of his tone told Ashburn he wasn't messing about.

"Faiza Amran."

"Really?" said Sharvari. "The Cartwrights' solicitor? Oh please."

"Okay, let's move on," said Price. "I'm sorry about that."

Ashburn couldn't believe her boss's apology, while

343

Sharvari positively lapped it up.

"Thank you," said Sharvari, knowing full well that they'd won that round. She glanced at Wordsworth. He didn't appear as gleeful as she did, but then, Wordsworth knew what was coming up next.

CHAPTER FORTY

Wordsworth arrived home with just enough time to grab the cheese and tomato sandwich that Wendy had already made. They were on their way to the theatre that night, and he had completely forgotten. Fairly standard: Wendy wasn't annoyed - at least he was there.

He then had to drag Izzy off the new electric drum kit they'd bought her for just short of £300 on eBay. William and Wendy thought the investment was worth it because Izzy could plug in her headphones and thrash hell out of the drums like some demonic child having a tantrum and nobody even knew. Then the whole family, except the seven-year-old Nathan who was left home with the babysitter, piled into their car and headed for the Alhambra in the city centre.

The show, *Bloodbath the Musical*, was loud and brash, the story - total escapism. The virtually full house went with it and the whole experience was just what Wordsworth needed. For a short time he forgot about work.

In the interval Wordsworth made his way into the

packed bar, his family following him. They'd pre-ordered their drinks and now all he had to do was to find them. It was intermission mayhem and Wordsworth told his family to hang fire by the entrance of the bar as he waded into the melee to get their refreshment. Just as he started to pick up the drinks, whilst working out the best way to carry all five together, he heard a voice in his ear: "Nice family."

Wordsworth turned to see Robin Adams staring directly at him.

"You have until the end of this week to drop the investigation into the Cartwright family, if not then I can't be responsible for the consequences."

Adams turned and started to walk away. Wordsworth replaced the drinks and grabbed him by the arm.

"Are you fucking crazy? Threatening a police officer?"

"This isn't a threat. Look on this as a genial gesture … a warning from someone who envies your domestic set up. Who wouldn't want to have your family? A wife that loves you, kids that are not on drugs … a new drum kit … it would be a shame to … well … you know."

And Adams was gone back into the crowd.

Wordsworth was still taking in what he'd said when he re-joined his family. He mentioned nothing to them about the encounter.

***

It was hard for Wordsworth to concentrate on the second

half of the show. His children didn't notice; they were just rocking along with the music and enjoying the story. Wendy however clearly did notice, though she waited until they were home and were alone in their bedroom to ask what the matter was.

Wordsworth explained how he'd found out about the property that Cartwright had abroad, and how he felt they were actually closing in on him, whilst admitting he wasn't even sure what he was closing in on. Had the girls been sold into sex slavery? How come two of them had turned up dead and the rest hadn't? Ethan was obviously the 'honey-trap' but he didn't actually know what for. Wordsworth was sure there was more to it than just a mad man manipulating everything for his own gratification. There were complex business dealings, shell companies, villas in foreign climes, all of which Wordsworth believed had something to do with the missing girls.

"But why the sudden change of mood tonight?" Wendy asked.

"I was threatened when I was getting the drinks – in the interval. But it wasn't just me he threatened, it was you guys."

"Me?"

"And the kids."

"What? Have him arrested. He can't get away with that," Wendy exclaimed.

"I have no proof. I've been accused of harassing them, it's going to appear I'm just trying to turn the screw."

"You can't do nothing."

"I know." Wordsworth paused for a moment. "Wendy, I'm going to drop the case."

"What?"

"The powers-that-be won't object. The Super will be over the bloody moon. He wanted me to drop it before it began. Girls in the care system … who the hell cares about them. It's how it's always been. They want an easy open-and-shut case; they want these girls to be runaways. It's why Lumb's given me a pathetic excuse for a team – he wants me to run out of resources, to close the case with an easy resolution. They certainly don't want to try and take on Prentice Cartwright. I'm a fool for trying."

"You can't just drop it."

"Why not? Would I have got so focused on it if it hadn't been for Steve's sister? Would I have been just like the rest? Would I be thinking it's just a few girls that nobody is going to really miss."

"You don't give up cases."

"Maybe that's because this is the first time my family have been threatened."

"He won't dare do anything."

"We don't know that."

"People make threats all the time."

"Not like this."

"Look I'll take the kids to school for the next few weeks. I'll make sure they don't talk to strangers. We'll give them each a panic alarm …"

348

"You have to take care as well," added Wordsworth.

"What's he going to do to me? If he comes near me, I'll scream so loud they'll hear me in Leeds."

Wordsworth still wasn't sure, and Wendy sensed his insecurity.

"Look, if anything does happen, anything at all, we get just a whiff of them anywhere near any of us, then hand the case over ... let someone else take it. But until then, you see it through."

CHAPTER FORTY-ONE

Ten days after their visit to the Alhambra Theatre, Wendy dropped the kids off at their various schools, just as she had done for the previous week and a half – Nathan at St Williams Catholic Primary School, the other three at the Hanson Academy. None of the kids complained and just got on with life as usual. Wendy had made arrangements at her work, so she was able to arrive late and leave early. They weren't too happy about it, but she said she had a family crisis, which wouldn't last forever. The dental practice knew she wasn't the type to try and get one over on them, so they accepted the situation.

She always parked on a side road on the other side of Manningham Lane from where she worked. The parking was restricted, sets of double yellow lines with odd parking here and there. Occasionally it proved problematic, but today she was fine. She had to cross over Manningham Lane to get to the practice, and as she did, she couldn't help but think of her parents' stories about a vanishing department store, a defunct Grammar School, and a Ballroom complete with besuited males, glamourous females and a glitter ball. All now gone.

As she started across the road, she became aware of something in the corner of her eye. She turned her head to check what had attracted her attention: there was a car, hurtling directly towards her.

She started to turn, to try and step out of its way, but was still half facing the vehicle when it struck her full on.

She flew up onto the bonnet and her face smashed into the front windscreen with such force it caused the glass to crack. The momentum spun her right over the roof of the vehicle, her body spinning like a top, crashed to the ground.

The car sped away.

**

For days now, Wordsworth felt he had achieved little. He was mainly trying to discover what he could about the villas Cartwright owned. At the same time Harvey and Cosgrove were looking into Cartwright's businesses in the UK. He owned various properties throughout the north, mainly derelict sites awaiting planning for redevelopment. He also seemed to have a number of properties that were individual retail units. Some were being rented from Prencart Holdings, others were leased, and there was one large site outside of Halifax that was apparently standing empty. It was approximately twenty industrial units that had been vacant for over six months and there was no planning application for the property or adverts offering the units for lease or rent. Wordsworth decided to take a look at it but before he could leave, he was called in to see Lumb.

He forgot all about Halifax.

"Sit down, please," said Lumb without his normal meet and greet style.

Wordsworth sat, sensing this wasn't any ordinary meeting.

"I've never been any good at this," continued Lumb with a sincerity Wordsworth had never encountered from him before. "So I just need to tell you … and I want to tell you in a way that … that …" Lumb's words dried up.

"What?" asked Wordsworth the concern and anxiety growing inside him by the second.

"There's been an accident."

"What sort of accident?"

"RTA."

"And?"

"Your wife was involved."

"Wendy?"

Lumb just nodded.

"Do you know how she is? Where is she?"

"I'm sorry, Bill … she …" Lumb looked down, took a deep breath and then looked Wordsworth in the eyes. "She died in the ambulance on the way to the hospital."

Wordsworth's head went light … and his sight blurred.

Had he heard right? He can't have. No … no … not Wendy.

"I'm really sorry." Wordsworth heard the words, but they were coming from another room, another time. "I'll get one of your team to drive you."

"Thank you … thank you. I just need a …"

"Sure."

Wordsworth just sat there. Lumb didn't know what to do. He watched him.

A long time passed in silence, and at last he eventually managed to say: "My children."

"Right … of course. I can send an officer to speak to them."

"No. No it has to be me."

"Yeah sure. Whatever you want, Bill. Let me get Steve Redhead in here."

Lumb opened the door of his office to speak to his PA working at a desk outside.

Wordsworth still didn't stir.

***

If anybody had ever asked Wordsworth to relate what happened directly after being given the news that his wife had been killed, he wouldn't have been able to tell them a thing. At the time his mind was just a pulsating mess. A scrambled brain trying to come to terms with what he'd been told. All he knew was he must have asked to go to the hospital, because that's where Redhead first drove him.

After neither speaking or seeing anyone Redhead persuaded him to let him take him home.

He must have arranged with someone to have the children picked up from school, though he couldn't remember doing it. Maybe Redhead had done it? He had no idea. Either way, before he knew it they were all gathered in the living room - Izzy, Molly, Oliver, Nathan, Redhead and Wordsworth. Wordsworth just looked at them, unsure what to say. Redhead wasn't sure what to do. Izzy, like only daughters can, sensed her father needed support and just quite naturally went and sat next to him, linking her arm through his, then she said, "What's happened?"

"It's your mum … She was … she was in an accident. She got hit by a car."

"She's all right, isn't she?" Molly knew the answer, just from her dad's face.

He found he couldn't speak. He opened his mouth but nothing came out. He was aware that Molly had started crying.

Redhead stepped forward, as if to offer to tell them, but Wordsworth held up his hand.

"I'm so sorry," he stuttered. "She's not with us anymore. She … she died … they say … she died …"

There was a stunned, shocked, devastating silence.

Wordsworth just repeated: "I'm sorry … I'm sorry … I'm sorry."

As he sat there, riddled with pain and disbelief, his

children gathered round him, all holding him, holding each other. Redhead stared on impotently, and then Wordsworth started to cry, for the first time since he'd heard of Wendy's death, he cried … uncontrollably.

**

That afternoon, the afternoon of his wife's death, was the last time his kids saw that naked pain. That doesn't mean it went away. Every night he lay in his bed, sensing the emptiness at his side and crying … the pain just as raw, just as exposed as it had been when he cried the first time.

The funeral was held at Scholemoor Crematorium. It was a humanist funeral, conducted by a close friend of theirs, Ellie Peterson. Wendy had met her at Uni, where they'd both studied sociology, Ellie went on to be a probation officer and as Wendy always used to say … she went on to have kids.

That night, after the funeral tea at the Bankfield Hotel, Wordsworth, Redhead and the kids returned to the house. If it had seemed quiet before, it now seemed positively void of noise, atmosphere, or any form of life. Wordsworth was still reeling from what had happened and hadn't attempted to try and piece it together.

Redhead on the other hand had been following the investigation. He was waiting for the right time to tell Wordsworth what he knew and inexplicably, it happened on the day of her funeral.

They were in the kitchen. It was late, gone midnight, and they were halfway through their third bottle of Merlot when Wordsworth suddenly said: "I know it wasn't an accident."

Redhead wasn't sure how to react.

"I'm right, aren't I?" continued Wordsworth.

"I don't think this is the right time to do this," replied Redhead.

"I do."

"Let's wait until tomorrow …"

"What have you found out?"

Redhead took a deep breath and looked at him. Should he tell him?

"Just fucking tell me!" said Wordsworth.

"I've seen the CCTV footage."

"And?"

"You're right, it wasn't an accident."

"Go on."

"Look Bill, I …"

"Don't fucking do this, Steve! I need to know."

"If I tell you, you have to promise you won't do anything."

"What am I fucking going to do?"

Redhead took another deep breath before speaking: "It showed Wendy starting to cross the road. The car that hit her was parked further up the road, not that far away. As soon as she steps out into the road, the car screams away from where it was parked. His foot must have hit the floor for him to get up to that speed so quickly …"

"How fast was he going?"

"Fifty … maybe sixty miles an hour is what they estimate."

"Plates?"

Redhead shook his head. "Nothing. The car was nicked just a few hours before. They've found it a couple of hours later … round the back of Valley Parade. It had been torched.

Wordsworth downed the rest of his wine. "I need to see the CCTV."

"No you don't."

"Who's got it? Are they treating it as murder? I have to see it."

"Trust me – you don't."

"You've got a copy, haven't you?"

Redhead was caught completely off guard. "I … I …"

"Where is it? Where you got it?"

"I haven't got a copy."

"Don't lie to me! Come on …" Wordsworth headed for the door.

"Where you going?" asked a bewildered Redhead as he stood up.

"Nelson Street … you're going to show me what happened."

Wordsworth was almost out of the door.

Redhead realised there was no stopping his boss. "I've got it here," he confessed suddenly.

"What?"

"I've got it on my phone."

Wordsworth moved back to the table. "Let me see it."

Redhead hesitated before taking out his phone. He looked up the video and handed the phone to Wordsworth. Wordsworth sat down at the table. For a moment it looked like he'd changed his mind; he wasn't going to watch it after all. He just kept staring at the frozen screen. Then without warning he hit play and the image came alive. Wordsworth didn't move a muscle, showed no signs of emotion as he watched his wife checking the traffic and stepping out onto the road. And there it was: the car in the background suddenly squealing to life as the tyres burnt into the tarmac.

Wordsworth watched as the hatchback roared directly towards her, watched as she was thrown into the air and over the car, crash landing in the middle of the road. The driver of the car didn't pause for breath, didn't pause to see the damage he'd done, didn't pause long enough for anybody to identify Adams as the driver. It just sped away.

Wordsworth handed him the phone back and quietly said, "Thank you."

"It's impossible to see the driver."

"It doesn't matter who the driver was, I know who was behind it."

CHAPTER FORTY-TWO

Prentice had been more vigilant than usual. The only places he'd been since Wendy Wordsworth had been killed were home and the office. That way it was easier to see whether he had been followed or not. He didn't think he had. And Ethan was doing exactly as he was told, not going anywhere. The morning after the funeral Virginia, her head spinning with the news of Wendy Wordsworth's death, trying desperately to figure out what was happening, ventured to ask her husband. He told her that it was still the business over the missing girl. The cops were just looking for a scapegoat and the richer they were – the better.

"It's a jealousy bust," said Prentice, trying to put an end to his wife's concerns. She seemed to believe him. Or, at least, she seemed to want to believe him. So she stopped asking and as often as possible went shopping in her new Porsche that had materialised on their drive two days previously – a surprise gift from her husband.

Cartwright arrived at work, later than normal, to find Adams waiting for him in his office reading one of his manga comics.

Adams closed the comic and placed it on the edge of Cartwright's desk. "We've had an offer …"

"For the full monty?" asked Prentice.

"Yeah," Adams verified, smiling.

"Is this for the Jodie girl?"

"Yeah. He'd seen the last few videos and is excited about actually participating, but at the moment he's not in the ballpark … financially."

"What's he offering?"

"Three hundred thou, but I'll get him way up on that."

"If you can't, take it. Then we should shut down Halifax. Move to another location."

"You still worried about the poet. He won't want to lose a child as well."

"I don't want to take any more needless risks. We get rid of the premises and we get rid of the girl. She's too high profile."

"It was you that wanted her."

Cartwright looked at him for a moment, he didn't need to be reminded of his mistake. "Just get shot," he said calmly. This was something that needed taking care of sooner rather than later.

***

"Gatesy wants to see you," said Harvey.

Everyone had been politely reserved when Wordsworth arrived back in the office and Harvey's message from Gatesy was the first work related exchange they'd all had. Wordsworth had said nothing about what he believed happened to Wendy – nothing to his colleagues and definitely nothing to Superintendent Lumb. If Lumb thought for one-minute Wendy's death was in any way linked to the case Wordsworth was investigating, he'd be sent home. Game over. Fortunately though, the Chief Super was still refusing to consider Prentice Cartwright as a suspect for anything, and definitely not murder.

Wordsworth stood up from his desk and headed out of the office. Harvey just naturally went with him.

"How's everyone doing?" she asked, her voice careful and full of concern.

"As you'd expect … devastated. The kids are with their gran." Although the words sounded quite natural, anyone that knew Wordsworth knew he was fighting to keep on track. "I thought she was the best person for them to spend time with … while I sort out what's to be done."

"With regards to …?" Harvey left the question hanging.

"Wendy's murder," replied Wordsworth as they turned into Gatesy's office.

Gatesy was in front of his computer as usual. Wordsworth and Harvey came into the office and Gatesy looked at Harvey. "Bill, this is really for your ears only."

Harvey held up her hands and just backed out of the

room. Once she'd gone, Gatesy said, "I've discovered something that will interest you."

"If it's anything to do with Prentice Cartwright then I'm more than interested."

Gatesy looked round to make sure no one was listening. "After your wife was murdered, I decided I should do some digging. Some, uh … *real* digging. I was disappointed that I hadn't been able to give you anything before."

"You were disappointed?" said Wordsworth unable to hide the surprise in his voice. He had always considered Gatesy devoid of any real emotion. "Did you find anything?"

"I realised I was being too selective and I didn't fully understand the complications of what I was reading. I'd been looking for tax dodges, VAT scams, that type of thing. Totally barking up the wrong tree."

Gatesy checked again no one else was around before clicking on a file and two sets of accounts appeared on the screen.

"I thought the idea was to delete these," said Wordsworth looking at the screen.

"I didn't."

"I can see that."

Gatesy then highlighted various figures in the Prencart Holdings account. There were a few dozen for £10,000, a good few at £20,000 and a couple at £50,000.

"See these?" said Gatesy.

"Yeah," replied Wordsworth scrutinising the figures,

"payments in to the Prencart Holdings account."

"They're transfers from other bank accounts," Gatesy clarified.

"And?"

"Originally, I thought these payments must represent rents, or deals connected to the sales of places – deposits or second payments … something like that."

"Ok. But now?" Wordsworth prompted.

"Well I traced one of the £10,000 deposits to try and give me an idea of what we were playing with. It came from a company based in Hong Kong, which I discovered makes a habit of helping people distribute their money. Before that it had been in the UAE and before that … any ideas?"

Wordsworth just shrugged.

"The Seychelles," Gatesy said, not hiding his joyful pride. "I traced another … that went a different route via South Dakota but before it got to South Dakota it had gone via at least Singapore and Switzerland … but the origin of the cash again was the Seychelles."

"You hacked into all these different accounts."

"Yes," said Gatesy. "Is … is that a problem?"

"Absolutely not," replied Wordsworth, "I'm impressed."

"I traced a few other sums as well and discovered they all didn't originate in the Seychelles …"

"Let me guess – the Cayman Islands."

"Exactly. The chances of this being a coincidence is less than two percent."

"You worked that out, didn't you?"

"Of course," said Gatesy.

"At least we know for sure now he's been pulling some sort of scam."

"If you look at the accounts more closely, it was really bail out money to keep Prencart Holdings going. Their total revenue looks fine, but that's because it's being propped up by these cash injections."

"What does the taxman think they are?"

"Just what we thought they were, rents, deposits … and what have you. There's obviously no uniformity to create suspicion."

"So. Money laundering."

"That's what I think. But we can't do anything, because I obtained all the information illegally."

"But if the illegal cash originates in the UK …"

"And that's what he's worried about us finding out. Ok, tens of thousands is small fry for him; he just needs that to survive. But the real estate ownership in the Seychelles and in the Cayman Islands? That's been paid for with serious cash. It involves millions. Find out the source of that cash, then we have him."

"Gatesy you're a fucking genius."

"I know," said Gatesy – deadly serious.

INTERVIEW ROOM. BRADFORD CITY CENTRE POLICE STATION, NELSON STREET.
14:03 p.m. 10th JANUARY 2020

"So you never pursued Prentice Cartwright in connection with your wife's death?" Ashburn said with a ringing doubt.

"No."

"What about the CCTV footage of the actual accident? Did you see that?"

"No."

"Did you ever ask to see it?"

"No."

"That doesn't strike me as very you," Ashburn stared at him.

"If your wife got hit by a car, would you want to see it?" was all Wordsworth said.

"You've always struck me as being more proactive."

"I'll take that as a compliment."

"When I worked with you … for that short time," there was a hint of bitterness in Ashburn's voice, "you were never the sort of copper that hung around waiting for something to fall into your lap. You always got out there, ruffled a few feathers, got your hands dirty and got to the bottom of whatever the case was."

"I was younger then, maybe now I just don't have the same get up and go."

"It was five years ago, hardly a lifetime."

"A lot can happen in five years," Wordsworth said with a slight smile. "Look how far you've come. But you always were ambitious … on every front."

For a moment Ashburn looked a little insecure, but she quickly regained her composure.

"I think if you'd have seen the CCTV footage of the accident …"

Wordsworth interrupted her: "You've seen it?"

There was a slight hesitation from the sergeant before she said, "Yes I've seen it. I would say there is no doubt that the action of the driver was deliberate. He deliberately targeted your wife."

"Sergeant," Price warned. "That's enough. DI Wordsworth – continue, please."

"I think it's relevant to the reason why we're here," protested Ashburn.

"And I'm saying – that's enough!"

"I have complete faith in the team that investigated the accident," Wordsworth said with a sense of gratitude.

366

"But you did continue to investigate Prencart Holdings?" asked Ashburn rhetorically.

"When I went back to work after Wendy had died, I took a back seat. I let Cosgrove and Harvey dictate how to proceed. Anything that happened from there on in, I was virtually a bystander."

Ashburn let a disdainful smile creep across her lips as she gave a little shake of the head. She didn't believe a word.

Wordsworth sat there, impassive.

"Then can you explain how the raid on Prencart Holdings came about?"

"Of course," replied Wordsworth politely. "It started when Herschel Berkowitz came forward with some new evidence."

"Which was …?"

"He'd heard Ethan speak to his stepfather on the phone, saying that he could, in his words, 'pick the girl up on Monday morning'."

"And why hadn't he told anyone this before?" Ashburn asked.

"I would have thought that was obvious. He was scared of Ethan Cartwright. But ironically, the fact Ethan had put him in hospital gave him the strength to come forward with the information. He realised there was no more damage he could do to him."

Ashburn knew that it all sounded plausible, but like a lot of what Wordsworth had told her that day, she knew it stank of shit.

CHAPTER FORTY-THREE

Since that first day when they arrived at Jodie Kinsella's house, Redhead and Wordsworth's relationship had developed into something neither of them had expected. They were friends – good friends.

Wordsworth had been back at work for nearly a week when Redhead felt it was okay to ask him out for a drink. Wordsworth didn't want to go. He was afraid if he started drinking, he might not be able to hold it together and he might never stop. Nevertheless, they ended up in their regular haunt – The Hare and Hounds.

Redhead bought the first round and as they sat there, neither feeling comfortable about the situation, he asked about Wordsworth's kids and in turn Wordsworth asked about Redhead's parents. Once the polite exchanges had been dispensed with, there was another uneasy silence before Wordsworth looked at Redhead and asked him straight out: "Steve ... could we have got this all wrong?

What if this is nothing to do with Cartwright, what if he's completely innocent?"

"What? You know that's not the case. I know that's not the case. What's this about?"

Wordsworth thought for a moment, then said, "If I tell you, you have to swear it goes no further."

"What am I ... five?" said Redhead with mock indignation. "Fucking tell me."

Wordsworth then related to him how Gatesy had hacked into Cartwright's accounts, traced the cash and come up with the money laundering theory.

"We find out where the cash came from then," said Redhead.

"Easier said than done."

"Someone will talk ... they always do."

"Well, we know his family are not going to say anything. Who else is there that's close to the action and might just give us something?"

Wordsworth and Redhead sat in silence for a while, before Wordsworth downed his drink and stood up saying, "Want another?

"Abso-fucking-lutely."

Wordsworth went to the bar and ordered the same again. As he waited for the drinks to be delivered, he looked round the pub. There was a television that seemed to have the attention of just one old lady perched on a stool at the end of the bar. Wordsworth had to wonder what she was getting out of the programme as the sound had been muted. On the screen were three boys all in school uniform … arguing. It was two against one. Wordsworth watched while their pints were being pulled, then he returned to the table and placed the drinks down saying, "I know exactly who I've got to talk to."

"Just like that."

"Herschel Berkowitz. He has an axe to grind."

"From what I understand he's also scared shitless. Somehow they got to him."

"Then I have to make him see reason. I have to make him realise we can look after him."

"Do you think you can?"

"*We* can, Steve."

And for the first time since the death of his wife there was a spark of the old Bill Wordsworth. And it wasn't just a spark, it was like a fucking firework which said the display was yet to come. In that moment Redhead knew whatever happened, Wordsworth was taking no prisoners … he wanted justice, but more importantly he wanted revenge.

CHAPTER FORTY-FOUR

Wordsworth had decided if he was to ever get anything out of Herschel Berkowitz, he needed to get him on his own. No friends, no teachers, no family. Herschel, still bearing the scars of his beating, had just started back at school. Newly acquired friends crowded round him like flies. Sebastian Mancini had immediately shown solidarity with Berkowitz. Now Ethan Cartwright's Machiavellian presence was no longer a factor in their relationship, their friendship was allowed to be honest.

Each day Berkowitz was driven to and from school by his mother and on his return home he just stayed in watching TV or playing on his Xbox. The trauma of the beating had left him mentally scarred as well as physically weakened. Wordsworth quickly realised his only window of opportunity was lunchtime. But here again there were problems, for a start Herschel never left the school grounds.

Still where there's a will …

***

It was Herschel's second week back at school. Like the previous week he was dropped off by his mother and there waiting for him, as usual, was Sebastian. Together they went in through the sixth form entrance. They were headed for their first lesson, when Sebastian's phone rang. Though the caller was *UNKNOWN*, he still answered it. On the other end was Wordsworth.

Sebastian was unsure what to say.

"Don't let Herschel know who you're talking to."

Sebastian wasn't sure why he went along with Wordsworth's request, but he did. Probably because he felt he must be under some sort of surveillance, otherwise how could Wordsworth have known he was with Herschel. In reality Wordsworth had seen Sebastian and Herschel enter the school together, just like they had done for the last week.

"I need to speak to Herschel by himself. I believe he has some information that can help in my investigation."

"Okay," was all Sebastian could say.

"I need you to deliver him to me this lunchtime."

Sebastian suddenly didn't like the sound of this.

"Hold on," he said into the phone. Then he spoke to Herschel, "Hershey go ahead, I'll catch up. It's … it's my mum. I don't know what she's wittering on about."

373

Herschel moved off and Sebastian turned his attention back to Wordsworth. "What's this all about?"

"Chloe Moreno."

"What?" Sebastian couldn't hide the panic that ripped through him. "Don't tell me she's missing? She can't be!"

"No, Seb, she's ok – for now. But I'm worried about her. I'm worried she might be going the same way as Jodie."

"No ... no way," Sebastian just dismissed the idea.

"Are you in touch with Ethan?"

"Why?"

"I was just wondering if he told you he's been meeting up with her."

Sebastian took a deep breath, trying not to allow his hatred of Ethan to seep into his voice. "Chloe wouldn't do that ..."

"Ask him ... ask him if he met with her the other night in Nero's. My guess is that he'll lie ... tell you he didn't see her, but I can assure you he did."

"Look, what's this got to do with Hershey?"

"I just need to find out what he knows. He's been keeping something from me. And he might just know what Ethan's playing at."

"He doesn't ... he hasn't spoken to him."

"Okay. But why would Ethan take out your girlfriend if he wasn't setting her up for something? You know how he can turn it on. If you don't believe me, ring her. Ask her."

There was a pause. Sebastian thought of hanging up on

374

Wordsworth and calling Chloe – but the sad truth was, he knew Wordsworth would be telling the truth. He knew Chloe had wanted Ethan all along and had settled for second best: him. He couldn't bear to hear her confirm it. So he simply said, "I'll see what I can do."

"I'll be just up the road, parked outside the cottages."

Sebastian hung up.

***

"The guy's all set for tonight," Adams told Prentice.

"That's quick," said Prentice, surprised. "Are we geared up for it?"

"Yeah. Not much to gear up really. And I've got the price up."

Prentice had just arrived at their office where Adams had been waiting for him in the car park. Prentice locked his car with his key fob, and headed into the office with Adams at his side.

"How much?"

"Another hundred thou … I'm thinking of buying *myself* a place in the Seychelles this time."

They passed Whitney.

"Morning Whitney. Any calls?"

"No."

"For me neither?" asked Adams.

"No," repeated Whitney with a smile that Adams loved but knew to leave well alone.

Prentice and Adams headed up the stairs.

"I'm guessing you've checked him out … this *client.*"

"Sure," replied Adams. "I know more about him than his parents do. He's a weirdo, into some serious S&M. His wife knows nothing about it. She's a strict Roman Catholic, never misses Mass. I'm thinking missionary only."

"Is he English?"

"Belgian … from Brussels. He's got all the instructions."

They reached the top of the stairs. Prentice halted momentarily.

"Will he go through with it?"

"Hundred per cent."

And with a definite air of anticipation, they went into their separate offices.

***

Wordsworth was waiting in his car. He wasn't sure whether Herschel would show or not, he was just praying he would. Then in his mirror he saw Sebastian step out of the school, alongside him was Herschel. He pointed to where Wordsworth was parked and then went back into the school. Wordsworth continued to watch via his mirror and for a moment Herschel hesitated. He half turned as if he was going to go back into the school, turned back again and this time took a long look at Wordsworth's car.

Come on, Wordsworth said to himself.

Then with a deep breath, Herschel headed up the street.

Wordsworth leant across and opened the passenger door. Herschel faltered momentarily before peering into the vehicle.

"What do you want to talk to me about?"

"Guess," replied Wordsworth.

"I've told you all I know."

"No … you told me all you wanted to. But things have changed. Get in, just for five minutes, and hear what I've got to say."

Once again Herschel hesitated, then let out a petulant grunt and got into the car. He sat there like a spoilt child, staring straight ahead.

"What's it like being back?" Wordsworth asked.

Herschel just shrugged.

"Better without Ethan Cartwright hanging around," continued Wordsworth.

"He'll be back," said Herschel with a dark foreboding.

"That's what I want to talk to you about. If we play our cards right, he'll never be back."

"Yeah right."

"With your help I can nail the Cartwrights. I just need that extra piece of information."

"What's that got to do with me?'

"You might have it."

"Me?" said Herschel derisively.

"You must have known something, or Ethan wouldn't have laid into you like he did."

"He thought I'd spoken with you lot, given you information about him and Jodie."

"But you hadn't."

"Of course I hadn't. What was I going to tell you? I don't know anything."

"You've been around Ethan for years ... what he did to you was unforgivable."

"I hate him."

"So why won't you tell me about what he's up to?"

"Are you deaf ... I – don't – know," he emphasised.

"The night you took Jodie to the bus stop, do you remember her saying anything else to you?"

"I told you everything."

"I know you were really fond of her ..."

"I was more than fond of her ... I would have made her a lot happier than that prick."

"So if I was to tell you Ethan was involved in her disappearance, would that jog your memory?"

Herschel didn't say anything.

"We know that at least three girls who were involved with Ethan have turned up dead. Another two, plus Jodie, are still missing, we have to assume the worst."

Still Herschel didn't say anything.

"Hershey – she could be dead, don't you care about that?"

"She's not," Herschel mumbled.

"Sorry?"

"I said she's not dead."

Herschel started to get out of the car.

"Whoa … whoa! How do you know that?"

"I just do."

"Tell me – how you know!"

Herschel still didn't move.

"Please … get back in the car."

Herschel looked down at the floor, trying to decide what to do. Then he climbed back into the car, closed the door, looked straight ahead and said: "The two dead girls… was one of them called Skye?"

Break through! Wordsworth tried to keep his cool. "Yes. Skye Chapman. You knew her?"

"He told me about her. He was showing off … making me feel small. Saying I couldn't even get a girl … and he had loads just hanging onto his every word. He told me this Skye had even done a picture of him, looking really cool. He had a copy on his phone."

"She was found in a squat in London - murdered."

Herschel, clearly shocked by what Wordsworth had just told him, for the first time turned and looked at him. "Look, if I tell you, will you promise me you'll find Jodie?"

"Yes."

"And … and you *promise* Ethan won't know what I told you?"

"I promise."

"I mean – you can't tell *anyone*!"

"I won't, Herschel. You can trust me. I want to help."

Herschel paused again, then: "I got a call in hospital."

Wordsworth didn't say anything, silently willing Herschel to continue.

"This man said if I didn't do what I was told then Jodie would be killed."

"Who said that?"

"I don't know."

"But you believed what he said."

"Yeah. I had to."

"How do you mean?"

"They … they put her on the phone. She was crying and she kept saying I had to help her … she just kept saying it … again, again and again …"

"Are you sure it was her?"

"It was her. I know it was her. They said if I told you lot it was Ethan that had beaten me up, then they'd kill her. They'd kill her and send me the video."

CHAPTER FORTY-FIVE

"We can't be sure it was her, can we?" Cosgrove pondered as he sat down.

"No, but we can't ignore it," said Wordsworth.

Cosgrove and Harvey exchanged a look, a look that Wordsworth witnessed, even though they hadn't intended him to see it.

"What? What's the problem?" he asked.

"It's nothing," replied Cosgrove too quickly.

"Bullshit … there's something. What is it?"

Cosgrove looked at him for a moment and then said, "We've run out of official leads. There's nothing we can take to the Chief Super. Okay there's this phone call but how do we explain how we know for sure that it came from within Prencart Holdings? That information was obtained illegally."

"Doesn't stop it being true," said Wordsworth not wanting to hear negativity.

"But doesn't help us get warrants … get phone taps …

make arrests. We can't do any of that. We have nothing," rationalised a frustrated Cosgrove.

"Let's just give up then. Shut up shop and call it a day. Is that what you want?"

"No, course not …"

"Then we keep going."

"But where do we go from here? We're chasing an impossible enemy. There's nothing else we can do."

***

Adams was waiting patiently in his Lexus on the fourth floor of the multi-storey park in the centre of Bradford. He'd been there about half an hour and there was just a slight sense of concern, which he was trying to suppress. He told himself that he'd done the right checks, he had to be right. The man from Brussels would turn up … he had to.

Another ten minutes went by and just as he was starting to really worry a figure emerged from the lift area.

This could be my man.

He flipped on his iPad and brought up a photograph with the name *Jan Elst* printed underneath. He studied the photo, then the man.

Yeah – that's him.

Adams flashed his headlights and Jan Elst immediately made his way towards the vehicle. As he approached Adams started to try and size him up. Adams was not a physical kind of a guy and if things did get awkward what he didn't want is some macho man kicking the shit out of him. Elst was far from macho, not too tall, tortoise shell round glasses, neatly tailored goatee. Adams knew he'd just turned forty-four because he'd done his research and Elst looked okay for his age. He climbed into the car next to Adams, placing his neat overnight bag on his knee.

"Hello," said Elst in his Belgium accent.

Adams nodded at him and they shook hands.

"What happens now?" Elst asked looking uneasily at his driver.

Without replying Adams started the vehicle.

***

Wordsworth, Harvey and Cosgrove were once again sifting through all the information they had about Cartwright. Wordsworth just moved pieces of paper around or scrolled down various documents or images he had on his computer, not really looking at them. This had all been harder than he had imagined.

Wordsworth felt a tap on his shoulder. It was Gatesy, who gave a slight twitch of the head indicating he needed a private word.

Once they were in Gatesy's office, Gatesy tapped his keyboard and up came a list of figures all suffixed with an assortment of letters and numbers.

Wordsworth squinted at them, not sure what he was meant to be looking for.

"I presume this means something to you," said Wordsworth.

"It didn't, but it does now," replied Gatesy with an edge of cockiness. "I continued digging … I actually got into the accounts of one of the offshore companies in the Seychelles."

"How?"

"Would you understand if I told you?"

"Point taken. Did you discover anything about the source of the cash?"

"Yeah. Not easy … but there it is." Gatesy indicated the figures on the screen. "I now know the source."

"Drug money?"

"No – not drugs. Something worse … something far worse."

Wordsworth looked at him, puzzled. Gatesy rapidly pressed a number of keys on his keypad. A website homepage for holiday properties appeared. Gatesy seemed to ignore the page and hit another combination of keys and another page came up … again referring to more property. This continued for a few minutes until a page came up, a black swirling vortex and then the word 'Onionland'.

Gatesy looked up. "Do you know what Onionland is?"

"Not a clue," replied Wordsworth.

Gatesy typed in an IP address and another site appeared on screen. It showed a room with a girl sitting on a bed, her back to camera. A caption flashed across the screen: *'TONIGHT. 11PM GMT – LIVE $1,000.00'*

"What the hell is this?" asked Wordsworth.

"This is Onionland or as most people call it – the dark web. This is where you can get anything you want for a price."

"A thousand pounds? What are they selling?"

"I don't know."

"I'm assuming it's not going to be a digitally re-mastered copy of The Sound of Music."

Gatesy didn't get the gag, he continued to look at the screen, he was obviously disturbed by what he was seeing. "There's a number of alternative bank accounts people can pay into to access the content. These change regularly, so there's never a sudden surge of money into any one account. Then as we'd already worked out, the monies go on some circuitous route, via other banks, and eventually arrives in the offshore accounts in the Seychelles or the Caymans. And they only deal in dollars, pounds and euros, no cryptocurrency. This is like the teaser, you can access a sister site where apparently the content shows round the clock. Whatever's happening here at 11 must be something different, something special."

Suddenly the angle of the camera pointing at the girl on the bed changed, and for the first time Wordsworth could see her face. She looked pale and vacant. She was obviously drugged. There was no fight in her. But she *was* alive!

"That's Jodie Kinsella." Wordsworth couldn't believe what he was looking at. *Jodie Kinsella*. He had come to accept that when he found her, it would be her corpse. But here she was … alive! "I need to look at the sister site."

"Seriously?"

"We need to see what the fuck is going on and whether there are any clues to where she is."

"This is the dark web. This is severe hard core … whatever it is. You know what would happen to me if I'm caught?"

Wordsworth, thought for a moment, then picked up a piece of paper, scribbled something down and handed it to Gatesy.

"A written statement, signed by me, ordering you to access the site as part of an ongoing investigation."

Both men, during their time with the police, had witnessed appalling atrocities and barbaric behaviour, nevertheless both men were tense an anxious about what they were about to encounter.

***

It was approximately five in the afternoon when Adams pulled up in the car park behind the industrial units. Elst looked round at the rather bleak and uninviting vista. He was expecting something grander, something that maybe had history, a little slice of England, not the arse end of West Yorkshire. Adams could see the disappointment on the Belgian's face.

"We don't want to invite attention," said Adams.

386

They both went through a door into one of the units and started to make their way through the labyrinth of corridors. Eventually they came to a room and Adams opened the door and ushered the Belgian in.

"Make yourself comfortable," said Adams looking at his watch. "You've got about six hours."

Elst looked round the room, which resembled a smart, functional hotel suite. It was in total contrast to the anonymous brick corridors he'd traversed to get there. There was a living/bedroom area, complete with TV, fully stocked fridge, comfy sofas, and en suite bathroom, all tastefully designed, down to the art on the walls. The only reason anyone would know they were not in some nice hotel, was the total absence of windows and a black silk dressing gown and a black leather mask cast casually on the bed.

***

Cosgrove and Harvey were still working their way through all the information. Cosgrove had just come across the notes he'd made about the industrial units in Halifax, when Wordsworth appeared.

"IT offices pronto."

As Cosgrove and Harvey followed Wordsworth in to Gatesy's office, he muttered apologetically: "This doesn't make for pleasant watching ..."

"Better shut the door," ordered Gatesy as he hit the

return key. The screen in front of him came alive.

There - being brutally raped by two men, both wearing black hooded masks to hide their identity, was Skye Chapman.

"Jesus," Harvey couldn't help herself. "Jesus," she repeated, "what is this?"

"Do you recognise the girl?" Wordsworth asked.

"It's Skye Chapman," answered Cosgrove. "What the fuck is this?"

"Whatever it is, it's real," Wordsworth said.

"Real? It can't be … it can't be real. No … it can't be," said Harvey horrified.

"That's what they're claiming. This costs two hundred pounds for one hour to watch."

"But it's a con … it's a set up," expostulated Cosgrove.

"Skye Chapman is dead … we know that. Now we know how she died."

Harvey unable to watch any longer, turned away. Cosgrove was visibly shaken.

"Tonight they're going to be doing something that's worth a grand to watch. Show them Peter."

This was the first time either Cosgrove or Harvey had heard Wordsworth refer to the computer man as anything but Gatesy, but neither noticed.

Gatesy brought up the screen showing Jodie sitting on the bed.

"That's Jodie Kinsella," said Cosgrove.

Once again the caption flashed across the screen:

'TONIGHT. 11PM GMT – LIVE. $1,000.00'.

"What sort of place would you say that was?" Cosgrove continued.

"Some sort of cellar," offered Wordsworth.

"It's not a cellar," said Gatesy who had studied the location the longest. "Those are breeze blocks. Houses with cellars are either brick or stone. You need to be looking for an industrial unit."

CHAPTER FORTY-SIX

Just off Keighley Road, one of the major thoroughfares out of Halifax, branches a smaller road called Shay Lane. Shay Lane is flanked with a mixture of different industrial units, and different-sized and aged houses.

Just a half a mile along Shay Lane was the industrial units Prencart Holdings had purchased some time ago. They stood away from the rest and were newer than the majority of other units on the road.

Two cars, one close on the heels of the other and breaking the speed limit, came to a sudden halt. One was being driven by Harvey, with Wordsworth as her passenger, the other was driven by Cosgrove. Cosgrove got out his car and climbed into the back of Harvey's, as Wordsworth looked at his watch: 10:35 pm.

"Do we have a plan?" asked Cosgrove, looking across at the industrial units.

Since seeing Jodie Kinsella on Gatesy's computer, he

had his team checking every piece of real estate Prencart Holdings had registered. They narrowed it down to three locations; Brigella Mills, which was still standing empty awaiting planning permission, a block of flats down Manchester Road, which still had a few flats occupied by tenants refusing to move out, and the industrial units that Cosgrove had been checking out in Halifax. The first stop had been Brigella Mills, but they had drawn a blank. Time was flying by too quickly. The deadline of 11:00 was rapidly approaching. So it was a toss-up – Manchester Road or Halifax. They decided on Halifax, because surely the premises Cartwright was using had to be totally vacant.

Now the three police officers were sat in a car, not knowing what to do.

"Fuck it, I'm going in. I can't just sit here," said Wordsworth.

"Let me at least check it out first," said Cosgrove, and he was out of the car before either of the other two could stop him. He ran over to the units and disappeared round a corner.

Just six minutes later he was back. He climbed into the car.

"There's a Lexus four-by-four parked round back, licence plate ..."

"I know whose it is," said Wordsworth interrupting. "Robin Adams."

"There's also a Mercedes."

"Cartwright's."

Wordsworth thought for a moment before saying, "Let's see if there's a way in. Pop the boot," he instructed Harvey.

Round the back of the car Wordsworth rooted through and found the lug wrench for changing a tyre. As he removed it, he saw Cosgrove standing, looking at him.

"We're going to need something to break in with," explained Wordsworth gently closing the boot of the car.

***

"Is the Belgian ready?" asked Prentice who was now wearing surgical gloves.

"Yeah." Adams responded.

"And the girl?"

"She's awake."

Prentice looked at the screens. There was the output on the sister site streaming a brutal rape by four men of two girls - Abigail Davies and Madison Bradshaw. Every time they tried to fight back fists lashed out at them and they quickly acquiesced. On another screen, Jodie, dressed in a summer frock, was lying on the bed in what appeared to be a semi-conscious state.

"We have nearly a half million subscribed already," reported Adams proudly. "Not bad for a night's work."

"When do you plan to show it again?"

"In a week. You better get the Belgian."

"What do you make of him?"

"Same as the rest. Rich, bored."

"Fucked up?"

"Totally, but then who are we to talk?"

***

At the far end of the building, the opposite end to where Adams and Prentice had parked their cars, Wordsworth, Cosgrove and Harvey were trying to find a way into the configuration of industrial units. They'd already checked and confirmed there were no cameras on this side of the building, but that didn't ease their anxiety about breaking in.

"This isn't going to go down well with anybody," said Cosgrove with more than a touch of concern.

"You don't have to do it. I wouldn't blame either of you if you walked away right now," said Wordsworth.

Harvey and Cosgrove exchanged a look, there was apprehension, a colossal amount of it, but neither were going to back out now.

They tried to force open a metal shutter which was barring the way into one of the units, but it wouldn't shift. Wordsworth looked around and, sticking the lug wrench in his belt, he asked Cosgrove to give him a leg up onto the roof.

Getting onto the roof was far from easy. A leg up from Cosgrove got him part way up the wall, to make it up the rest he had to hang on to the gutter and pull himself up.

Eventually he managed to clamber onto the roof. He looked around and spotted just what they needed: a skylight. He crawled up the slanting roof to the window and tried to push it open. It wouldn't budge. He slipped the lug wrench under the PVC trim which framed the window and it easily came away. He worked away at the sealant surrounding the frame, digging it out. After some time, and what seemed a ridiculous amount of sealant, Wordsworth stood up, balancing carefully on the sloping roof, he then took a deep breath and smashed his foot into the window, causing him to lose his balance. He slid down the roof, clawing furiously at the corrugated asbestos, whilst his feet and legs flayed around, but he couldn't get any kind of a grip. He braced himself for the impact of the fall when his body suddenly jarred and his descent abruptly stopped. One of his feet had hit the guttering that skirted round the edge of the building.

Cosgrove and Harvey stared on in helpless horror.

Wordsworth without taking time to regain his breath, started to claw his way back up the roof towards the window, only there was no longer a window there, just a gaping hole. He looked through it and saw the smashed glass on the floor below.

Gingerly, he lowered himself through the hole and dropped to the ground. It was pitch black so, using the torch on his phone, he located the shutter, and the bolts which were keeping it firmly closed. He quickly released them and there was Harvey and Cosgrove.

394

With the shutter open, the moonlight illuminated the inside of the unit and they found themselves looking at bits of car parts hanging around and lots of oil stains on the floor. The space had obviously been used as some sort of garage. Then Wordsworth noticed there was a door at the back of the unit which had been temporarily hidden by some metal shelving. They started to drag the shelving out of the way, the metal legs scraping along the concrete floor.

"Lift it … Lift it," whispered Wordsworth.

It wasn't heavy and quickly they had access to the door. Using his lug wrench again, Wordsworth prised open the door and, followed by the other two, set off into the main section of the complex.

***

Prentice and Elst made their way down a corridor. Elst was wearing the black silk dressing gown and carrying the black leather mask. Prentice was wearing a similar mask, one he'd first put on before entering Elst's room. He was not going to be recognised. If things went wrong, then Adams would be the only one Elst could identify.

"You must put the mask on before entering the room, the cameras are already live."

"Of course," said Elst in his clipped English.

"Have you any tattoos or recognisable birth marks …?" inquired Prentice.

Elst shook his head. His nerves were showing. Prentice

worried he might be starting to have cold feet.

They arrived at a door and Elst put the mask on, reached round the back of his head and pulled the zip down.

"Okay?" asked Cartwright trying to sound like he cared. Elst nodded. Prentice pushed open the door.

* * *

Adams watched the screens as Elst tentatively entered the room. He checked the time – six minutes past eleven. A touch of viewer anticipation was never a bad thing. He checked each camera. There were five in all, one in each corner of the room and one directly over the bed. Adams, with the controls in front of him, was able to pan and tilt the cameras as well as being able to zoom in and out.

He watched as Elst stood motionless in the doorway. There was always this brief moment when you could see the indecision. These men had never done anything like this before, never gone this far, and once they were presented with a real girl, there was always a chance they'd chicken out. To date, no one ever had. For Adams it was purely a money-making exercise and justified it to himself by saying that if they didn't do it, then somebody else would – after all, life was all about supply and demand. Prentice had come up with the idea after visiting strip joints and lap dancing clubs with clients. Attention to the female 'performers' had often edged towards being violent. Prentice, never slow to spot an opportunity, decided to take it to what he considered to be the next logical step. 'Give the paying customer what they can afford' At the moment Prentice was taking the lion's share of the revenue, but Adams wasn't going to tolerate that for long. He knew Prentice couldn't do it without him and very soon he was going to demand more ... and more.

After maybe 30 seconds of hesitation, Elst moved towards the bed.

Jodie didn't stir, she didn't seem aware there was anyone else in the room. There was nothing preventing her from moving, except for the heroin she had coursing through her body, which had put her into a state of total apathetic lethargy. Elst got nearer and nearer, his masked face slowly coming into Jodie's line of sight. Her eyes widened in fear at the sight of the mask. The mask meant one thing – torture. She screamed - instinctively, as Adams zoomed in on her face to capture her horror. This is what the people were paying to see.

Elst continued to look down at her and then he just lashed out with the back of his hand hitting her across the face. Jodie still attempted to break free from her attacker. But Elst was much quicker than the drugged teenager and quickly had her wrists handcuffed to each side of the bed head. The more she struggled the more aroused he became and the more he considered the experience was worth the money. He'd had a nervous start, but now he was beginning to enjoy himself.

Jodie's legs were flaying away, but Elst just knelt on

them, grabbed the front of her frock and ripped it off. He loomed over her, his robe falling open revealing him to be naked underneath. Jodie tried to fight him off by moving as erratically as she could, but Elst just hit her again … and again … and again until the fight was beaten out of her. He then grabbed her see-through bra and ripped it off. He threw it aside and violently grabbed her breasts. Jodie once again screamed in pain.

***

Prentice was standing just outside the door. He'd taken off his mask and stuffed it in his jacket pocket. He had his phone on and was watching, almost dispassionately, what was going on inside the room. He was about to go join Adams in the control room when he heard a noise. He looked up from the small phone screen and listened. All was quiet. Nothing - he must have imagined it. He put the phone in his pocket and started to move off, then the noise again.

What the fuck?

It could be a rat of course, or a cat maybe. Cautiously he set off down the corridor.

As he made his way through the breeze block maze, he suddenly stopped. Voices … speaking in hushed whispers. There were people in the building, but he had no idea who they were, what they were doing there or even more worryingly how they'd manage to get in. There were cameras, steel doors, combination locks and both getting in and out was a process you needed to learn. There was no way anyone could just walk in. The voices became closer. He tentatively looked around a corner and saw three figures in the dark. He was fairly certain they hadn't seen him, because there was no sudden reaction. However, in that fleeting moment, he'd recognised one of the trespassers. A figure he would have known anywhere: Wordsworth.

What the fuck is he doing here?

Prentice's first and only thought was self-preservation. Quietly he headed off back down the corridor. He knew if the police were in the car park, then Adams would have spotted them on his cameras and raised the alarm, therefore he had to assume that his exit route was clear. He could escape.

He looked back and saw shadows at the end of the corridor; the three police officers were still coming. With no thought for Adams, he started to run.

***

The police officers still didn't know whether they were in the right place or not, that is until they heard the noise of feet hitting the ground. Someone was running away from them. No need for stealth any longer, Wordsworth started to run down the corridor, Harvey and Cosgrove hard on his heels. In a matter of seconds they arrived at a door.

Wordsworth stopped, trying to figure out if they were going in the right direction. He listened for the footsteps.

Nothing, then a sound from behind the door they were standing next to. Without hesitation Wordsworth threw open the door and there was a naked Elst in the process of having sex whilst strangling a blood covered naked Jodie. Without a moment's hesitation, Wordsworth grabbed Elst by his mask and threw him against the wall, his head hitting it with force, immediately rendering him unconscious.

As Cosgrove and Harvey stood there in shock, Wordsworth quickly took in the room and realised whatever this was, was being filmed.

"CPR!" he ordered Harvey pointing at Jodie who was lying like a crumpled rag doll on the bed. Then ripping the mask off the unconscious attacker, he said to Cosgrove, "Break his legs if he tries to leave."

"Where you going?"

If Wordsworth had heard the question, he was wasn't going to take time out to answer it and he was gone from the room.

***

Adams was staring with shock at the screens in front of him. It took him a few seconds to process what exactly was happening. He stood up, as his breathing became shallow, and he felt his legs give way beneath him. He was in shock … clinical shock. This wasn't part of the scenario. This was way off piste, this was dangerously wrong. He had to get his shit together and do it fast. He hit a series of keys on the keyboard and the hard drives instantly started to erase everything, while all the cameras went blank, including the CCTV cameras. If they'd still been live, he would have seen Prentice appear out of the building and disappear down the road in his car.

As Adams grabbed his leather messenger bag he did think of Prentice; he thought there was nothing he could do for him. It was now every man for himself. He stuffed in a number of manga comics, and flung open the door of the control room. No sooner had he stepped into the corridor than he heard Wordsworth's voice.

"Police! Don't move!"

He looked down the corridor and there was Wordsworth striding confidently toward him.

Adams knew he could get to the back door before Wordsworth, he was sure of it. And if he did, then he could just disappear … he had the cash. No choice, he had to go for it.

He turned and still clutching his bag headed for the exit.

"Shit!" was all Wordsworth could say as he took off after him.

The back door of the complex was flung open, and Adams came charging out. He headed for his Lexus, fumbling for his keys which were in his bag. He didn't dare look behind him; he just had to keep going. What he did notice was that Prentice's car wasn't there. He had already escaped. Hitting the key fob, he jumped into the driver's seat, pushed the starter button, the rev counter needle spun round to the red, he engaged 'drive' and started to leave the car park. The car had hardly gone a metre when the passenger door flew open and in scrambled Wordsworth. He didn't waste any time. His fist flew across, connecting with the left side of Adams' head. Adams reeled with the impact and before he could recover Wordsworth landed another blow. Somehow Adams managed to steer, the car doing a sharp left turn. The sudden movement caused Wordsworth to be nearly thrown out of the vehicle, but he hung onto the passenger door, only just clambering back to safety as the door was ripped clean off as it caught the corner of the building.

As the vehicle sped down Shay Lane, Wordsworth went to grab Adams again, causing him to lose control and send the Lexus careering into a number of parked cars.

The 4 x 4 screeched out onto the much busier Keighley Road, hitting an oncoming car, but still managing to keep on going. The impact with the other car nearly threw Wordsworth out again, but again he managed to hang on, grabbing the gear selector. Adams saw there was a possible opening to get rid of him, now there was no longer a passenger door he could force him out of the car. He smashed down on Wordsworth fingers, trying to loosen his grip on the automatic gear lever. Adams kept hitting him and hitting him. Wordsworth knew he had to do something. Grabbing the seat with his left hand he let go of the gear lever and grasped the little park lever. The parking brake engaged. The car suddenly started to spin round and round, smashing cars lining both sides of the road and eventually coming to a halt by colliding with the side of a bus.

Adams was dazed and stunned, but he managed to try and open his door. It was totally smashed in. He couldn't shift it. He turned to check to see if he could escape through the passenger side, when his face met with Wordsworth's fist. It knocked him clean out.

***

Wordsworth sat in the back of the ambulance being checked over by a paramedic. He was bruised, battered and bleeding, but all his thoughts were about what he'd witnessed in the industrial unit. His mind was trying to get it into perspective. From what he now knew, Cartwright and Adams were abducting girls, subjecting them to rape, physical violence and in some cases death, so the acts could be then viewed for a high price, by sick voyeurs, on the dark web around the globe. At this point he had no idea if Jodie was alive or dead, or whether they'd managed to pick up Cartwright.

As the paramedic stepped out of the ambulance to consult with his colleague, Wordsworth, unnoticed, climbed out of the vehicle and headed back towards the industrial unit. The roads had already been cordoned off, and forensic had already started doing their job. He was confronted by a uniformed policeman, but he just flashed his warrant card and continued to limp along the road. He arrived at the car park just as an ambulance was pulling away watched by Harvey and Cosgrove. The look of relief when they saw the damaged but mobile Wordsworth was obvious. Before they got a chance to ask him anything, Wordsworth asked them: "How is she?"

"She's alive," Harvey said simply and quietly. Wordsworth had to bite his lip; he was shaking, he couldn't have handled it if their arrival had been minutes too late. After the death of Wendy, another blow like this would have been too much. Emotionally he wasn't sure he was strong enough.

"They're still searching the building," added Cosgrove, "it's like a rabbit warren in there."

"We got lucky, boss," said Harvey as she watched blood drip from a cut on his head and land on the tarmac of the car park. "We should get you to hospital."

Wordsworth didn't object, he'd found out what he needed to know.

CHAPTER FORTY-SEVEN

In the days and weeks that followed, Wordsworth and his team were grilled about the night they ended up at the industrial unit. They were no longer on the investigation – something that angered them all. They'd done the work, they knew the case like no one else, their information could be vital, but it was thought that their actions had been too Maverick. They'd had no search warrant and their story of how they entered the building was dubious at best.

Wordsworth, Cosgrove and Harvey had come up with their own version of events and they'd stuck to it rigidly.

On that fateful evening they'd decided to have a drink after work at The Moorlands on Keighley Road. En route they realised they were very near one of Prencart's properties. They thought they'd just take a quick look, their excuse being that they wanted to try and work out why it had been on the market so long. When they arrived, they discovered that one of the shutters on the side of the building was open and a door that led into the rest of the complex had been forced. They did what any self-respecting police officer would have done; they checked the place out. But they hadn't bargained for what they found.

This was their story and none of them swayed from it, despite the fact those in charge didn't believe a word of it.

At the first possible opportunity, Wordsworth visited Jodie in the BRI. She was still disorientated and confused, but she was just grateful she was away from Shay Lane. Wordsworth didn't want to pressure her, but he had to ask her one question: "Is there anybody you would be able to recognise?"

"Just the man who picked me up."

"What was he like?"

"Thirtyish … glasses, beard … He was the only person I ever saw. Everyone else wore masks."

Prentice Cartwright was no idiot. He'd played his cards perfectly.

***

At the station, the whole extent of what happened at Shay Lane came to light. The dark web revealed 'snuff movies', showing the deaths of both Britney Atkinson and Skye Chapman. Madison Bradshaw and Abigail Davies were found alive in two separate rooms; both having suffered terrible abuse and both were addicted to heroin.

In another room, which had been Jodie's, scratched on one of the walls was the inscription:

> *These things I have spoken onto you,*
> *That in me ye might have peace.*
> *In the world ye shall have tribulation:*
> *But be of good cheer*
> *I have overcome the world*
> *JOHN 16.33.*

When Wordsworth saw photographs of the room and the inscription, his eyes filled with tears, not out of sadness, but out of sheer admiration of a girl who seemed to be determined to battle through everything.

Adams was interviewed at length, most of which Wordsworth watched from the observation room. A lawyer from Kahn's Solicitors was present, but it seemed a bit of a pointless exercise, because Adams refused to speak. They had plenty of evidence to convict him of abduction, exploitation, trafficking, drug possession, accessory to murder … the list was endless, but nothing he said or he'd done gave them enough to charge Prentice Cartwright.

Elst was a gibbering wreck. He told his interrogators everything … how he'd regularly visited the dark web where he indulged himself by watching hours and hours of child and teenage porn. He'd no idea the number of times he'd visited the 'snuff' site, but it was certainly in the hundreds, as was backed up by his bank records.

When the opportunity arose for Elst to actually partake in one of the 'snuff' films, he jumped at the chance. The amount he eventually paid was close on a half a million dollars. When his interviewer asked him if he thought it was worth it, he just stared at the floor.

But still Cartwright wasn't implicated. The only person Elst could describe was Adams. There was another man, but he wore a mask.

Adams and Elst were both charged and held on remand waiting their respective trials. Prentice Cartwright was brought in and grilled. With Faiza Amran advising him all the way, he claimed to know nothing of the operation at Shay Lane. He denied categorically that he had involved his son in these nefarious activities, and he feigned shock and disgust when he heard what Adams had been doing.

When asked about the Shay Lane industrial units and why they had been held off the market for over six months, Cartwright said that was down to Adams. "Do you know what an algorithm is …?"

"Yeah – I know what an algorithm is …" replied the DC interviewing him.

"Robin developed one that can predict the optimum moment for putting a property to market. That's why I employed him. I rely on him completely. If he says don't sell, I don't. I had no idea he was using the place for whatever you say he was using it for."

"Forgive me Mr Cartwright," said the DC, "but I find that just a little hard to believe."

"Believe what you want. I'm telling you what I know."

"You're claiming you didn't know anything about what Adams was up to. You knew nothing about the abduction of teenage girls, nothing about the making of pornographic films ... nothing about the murders?"

"Absolutely ... do you think I'd have just ignored it if I had?"

How many girls had died to provide the money for your empire? Wordsworth thought bitterly as he watched the interview. They'd almost certainly never know. Prentice had chosen carefully, vulnerable girls from care homes, just at the age when the authorities were happy to abdicate any responsibility. They could simply just let them disappear. Who was going to go looking for them? No one.

Ethan, under the watchful eye of Faiza, admitted knowing Jodie, but not any of the other girls. He was adamant that he did not encourage Jodie to meet anyone and didn't even waiver when confronted with Chloe's statement, that she had at last decided to make, stating it was Ethan that had set up her friend for the meeting on the morning of her disappearance.

A major effort had been launched to discover the other masked men in the videos, the ones that had been involved in the multiple rapes and also the ones responsible for the murders of Britney and Skye, but doing so had proved impossible. Some of the other girls were identified, all from care homes, all vulnerable, but none were actually found. It was estimated that over a two to three-year period, at least twenty girls had been abducted and killed by Prentice and Adams.

After a number of interviews, the CPS decided that no charges were to be brought against Prentice. They had no forensics linking him to the crime, they had no witnesses, and neither Adams nor Elst were implicating him. Prentice Cartwright was a free man. He'd got away with it and so had his son, who along with his mother had stood steadfastly behind his step-father.

So, the only thing left for Wordsworth and the team to do was to drown their sorrows at The Hare and Hounds.

During the course of the evening the conversation never veered far from the 'snuff' topic. Everyone had heard of 'snuff' movies, but all thought they'd not yet crossed the pond from America. Now they knew otherwise and couldn't help but think that society had plunged to a new low, a level of depravity that they couldn't possibly have imagined.

On arriving home, worse for wear, Wordsworth checked all the kids were safely asleep and then crashed in a chair in the living room, like he had been doing for the last month or so; his marital bed no longer had the pull it used to have. Two hours later he suddenly awoke. Raging through his sleeping mind was one thing and one thing only – Cartwright couldn't be allowed to get away with it. He couldn't be allowed to get away with the abuse and murder of god knows how many girls, and he couldn't be allowed to get away with killing Wendy.

"What was your overall feeling with regards to the investigation and its outcome?" asked Price – he knew they were coming to the end and he just wanted to go home.

"I felt that the conviction of Robin Adams and Jan Elst went some way towards justice, but nowhere near far enough." Wordsworth said. "It's our job to protect the public, but we didn't. We failed. Most of those girls were in care homes, already vulnerable. No one cared enough to even try to look for them. Even in death who cares …? And for those that survived … well, what kind of life are they going to live now? We didn't do our job. We didn't protect any of them."

"What about Zara Redhead? She came from a middle-class family, not a deprived background or an abusive environment.   She was far from vulnerable. Or are you

411

saying her death wasn't connected to Adams?" asked Ashburn, still looking for cracks in Wordsworth's account.

"She got hold of those drugs, didn't she? She was intelligent, smart, together and we still let her die. We didn't protect her. Again, we failed."

"And that's your mission from now on, is it, to be the great protector?" Ashburn rolled her eyes.

"My mission is to raise my children to the best of my ability. It's the Government's job to fix society – not mine."

"And Prentice Cartwright …?" Ashburn went on.

"What about him?"

"How do you feel about what happened to him?"

Wordsworth looked her directly in the eyes.

"You don't have to answer that," warned Sharvari.

CHAPTER FORTY-EIGHT

Since the night they managed to free Jodie and the two other girls, Wordsworth had spent all his free time going through the case to try and find evidence to bring Prentice Cartwright to court. Each night he spread the files and documents over the dining table, hoping that something would leap out at him and give him the information he prayed for. He was doing just that, when unusually for that time of night, the doorbell rang.

Izzy answered it. He listened out, trying to figure out who was at the door. He heard his name, then Izzy appeared back in the room.

"Someone to see you," she said, with no hint of what was to follow.

Into the room walked Ethan Cartwright. He looked a lot older, his peaches and cream complexion now lined and pale. He was still wearing designer clothes, but because of his weight loss, they didn't fit as well. Wordsworth closed

413

the file in front of him and turned it over so Ethan wouldn't be able to read what it said.

"Do you want a drink of something?" asked Izzy, who had now assumed the role of matriarch in the family.

"No, I'm fine thanks," replied Ethan his voice tired and depressed.

"I'll be in my room if you need me." Izzy turned and disappeared into the house.

"I h-h-hope you don't mind me coming to see you," Ethan stuttered.

"Sit down," instructed Wordsworth, not letting him know if he minded or not.

Ethan perched on the edge of an armchair. "I had to come and see you," he said. "I need to explain to someone."

"Explain what?" asked Wordsworth with a cold ring in his voice, yet inside he was both intrigued and nervous. What had motivated Ethan Cartwright to turn up on his doorstep?

"I didn't know what was going on."

Wordsworth said nothing.

"Really I didn't," pleaded Ethan. "If I'd known … I would never have done it."

"You didn't know you were setting up Jodie … or Britney, Madison, Skye Chapman or Abigail Davies? If you're trying to tell me that … then forgive me if I say I don't believe you. What about the message Jodie sent to you the night before she was abducted?"

"I … I …" Ethan was struggling to remember it.

414

"'I know you're angry with me, but just remember I love you, please believe me.'" Wordsworth had no trouble remembering what the message said. "When I first read it, I thought she was trying to appease you, trying to not lose you because she was meeting another man. Trying to calm your jealousy. But I was wrong. You were angry with her because she didn't want to do it. She didn't want to go. But you'd promised her to your father like some sacrificial lamb. And you were angry because she'd tried to say no."

Ethan hung his head. "I didn't know … I swear I didn't know."

"Didn't know what?"

"What I was setting her up for. I didn't know anything about it."

"Really? You just thought that Prentice wanted them to hand out drinks at cocktail parties. Do me a fucking favour. You knew exactly what you were doing."

"I thought he wanted them as drug mules. That's what I thought – I swear it!"

"Drug mules?"

"That's what I thought. He told me he could fly them back and forth to various places, give them the first-class treatment … and they'd bring back drugs for him. He told me he was offering them a better life. A life they could only dream of if they stayed where they were."

"Did you still think that when Britney Atkinson and Skye Chapman both turned up dead?"

"He told me that they'd got greedy. Weren't happy with

415

what they were making and had tried to smuggle more back. They'd swallowed it and it'd burst in their stomach."

"And you believed him?"

"Why not? It sounded feasible to me. And … and … "

"What?"

"I needed to believe him. Because if I didn't how was I ever going to be his son." Ethan paused for a second. "I just wanted to be his son … a real son … that's all I ever wanted. I wanted him to be proud of me."

"My heart bleeds for you …" said Wordsworth sarcastically. There was no sympathy … how could there be.

"I know I was stupid … I know that. But if I'd have known what was really happening, then … then … I promise you … I promise you, I would never have done it."

"You'd have stood up to him?"

"Yes, I would. Those girls were my friends … they trusted me."

"Does that include Zara Redhead? Did she trust you when she overdosed?"

"She … she …"

"She what?" demanded Wordsworth.

"When I met her, she told me she was nearly sixteen …"

"Where did you meet her?"

"At a party … some girl, Catherine something – Pizza Boy knew her."

"And you thought she was right up your dad's street – yeah?"

416

"To begin with. She said she wasn't happy at home … she lived with her uncle that abused her …"

"She lived with her mum and dad who loved her. Who miss her every fucking day."

"I know that now … but at the time …" Ethan paused for a moment trying to collect himself, before launching back in with a plea, "When I found out her age … I swear I called it a day."

"You can say what you want … you sold her the drugs that killed her."

"I gave them to her … "

"Just like that."

"She said she'd had plenty before and she knew what she was doing. I didn't know she'd take them all at once."

"You saying she overdosed on purpose?"

"I don't know … I just know I got it all wrong. I should never have given her the stuff … I shouldn't have led her on … I should have seen …" Tears welled up in Ethan's eyes.

"She was fourteen … she was a child …"

Wordsworth looked at him for a moment then got up from his chair and walked round the room. He had to clear his head. He was starting to have some sympathy for this boy. Ethan's need to impress his stepfather was something Wordsworth recognised and empathised with. The relationship with his own father had never been smooth, he always thought he was a disappointment to him, but that had never stopped him wanting to impress him. "When did

417

you find out the truth about what was actually going on?"

"He finally told me when the journalists started turning up at the house. I didn't want to believe it and at first he denied it. I told him I was going to the police, tell them all I knew. He told me if I ever said anything to anybody, he would have me killed … and my mother."

Wordsworth slowly sat down again and quietly said, "Yet you're here now."

"I had to tell someone – I just had to, before …" Ethan stopped mid-sentence.

"Before what?"

"I don't know. Before … I go insane … I guess."

"What would you like to see happen to your stepfather?"

"I want to see him arrested. I want to see him in jail. But that's not going to happen, is it? He's too smart for that. He gets everyone else to do his dirty work – pick up girls, set up porn sites, even kill people …

Wordsworth looked at him – he knew what he was saying.

"He controlled everything. My real dad went off with my mum's best friend and we had to live in some shitty hostel … Then suddenly there was my stepdad. I don't know how they met, but I do know our lives changed just like that … overnight. If I wanted anything … anything at all … I got it. But that's what he does with everyone, he makes you in indebted to him. It's like you always owe him and he always owns you."

"But you don't feel like that anymore," stated Wordsworth.

"I fucking hate him. Hate what he's done to me, what he's done to my mum. She's not stupid. But she can't do anything. We're in this till the grave … If we try to leave, he'll kill us. I know he will. He won't risk the truth getting out."

Ethan looked at Wordsworth for a few moments before he stood up and very politely said:

"Thanks for listening. I had to tell someone. I can't stop thinking how stupid I was … how naïve I was. How could I have done what I did? Hershey … poor old Hershey what had he ever done to me except be a really good friend? And look what I did to him. I was turning into … I was turning into Prentice."

Ethan headed back into the hall, where Wordsworth opened the front door for him. Ethan stopped, turning back to Wordsworth, "How's Jodie?"

"How would you expect after what she's been through."

"I can't imagine … I can't …" he said quietly. "I can't believe how much I miss her. I can't stop thinking about her." Ethan paused again, Wordsworth said nothing. "If you see her … would you … please … tell her how sorry I am. I really am sorry …"

Then with a slight nod of the head, Ethan was gone into the night.

***

The following day at the office Wordsworth was supposedly working his way through the previous night's list of burglaries and offences, but really his mind was fully occupied with Ethan's unexpected confession. He was desperately trying figure out how he could use it to nail Prentice, but he was getting nowhere.

"You heard?" Redhead interrupted his thoughts.

"Heard what?" replied Wordsworth.

"Ethan Cartwright topped himself."

Wordsworth physically reeled with the news.

"This morning … headphones on, he walked out in front of a train. No messing about."

Wordsworth started to think about the encounter he'd had with the youth the previous night. He remembered him saying *"I had to tell someone – I just had to, before ..."* Wordsworth now knew what he'd been about to say.

CHAPTER FORTY-NINE

Between the kids and handling everything from burglaries to assaults, from conmen to drug dealing, Wordsworth was kept busy. But every night, when he closed his eyes, all he could see was Wendy lying in a tangled mess on the road. With this thought the incapacitating feeling of impotency just grew and grew. He couldn't get past it; he couldn't move on and the person who coldly premeditated her murder was still walking free.

His colleagues constantly asked him to attend various functions or get togethers, most of which Wordsworth declined. However, when Joe Carter, the oversized DI, asked him to his leaving bash, he didn't feel he could turn him down. Joe had his faults, but he'd been a voice of reason when Wordsworth had first joined the Force.

Joe's farewell was held at Jacob's Well, or as it was known by some – Jacob's Beer House. Joe liked his pubs

421

old fashioned, and this pub was certainly old fashioned, being one of the oldest in Bradford. Joe drank more than normal that night, he was one of those drunks that never fell over, never even stumbled, but did get progressively louder as the night went on. And with the volume often came the confessions.

Wordsworth didn't arrive until late, and Joe was at the bar holding court. Once again, as in the night at the Hare and Hounds, the main focus of his stories was the Ukrainian Sergey Klochkova. He'd now gone down for fourteen years. According to Joe right up to sentencing he was trying to do a deal with him. Kept on about the firearms he said he had.

"That's them Eastern Europeans for you," said Joe, "they'll do a deal out there for 50p. Whatever I couldn't be arsed, all that paperwork, fucking things might not even exist."

Later on, Wordsworth, who had started to piece together the foundations of a plan, found himself at the bar with Joe. He wanted to know more about Klochkova's mystery stash of weapons. Did Joe have any idea where they might be? Joe, now very drunk, just blurted out: "He said they was in Leeds, in some storage place, but that's all I know. By the time that bastard gets out, he'll have probably forgotten where they are himself. Bang bang … Sergey … game over."

The following day Wordsworth sat down at a hot desk computer and pulled up the Klochkova file. He went through it, trying to find some clue about this stash of weapons. Nothing. Klochkova was just a two-bit hoodlum who liked to think he was some sort of godfather figure. His compatriots in crime, six in all, were arrested with him and now were serving prison sentences of varying lengths, the shortest being eight years. It seemed the only link Klochkova left behind was his girlfriend. According to the file she was never suspected of any involvement with her boyfriend's nefarious activities and after initially being taken into custody, was quickly released. However, there was an address for her, which at the time of Klochkova's arrest, placed her in Eccleshill, a suburb of Bradford. Wordsworth had to hope she hadn't moved.

The girlfriend, Poppy, was in her late twenties and naturally looked nervous when Wordsworth showed her his warrant card. She wasn't at all what Wordsworth had expected. She looked too meek and timid to be a gangster's moll, in fact she worked on the checkouts at the local Morrisons Supermarket. She claimed the night Klochkova was arrested, was the first time she knew anything of his misdemeanours, up until then she'd thought he was a white van man.

Sensing Poppy's nerves Wordsworth didn't mess about, he got straight to the point. "I'm looking for information."

"What about?"

"Sergey Klochova."

She moved away from the front door of the small terrace house, returning to a computer she'd been on when

Wordsworth knocked. "Nothing to do with me," she stated.

"But he was."

"Once upon a time ... but I'm with someone else now."

Wordsworth entered the house, which had no hall, the front door opened directly into the living room.

"And how's Sergey about that?"

"He doesn't know. And he isn't going to find out."

Poppy started to shut her computer and as she did, Wordsworth caught sight of details for a domestic property.

"Six weeks and we're out of here. He'll never find us," she continued.

"Where you going then?" asked Wordsworth.

"Do I have to tell?" Poppy's concern was obvious.

"No – but I can always find out."

Wordsworth moved to the computer that only seconds a go she had closed, and without asking, opened it up again.

"Hey ...! You can't do that!"

"Just have," said Wordsworth, looking at the details of a property on the computer screen.

"Bishop Auckland," he continued. "That's certainly getting away."

Wordsworth continued to look at the property details, as Poppy stared on helplessly.

"Don't tell him – please," pleaded Poppy. "If he found out ..."

"I won't tell him ..."

"Thank you ... thank you ..."

"Just as long as you're straight with me."

"I've nothing to hide."

"This house … the one we're in at the moment, do you own it?" Wordsworth asked.

"No – it's rented."

"And what does your boyfriend do?"

"Delivers for Just Eat," replied Poppy, wondering why Wordsworth was asking.

"'A two-bedroom, one reception, terrace property in need of extensive renovation. £36,500.00.'" Wordsworth read from the screen. "This where you're moving to?"

"Yeah."

"Great price. But needs a lot of work."

"My boyfriend's very good at DIY."

"He'll need to be. Must have been difficult … getting a mortgage."

Poppy hesitated before replying, "It was."

"Who's it with?"

"Er … I forget now …"

"That would be like forgetting your middle name … nobody forgets who they owe money to. Unless the truth is you don't owe anybody anything. You're paying cash for your new home."

"What does it matter to you."

"I'll tell you why it matters … because I want to know where you got thirty-six grand from."

Poppy looks at him for a moment, not sure how to reply.

"You didn't get it working shifts at Morrisons or

delivering curries to students. So where's it come from?"

Poppy said nothing, but she was clearly worried. She hadn't foreseen this development.

"Look how about this – let's do a deal. You tell me where you got the money and … and this is me being really fair … I'll let you keep it, move to your dream house in Bishop Auckland and I won't say a word to Sergey. If you don't tell me … well …"

Wordsworth looked at her, watching her slowly realise she had no choice.

"Sergey opened five bank accounts in my name. Two with ten grand in each and three with eight."

"When was this?"

"Just after we first met. He said it wasn't really illegal, he was just keeping it from the VAT man."

"And you believed him?"

Poppy just shrugged.

"Whatever - you've now decided to spend it."

"Sergey is crazy … if he found out I'd got a new fella, he could do anything. Anyway, he can't spend it where he is. He can't even own up to having it."

"So he just left you taking care of his forty-four grand – a nice little nest egg for when he gets out."

"If that was his plan, it shows what a moron he is."

"How do you mean?"

"Even if I hadn't have started spending it, there wouldn't have been that much left."

"Why not?" asked Wordsworth – intrigued.

"There's a direct debit that's paid out every month for £320. If he does the whole fourteen years, there's not going to be much left."

"Three-twenty a month? Just cancelled it."

***

Wordsworth, after calling in home and slipping into a black hoodie, drove as fast as the speed limit allowed to SeaCroft Storage in Leeds. This was the facility linked to the monthly payments made from one of the five bank accounts. Poppy also furnished him with two other numbers that had been texted to her on an illegal mobile from prison. Klochkova had told her to keep them safe, he would need them when he was released, and he was convinced that would be sooner rather than later.

Wordsworth pulled up in the virtually empty car park. He'd stopped some five minutes away, put on a baseball cap and pulled a scarf around his face. He knew there would be CCTV cameras and avoiding them would be impossible. His only option was a disguise. He slipped on a pair of sunglasses he kept in his car, pulled up his hood and headed for the storage facility's reception.

It was late and there was no one on the reception desk. There was a keypad which was used to allow access to the storage lockers and Wordsworth, making sure to keep his back to the CCTV cameras, checked the numbers that he'd noted on his phone. He tried the shorter one, and the door

427

clicked open immediately. He entered the building and looked down the long corridor stretching ahead of him.

Each storage unit had a letter and a number on it. He looked at the second number Poppy had given him: 'J5058392'. After a little checking of lockers, he figured out that J505 was the number of the unit. It took him a little while to find it, it was one of the bigger ones, but then quickly realised the 8392 was the code for the combination lock on the door. Slipping on some purple nitrile gloves, which he normally used for scenes of crimes operations, he swiftly lined up the numbers and the lock sprung open. The night Joe Carter spouted his mouth off in the pub, was the night Wordsworth had formulated his plan. Now he was about to enter the locker that he hoped would yield him what he wanted and if it did, then all had gone better than expected.

Wordsworth stepped inside.

It was a proverbial Aladdin's cave full of stolen goods, everything from jewellery to high-end designer handbags. But Wordsworth wasn't interested in any of that. He started to root through the boxes and bags and very quickly he found what he was looking for. Under a pile of black plastic bin liners containing numerous pairs of Timberland boots, was a large cardboard box. He peeled back the lid, looked inside and there was what he wanted – firearms.

Wordsworth stared at the guns for a minute. The guns seemed to stare back at him, metal and dangerous. These were killing machines. There were about a dozen weapons in total, mainly pistols - Lugers, Berettas, even a sawn-off shotgun, along with various attachments, bullet clips and suppressors. Wordsworth reached into the box, took a deep breath and picked up a Glock 17 handgun, the only weapon he was really familiar with having been on a police training course and this was their weapon of choice.

Nervously he checked it was loaded; it had four bullets in the magazine, which was enough for Wordsworth's purposes. Now all he needed was a suppressor, without it the risk was too great. The Glock already had an adaptor screwed into its barrel; he just needed a silencer to fit it. The choice was limited. Wordsworth tried a couple, before finding one that fit snuggly. He then removed the suppressor, slipped it into one pocket and the gun safely into the other, checked his disguise was in place, left the unit, relocked it and calmly departed the building.

CHAPTER FIFTY

The weather was turning wintery, in fact snow was falling. Wordsworth watched the first few flakes hit the ground as he sat in his car outside Prentice Cartwright's house. He was neatly tucked out of sight, as he had been for the last six weeks, whilst tracking the comings and goings of Mr and Mrs Cartwright. He knew every Thursday evening, religiously, Virginia went to her book club, held at the home of one of the other readers.

Since the arrests of Adams and Elst, life in the Cartwright household had become uneasy. Virginia was fairly sure that her husband had been involved with the horrific atrocities at Shay Lane, but dared not say anything. Their relationship had become brittle, even more so after Ethan's suicide. They barely talked to each other, slept in separate rooms and spent as little time as possible with each other. But Virginia knew Prentice would never let her leave him, and anyway she was too scared to even try.

Wordsworth watched Virginia get into her Porsche and

drive away. He sat there for a further twenty minutes, just to make sure she didn't come back for something she'd forgotten. He then got out of his car, pulled up the hood of the same hoodie he'd worn at SeaCroft Storage and headed across the road. He knew, because he'd already done a recce, that there we no cameras on the side of the property, only the front and back, and as luck would have it, down the side of the house, the fencing was just short of two metres. Not easy to climb over, but not impossible. His only impediment were his size twelve boots, which were two sizes larger than what he normally wore.

Checking there was no one watching, he grabbed the top of the fencing and pulled himself up. He then managed to swing one leg over, straddle the fencing for a moment, before hastily dropping down onto the drive, his size twelve boots leaving a clear imprint in the light covering of snow that had fallen. Wordsworth made his way round to the back of the house. He was now entering into the unknown. He knew where the security camera was positioned and made sure he safely ducked underneath it. He had no idea how he would progress from here. He tried the back door, which was locked. He'd studied a floor plan of the house, so he knew the lay out and entry through the back door would have been perfect, but it was not to be. He had to find another way in. He'd come this far, he couldn't back out now. Then he had an idea. In the back garden was a metal rotary washing line. It was not splayed out, but closed, so it was a pole. He crawled on his hands and knees to the rotary line, keeping out of sight of the camera. Trying to make as little sound as possible, he eased the pole out of the plastic socket. Up it went and he couldn't help but think that if anyone was watching the monitors in the house, they would have witnessed what looked like a miracle – a self-rising rotary washing line. Holding it under his arm, he again crawled towards the windows at the back of the house, the windows that belonged to the dining room.

Out of sight of the camera, he stood up to do one last check. The Glock 17 was tucked neatly into his belt. This was the first time Wordsworth had ever carried a firearm and if everything went to plan, it was going to be the first time he'd ever used one – for real. Then with all his might he smashed the washing line right through one of the dining room windows. The noise in the empty night was piercing. He then slipped round the side of the house and waited.

Prentice had rushed into the dining room to find out what was happening. There was the washing line half in, half out of the smashed window. Confused about how this could have possibly happened, he hurried round to the back door, stepped outside and went to remove the washing line from his window. But he never got there. He was stopped by Wordsworth's voice.

"Leave it. Someone will see to it later."

Prentice turned and saw Wordsworth standing there holding the semi-automatic. He watched as the police officer slowly took the suppressor from his pocket and screwed it onto the barrel of the Glock. Prentice couldn't

432

quite believe what he was looking at. Wordsworth motioned for him to go inside. Prentice obeyed.

They went into the kitchen and for a moment it looked like Prentice was going to make a run for it, but he didn't. He turned to look at Wordsworth. He was scared ... there was no doubt about that.

"I need you to tell me a couple of things, then I'll get out of your hair."

"What ... what do you need to know," Prentice uttered nervously.

"The whole 'snuff' website, the abducting the girls, the murder and the abuse, whose idea was that. Now if you lie to me, I'll shoot you."

Prentice decided the best form of defence was attack, so he hit back, "Why should I tell you anything?"

Wordsworth took aim and fired at Prentice's leg. Prentice screamed in pain as the bullet lodged in his thigh. His leg buckled and he went down on one knee, his cockiness now totally disappeared as he looked with shock at Wordsworth who still had the gun levelled at him.

"Okay ... okay. It was me ... it was my idea. But I ... *I* ... never killed anyone. I never harmed anyone."

"What do you fucking want - an OBE?"

"I regret it ... I really do. I wish I hadn't done it."

"Oh please," said Wordsworth, the gun steady in his hand. "Don't fucking insult me. You regret nothing. You don't even regret that Ethan threw himself under a train."

Prentice said nothing as Wordsworth lowered the gun.

"One last question and I will leave you alone to contemplate our conversation. Did you kill my wife?"

"No ... no. No, I didn't."

"Did you order her to be killed? And think carefully. The wrong answer could be fatal."

For thirty seconds or more Prentice said nothing, whilst all the time just staring at the gun. Then he spoke, "I had to protect my interests and you were getting too close."

Without another word Wordsworth strode towards the incapacitated Prentice, lifted the gun, forced the silencer against the quivering man's forehead and pulled the trigger. Prentice's brains splattered all over the walls. Wordsworth was taking no chances. He pushed the gun against Prentice's chest and pulled the trigger twice. Four minutes later he was climbing into his car and driving away.

***

Over the next few hours Wordsworth systematically destroyed all the evidence. He was fairly confident that he hadn't been caught on camera. He smashed the gun to pieces and disposed of the odd bits of metal in various refuse bins. His clothes were ripped to shreds and his boots hacked to pieces with a Stanley knife. Then the whole lot was distributed into various bins across Bradford, Leeds and Halifax. The false number plates he'd had on his car were smashed up and also disposed of, whilst the plastic that covered the inside of his car was, by the next day, in a land fill. There was nothing left that could be connected to him.

SOCO were all over the murder scene and found there was not one witness that could give them any useful information. They'd all had their doubts about his denial of any involvement with what happened at Shay Lane. Now they just believed their suspicions had been verified, because as far as they were concerned this was an assassination.

As for the police they were looking for someone with size twelve feet.

INTERVIEW ROOM. BRADFORD CITY CENTRE POLICE STATION, NELSON STREET.
15:07 p.m. 10th JANUARY 2020

Ashburn was talking quietly to Price. Wordsworth and Sharvari waited patiently, listening, but they were only able to make out the odd word.

"Are we just going to take his word for it?" whispered Ashburn.

"He's a police officer …"

"He's lying. If he didn't actually kill Cartwright, if he didn't actually pull the trigger, he was certainly involved."

"What are you basing that on?"

"Everything he's said."

Sharvari decided it was time to intervene. "Is it okay if we go now?"

"I have some more questions …" Ashburn declared loudly and positively.

"Ashburn …" It was a warning from Price.

"DI Wordsworth, are you honestly asking us to buy the

notion that you had nothing to do with the murder of Prentice Cartwright?"

Wordsworth just looked at her. He knew she was striking out by herself from the expression of frustration on Price's face. He knew he was in the driving seat.

"I believe you're lying ... I believe you've done nothing but lie all day. Now it's time to tell the truth."

"Are you accusing him of something, Sergeant Ashburn? If so you need to tell us exactly what and provide some evidence to back up your accusation," said Sharvari calmly. Like Wordsworth, she knew they were in the driving seat.

"You're not fit to be a police officer ..." Ashburn spat the accusation directly at Wordsworth.

"Sir ... are you going to allow this?" Sharvari appealed to Price.

"That's enough."

"Is everybody blind round here?"

"Sergeant!"

"What have *you* got against him?" asked Sharvari.

"He masquerades as a cop who cares, a cop who's honest, a cop who has integrity and all the time he's worse than any villain."

"No. The truth is you wanted to be a detective and I wouldn't have you on my team," Wordsworth calmly stated. "Do you know why? Because you just don't get it. It's not all black and white. There are shades of grey. But you don't see them. And you don't see them because you don't want to see them."

"You killed Prentice Cartwright …"

"Believe what you want," said Sharvari.

"Am I the only person here that can see it?! Is everybody else fucking blind?"

"Sergeant Ashburn … you need to leave the room," Price ordered.

"But …"

"Now! Go!"

Ashburn looked like she was still going to fight on, but then without even looking at Wordsworth she picked up her papers and left the room.

"Sorry about that," apologised Price. "I'm not sure what got into her. If you want to make a formal complaint …?"

"No, let's just leave it there shall we," said Wordsworth, standing.

"I take it that this is now put to bed?" Sharvari asked.

"Yeah, that's the end."

"Good."

Wordsworth and Sharvari started to leave the room.

"I'm sorry about your wife, Bill … I really am. I'm ashamed we never caught the driver," Price said genuinely.

"Thanks," said Wordsworth. "I'm sure by now whoever did it is rotting in hell."

And Wordsworth and Sharvari left the interview room. Price watched them go, thinking about what Wordsworth had just said. Could he have done it?

CHAPTER FIFTY-ONE

Jodie was in hospital for weeks ... twenty-three in total as the medics tried to deal with her physical state, her mental state and her heroin addiction, something that had been forced on her. All her life she had promised herself she wouldn't end up like her mother.

Fuck – how unfair can life be.

Eventually she was discharged, but she wasn't able to join the mainstream of life. She was mentally scared, still fighting her drug dependency and also terrified that something similar might happen again. Looking over her shoulder became a way of life for Jodie.

The system wasn't sure how to deal with the problem, she was no longer a child and yet she wasn't an adult either. She was moved from pillar to post and ended up being 'fostered' by a family in Baildon. They lived in a large house and had fostered many kids before, but never one as old as Jodie, or as damaged.

Chloe Moreno, her school friend, knowing she could have brought the situation to end as soon as Jodie had gone missing, got in touch with her. But Jodie wasn't really able to communicate with her, and Chloe felt she was doing more harm than good, so she stopped calling.

By the time Jodie was ready to return to full time education, she was a year behind where she should have been. Her desire to educate herself had also disappeared along with her zest for life, but nevertheless she enrolled at the Bradford College and worked for her GCSEs. However hard she tried she was unable to fulfil the potential she showed before her abduction. Her ability to concentrate had been shattered and the academic life she and others once saw for her, seemed to have faded away along with any trust she once might have had.

All the time Wordsworth was keeping an eye on her. He for some reason felt he'd let her down. He should have been there sooner. He should have worked it out quicker. When she started at the Bradford College his continuing observation of her was made easier because he had his own little spy in situ. Izzy was doing her 'A' levels there and regularly reported back to her father about Jodie's movements and disposition; how she remained on the fringes of everything, engaging with no one.

Of course, most people didn't know what had happened to her, what she had gone through, so they just thought she was a bit weird. Izzy would watch on as other students sniggered and made comments about her as they passed her in the corridor.

Jodie had been there just over a year when she was cornered in one of the classrooms by a group of male students led by Martin Dyer, a smart ass who really fancied himself. Egged on by his mates he started to ask Jodie what turned her on. He could dress like an Amish if that would do it for her. In no time at all Jodie had started to crumble. She began to collapse and cry. This didn't stop the group of morons grabbing and touching her. The taunting was eventually stopped by the arrival of a teacher. The boys quickly dispersed, and the teacher helped Jodie to her feet and took her along to the nurse's office.

The taunting of Jodie became public knowledge and Dyer made no attempt to try hide his role in the action, in fact he was proud of it. Naturally Izzy heard about what had happened. She had become more and more her father's daughter and the need to be proactive and not reactive was so strong it was inevitable she would do something – but what?

A week later Izzy was in the refectory and she noticed Jodie sitting by herself sipping on her diet coke. Dyer and his cronies spotted her and they placed themselves directly opposite her. Dyer sat on the edge of the seat, rocking the chair forward onto the two front legs, so he was right in Jodie's face, right in her space. Izzy watched, not hearing what he was saying to her, but it was obvious whatever was being said was upsetting Jodie. All Izzy could see was Jodie's terrified face and the back of Dyer as he continued to rock backwards and forwards.

Dyer never saw her coming and was caught totally unaware. Izzy with one swift pull on the chair sent Dyer crashing forward smashing his chin on the table in front of him. He hit it with such force that he bit his tongue, causing his mouth to fill with blood. The anger immediately superseded the shock and just as he was about to turn to confront his assailant, Izzy quickly grabbed him by the hair and smashed his face down onto the table, breaking his nose. She then signalled for Jodie that it was time for them to leave, which they did to resounding applause from the other students in the refectory.

When Dyer was asked by the teachers what had happened, he claimed his chair had just slipped ... In no time the truth had spread round the college and from then on there was no more bullying of the 'odd girl' studying psychology and sociology.

Naturally Izzy and Jodie talked about the incident, Jodie wanting to know why Izzy had defended her. At first Izzy didn't admit to who her father was and simply told Jodie that she'd never been able to stand Dyer. It wasn't until a couple of weeks later, while they were having an afternoon coffee, Jodie for the first time mentioned that she'd been involved in an 'incident,' which is why she was like she was. Izzy felt instinctively this was the right moment to tell her about who her father was and that she knew all about what had happened. Jodie wasn't sure how to handle the news. She certainly didn't want what happened to become public knowledge, but at the same time she felt a sense of relief that she could talk to someone her own age. She'd been seeing a counsellor every week since leaving hospital, but this one moment with Izzy gave her far more mental freedom than all the counselling sessions put together.

Izzy and Jodie spent more and more time together, and Jodie started to show interest in the man who had saved her. She had been told if it hadn't been for Wordsworth her life would have ended in that warehouse and she knew that had to be true. It was Izzy who suggested she should meet him. At first Jodie was reluctant, but nowhere near as reluctant as Wordsworth. He was unsure how she'd react and he was even more unsure how he'd cope. The whole case had had such a profound effect on him that it had been only recently he'd stopped having nightmares about it. And, of course, there was no counselling, he couldn't risk his involvement in Prentice's death slipping out. He knew a secret was only a secret if he told no one. Now here was the girl who started it all wanting to meet him. He didn't know if he could face it.

Nevertheless, a couple of weeks later Izzy arrived home with Jodie. Molly, Oliver and Nathan were all there too, with only Nathan putting his foot in it by asking if this was the girl that nearly died.

Wordsworth arrived home from work and they sat down to have a supper that Izzy had made with Jodie's help. After the meal the younger kids vanished to either do homework or just play on the X box. Izzy made herself scarce with the excuse of making coffee. Jodie and Wordsworth sat in silence. After a while Wordsworth said, "I had Izzy spy on you."

"I know. She told me," replied Jodie.

"I needed to know you were all right."

"Thank you."

They sat again in silence for a few more moments. Wordsworth felt he had to say something or the situation would just become too uncomfortable. "The verse in your bedroom and on the wall, I've often wondered what that was about."

"These things I have spoken onto you, that in me ye might have peace. In the world ye shall have tribulation: but be of good cheer I have overcome the world." For a moment Wordsworth thought she smiled. She continued: "When I was living with mum, I just needed something to say whatever happened I could make it through ... I could beat it. I'd win."

"And that's why it was in the room in Shay Lane – you knew you could beat them."

Jodie shook her head. "I thought it was all over. I scratched the words on the wall so I was prepared for another life ... a life after death."

Wordsworth couldn't think of what to say, what this girl had suffered, all her life, was impossible to imagine.

"I can't thank you enough," she said quietly.

Again Wordsworth - unsure what to say just looked at her.

"Did you meet my mum?" continued Jodie.

"Yeah – I met her … briefly."

"She wasn't a bad person."

"No … I'm sure she wasn't."

Then there was a long silence as Jodie picked up the courage to say what had been on her mind from the moment she'd heard who Izzy's father was.

"Your wife … Izzy's mum … He killed her didn't he?"

Wordsworth just nodded.

"I'm sorry."

"It wasn't your fault."

"If I can do anything to make up for it …"

"You need do nothing," Wordsworth assured her. "We've both lost so much, we're both still hurting, but you know if we let them break us then they've won. And I'll never do that … I'll never let that happen." Then he gave a slight laugh. "Do you know why?"

Jodie just shook her head.

"Because Wendy would never forgive me … I have four children who I need to look after … I can't let them down."

Jodie had tears in her eyes as she spoke softly, "I wish I'd had a dad like you. I just wanted to make something of my life. I just wanted to achieve something. Not spend my life wondering where I could get the next fix. And here I am … a wreck … a broken shell. I have nothing … nothing."

Jodie broke down in tears … uncontrollable tears. Wordsworth went to her and held her, held her like she'd wanted to be held all her life. She let out all the pent-up pain she'd been unable to release since being rescued … and she felt safe. For the first time since the morning she was abducted, she felt there maybe … just maybe, some kind of future for her.

Izzy returned with the coffees and found her dad and her new friend huddled together. She was surprised she wasn't jealous, any other circumstance she would have been. She knew this was good for both of them. When Wordsworth saw his daughter just standing there, he knew how much she must be hurting. How much she missed her mother. He held out his hand and she went to join them. Wordsworth held both girls - tight. Both these girls he felt he'd failed, while they both felt he'd made it possible for them to go on.